GLENN TRUST
ROAD TO JUSTICE

By Glenn Trust

Sole Justice

Sole Survivor
Road to Justice
Target Down
The Ghost
Dark Winter
Shadow Man

For those who go into the storm

Vinci Books

vinci-books.com

Published by Vinci Books Ltd in 2025

1

Copyright © Glenn Trust 2019

The author has asserted their moral right to be identified as the author of this work in accordance with the Copyright, Designs and Patents Act 1988. This work is a work of fiction. Names, characters, places and incidents are the product of the author's imagination or are used fictitiously. Any resemblance to actual persons, living or dead, places and incidents is entirely coincidental.

All rights reserved. No part of this publication may be copied, reproduced, distributed, stored in any retrieval system, or transmitted in any form or by any means, including photocopying, recording, or other electronic or mechanical methods, nor used as a source for any form of machine learning including AI datasets, without the prior written permission of the publisher.

The publisher and the author have made every effort to obtain permissions for any third party material used in this book and to comply with copyright law. Any queries in this respect should be brought to the attention of the publisher and any omissions will be corrected in future editions.

A CIP catalogue record for this book is available from the British Library.

Paperback ISBN: 9781036704353

Printed and bound in Great Britain by Clays Ltd, Elcograf S.p.A.

ONE

The Light Was Gone

He was going to be a rich man. A broad grin spread across his face as the cantina door slammed shut behind him. The music and din from inside faded. The grin remained. Visions of the US dollars that would soon fill his pockets fluttered around in his alcohol-fogged brain.

He stumbled a little in the dark, making his way toward the curb, feeling the desperate urge to take a piss. He looked up and down the narrow street. It was empty.

"Not here, in front of the cantina, you *tonto*," he mumbled to himself, lifting a finger to his head and tapping it to remind himself that good manners required him to at least move away a few feet.

With his hands at his crotch working down his trouser zipper, he shuffled stiff-legged to a point about ten feet down the street from the cantina entrance. A final look around to ensure no one was watching, and he exposed himself, letting loose a stream that splashed happily in the gutter. Mario Acosta sighed and smiled, a happy man.

Shaking out the last few drops, he zipped up and arched

his back with a pleasing shiver he always got after a good piss. Then he wiped his hands on the sides of his pants and turned to stagger toward his car parked in a side alley halfway down the block.

He passed the stuccoed wall of a residence, and the fragrance of gardenias hit him in the face. The sickly sweet odor on top of the tequila made the bile rise a little in his throat, and he hurried past the house. Pissing in the street was one thing, but puking out your guts was something else. He was no little girl whose stomach was turned by a few shots of tequila.

Of course, *a few* was a relative term, and Mario had lost count hours ago. He had been drinking at Rosita's, his favorite cantina in Torreón since noon. It was now past eleven in the evening.

He stumbled along the pavement, squinting with one eye shut at a single street light. There, he thought. There in that bright light, just in the alley is where I left my car. Not so far, is it? First, move one leg and then the other.

Like a man on stilts, Mario wobbled and walked, two steps, then three then, *mierda*—shit, a step backward and to the side. He put a hand out to steady himself against a building. For a moment, he considered resting his back against the wall and sliding down to the pavement to relax a little, maybe take a short nap.

No. He shook his head. No. Get to your car. You can sleep there until you feel better. If you sleep here on the street, *los policías*—the cops—will find you.

Yes, but they probably won't arrest you, he thought, reasoning with himself. That would make too much work for them.

True, but it was more likely they would take turns

pissing on you as you slept. That would be sport for them, not work.

Mind made up, Mario continued his slow, unsteady progress toward the street lamp and his car in the adjacent alley.

"Too much tequila," he mumbled and laughed. "But why not? I am going to be rich! I deserve a night to party. No working in a grimy factory making car parts for American Chevrolets like *mi papa.*"

Not Mario Acosta. No, Mario Acosta had found a way to become rich, and by the grace of God and the Virgin Mary, he was going to be un *hombre rico como un puto rey!*—rich as a fucking king!

He grinned and pushed himself forward. Almost there, a few more steps and then…

Mario stopped just outside the circle of light thrown by the street lamp and breathed in the warm night air. With great deliberation, he lifted his right leg and planted his foot in the light. He stood for a moment, relishing his victory at navigating all the way down the street without falling and breaking his neck.

He turned to the alley. Sure enough, there was his car, a cheap Japanese model ten years old. That would change, he thought. Soon a better one that always starts and with tires that don't go flat from driving over stones in the road.

With a hand extended, he leaned toward the car until his fingers made contact with the warm metal. Ah, success. He rubbed his hand back and forth over the dusty surface as he searched with the other for the keys in his pocket.

There, they are. He pulled the leather key fob out and held the jingling bits of metal, sparkling in front of his eyes, squinting at them in the light from the streetlamp.

"There you are," he giggled.

A rush of feet over the pavement behind him caught his attention. He turned in time to glimpse three figures in dark clothes run into the circle of light and toward him. Something heavy and hard, struck him in the temple, sending blinding white pain through his eyes. Then the light was gone.

TWO

Meanest Son of a Bitch Around

The rifle shot cracked like a bullwhip in the hot, dry air. Across the green ribbon of water, a half-dozen people scurried around on the bank searching for what scant cover there was. There wasn't much along this part of the Mexico-United States border.

A woman waved a hand from behind a low, dense pile of brush. Her voice carried plainly across the river. "*¡Por favor! No dispares ¡Hay niños aquí!*"

"What she say?" Ralph 'Lucky' Martin levered another .30-30 round into the Winchester Model 94, western-style carbine and squinted through the scope, sighting on the pile of brush.

"Didn't get it all, but I heard *niños*. That means kids. They got some young'uns with 'em, I suppose." Stu Pearce stood up on the toes of his boots to peer across the hundred yards of water. "I don't see 'em, but there's a lot of rustlin' about in the brush."

"Fuck, I didn't hear no shit about no kids. Maybe she

was trying to say she got beenos ... you know, *frijoles* for super." Martin gave a mean, short laugh.

Kneeling with one knee on the ground and the other supporting his elbow, he settled the butt of the Winchester into his shoulder. With a quick turn of his head, he shot a stream of tobacco juice from his brown-stained lips. It sailed in a long arc into the dust as he turned back to the scope and rested his finger on the trigger.

"Hold on, Lucky!" Pearce stepped closer and looked down at Martin. "I heard her say *niños* ... children. We ain't supposed to be shootin' children. Shit, we ain't supposed to be shootin' no one."

"I ain't shot no one ... yet." Martin looked up, and the same nasty smile was on his face. "Besides, who's gonna tell? You?"

"Boss says hold 'em on the other side of the river. That's all." Pearce shook his head. "No bloodshed and no killin'. Just make 'em cross like they's supposed to ... where they's supposed to."

The woman who had called out took advantage of the interlude to change position. She scrambled along the ground towards a mesquite that would offer more protection than the pile of brush and river grass along the bank.

"Fuck!" Martin jumped to his feet.

He let loose a shot that kicked up dirt about a yard from her feet as she scurried towards the tree tugging two small children by the hands. They were toddlers and couldn't keep up. By necessity, the woman dragged them over the stony ground through the briars and brush as they wailed in pain from scratches and bruises.

"Dammit, Lucky!" Pearce shouted. "Range is too far for that cheap-ass scope of yours. Hold your fire, or you're liable to be off and hit one."

He'd seen Martin like this before. When his blood was up there was no calming him down short of killing him, and Stu Pearce was not going to try that.

"Who gives a fuck?" Martin shouted back.

He jacked another round into the chamber and fired at the mesquite. The smack of the bullet into the trunk was audible on the U.S. side of the river.

A man stood up from the brush and waved his hands. "Hey, *gringos*!" He jerked his forearm up in the universal obscenity. "Fuck you, *gringos*! *Vete a la mierda Tu madre es una puta!*" He jumped up and down to draw Martin's attention away from the woman trying to conceal herself and her two children behind the small tree. "Fuck you, man! Your mother is a whore!"

It worked. Lucky Martin levered round after round into the Winchester, firing them off in rapid succession.

"Son of a bitch," he muttered as he tracked the man scrambling along the river bank on his hands and knees away from the mesquite.

Some of the rounds hit the water along the shore, raising little geysers that sprayed down on the man. Others thudded into the surrounding mud.

A howl of pain echoed across the water. The man rolled over on his back, his hands holding a bloody knee as he rocked back and forth in pain.

"*Hijo de puta!* You son of a bitch!" he shouted then turned on his side to stare at the rifle pointed at his face from three hundred feet away.

"Goddammit, Lucky!" Pearce shouted. "You hit him! How we gonna explain that to the boss?"

"Ain't gonna be nothin' to explain when I finish them off."

"Be sensible," Pearce tried to reason. "Somebody will report it. Word will get out."

"Won't be no one to report it."

"You mean …" Pearce shook his head. "No, Lucky. You can't do that. I don't want no part of murderin'."

"Then stay the fuck away, and you won't have no part in it." Eyes on fire with rage, he turned to Pearce. "Don't get in my way, Stu."

The man on the ground shouted something toward the pile of brush. Two more children popped up, these older, nine or ten, Pearce figured. They ran headlong to the mesquite where they huddled down beside their mother and siblings. The narrow tree could not hide the squirming mass of bodies that sought cover there from the Winchester's bullets. It was only a matter of time.

Pearce tried one more time. "Lucky, you can't do this. I know your blood is up, but later, when things calm down, there'll be hell to pay, and you'll be wishin' you hadn't."

Martin swiveled, bringing the rifle to bear on Pearce from a distance of three feet. Hands stretched out, palms up, Pearce shook his head and backed away. "Take it easy, Lucky!"

"Warned you once, Pearce. I won't say it again. Get in my way, and I'll put one in you and tell the boss them Mexes over there did it, and I had to take care of them for it." He sneered. "I'll bet there won't be no problem then … me defending one of his men and all. Probably give me a bonus for it."

Pearce wished he hadn't left his rifle in the truck. He wouldn't have used it except in self-defense, but right now, he was defenseless. He backed up another ten feet, watching the muzzle of the rifle and Martin's finger on the trigger.

The argument was over. Lucky Martin had won, as he

always did. It was one of the reasons he had earned his nickname.

Thick and stocky of build Martin was a bully at heart. Most people gave him a wide berth, but that wasn't why they called him Lucky. In truth, although he was far from being the smartest man around, he still managed to win at things, whether it was cards, betting on horses or claiming the prettiest, youngest whore for himself over in Creosote. He always managed to come out on top.

Today he won the debate with Stu Pearce. What started as some mean spirited, but harmless, plunking with the rifle to scare them was about to turn into a blood bath. Pearce knew that Lucky wasn't really all that lucky. He was just the meanest son of a bitch around, and most people gave him a wide berth, for safety's sake.

Lucky turned back to the man still lying across the river, holding his leg. Their eyes met across the distance. The man was unflinching, awaiting his fate.

"That's right," Martin whispered, resting his cheek on the butt stock. "You hold still for just a minute."

The man did. It was the only means he had left to protect his family.

Lucky Martin raised his nose for a second checking the wind. There was none.

At a range of a little over a hundred yards, there was no need to adjust the scope's elevation for the angle. He let the crosshairs rest on the center of the man's face.

Through the scope, he could see the man's eyes, intent, watching, waiting. He nodded. Martin jerked his eyes away from the scope.

"What the fuck does that mean?"

"What?" Stu Pearce asked, hopeful that Lucky had changed his mind.

"Motherfucker nodded at me like I need his permission to put a round through his head."

"He's just trying to protect the woman and little ones."

"Yeah, well it's too late for that."

Martin settled the rifle back on his shoulder. "You think I need your fucking permission," He shouted across the water. "I don't! You're a dead man!" Eyes squinting through the scope, his finger touched the trigger.

THREE

Creosote

She walked down the center of the gravel road that passed through town. The gravel was firm there, packed down by the trucks and cars passing over it and made for easier walking.

The red glitter polish on her toenails flashed in the sunlight with each step. The polish was the reason she wore sandals with thin leather soles. On most days, she would have been barefoot.

The soles of her feet were tough enough to walk along the road without protection. She'd grown up here, had walked these roads and surrounding scrub country since she was old enough to stand on two feet. But the polish was new, just applied after her shower this morning, and she wanted to protect it, at least for a day or two.

Isabella Palmeras had lived in the tiny backwater place called Creosote, Texas all of her life. Calling it a town would have been too grandiose. The collection of dusty block buildings and frame houses that made up the community did not even appear as a dot on maps.

Creosote was a gathering place more than anything else, a stopping place where people looked around and took stock before continuing on. Some worked their way farther west to the Rio Grande and Mexico beyond. Others saw nothing here but scrub and dust and moved on to Laredo to the north or Brownsville to the south.

A few stayed. When they did, it was because Creosote was what they were looking for. There was no newspaper, no law enforcement, at least not within twenty miles, no town council, or mayor. No website or Wikipedia entry would show up for anyone searching the place online. For all practical purposes, Creosote was nowhere.

Over the last century and a half, the ones who did stay arrived without fanfare. Mostly, they just showed up one day, stumbling across the place as they made their way across the vast South Texas plains. If ever there were an accidental assemblage of persons congregated in one place for no apparent reason, it was the community of Creosote.

As in most out of the way places, order was arrived at through mutual agreement. That doesn't mean that everyone got along. They didn't.

There were disagreements, and when no satisfactory solution to disputes could be arrived at, the issue was frequently settled by force. In the old days, Creosote had seen its share of gun battles in the street. These were not the fast draw duels pictured in Hollywood movies. They were dirty, messy affairs, with blood being shed at close quarters in an unspeakably brutal fashion.

That is not to say that Creosote was lawless. There was law of a sort. There had always been some local Texas lord who ruled over things, serving as judge, jury, and executioner when necessary. These days Tom Krieg and his partner Raul Zabala sat enthroned as the lords of the prairie, enforcing their own form of justice.

Dressed in denim shorts and a flowered cotton halter top, Isabella swung her long brown legs through the morning air, relishing the sun on her bare shoulders. A breeze blew in off the plains carrying with it the scent of sage and the acrid taste of the dry dust that was everywhere. She sucked it in savoring the smells and tastes like a person sampling a favorite wine.

The quarter-mile walk from her small frame home at one end of town to the place where she worked took only a few minutes. The business had no name. There was no need for one. Everyone knew what it was and who owned it.

Isabella's grandfather started it after he came back from the war in 1945. If someone had to say where they were going, they would just say, "To the café."

Like her grandfather, Isabella served two meals a day for those interested. These consisted of a breakfast of eggs, bacon, black beans, and tortillas and an afternoon meal of hamburgers. The evening was reserved strictly for drinking. It was seven AM, and she walked down the center of the road to prepare the morning meal for the hungry and those just looking for something to fill their guts and ease their hangovers.

She stopped on the concrete block in front that served as a step, turned the knob, and pushed the door open. There were no locks. They wouldn't have done any good anyway. If someone wanted to get in, they could, but no one ever had. By mutual agreement among Creosote's residents, the café was Isabella's and not to be touched or disturbed in any fashion on pain of having your ass beaten by the rest of the inhabitants.

A noise on the morning breeze caught her attention. She turned her eyes out toward the open plains.

Vehicles approached. No doubt Krieg or Zabala or some of their men. Plumes of dust billowed high behind three fast-moving trucks, hanging in the air for a minute before dissipating in the breeze.

A frown crossed her face. "Wonder what they're in such a hurry for?" she muttered.

She glanced across the road to another low-walled block building. Oh, that.

Mazey's whore house was already open, the door flung wide in welcome to the approaching customers. The girls could be seen moving about inside cleaning things up from the previous night's festivities. Mazey herself sat in a rocker on the ground outside the front door. She lifted a hand and waved.

"Mornin' Isabella."

"Mornin' Mazey. Looks like you got business coming."

"Yep." Mazey nodded. "For both of us, I expect."

Like Isabella, Mazey Higgins had lived in Creosote all of her life. Older than Isabella by twenty years, she had seen the boom days when drill crews had come through looking for oil. They had stayed for a while then moved on. Many of the shacks and buildings in town had been left by the drill crews, taken over by various residents and newcomers as needed.

"Guess I better, get some food going inside. Talk to you later, Mazey."

"Yeah, me too. Gotta make sure the girls got things in order." Mazey lifted her sturdy bulk from the rocker, pulled her bathrobe tighter around her, and shuffled inside in her slippers. She called over her shoulder, "Have a nice day, Isabella."

The sound of a compressor and air wrench vibrated through the air. Isabella walked around to the shed at the side of the café and peered through the open door.

"Sandy, come help with breakfast. Looks like a crowd coming."

A blond boy of eighteen poked his head above the engine cowling of a four-wheeler. "Be there in a minute, Mom. Just got to put this back together for Mr. Westerfield. He said he'd pay me thirty bucks to get her running."

Sherman 'Sherm' Westerfield lived in the backcountry about five miles out of Creosote. He had become a sort of grandfather figure to Sandy, always finding some small job for him so that he could pay him for it. For some reason, he had developed a soft spot for the boy. People thought it was because old Sherm's own boy had died in Afghanistan some years back. Whatever the reason, Isabella suspected that he would just dole out money to the boy if she weren't around to make sure he earned it.

"Did you get it running?"

"What do you think?" Sandy grinned.

Isabella smiled. Her son had a gift for tinkering with engines, continually pulling things apart to see how they ran, and reassembling them, so they ran even better.

"Alright, then. Put it back together. I expect Sherm will be in this morning for breakfast." She looked across the plain at the approaching dust cloud kicked up by the trucks. "They sure as hell are hauling ass. I better get moving."

She turned toward the café door, calling over her shoulder. "I could use a hand cleaning up after breakfast."

"Yes, Ma'am. I have to take this old buggy out for a spin first and make sure it runs."

"Take it for a spin, but don't get lost for the day."

"Yes, Ma'am."

Sandy disappeared behind the engine cowling. Isabella went into the café and began breaking eggs into a bowl. Across the road, Mazey had the girls cleaning themselves up for the approaching clientele.

Other residents slept off their hangovers or sipped their morning coffee on the cinder block stoops of their dusty shacks. Life continued in its typically slow fashion on the little patch of Texas dirt known as Creosote.

FOUR

Encounter on the Rio Grande

The sun had risen. John Sole settled himself farther back in the pickup's seat, arms folded across his chest, his eyes closed. He wanted to sleep. This spot was good. He had pulled off U.S. 83 a little after four in the morning and had been sleeping since.

In the last day, he had covered a thousand miles or more, uncertain of his destination, but determined to get closer to his goal.

His eyes blinked open at the first crack of the rifle, echoing through the air like a distant, muffled thunderclap.

He sat up. Gunfire was an excellent alarm clock.

Immediately alert, his senses reached out, gathering every bit of data they could about his environment, searching for threats. There didn't appear to be any.

The fatigue of his sixteen-hour drive the day before was forgotten. He was focused. Gunfire tended to do that to a brain, even one that had been asleep seconds before.

He turned to scan a full three hundred and sixty degrees, pushed the door open, and stepped out. The Texas scrub brush country afforded him a view to the horizon in all directions. Another shot sounded, followed by another. It was definitely a rifle, not a handgun.

Not a .22. The shots were not from kids plunking at cans and bottles. This was bigger, but not quite .30-06 heavy game caliber. Something in between. .30-30 possibly, something traditional and not an AR-15. People out fun-gunning with ARs tended to spray ammo just for the hell of it. These were deliberate shots, fired at something, or someone.

The slight pause between rounds indicated a manually operated rifle, bolt or lever action, not a semi-auto. Hunters? He wondered what they were hunting. Apparently not him, since none of the rounds seemed aimed in his direction.

He reached into the cab to retrieve the Colt 1911, .45 ACP, he kept under the driver's seat. He had other weapons, but this one was handy, and the .45 had a way of making a statement if it came to that.

A rapid series of shots rang out across the plains, pulling his eyes to the west. Instinctively, training and experience took over, and he began moving.

A couple hundred yards distant, a belt of green stretched along the banks of the Rio Grande River. He couldn't make out the shooter, but the shots had definitely come from that direction. He started off at a trot, clipping the Colt's holster to his belt as he moved.

What are you doing, John?

It was a question he asked himself a lot these days. Not sure, he answered the voice in his head. Someone's shooting. Could mean trouble.

Someone else's trouble, buddy. Not yours.

I'll just check things out.

And do what? You are not a cop. Remember?
I remember.

The voice in his head was right. He wasn't a cop anymore. Hadn't been one for over a year. What the hell was he going to do?

Another shot, this one a deep-throated roar. He was closer now, and the sound of the gunfire had lost its distant cracking quality. It was a phenomenon he had experienced in the Gulf War and in confrontations since. The closer you got to gunfire, the more alive it became, not just because the volume was louder. The sound took on a personal, threatening quality as if every bullet was searching for a home in your brain.

He saw movement ahead in the brush. If it's nothing, he reminded himself, I turn around and get back to the truck and hit the road.

He slowed and advanced in a crouch staying as close to the sparse cover as possible. He could see the river now, below the small rise where two men stood looking out across the water. A white Chevy pickup sat nearby in the brush.

One spoke to the other who had a Winchester raised, sighting across the river. The one with the rifle ignored him focused on his target. It was a man, lying on the opposite bank, apparently injured.

Sole slowed to assess the situation and noted the jumble of bodies, arms and legs jutting out, squirming for cover behind a nearby mesquite. Their size indicated they were children. The man with the Winchester shouted.

"You think I need your fucking permission? I don't! You're a dead man!"

It was a long shot, too long for the Colt. Sole took it

anyway. He wasn't trying to hit anything, just get the man's attention. The .45 slug flew in an arc and kicked up gravel ten feet from the men on the U.S. side of the river.

It was enough to startle Winchester-man as he pulled the trigger. His shot went wild and sent up a small geyser of water from the river. The man on the opposite bank started scrambling toward the mesquite.

Winchester-man spun with the rifle held out at waist level, levering a round into the chamber as he searched for a target. It was not a very accurate method of firing a rifle, at least if you planned to hit anything. A couple of wild shots rang out, whizzing far wide.

Sole knew he had to close the distance before Winchester-man decided to slow down and put one between his eyes. He moved forward at a run, and let another round off, still not intending to hit anything, but just to keep the shooter off-balance and to remind him that he was armed as well. He was almost there, a few more feet and he would have the advantage over the rifle.

He made it as the man started to lift the rifle back to his shoulder to take an aimed shot.

"Lower it or die!" Sole shouted. "Do it now!"

He took a point-and-shoot stance, ten feet from his target, both hands holding the Colt out in front, the sight centered on the man's chest. At that range, the .45 caliber muzzle looked like a cavern.

"Who the fuck are you?" Winchester-man said, trying to retain some bravado as he complied with the order to lower his weapon.

"Put the rifle on the ground." Sole kept the forty-five pointed at the man's center body mass.

"On the ground! Hell no, I ain't putting my rifle in the dirt."

Sole took one step forward, closing the distance to about eight feet. To the two men he faced, the Colt's muzzle bore grew about two feet in diameter.

"Won't say it again. Lay it on the ground. Do it gentle so you don't get the mechanism jammed with dirt, but you are going to put it down, one way or another." He motioned down with the Colt. "After that, we can talk about what happens next and what you're doing here."

"Lay it down, Lucky," Stu Pearce said. He had remained silent since the confrontation began, but someone had to reason with Lucky before he got them both killed. "He means business."

"Listen to your friend, Lucky." Sole smiled. "And you'll stay lucky."

"Shut up, Stu," Lucky snarled, keeping his eyes on Sole. "How do I know you won't shoot us if I do like you say?"

"If I wanted to shoot you, I would have already done it and gone off to find some breakfast." Sole shrugged. "I don't want to … yet. So, do like I say and place your rifle on the ground before I change my mind."

With the Winchester's muzzle pointed at the ground in the direction of the feet of the man with the big ass Colt, Lucky considered his options.

It was a standoff. He might be able to raise the rifle enough to get a shot off to hit the man before he drilled him with the forty-five. Then again, he might not. It was a chancy thing, and despite his name, Lucky was not much of one to take chances with his own skin.

His eyes darted from the forty-five's muzzle to the hard eyes of the man holding it. The man took another step, closing the distance to six feet. The Colt's muzzle yawned open at him. Lucky bent and gently placed the rifle on the ground.

"Good." Sole nodded. "Now, step away from it."

Lucky shuffled back a few feet, watching the forty-five all the while. Sole knelt to one knee and picked up the Winchester, keeping the Colt pointed at the two men. Resting the rifle over one arm, he holstered the Colt.

"Okay," He said with a smile. "Now, we can talk. What's going on here? Why'd you shoot that man over there?"

"Didn't shoot no one," Lucky muttered.

"How'd that man get injured?" Sole motioned to the mesquite where the mass of bodies remained huddled. The man had crawled there now and tried to push the others behind him, so they weren't exposed to the rifle fire.

"Don't know."

"Bullshit. I saw him drag himself to the tree. I know a gunshot wound when I see one."

"Look, mister," The one called Stu said, trying to reason. "It was accidental. He was just firin' roundabouts in the area to scare them back away from the river, that's all. A round flew wild, and that fella over there got hit. It wasn't intentional."

"Shut up, Stu." Lucky glared at his companion.

"So, if I understand," Sole said nodding. "You were trying to keep them over on the other side of the border and accidentally hit one. Then you decided that it was best to cover up the incident by removing the witnesses ... killing them so no one could say who shot them."

"Well, no ..." Stu's brow wrinkled trying to think of a way to explain things so that it didn't look so bad. He couldn't, and his mouth closed shut.

"Why?" Sole asked.

"Why what?" Lucky glared at him.

"Why shoot at them to keep them there? Why not just

watch them come over and call in the Border Patrol to pick them up?" He nodded at the mesquite across the water. "You can see it's a family, a man with a woman and children. They aren't going to be running very far. You could have called in the Border Patrol while they were swimming across."

"Well …" Stu began, thinking things through. "You see, it's like this. Our boss don't want them over here. Says they got to come over the right way. So, he sends us out to kind of patrol around the river and send any we find back across. You know, so they come over right."

"Who's your boss?"

"K and Z Trucking," Stu said. "Tom Krieg and Raul Zabala.

He said the names like they should mean something to Sole. They didn't.

"Who are they? Krieg and Zabala?"

Stu nodded at the Chevy, fifty feet away. "Krieg and Zabala Trucking. There, it's printed on the side of the pickup. That's who we work for."

"So Krieg and Zabala don't want any illegals coming across the border around here." Sole nodded. "Why?"

"Why?" Stu said, looking uneasy. "It's their … policy."

"Seems like I keep asking the same question." Sole sighed. "Why would a trucking company have a policy about illegals swimming the Rio Grande?"

"Just the way they do business, I suppose." Stu shrugged. "You know, concerned citizens."

"Sounds like a fucked up way to do business, shooting at folks who can't shoot back."

Sole turned to the mesquite a hundred yards away across the river and raised a hand to the side of his mouth so his voice would carry.

"Usted allí!" he called. *"Vete a casa. Obtenga atención médica y no intente cruzar aquí de nuevo. Ve ahora. Nadie disparará."*

You over there! Go home. Get some medical attention and don't try to cross here again. Go now. No one will shoot.

He hoped the Spanish he had been practicing for the last year was understandable.

The family behind the mesquite huddled together. Sole could see the man talking to the others. He inched away from the tree, testing to find out if anyone was going to fire at them. After moving several feet without a shot ringing out, he motioned to the others. One by one, they scrambled to him, and he pushed them ahead into the brush, where they disappeared. The woman came out last and turned to look at the man who had stopped the shooting.

"Gracias Señor," she called out and disappeared behind her children.

The wounded man gave a short wave and nodded, then dragged himself into the brush behind his family.

"You don't know what you done," Lucky said through gritted teeth. "You shouldn't a butted in."

"Yeah, maybe not. We'll see." Sole nodded and stepped forward, holding the rifle out at port arms. "I suppose you want this back now."

"Yeah, and when the boss finds out what you done, you're a dead man." Lucky sneered. "And I'll be the one to cut your fuckin' heart out."

"That a fact?" Sole smiled, as he swung the butt of the Winchester, landing a blow that broke Lucky's jaw and sent him to the ground.

"Goddamn, you son of a bitch!" Lucky mumbled through a mouth full of blood and loose teeth

Sole looked down at him as he levered the rounds out of

the Winchester, letting them fall on Lucky's bloody face. He nodded his head in the direction he had come.

"Couple hundred yards that way is my truck. I'll take the Winchester with me and leave it where my truck sits now. You can pick it up there." He nodded at the Krieg and Zabala pickup. "There's one round left in the chamber of this rifle. I see you coming after me, and I will put a bullet through the skull of whoever is driving. Understood?"

"Understood," Stu replied somberly.

Lucky moaned.

"Good," Sole said.

Now that the issue was resolved, his other senses began to kick in, and he realized he hadn't eaten since breakfast the day before. He looked at Stu. "You seem to be more reasonable than your partner."

"Don't see no reason for there to be trouble between us." Stu glanced down at his partner, still sprawled in the dirt. "Lucky, he ain't so bad, sometimes."

"Hmm." Sole shook his head at the man on the ground. "Guess sometimes wasn't today."

"Nope." Stu grinned for the first time. "He definitely overplayed his hand. Anyway, thanks for not killing us."

Sole examined Stu's face. He realized the gratitude was real. Stu was glad not to be killed out here on the plains, as if that were not an uncommon occurrence. *What the hell kind of country have you wandered into, John-boy?*

His stomach growled, reminding him it needed to be fed.

"Well, Stu, maybe you could tell me where I can grab some breakfast around here. I'm starving."

"Not much around," Stu said, relieved at the sudden change in tone from threatening to put a bullet in his skull to asking about the local cuisine. He pointed to the south.

"About fifteen miles down the highway you come to a turn-off. There's a sign, says Creosote … not official or anything, just something the locals painted on a board and put up."

"Creosote," Sole said. The name conjured up images of railroad ties and telephone poles strung across vast open spaces. Looking around, he figured it fit.

"Yeah." Stu nodded. "Not much there, really. A little shithole of a place, but the café serves up decent food."

"Thanks, Stu. I'll give it a try." Sole turned toward his pickup.

"Maybe we'll be seeing you around," Stu called after him.

"I wouldn't count on it," Sole replied over his shoulder.

The Winchester resting over his forearm, he strode with purpose, his boots kicking up dust with each step. He was hungry. A little gunplay always sharpened his appetite.

FIVE

Business is Good

"*El gringo no confía en mí.*" The gringo doesn't trust me.

Pepe Lopez folded his arms and sat back annoyed as the bills were counted out on the table.

"*Es negocio.*" It's business. Raul Zabala cast a hard look at the young *coyotaje*—smuggler of persons. "*Tú lo sabes.*" You know this.

"*Sí, lo sé, pero después de tanto tiempo trabajando juntos, debemos tener cierta confianza entre nosotros.*" Yes, I know, but after so much time working together, we should have some trust between us.

"I speak Spanish," Tom Krieg looked up from the stack of bills he was counting. "You might keep that in mind before you mouth off in front of me."

"Sorry, Tom," Pepe said in accented English. "You are right. I should not have said what I said. It's just that we have been doing this now for two years. I thought you trusted me by now." A broad smile filled his face. "We are partners, no? I would never cheat you and Raul."

"Damn right, you won't," Zabala interjected. "That's

because once a month you have to come in for the count to settle up." He grinned. "Otherwise you would find a way to cheat us. The more we count, the more honest you are."

"How can you say that?" Pepe was offended. "I have never cheated you or even thought of cheating you. We have a good thing here. I won't fuck it up." He shook his head in dramatic fashion and gave Zabala a hurt look. "That you would think such things of one of your countrymen ... it is regrettable."

"Let me make something clear for you." Zabala leaned toward the young man, his eyes narrowed and hard. "I am not your countryman. I am *Tejano*. My family has been in *Tejas* since the days of the conquistadors when yours were still Aztec peasants digging in the ground." He shook a finger in front of Pepe's face. "Do not think we are the same."

"My ... apologies," Pepe stammered. "I meant no offense."

"I'm not interested in your apologies." Zabala waved a hand, dismissing the young smuggler's words. "We do business together. Nothing more."

Tom Krieg ignored the confrontation. With his finger on a line in a ledger book open before him, he made a note. Then he shuffled the stack of bills together on the desk and began counting out a pile.

"It's all there, right, Tom?" Pepe asked nervously.

Krieg ignored him and continued counting. When he was finished, there were two piles on the desk. He pushed the smaller one toward Pepe.

"That's yours. We're square."

"Good, good." Pepe nodded with an enthusiastic smile. "Thank you, Tom. Business is good, no?"

"Good enough," Krieg said and turned to a safe behind the desk where he placed the ledger and the cash.

"That's what I keep telling my buddies in Monterrey," Pepe said rapidly, a nervous grin on his face, trying to make up for his initial comments about trust. "They should do business with you. That's what I always say. They should come and do …"

"We're done," Krieg interrupted, nodding at the door.

"*Sal de aquí insignificante*—get out of here, pipsqueak," Zabala growled.

"Yes, yes." Pepe jumped to his feet, scooping up the pile of cash. He bowed his head. "Yes, I am going. Thank you again, Tom … Raul."

Another brief bow of his head and Pepe scurried out of the door.

"That little pissant thinking we are the same, him and me! Ha!" Zabala laughed, then continued with a nod. "Still, he is right. Business is good, Tom."

"Yes, it is." Tom Krieg looked out of the office window to the K and Z Trucking lot. It was empty except for two refrigerated haulers parked for minor repairs and service. The rest were out picking up cargo or making deliveries. "Business is very good."

SIX

Unfinished Business

Fifteen miles down U.S. 83, Sole found the turnoff to Creosote. As Stu had promised, the sign marking the road that led off to the east was nothing more than a hand-painted piece of wood with a large red arrow pointing to the left under the town's name.

He spun the wheel, and the pickup bumped down onto the dirt road that ran in a straight line, disappearing over the horizon. The brush country spread out on both sides, offering an endless vista. There was no sign of a town.

He settled back. It was as good a road as any this morning and in the last year he had traveled many empty roads. Besides, he was hungry.

Since leaving Atlanta, he had spent time in all the southern states except Florida. Florida was in the wrong direction for his purposes. The money from the sale of his house in Georgia was deposited into an account he drew from occasionally when he needed cash, but mostly, he worked itinerant jobs and wandered from city to city, learning the ways of the road and how to survive.

There was a different world, he discovered, existing in the shadows. The inhabitants of that world did not share the traditional values held by mainstream society.

What did the word mean, anyway? One person's tradition was another's oddity. It was just a matter of perspective.

There was the non-traditional woman he met on a street corner in Birmingham. If he'd met her as a police officer in Atlanta, he would have at least told her to move on. He might have arrested her, depending on what was going on that day. She propositioned him.

"No, thanks."

"Why? You gay?" she snapped at him.

"Nope, just looking."

"Looking for what?"

"I wish I knew."

And that started a conversation that lasted all night. Her name was Louise, and she took him to her apartment. They talked. He bought food, and she cooked him a meal. They ate it together and talked some more.

He said little about himself but listened for hours as she talked of her life growing up in a small Mississippi farm town. She ran away from a father who abused her. Selling her body became her road to survival.

He did not pass judgment. He merely listened. Who was he to judge? What the hell did he know about her life and what she had to do to survive?

She asked about him, but he said nothing.

"You got something inside gonna kill you, you keep it bottled up like that," she said and touched his face gently as they sat on her sofa after dinner. "One day, it's gonna bust out, like that alien thing bustin' out of a man's chest in the movies."

They both laughed at that, but he remained silent about his demons.

She turned on the sofa to look into his eyes, and made a prediction, "When it happens, when that thing busts out, it's gonna kill you and everyone it touches."

She smiled and laughed again, patting his face with her dark, warm, smooth hand. "But not tonight."

"Not tonight," He agreed, nodding.

They held each other through the night, talking, mostly about life on the streets. After a while she fell asleep, and they stretched out on her sofa, her head on his chest.

Their time together was a mutual exchange of equal value. Lying with this white man who didn't want anything from her except to talk and be with someone for a spell, Louise felt truly safe for the first time in a long while. In return, John Sole felt the bond of human closeness for the first time since the terrible day in Atlanta.

When daylight came, she fixed him breakfast. Then they hugged, and he left.

There was the non-traditional salvage yard owner outside Memphis who found him asleep in his truck, backed up against the lot's chain-link fence. He poked him in the cheek with the barrel of a shotgun to wake him.

"What you doin' here, fella?"

"Just sleeping."

"Private property. Can't sleep here. Move on."

"Okay," Sole nodded, trying to shake the grogginess from his head. He fumbled for the key in the ignition.

Maybe it was because he didn't argue, or had the look of a man waking from a coma—who knew? People had their own triggers and their own demons—but the man lowered the shotgun and asked a question.

"Hold on. You got any money?"

"A little."

"Got any way to make money? Got a job?"

"Not at the moment."

"Want a job?" The man eyed Sole up and down and figured he had better add a disclaimer. "Not anything permanent. Just something to put some cash together so's you can move on."

He was about to say, no thanks, but instead, for some reason he still didn't understand, he said, "Thanks I could use some work. I'll pay you some rent to sleep out here in the lot if that's alright."

The man gave him a final appraising stare and stepped back from the truck. "Come on inside. Got coffee and doughnuts in the office. Then I'll put you to work."

For two weeks, Sole wrenched parts off of wrecked cars and piled them up for the old man. He learned the man was a widower of forty-five years. His wife died in a car crash just eighteen months after their wedding. Their unborn child died with her. Since then he had lived alone in a shack behind the jumble of wrecked cars in his lot. Like John Sole, he had no one.

People came and went, buying used parts for used cars. None ever stayed to chat. No one called him to go out and have a beer. He was alone. Sole understood being alone.

After two weeks, they shook hands. The man gave him one of his rare smiles.

"You could stay ... if you want," the old man said, shy almost.

Sole hated that he had said it. He hated it because we wanted to stay and not break the old man's heart again, but he couldn't. He had unfinished business.

"I'm sorry. I can't there's something ..." He didn't know what to say or how to say it to the old man.

"Never mind." The old man gave his hand a final pump, turned, and walked away. "Good luck to you."

Then he went into the office and closed the door. John Sole got into his pickup and drove away.

There were a hundred others in the last year, non-traditional people living on their own terms. Each one had a story. Each one lived outside the boundaries of what others would call traditional. Each one taught him something about surviving outside the conventional world.

A dusty clutter of small buildings appeared on the horizon. Creosote was even less impressive than its name sounded.

It didn't matter. He wouldn't be there long. He would keep moving toward the unfinished business he knew waited for him. After, he might go back to the old man and salvage yard, or somewhere else even. Someplace new, not dirtied by everything that had happened, not cluttered by memories. If he survived.

SEVEN

Another Niche

The Krieg and Zabala families had known each other for more than a hundred years. Sometimes they worked together. Sometimes they were at war, depending on the fortunes of their respective patriarchs at any given time.

Now, they worked together. Both had ranches that had been in their families for generations. The Zabala deed was from a land grant issued by a Spanish royal commission in the 1700s. Krieg's claim to his land only extended back to the mid-1800s and the founding of the Republic of Texas. Both families had profited over the years from the turmoil that surrounded the separation of Texas from Mexico.

Tom and Raul grew up together. They attended the same schools, fought each other over the same girls, drank beer together, and fought some more.

After their teens, they drifted apart, going off to college, Tom to UT, Austin, Raul to Texas A&M. On their return to their ranches in the south Texas country along the border with Mexico, they decided over beers one night to go into business together.

At first, their plan was simply to establish themselves independently of their domineering families. They had lived along the border all their lives, and both had extensive contacts on the Mexican side. Raul, in particular, had socialized with many of the Mexican farmers in the northeastern part of the country, or more correctly, with their daughters. Some were wealthy, some were little more than peasants, but the vegetables and tropical fruits they produced were in high demand in the States.

Mexico had been the largest exporter of fruits and vegetables to the U.S. for years, but Krieg and Zabala Trucking established themselves as importers of only the finest produce for the finest restaurants, hotels, and specialty markets. While Zabala handled the supply side of the business with the farmers, Krieg took on the demand side, building a customer base across Texas.

Their reputation grew over time. They had found a specialized niche in the import business, and while their trade wasn't massive, and the market was somewhat limited, it thrived. Chambers of Commerce from El Paso to Brownsville looked upon the young men as exemplars of entrepreneurism and the true Texas spirit of achievement.

Of course, what those who admired their success didn't suspect was that their business included transport of another more lucrative product. Krieg and Zabala's drivers were familiar faces at the crossings along the U.S. Mexico border. Over the years, they established friendly relations with the Border Patrol and Immigration officers up and down the Rio Grande.

A case of avocados or tomatoes left at a crossing station as a gesture of appreciation for the hard work of the officer became common practice. In fact, Tom and Raul required their drivers to always leave something for the officers on both sides of the border crossings they used. It was never a bribe, just an expression of thanks from Krieg and Zabala Trucking. It was good for business to have friendly relations, they said.

Out in the remote farm districts in the Mexican backcountry, Krieg and Zabala loaded their trucks with fruits and vegetables for their northern customers. Then one day, they discovered another specialized niche. It happened by chance.

"What's that up ahead?" Darnell Purdy took his foot off the accelerator and downshifted to slow the truck.

"People walking in the road." José Martínez looked up from the dog-eared Sports Illustrated swimsuit edition that had been riding back and forth in the truck for eight months. "Illegals headed to the border, probably."

Darnell touched the brake.

"Why are you slowing?" José asked, placing a hand on the shotgun they carried in the cab for security.

"There's a girl standing in the road."

The group huddled close on the side of the road while the lone female with them stepped out in front of the truck. Five men, one older, in his fifties, and the others ranging from sixteen or so to about thirty in age waited while the girl approached the passenger window.

Darnell brought the truck to a stop. José leaned out to speak to the girl.

They exchanged words in Spanish for a minute, and José turned to Darnell. "They want to get to the border. They want us to take them."

"They must be crazy," Darnell shook his head. "It's

another three hundred miles to the border. Out here like that, no provisions, just the clothes on their backs."

"She says they were to meet someone in Torreón ... a *coyotaje* ... but he took the down payment they gave him and disappeared."

"That's a tough story, but I don't see how we can help. Tom Krieg finds out he'll skin us alive while Zabala looks on and smiles."

José leaned out the window and spoke to the girl. She started crying. The men on the side of the road hung their heads. The older man stepped forward to take her by the arm and lead her away from the truck.

"Shit." Darnell shook his head at what he was about to say. "Goddammit, I can't stand to see a woman cry. Let's make room for them in the back. We'll put them all the way in behind the crates of tomatoes. They stay down; no one will ever suspect they're there."

"Unless the Border Patrol gets on and does a visual check," José reminded him.

"That ain't gonna happen. Most they ever do is open the back door and shine a light around a little. If they keep their heads down, no one will see them. We can let them out when we get back to the lot. After that, they're on their own."

"I don't know, Darnell. This could cost us our jobs."

"Maybe, if we get caught, but hell I can't leave a girl crying like that on the side of the road. Can you?"

José looked out the passenger window at the faces staring back at them from the shoulder. The old man patted the girl's arm while she wiped the tears from her eyes with the back of her hand.

"Aw hell," José said and opened the door, jumping to the gravel on the side of the road. "*Espera un minuto. Te llevaremos a través de la frontera.*" Wait. We will take you across the border.

The girl's brown eyes opened wide. "*De Verdad?*" Truly?

"*Sí.*" José nodded.

Darnell got out and helped them load into the back of the refrigerated truck. José explained that it would be chilly, so they would have to huddle together for warmth. The border was five hours away, and they must remain silent. Their new passengers didn't care.

"We have money," the old man said.

Surprised that he spoke English, Darnell shook his head. "We don't want your money."

"How much money?" José asked, casting a hard look in Darnell's direction.

"The price was a thousand U.S. dollars for each," the old man explained. "Six thousand dollars in all. We worked for a year, saving for it and then sold everything we had to get the rest of the money. The *coyotaje* got half and left. We will give you the other half, three thousand dollars for taking us. That is fair. Just don't report us when we get to the border."

"No," Darnell said, shaking his head firmly. "We won't report you. You'll need the money when you get where you're going."

"You sure?" José asked. "I mean that's fifteen hundred apiece if we split it."

"Let's go," Darnell said, ending the discussion of money.

Like most crossings by K and Z trucks, this one was uneventful. They stood to the side and chatted with the U.S. Customs agents while they performed a perfunctory inspection of the truck. Darnell and José made this run regularly and knew the agents who worked this station.

José held his breath when the agent opened the truck's rear door and shined a flashlight beam over the crates of tomatoes. Satisfied, he closed the door again, and José resumed breathing.

Two hours later they pulled into the Krieg and Zabala lot off Highway 83 fifty miles north of Brownsville. When they opened the rear door, they had to reassure their passengers that they were safe and not being turned over to the immigration authorities. It took a few minutes, longer than they had wanted, and by the time the young men jumped down and turned to help their sister and father down, Raul Zabala stepped out onto the loading dock.

"What the hell's going on?" he snapped.

Caught in the act, Darnell and José had no option but to confess. Zabala listened with interest, casting a stern eye over the six illegals standing, heads bowed before him.

When Darnell finished explaining, Zabala looked at the old man and asked, "Where are you going?"

"To Dallas," the man replied. "My brother is there. He says he can find work for us."

"Alright," Zabala said. "Let's take this inside."

He directed them to the office in the back of the warehouse where Tom Krieg was going over the books. He looked up when they piled into the cramped space.

"What the hell, Raul?"

Darnell repeated the story for Krieg. When he finished, Krieg asked the old man, "You said you had money?"

"Yes, a thousand each." He shrugged. "But now only five hundred each. We will pay you."

Krieg's eyes narrowed. He looked at Zabala. "We need to talk."

Darnell and José were sent on a run to Dallas that night

with instructions to drop their passengers in a quiet spot without being seen.

Tom Krieg and Raul Zabala spent the night running the numbers. A thousand dollar fee was far below the standard four thousand they knew most *coyotajes* required. It was apparent the family had been scammed and left to fend for themselves.

"So what if we set up a real network of *coyotajes*?" Tom asked. "Our own network."

Raul was silent for a moment then nodded. "It could be done. I have contacts, people who do such things."

"Then we charge three thousand each. Not scamming anyone, we guarantee delivery across the border."

"I'm listening," Raul said.

"We give the *coyotaje* one thousand and keep two thousand for ourselves."

"Why would they take only one thousand?" Raul asked.

"Because we are eliminating their risk and overhead. We handle all transportation expenses. They are our procuring agents, and when they deliver them to us, they go procure some more."

"Assuming we can convince them to do that, six people at two thousand brings us twelve thousand." Raul shook his head. "The risk is still too great in my opinion."

"You're thinking too small." Tom nodded as the plan materialized in his mind. "I'll bet we can fit twenty in a load, behind our regular cargo. It would be cramped, but they would only be there a few hours, and we won't be dumping them out in the desert somewhere to die."

He grabbed his calculator. "Now we're up to forty thousand a load." He keyed some numbers. "Say two loads a week, that's eight a month. Now we're up to three hundred twenty thousand a month and …" He punched a final number into the calculator. "Three point eight million dollars a year." He looked up from the calculator. "Nearly four million dollars, not reported and not taxed, in our pockets. What do you think about the risk now?"

"I think we may have found another niche for our business." Raul grinned.

EIGHT

Networking

Even in the dark, his head covered with a hood, hands, and feet bound with zip ties, stuffed into the narrow compartment concealed below the floor of the van, he knew they were crossing the border. The sounds were unmistakable.

After driving for hours, the van slowed. Then it moved a few feet and stopped, moved a few more feet and stopped again. Then he heard the Customs and Border Control agents speak to the driver and occupants. Mario Acosta was surprised that the men who had abducted him spoke in English, not Spanish.

"How y'all doing today? Need to see your identification," the agent said, his voice muted but understandable through the floor.

"Sure, sure," the driver responded. There was shuffling as the three men pulled out their passport cards. "Here you go."

There was a pause, then the agent asked, "What you boys up to today?"

"Had a special pickup down in Torreón," the driver responded. "Client had to have melons for tonight's menu from one particular farm." He laughed. "Some sort of special melon. They all look the same to me, but they pay, and we deliver. Crazy *gringos*." The driver grinned.

"They pay you for that?" the agent asked chuckling. "For watermelons?"

"Fucking rich people have more money than they know what to do with." The driver said and then added with a laugh, "But that's what we do. K and Z trucking, only the finest imports."

"What's so special about these melons?"

"Damned if I know." The driver lowered his voice as if sharing a secret with the agent. "I think the farm belongs to the brother of the restaurant owner. Trying to keep things in the family, but tells his customers the melons are special and come from only one special farm. It's all a scam."

"Sounds like it." The agent handed back the passports. "I have to look."

"Sure," the driver said. "Door's unlocked."

Footsteps moved around the side of the van, and the back door opened.

"These are special melons?" The agent asked chuckling. "Look like plain old watermelons to me."

"Me too." The driver called out. "We got plenty. I'll grab a couple for you and your partner."

"You sure?"

"Why not? There's no count, and we have more than enough for the order."

"Thanks. I appreciate that."

Mario heard the van door open, and then someone moving melons around. A minute later, the door closed.

"Here you go. Special melons from a special farm in Mexico." The K and Z man laughed.

"Thanks. My wife will be happy to see these tonight."

"Enjoy," the driver replied. "Next time, I think we'll be bringing back some avocados. Another small special order."

"I'll keep that in mind," the agent stood aside, a large melon under each arm. "Have a good day."

The van was moving again. They rode another hour before Mario heard and felt gravel crunching under the tires. Then they rocked to a stop. A few seconds after, the door opened, the floor panel was lifted and light filtered in through the hood.

Hands grabbed Mario and jerked him upright, then dragged him out, dropping him on the ground. He managed to right himself, but the men forced him to kneel. The gravel dug painfully into his kneecaps.

The hood was pulled from his head. He blinked in the bright light, turning his head to squint at his surroundings while they cut the zip ties off his wrists. The three men surrounded him. Each had a hand resting on a pistol in their belt.

They stepped back. This is it, Mario thought and began praying. Tears fell down his face.

"*Por favor. ¿Por qué me estás matando? Que hice?*" Please. Why are you killing me? What did I do?

The men laughed. One, the one with the driver's voice said in Spanish, "On your feet."

Mario rose, and stood, wobbling under the sun. At any minute, these men were going to shoot holes in him, and the worst of it was he could not even say why?

He shook his head. No, that wasn't the worst of it. That was just the puzzle. The worst of it was that he would be dead. He wept more now, shaking his head in denial.

He wasn't religious but, he began saying a Hail Mary. Maybe they were religious. Maybe they would hear his faith and not kill him.

Dios te salve, Maria. Llena eres de gracia: El Señor es contigo. Bendita tú eres entre todas las mujeres. Y bendito es el fruto de tu vientre: Jesús. Santa María, Madre de Dios, ruega por nosotros pecadores, ahora y en la hora de nuestra muerte. Amén

Hail Mary, full of grace. The Lord is with thee. Blessed art thou amongst women, and blessed is the fruit of thy womb, Jesus. Holy Mary, Mother of God, pray for us sinners, now and at the hour of our death, Amen.

They were not religious. They laughed.

"That way." The man who had been the driver pointed at a building nearby.

Mario turned and walked. His numb legs felt as if they would collapse under him. They were taking him inside out of view to kill him where no one would see, and he could do nothing about it.

He prayed a Hail Mary again, for real this time, feeling more religious with every step he took.

One of the men stepped up onto the small loading dock attached to the building and pushed open a door. They pointed, and Mario managed to make his legs move forward, weeping silently as he walked. As the door slammed behind him, his hope was lost. There was no escape now.

Two of them took him by the arms and pushed him into another room at the back of the building. The moment was here. Mario thought his bladder would empty on the floor, but he clenched his legs together hard because he knew they would just laugh more at him for his fear.

He entered the room. It was an office. Two men sat on

either side of a wide desk. One was white, *norteamericano*. The other was brown and looked to be *Mexicano*.

The brown one spoke first. The words were in fluent Spanish but with an accent of one who does not live in Mexico. "What is your name?"

"Mario Acosta." His voice trembled. They were verifying that he was the man they sought so they would kill the right person.

The brown man nodded. "Good. Do you know who we are?"

"No, *señor*."

"We are your new employers."

"My employers ..." Mario's eyes opened wider, confused. "I do not understand."

"I will explain," the brown one nodded, speaking quietly. "You have found a way to make money. You are smuggling people across the border from Mexico."

"I did not ..."

"Do not lie to us." The man's voice was harder now. "We are aware of your activities and what you are doing. It is our business."

"Yes, I took some people across the border ... on a trail I learned when I was a boy." He shook his head. "I promise I will not do it again."

"Yes, you will do it again."

The expression on Mario's face reflected his utter confusion. Who were these people? They kidnapped him from the alley by his car. They knew about his plan to be rich, taking people across the border. Now, they told him he must continue to do it. That was his plan all along. He wanted to say to them that they were *jodidamente loco*—fucking crazy.

Instead, he said, "I do not understand."

"You might say we are competitors." The brown one shook his head. "We cannot allow that."

Mario paled. The bullet was coming any moment now.

"What we can allow," the brown one continued. "Is for you to work for us. Are you willing to work for us?"

Mario looked around the room. The large white man behind the desk had remained silent, but his hard eye never left Mario's face. The three men from the van stood respectfully to the side but nearby. He nodded.

"Yes … I am willing, I think. What must I do?" He hoped the work was not to kill someone. He was not a killer and hated the sight of blood.

"You continue doing what you have already started. Find people to take across the border, except you will not take them on the trail you played on as a boy in Chihuahua."

"No?"

"No. You will deliver them to us. We will tell you where and when. For this, you will be paid a thousand dollars for each person you bring." The brown one smiled. "You see, you will still be rich, and you will have little risk. No other *coyotaje* will molest you, and you will not have to make the trip yourself across the frontier and risk being arrested."

"Yes, but …" Mario hesitated. "But if you pay me a thousand, how will you be paid?

"We will be paid two thousand each," the brown one said. "You will charge each three thousand."

"Three thousand?" Mario's eyes opened wide. "But such a sum, I don't think many will be able to pay. How will I find people to pay this much?"

"You will. Take this." The brown one handed him a card. It was green, like the green in the flag of Mexico with a large red circle in the middle. There were no words on it.

"People know this card. They will see that you work for us and that you can guarantee they will be safely transported across the border and delivered to a city inside the United States. They will not be molested, their women will not be raped, their children not abused. For this guarantee, they will pay."

Mario took the card, turning it over in his hand, examining both sides. "Just this card? This is all I need?"

"That is all you need." The brown one smiled. "That and you must make more contacts, spread the word, bring more people to us."

"More people, but how?" He shook his head. "I know of those who want to cross the border, but not so many."

"Don't sell yourself short." The brown one laughed. "You will do fine. You just need to get out and work. Remember riches do not come for the idle. We will make you rich, but you will work for it."

"I am not sure where to start, *señor*."

"I suggest you give it some thought on the way back to Torreón. By next week we will expect ten who are ready to cross and who have paid their money to you. We will contact you, and you will bring the money and people to the place we say. Once a month, we will settle the accounts, and you will receive your share, one thousand apiece."

"But ..."

"No buts. Should you decline our offer ..." the brown one raised his hands shrugging. "Well, as I said. We cannot have you competing against us. You either work with us, or your father who works in the car factory will wonder where you have disappeared to. *Comprende?*"

Mario nodded. "*Comprendo*."

"*Bueno*. Take him home so he can become a rich man."

The three men from the van approached. The hood was

placed over his head, and he was bound once more and stuffed in the compartment under the van floor. They used a different crossing to go back to Torreón.

In the office, Raul Zabala leaned back in his chair, hands folded behind his head, relaxing. "That went well, don't you think?"

Tom Krieg smiled at his partner. Networking was Raul's favorite part of their operation.

NINE

Welcome to Creosote

A dust devil spun down the middle of the dirt road, its forty-mile-an-hour whirlwind sucking up sand and every bit of debris in its path. Twenty feet away from the mini-tornado, a pile of old newspapers stacked by a building lay undisturbed by its passing.

John Sole was in its path. With one hand on the steering wheel, he cranked the driver's window on the old pickup as fast as he could. It was too late.

Sand and grit swirled through the truck cab, filling his nose and peppering his face, coating everything. As suddenly as it came, it was gone, bouncing down the road, a thousand-foot tower of spinning dust that seemed to have a life of its own, spewing everything it picked up out the top to settle back to earth a half-mile away.

It was an inauspicious welcome to Creosote., Texas. Sole followed the dust devil as it passed down the road between the rows of buildings and pulled to a stop in front of a collection of pickups and rusty cars at the end of what passed for the main street. The dust devil continued out across the plains.

He pushed the pickup's door open and stood for a moment in the street, blinking the dust out of his eyes. A bit of unlit neon tubing in the window of an adjacent building was curled into the word 'café.' The place looked closed.

He stepped to the door, brushing the sand from his hair with one hand as he grabbed the door handle with the other. To his surprise, it opened. Inside, the air was thick with the aroma of fried bacon and eggs spiced with chilies and cilantro. He stood with his back to the door allowing his eyes to become accustomed to the gloom.

"You comin' or goin'?" The old man at the counter swiveled on a stool and squinted at the silhouette in the doorway.

"Coming I suppose," Sole said and walked to the counter. He looked at the empty tables scattered around that took up nearly the entire interior space of the building. "Where is everyone? From the cars out front, I figured the place would be packed."

"Oh, them ..." A woman came from the small room on the other side of the counter, wiping her hands on a dishtowel. "They've already eaten." She nodded at the window and the building across the road. "They're all at Mazey's."

"Mazey's?" Sole followed her gaze through the dust-covered window to the shack with the front door propped by a cinder block.

"Whorehouse," The old man chuckled. "Came in for breakfast, now they're at Mazey's taking care of another kind of appetite, you might say."

"Oh." Sole nodded, indifferent, for the moment, to that type of appetite. He smiled at the woman. "Is it too late to get some breakfast?"

"Nope. Just in time. Was washing up, but there's enough left for one more." She rested her elbows on the counter, brushing at a wisp of hair that hung in front of her brown eyes. "I've got bacon and eggs, or eggs and bacon. Which'll it be?"

"I'll take one of each."

"One of each," the old man chuckled and slapped a knee. "That's a good one, young fella. One of each."

"Coming up," the woman said.

She smiled, and her dark eyebrows rose, making little lines around the corners of her eyes. It was a welcoming smile with a familiarity that held his gaze for a moment.

John Sole knew nothing of her background, didn't even know her name, but he was drawn to the smile. He realized others must have been touched the same way, looking into those soothing brown eyes, feeling the smile shining on them.

"Pour yourself some coffee from the pot there on the counter. I'll get your breakfast."

She turned, throwing the dishtowel over her shoulder and walked back to the small room behind the counter. Sole's eyes followed.

There was more than a smile there. The curve of her hips under the denim shorts, the graceful stride, the long legs swinging rhythmically as if she were moving onto a dance floor and not to a kitchen to fry bacon and eggs. There was a womanly familiarity about her that reminded him of … he pushed that memory away, reached for the pot, and poured black coffee into one of the mugs stacked beside it.

Eat your breakfast and get out, John, he told himself. No distractions.

The sounds of his meal being prepared came from the

small kitchen, and he couldn't help looking in that direction, hoping to catch a glimpse of her, and not wanting to at the same time. He forced his eyes away and down at the coffee, circling his hands around the mug as if to steady himself.

What the hell's going on with you today, John? Too much driving and not enough sleep, that's what it is. She's just a woman. She's not … he shook his head. She is not someone you have ever known or will ever know.

The old man watched the emotions play across his face. "Isabella does have a way of touching a man without ever laying a hand on him."

"Does she?" Sole turned and looked up from the coffee. "I hadn't noticed."

"Bullshit!" The old man gave a friendly laugh. "Don't know anything about you mister, but it was there all over your face for a second. Nothing to be ashamed of. Isabella is one hell of a woman. The man that can match her spirit and win her as a partner will be one lucky man."

"I suppose so," Sole said, wishing the old man would change the subject.

The old man had other ideas. He fixed his eyes on the newcomer, giving him an appraising once over. "There's someone else, ain't there."

Sole started to turn to the window, thought better of it and tried to freeze all emotion from his face.

The old man wasn't fooled and would not be denied. He nodded, sure of himself now.

"That's it. There's someone else, and you had a second of guilt for looking at Isabella the way any man would look at her." He nodded. "That's it, right?"

Sole sighed and nodded to appease the old man. "That's it."

"Thought so." The old man's eyes remained uncomfortably fixed on Sole's face. "Is she around here? The other one?"

"No." Sole shook his head and looked down at the counter. "Not around here." Not anywhere, he thought.

The old man paused, his eyes narrowed to stare at Sole from under his bushy eyebrows. "She's gone. That's it. Left this world." He smiled, sure of himself. "How long's it been?"

Sole's eyes hardened. The old man's gaze was fixed and undeterred.

"I'd rather not talk about it."

"I understand." The old man nodded. "Lost my wife twenty years ago this month. Still hard to think about it." He extended a hand toward Sole. "Name's Sherman Westerfield, but you call me Sherm. Everyone else does."

A second passed, then two. Sherman Westerfield's hand remained outstretched, his eyes friendly and without guile. Sole relented.

"Bill Myers," he said, giving Sherm's hand a pump.

"Glad to know you, Bill Myers."

"Same here, Sherm."

"What brings you to Creosote?"

"Breakfast."

"Breakfast?" Sherm laughed and shook his head. "You're surely one for mystery, Bill, and a hard one to pull a story from."

"Sorry." Sole smiled for the first time. "I was sleeping in my truck when I heard some shooting out by the Rio Grande. Went to check it out and found a couple of boys firing across at a family of Mexicans."

"That would be Krieg and Zabala's men, assholes most of them."

"Can't disagree with you there."

"So what do a couple of men shooting at Mexicans have to do with breakfast?"

"Told them I was hungry and asked where I could find some food. One of them … Stu was his name … told me about this place."

Sherm nodded. "Stu's a good man, just in with a bad crowd. Who was he with?"

"Fella by the name of Lucky."

"Lucky Martin." Sherm's lips curled as if he'd tasted something sour. "Biggest asshole of them all. You're fortunate he didn't turn the rifle on you."

"Yeah, I got the impression he might have if I'd given him a chance."

"There you go again, saying things like there's a story there, but you're not telling it."

Isabella walked from the kitchen carrying two plates loaded with bacon, eggs, tortillas, and black beans. "Here's your breakfast." She stopped and looked at him, the smile back on her face. "I know everyone around here." She laughed, and the smile became even more enticing, beckoning to him to smile back. He resisted.

"Not too many to know in Creosote," she laughed. "But I didn't catch your name."

For an instant, he thought he might blurt it out—John Sole. Get a grip, he thought. You're acting like a teenage boy, tongue-tied and confused.

"This here's Bill Myers," Sherm piped up, filling the brief silence that passed between them.

"Here, Bill Myers. Eat your breakfast."

She placed the food in front of him, and for a moment, her hand rested beside his on the counter. He wondered what it would be like to let his hand touch hers, soaking in the feel of her skin against his. Would she pull away from him?

The muscles in his arm tensed. It was as if his hand was being pulled toward hers. He picked up the coffee mug, to break the magnetic attraction.

You're being ridiculous, he thought. She was a woman, like any other, and she was not ... Damn it. The memory forced its way in again. He gave in, saying the words to himself. She was not Shaye.

No one is, a voice inside reminded him. No one ever will be. But this woman is real, and she is here. Shaye is not. See, she's smiling at you, waiting. Her name is Isabella. Say it. Go on, say her name.

He put the coffee mug down and said, "Thank you, Isabella. It looks good."

"Eat," she said, and the smile was back, warm and knowing, the brown eyes watching, curious and friendly. "And tell us the story, the one Sherm was trying to coax from you."

He managed to pull his eyes away from hers, lifted a fork, and began shoveling food into his mouth. In between bites, he told the story. It only took a few minutes to finish the meal and his account of the encounter on the Rio Grande.

"You butt-stroked, Lucky Martin," Sherm chuckled, shaking his head. "Boy, you got some balls on you. That's all I can say. I'd a given a month's pension to have been there."

"Just happened," Sole said, shrugging.

"Well, just the same, you keep an eye out," Sherm leaned toward him, shaking a finger. "Lucky Martin is not one to forget a grudge."

"I'm not hard to find." Sole forked in the last mouthful of egg, scooped up some beans in a tortilla, and shoved it all in his mouth. "Good food," he mumbled, cheeks bulging.

"Thanks." Isabella leaned against the counter and grinned, nodding at his plate. "Good eater."

They laughed together this time.

"Yeah. Guess I made a pig out of myself."

"Nice to have the cooking around here appreciated," Isabella said, wiping the counter in front of Sole with the towel. "Usually they come in slam down some eggs and trot their horny asses over to Mazey's." She grinned. "Not always in that order, of course."

Arms folded, she gave him an appraising look. "So, besides breakfast and the usual gunfire on the Rio Grande, what brings you to Creosote, Bill Myers?"

"Chance," he said with a shrug. "Just wandering the country."

"Hmm. I don't think so." She shook her head. "No, there's another reason … something more."

She leaned toward him, resting her hip against the counter. For a moment, he couldn't control himself, and his eyes rested on the curve of her bare shoulders and swelling of her breasts under the halter top. He jerked his head to the side to break his gaze away.

"No, there's more," she repeated, leaning closer, curious, studying his face.

He could feel the warmth of her breath in the air before him. Her fragrance surrounded him.

"You aren't a man who just wanders," she said, making up her mind about it. "You're searching for something."

Her eyes rested on his for seconds. He was powerless to turn away, feeling them probe, turning things over, searching for a key to unlock whatever he was hiding inside.

Then all at once, she stood up straight, the smile spreading across her face again. She extended a hand.

"Well, whatever the reason, welcome to Creosote, Bill Myers."

He took her hand in his, holding it a second longer than necessary. The feeling was intense. It was strong and firm, warm and feminine at the same time, a hand accustomed to work, but that also knew other things. It was a woman's hand, and John Sole lingered, clinging to it for as long as he dared.

"Thank you, Isabella."

TEN

Time to Go to America!

It was cold and gloomy, and she was frightened. She wasn't alone.

Twenty-two others were jammed inside the cramped space behind the false walls of the K and Z refrigerated truck. Before boarding at a remote farm in the Mexican State of Sinaloa, they had been told the trip to the border would last twelve hours. There would be two stops along the way, for water and to allow those hiding behind the walls to relieve themselves in the brush.

At the first stop, Jacinta Martinez took the bottle of water the driver offered but had been too shy to squat behind a bush and empty her bladder as the other women had done. Now she regretted her inhibitions. She squirmed and bent over in the small space, trying to squeeze her legs shut and stop the urge to release her water on the floor.

"You should have let it go when we stopped, little one." The woman who spoke was older, in her fifties. Jacinta had learned that her name was Inez. She stood against the outer wall to the left and patted Jacinta's arm, speaking gently. "No one would have thought anything about it."

Jacinta nodded without speaking, focused on holding her bladder shut. Tears of frustration and embarrassment rolled down her face.

"All I can say is you had better not let it go down your leg in here. It smells bad enough already with all of these bodies." This woman's voice was cold, with no sympathy for the young girl's plight.

"Quiet!" Inez snapped. "You can see she is doing her best to hold it. She doesn't come from the same sort of life we have had. These things are new to her."

"Just the same," the cold-voiced woman said, turning away from Inez's stare. "She better not let it go in here."

Jacinta looked up at Inez. "I won't let it go. I promise, but it hurts so."

Inez moved closer in the dim light. Two small light bulbs mounted in the walls of the truck provided a yellowish glow. She put an arm around Jacinta.

"Relax, child. Ignore that old hag."

The cold-voiced woman turned her head and glared at Inez, but she said nothing.

"Try not to think about the urge to go, and it will pass," Inez said and added with a shrug, "Besides, we've all slept on the floor with the dogs or in the barn with the animals. A little piss on the floor isn't going to bother any of us."

There was muted laughter from the other women lining the truck wall. Only the cold-voiced woman remained silent, scowling at Inez.

"How did you come to be here?" Inez asked, more to take Jacinta's mind off her discomfort than for any other reason.

"My mother's brother lives in Houston in Texas. I have

a picture." Jacinta reached in her pocket and removed an envelope, forgetting the urge to pee for a moment. "Here it is."

She held it out to Inez who squinted at the image of a round-faced, smiling man in his fifties. "Your uncle is a nice looking man. He has a pleasant smile."

Jacinta turned the picture to see it better and nodded. "Yes. His name is Arturo Cardozo, and my mother always said he is the happiest of men, always laughing and making others laugh." She placed the photograph back in the envelope, closed the flap, and slid it back in her pocket. "I am going to find him and tell him that I am his family. He will welcome me, and I can work for him and be with my family there in America."

"Your mother sent you away from her to your uncle for this?" Inez looked into the young girl's face, sensing that there was more to the story.

"No." Jacinta shook her head, and a tear appeared at the corner of her eye. "My mother has passed."

They made the sign of the cross together at the mention of her mother's death. "God calls those he loves," Inez said.

"Yes." Jacinta nodded. "And those I loved as well. She died two years ago. I have no other family, but ..." She patted the pocket where the picture of her uncle was secured. "But my uncle will welcome me. My mother loved him very much, and he is such a good man."

"I'm sure your Uncle Arturo will be glad to see his niece. He is sure to throw his arms around the daughter of his beloved sister." Inez smiled. "But where did you get the three thousand American dollars to pay the *coyotaje*?"

"I have been working. It was hard to find a job that would pay more than it took for me to live, but the priest who buried my mother knew a family in Culiacán. They said I could live with them and care for their three small children. The pay was not so much because they fed me and gave me a bed to sleep on, but in two years, I was able to save the money."

"They sound like nice people. Could you not have remained with them until you met a man to marry?"

"Perhaps." Jacinta shrugged. "I thought of that at first. The woman was very nice. The man too ... at first."

"He changed, the man?"

"He ..." Jacinta hesitated. "He wanted things from me ... when his wife was not around."

Inez's eyes narrowed. "What sort of things," she asked, suspecting the answer.

"He came to my bed when the children were sleeping. He ..." She shook her head. "I didn't understand at first. He did what men do with their wives. Made me do things for him ... to him. Terrible things that will send me to hell."

Sobs shook Jacinta's shoulders. Inez held her close in the tight space, letting her cry out the tears she had been holding.

"There, there, little one. You are not going to hell. Did the priest not tell you? You were raped. The man who raped you will go to hell for sure, but you are still innocent."

"*El hijo de puta!*" The cold-voiced woman's voice was less icy now, and she turned back to Inez and the girl, Jacinta. "The son of a bitch! If there is any justice, he will have his balls cut off before he goes to burn in hell," she hissed.

"I agree. He is the evil one, not you," Inez said. "And your priest? You told him, of course, and he did nothing?"

"Yes." Jacinta lowered her head, ashamed. "I confessed my sins."

"Your sins?" Inez raised her voice for the first time. "How can there be a sin when you are the victim?"

"It is what I was taught as a child … when a woman lies with a man she is not married to it is a sin. So, I confessed my sins to my priest."

"And this priest of yours, what did he do?"

"He was very kind and forgave me. I only had to say four Hail Mary's,"

"How kind of the black-coated bastard," the woman with the cold voice interjected.

Inez nodded agreement but drew the line at speaking evil of a priest.

"It was the priest's idea for me to leave," Jacinta said. "Father Alfonso said it was best to get away so that the sinning would stop. He introduced me to the *coyotaje*, *Señor* Lopez."

"*Señor* Lopez?" Inez laughed. "Such a grand title for a gutter rat like Pepe Lopez."

"Father Alfonso said you had to find someone to trust to take you over the border. Otherwise, they might take your money and leave you in the desert or do terrible things to you. He said that …" She hesitated and then whispered, "*Señor* Lopez would see that I was safely across."

"Well, at least he was right about that," Inez said, patting her hand. "Pepe Lopez is better than the others who take people across." Her voice went low, remembering something unpleasant from her past. "I have made the crossing five times to be with my son in Nevada. Each time, I stay for a while, earn money, see my grandchildren, and then go back to Mexico with the money to see my sisters and help them. The first time, I was dropped off in the middle of the desert without water or supplies. There were ten of us. Four died. We didn't even know if we were over the border. As it turned out, we were in Arizona. I made it to a town and called my son who drove all night to come pick me up, or the Border Patrol would have found me and sent me back."

"You must have been frightened," Jacinta said.

"*Ay!* I was angry." Inez shook her head in disgust. "The next time we made it safely across, but there was an extra charge before we could leave."

"An extra charge?" Jacinta's eyes opened wide. "After you already paid?"

"Yes." Inez nodded somberly. "That time, the women in the group had to pay with their bodies. The *coyotajes* gathered around and took turns with us. When they were done, they let us go."

"*Madre de Dios!*" Mother of God. Jacinta crossed herself.

"After that, I found the *coyotaje*, Pepe Lopez, the one who has arranged this trip. They promise safe delivery, no rape, no being left in the desert to die of thirst. The Americans he works for make sure that no one is hurt. Since I found them, it is safe to cross. Sure it is a little crowded and cold in the truck, but you get there in one piece."

"It is true," a voice agreed in the dark.

"Yes, for me, this is the fourth time with Pepe and no problems," another said.

"Your priest did one thing right," the woman with the cold voice said. "Look around. Why do you think there are eighteen women in a group of twenty-three? Because they know this is the safe way to cross."

The truck shuddered and slowed. Brakes squealed as they bumped and swayed in the back. The driver steered off the road and down a dirt trail until they were out of sight of the main road. A murmur went up among the women and the few men on board. Finally, they could have some water and get out to stretch.

The truck rocked to a stop. A minute later, the back

door was thrown open, and one of the panels that concealed them behind the wall was removed. The passengers made their way through the narrow opening and weaved through a path that had been made between the crates of tomatoes.

The crates were arranged strategically so that from the outside, they appeared to be stacked all the way to the back. Even if someone came onto the truck to inspect, they would have to remove every crate to discern that there was a winding passage between them. Even then, they would not know about the wall panels that concealed the illegal border crossers.

One by one, the passengers jumped to the ground. The sun was rising and, a fresh breeze, dry and warm, but clean, blew over the desert.

"Come, little one," Inez said and took Jacinta by the arm.

They walked thirty feet away from the crowd that gathered around the truck to receive their bottles of water.

"Good. *Hierba del vaso*—vase grass. This will do." Inez stopped and with the toe of her shoe carefully lifted the outlying stems. "No snakes," she said, satisfied. "Squat and do your business here. I will watch and see that no one disturbs you."

Jacinta did not need to be coaxed. Moving behind the four-foot-tall shrub, she dropped her pants and squatted. Relief washed over her, taking with it any remaining delicateness about relieving herself in public.

For nearly two minutes, the flow ran onto the ground, splashing at first, then soaking into the parched soil. When it stopped, Jacinta stood and adjusted her underwear and pants. She looked at Inez over the bush, a smile on her face and the embarrassment gone.

"Now you watch for me," Inez said, dropping low on the other side of the vase grass. As she peed, she chatted as if they were two women leaning over a wall talking about the weather. "The *norteamericanos* call this shrub bristle brush. I think our Mexican word has a nicer sound, don't you?"

"Yes, vase grass sounds like something you would find in a garden."

"Exactly. In fact …" Inez stood, pulled her pants up, and leaned toward Jacinta. "Some call it *incienso* because in the old days the priests would burn it as incense during the mass. What do you think your priest would say to that? That we took a piss in his incense!" Inez threw her head back and laughed.

Jacinta couldn't help but join in. For the first time since her mother's death, she felt free to laugh. There were no children to care for, no rules to follow in a stranger's house, and no man coming to her bed in the night. There were only the new day, the laughter, and the relief after a good pee.

They walked back to the truck. The driver and the man who rode up front with him handed them each a bottle of water.

A car approached down the dirt road, the tires crunching over the rocks. Jacinta tensed and reached out for Inez's hand.

"Relax, child," Inez said. "He always comes just before the last part of the trip."

The car brakes squeaked, and the door opened. It was the man the priest had introduced to her, the one who would get her across the border. Pepe Lopez walked up smiling.

"*Bueno mis amigos*. I hope all is well. Have there been any problems?"

Heads shook.

"Good. That is good. So, I am here to tell you what will happen next."

Inez whispered to Jacinta, "He always does this. I think he likes the show, to be the big rooster and show us how he has taken care of everything." She shrugged. "Still, it is his show, and he *has* taken care of everything, so we listen and smile."

"From here," Pepe said. "It is only four hours to the border. They know us there, but they do not know about you, so one thing is most important. When you hear the men in the front knock on the wall behind the cab …"

He stopped and gave three hard raps on the side of the truck to demonstrate. "When you hear these knocks, you must be completely silent. There can be no noise."

He placed his finger to his lips. "Total silence This is most important. Absolutely no sound, not a sneeze, a cough, or even a whisper."

Heads nodded their understanding.

Pepe smiled. "Excellent. So, we all understand. Now stretch your legs for a few more minutes, and you will go back into the truck to cross the border."

Two of the men lit up cigarettes and leaned against the truck. The women gathered in small groups, chatting about where they would go and what they would do once across the border.

Pepe approached Jacinta and Inez. "*Hola abuela*—hello, grandmother."

"Phht," Inez hissed. "I am not your grandmother."

"True enough," Pepe nodded, the ever-present smile not flinching under the woman's rebuke. "But I trust you have taken good care of our youngest passenger, perhaps been a grandmother to her."

"I have been a friend."

"What more can a person ask?" Pepe oozed. "True friendship is everything, is it not?" He turned to Jacinta. "Father Alfonso sends his greetings and a prayer that you are well."

Jacinta smiled. "I am well. Please thank Father Alfonso, for all he has done for me."

"I will do that." Pepe gave her a pat on the shoulder and turned. "¡*Vamos!* Let's go! Everybody in the truck. Time to go to America!"

ELEVEN

Not Overloaded with Brains

"What the fuck happened to you?"

Raul Zabala stood on the loading dock to the refrigerated warehouse at K and Z Trucking, watching Stu Pearce and Lucky Martin get out of their pickup and walk toward him.

Stu had the sad dog look of a mutt about to take a beating. Lucky supported his broken jaw with one hand as he walked, wincing at every step. When he reached the dock and tried to climb the short iron ladder up from the pavement, he moaned.

"Go around to the front and come in through the door," Zabala ordered. "Meet us in the office."

Martin nodded and walked around the side of the building, stepping gingerly to avoid any jarring of his injury.

"What happened?" Zabala snapped at Pearce.

"Met someone," Pearce said matter-of-factly and shrugged. "He didn't like Lucky shootin' at a Mex family across the river."

"Let's go." Zabala turned and led the way inside to the office.

By the time they arrived, Martin was sitting across the desk from Tom Krieg whose steely eyes bored into the luckless Lucky. "What happened?"

"Got my jaw broke," Martin managed to whisper through clenched teeth and then whimpered in pain.

Zabala elbowed Pearce as he took his customary seat to the side of Krieg's desk. "You tell it, Pearce."

"Me?"

"You." Zabala nodded. "Just spit it out."

"Well, Mr. Krieg," Stu Pearce said, swallowing down the butterflies rising in his gut. There was no telling how the boss was going to take this, two of his men outdone by a drifter sleeping in his truck and looking for breakfast. "Like he said, he got his jaw broke."

"I can fucking see that. You tell me how it happened. Start talking."

"Well, we was out by the Rio Grande, like you said … followin' orders, doin' what you told us to do … what we always do."

"Get to the point, dammit!" Krieg leaned forward, elbows on his desk, glaring at Pearce.

It didn't seem fair to put the pressure on him, Pearce thought. He thought of protesting. After all, he didn't do anything. He didn't shoot down some Mexican and get a drifter pissed off at them. He sure as hell didn't get buttstroked with his own rifle. Then he looked into Krieg's eyes and put aside any idea of protesting.

"Right," he nodded and took a breath. "So we see some Mexicans about to swim across. Don't know where they was headed, didn't seem to be nobody waitin' for them. I reckon they was gonna walk a ways and meet someone when they got over."

Pearce cast a sideways glance at Martin, still whimpering in pain. He didn't like turning on a partner, but there was no putting off the boss. Besides, he was not going to take the blame for Martin's hotheaded nature.

"So, Lucky, he puts a few rounds in the water in front of 'em, but they keep comin' on, like they knew we wasn't really gonna shoot 'em. So, he puts a few more rounds in the mud around 'em on the bank over there." Pearce lifted a finger to emphasize that this was all within their operating orders. "Not too close mind you. Just close enough to get their attention."

"And they still came on?" Krieg's eyes bored into him, looking for some sign of deception.

"Well, no, sir." Pearce could feel Martin's eyes glaring at him. "They sort of stopped about then."

"So, what was the problem?"

"Well, they was walkin', along the bank sort of … maybe they was lookin' for another place to cross, you know, away from the shootin'. That's when … well, I suppose that's what did it … what caused it to happen."

"What, Goddammit!" Krieg's fist slammed down on the desktop.

There was no stopping now, Pearce told himself. Just get it out.

"That's when Lucky here reloaded. I guess it pissed him off that they wasn't payin' us no mind. So he puts seven rounds in the magazine and one in the chamber. Then he lifts and starts levering them rounds in and spraying the far bank to scare 'em back for real. And that's when …" Pearce hesitated and took a breath and lowered his head, avoiding Krieg's icy stare. "I mean, he didn't mean to or nothin', least I don't think so. You know they was all movin' around so much over there, but that's when he hit one."

"What!" Krieg spun towards Martin. "You shot someone trying to swim across? Are fucking out of your mind?"

Martin tried to answer. "I was only …" he shook his head, the pain of trying to speak too much for him to bear.

"And you?" Krieg swung his stare back to Pearce. "What did you do during all the shooting?"

"Well, I tried to tell him to stop … that we had done what we was supposed to, but he didn't." He was committed now. Best to just spit it all out. "I reckon his blood was up about them ignorin' the warning shots and all. You know how Lucky gets. Anyways, he wasn't listenin' to me. He just commenced to shootin', sprayin' the other bank."

"And he hit someone," Krieg said, disgusted.

"Yes, sir." Pearce nodded solemnly. "He did for a fact."

"Who?" Krieg shook his head. "Tell me he didn't shoot one of the children."

"Oh, no, sir." Pearce grinned, happy to have some good news to report. "Not one of the kids, or the mother either. Hit a man. I suppose he was the father of the brood."

"How bad?"

"Not so bad he'll die," Pearce said, giving the man's wound serious consideration. "From what I could see, at that distance and all, I'd say he'll be limping for the rest of his life, but he should make it fine if he gets some medical attention."

"You stupid son of a bitch." Krieg glared at Martin. "You're supposed to scare them off from crossing, not shoot them. What happens if the Mexicans pull your bullet out of that man's leg and pass it over to the Border Patrol with a grievance? They match the bullet to your rifle, and we're all fucked!"

Lucky Martin could do nothing but stand there and take his punishment. He prayed now that the ordeal would end so that he could get some liquor in him and try and kill the pain.

"Alright," Krieg sighed. "He shot a Mex, but who broke Martin's jaw."

"Well, that's when he showed up, when all the shootin' commenced."

"Who?"

"Some drifter. Said he was sleepin' in his pickup off the highway and heard the shootin'. Come to see what the fuss was about. Had him a pistol, a big Colt 1911." Pearce shook his head. "That damned bore looked wide as a badger hole and twice as mean."

"So he got the drop on you … both." Krieg's eyes narrowed. "What did you do?"

"Me? I didn't do nothin'. Like you said he had the drop on us. Lucky, he thought about it, but after a bit, he laid his Winchester on the ground and backed away."

"What about your rifle?"

"Mine?" Pearce raised his eyebrows in surprise. "Oh, it was back in the truck. I don't much care to shoot at them Mexicans. I always let Lucky do the shootin'."

"So a drifter disarmed two of my men." Krieg sighed, shaking his head. "Go on."

"Well, he talked alright, you know not ruffled or anything. Just wanted Lucky to stop shootin' at the Mexicans." Pearce nodded. "I think it was mostly 'cause there was kids and the woman over there."

"Alright, so you stopped shooting. Sounds like he had

more brains than the two of you." Krieg looked at Martin. "And his jaw? How'd that get broke?"

"Well, I reckon it was something, Lucky said." Pearce hesitated.

"Finish it," Krieg said, disgusted. "It can't be any worse than what you've already said."

"Well, he was holding Lucky's rifle, the drifter was, and he sort of took a step forward, and butt-stroked Lucky in the jaw." Stu Pearce shook his head, repressing a smile at the memory. "I swear he dropped like a rock."

"Why?"

"Why what, Mr. Krieg?"

"Why did he butt stroke Lucky?" He cast a disgusted look in Martin's direction. "With his own rifle?"

"Oh that. Well, like I was sayin', it was somethin' Lucky said."

"What?"

"He ... uh ... he told him he was a dead man when you found out and that ..."

"Go on."

"And if I remember right, Lucky said he was goin' to cut the drifter's heart out."

"And the drifter gave him something to remember him by for that." Krieg laughed. "Don't blame him. Did you happen to catch this drifter's name?"

"No, sir. We talked for a bit after that, but he didn't never say his name, and he had the Colt and Lucky's rifle, so I wasn't pressin' the issue."

"Sounds like the first smart decision you made," Krieg said. "Anything else you can tell me about him?"

"Well, he was hungry. Said he hadn't eat in a day, so I sent him over to Creosote to the café."

"And he said he was going there for breakfast?"

"Yes, sir. Near as I could tell, he left us and went to find him some breakfast. He didn't seem like all that bad a fella. Talked nice once the shootin' stopped and Lucky hit the ground. Even left Lucky's rifle for him out where he had parked his truck. Took real good care not to get dirt in it."

"Alright." Krieg stood. "Stu, go wait outside. Got a load coming in. You help with it when it gets here." He turned to Martin. "You drive your dumb ass down to Brownsville and get patched up. Then you meet us back here."

"Yes, sir." Stu Pearce said.

"Yeph, thur," Lucky Martin hissed from his broken mouth.

The two men left the office.

"What do you think?" Krieg looked at Raul Zabala who had remained silent during the inquisition, trying hard not to laugh out loud.

"I'd say those boys are lucky to be alive. This drifter sounds like a serious man."

"Someone we could use, maybe?"

"Well, as you can see," Zabala said jabbing a thumb at the door where Pearce and Martin had exited. "We're not overloaded with brains around here. If he's smart as Stu made him sound and half as tough, we could use him ... if he's on board with our operation."

"Yeah, that's the kick." Krieg nodded as he considered the dilemma Lucky Martin had faced. "It is getting harder to keep them on the other side, and make them pay up and go through one of our contacts."

"I imagine that Mex who got shot in the leg will spread the word. Mean and dumb as he is, Lucky may have done us a favor."

"Maybe." Krieg grabbed his keys off the desk. "We'll check the load coming in first. Pepe said he packed something special for us. After, we'll head into Creosote and meet this drifter and see how he liked his breakfast."

TWELVE

Die Now, or Die Later

Once again, there was a rush of feet from behind. Strong hands gripped him by both arms as he left Rosita's Cantina again. This time it was in broad daylight.

¡Mierda!—Shit! This was becoming ridiculous. He was going to have to find another cantina if they kept this up.

"Come with us."

"There is some mistake," Mario Acosta said, sighing as he tried to pull his arm free. "I have already been to see your *jefes* in Texas."

"Shut up." The man who spoke stood behind the two who held his arms.

Half dragging, half carrying him, they walked to the end of the block away from the direction of his car. An old Chevrolet minivan waited there. The door slid open as they approached and the men holding his arms shoved him in ahead of them, pushing his face down on the floor. They climbed in and sat in the seat, side by side with their feet on his back, pinning him down.

"I'm telling you, they already did this to me ... *sus socios de negocios!*" Your business associates!

The man with his foot closest to Mario's head gave him a kick in the ear. "We told you to shut up."

Mario shut up. The van swerved through city traffic for twenty minutes then pulled onto a dirt road. The bouncing thumps knocked the breath from him several times as he was lifted from the floor and then thrown back down with the men's feet still on his back.

He began to feel nauseous. What would these assholes do if he puked up the tortillas, beans, and Victoria beer he had downed for lunch at Rosita's? He didn't want to find out and swallowed back the rising bile.

Just when he thought the fight to hold on to his lunch was lost, the minivan skidded to a halt in loose gravel. The door slid open, and the men in the seats climbed out, dragging him with them. He stood blinking in the bright sunlight, surrounded by four men. The three who had abducted him and the van's driver. He recognized none from his previous encounter with the men sent by Krieg and Zabala.

Who were they? Fear rose in his throat, but he managed to squeak out a question. He wasn't sure he wanted to know the answer, but he asked, "Why have you brought me here?"

"There." The man who had been sitting in the front seat with the driver pointed at a small adobe shack fifty yards away. "Move."

Mario stumbled toward the shack, his knees threatening to buckle under him with every step. It was certain that these were not the *gringos'* men.

His head pivoted on his neck as they walked to the shack. They were in the desert, an hour or more out of

Torreón. The high mountains in the distance told him they were south of the city, but he was clueless as to where in the vast expanse of desert. No one would find him here if these men did not want them to.

The man in front pushed the door of the shack open and stepped aside for Mario to enter. He stooped to pass under the low door sill and then stopped to accustom his vision to the gloom. The place smelled of wood smoke, fried meat, and onions.

"Sit."

The command came from a man seated at a table before the small fireplace. An iron skillet containing the remnants of breakfast sat on rocks beside the ashes of the morning fire.

Even sitting, Mario could tell he was of short stature. His brown complexion, high cheekbones, and thin prominent nose showed that he was no *mestizo*—mixed blood Mexican. No Spanish conquistador or missionary had found his way into the man's parentage.

Probably Yaqui, Mario thought. They didn't get along with anyone.

A hand on his shoulder pushed Mario toward a chair across the table from the man. He sat and waited, afraid to look him in the eyes, but unable to avoid his stare.

"I see you have met my sons," the man began.

Mario looked around at the faces, noticing for the first time the resemblance between them and the man at the table. He nodded.

"My name is Benito Diaz. You will remember this name."

Mario nodded.

"Do you want to know why you will remember it?"

Marion nodded. It seemed the safest thing to do.

"You will remember it because you now work for me." Diaz nodded at his sons. "And them. What they say, you will do."

His head swam with the absurdity of what the man said. First, the *gringo* and *Tejan* threaten him, and now this Yaqui gangster. His plan to get rich was definitely becoming too complicated.

Diaz waited for him to acknowledge his instructions. Mario had no choice but to nod once again.

"We are aware that others have approached you," Diaz continued. "The *norteamericanos* are cutting into our business. This is our country, and if anyone is to send people north for profit, it will be us. Do you understand?"

Mario nodded.

"Say it."

"I understand."

"Good." Diaz nodded this time. "Now, tell us what they have instructed you to do."

"But …" Mario hesitated. "They are very … serious … men. If I say anything, they will …"

"We are also very serious men." Diaz leaned close across the small table, the lids of his eyes narrowed until they were just slits with black dots in the center. "And we are here now with you. They are not."

"Yes, I understand. It's just that …"

"They will kill you?" Diaz's lips parted, revealing a line of white teeth. "What do you suppose we will do if you choose not to cooperate?"

It wasn't much of a choice. He could die now or die later. Mario chose to die later.

"What do you want to know?" he said.

"Tell us everything."

Mario nodded and told them everything.

THIRTEEN

Soon

Three metallic raps sounded through the wall of the truck.

"We're close now," Inez leaned toward Jacinta and whispered, putting a finger to her lips.

Jacinta nodded without speaking. Her heart beat like a drum in her chest, and she worried the others might hear it. Worse she thought it might be so loud the men outside could hear, or that it might make her so nervous, she would make some small sound that would draw their attention.

Stop, she said to herself. You worry for no reason; look around. See how Inez rests her head back against the wall napping. Others do the same. Even the woman with the cold voice and icy stare had closed her eyes in peaceful repose, unconcerned with what was happening outside the truck.

Five minutes passed in silence. Most did as Inez and rested their heads against the wall or on their knees, dozing, waiting for the truck to move forward across the border.

Jacinta felt the truck inch forward, the engine whining a little, then stopping. Then a pause for a minute and move forward again. Another stop. Then move forward, and the truck stopped once more. She heard voices outside now, speaking in English, close to the truck.

"How ya doin', Sam," the driver called down. "Missed you last trip through."

"Not bad." The Border Patrol agent stepped up to the window. "Had a cold last week. Seems like it's taking forever to get over it. Still coughing and sneezing."

"Yep," the driver nodded and chuckled. "Grandma always said a cold is three days coming, three days with you, and three days going. She called it a nine-day event."

"Seems like nine weeks," Sam muttered and sniffed. "Need to look at the manifest, Louie."

"Sure, sure. Here you go."

Louie handed the clipboard with the load manifest out the window. Sam, the agent, watched and looked over at the man sitting in the passenger seat. He took the clipboard and then called over to the passenger.

"Heard you had some trouble over in Webb County, Jake. Wouldn't have expected to see you this trip."

"Just a run-in, not much," Jake replied, his tone indicating he didn't want to discuss his absence.

Sam, the agent, didn't care and persisted. "The way it was told to me, you had a run-in with a couple of deputies."

"Said it wasn't nothin'." Jake's tone was downright surly.

Louie, the driver, decided he'd better intervene. "Ole Jake got liquored up. That's all it was to it, Sam. Tussled with a couple of deputies outside Bigguns Bar. They tossed him for public drunk. Spent a night in jail." Louie laughed. "You know what the worst of it was?"

"What's that?" Sam said as he looked over the manifest.

"Mr. Krieg had to come bail him out." Louie laughed. "Hell, I thought he was gonna tie a knot in Jake's neck. Probably would have, if it wasn't so damn leathery."

"Manifest looks good," Sam said, chuckling at the story. "Pull up so I can check the back."

"You got it." Louie shifted into gear, and the truck rolled forward a few feet and turned into a pullout on the right.

While one officer walked a drug-sniffing K-9 around the truck checking for illegal narcotics, Sam went to the back door and opened it. Climbing onto the bumper, he looked over the stacked crates of tomatoes then jumped down to the ground.

"All clear," he said, walking up to the driver window. He handed the manifest back through the window.

"Thanks, Sam. See you next time."

"Yep." Sam nodded and waved forward the next vehicle in line as Louie put the truck in gear and began to move away from the crossing.

In the back, Jacinta looked around at the others. They began to stir, lift their heads, and open their eyes. They smiled, relaxed, and raised their arms stretching as much as they could.

"What does it mean?" Jacinta whispered to Inez.

"We are across." Inez smiled and patted her knee.

"Across the border? So easy?"

"I told you it was nothing to be worried about as long as you are quiet."

Jacinta looked around, thinking that everything should look different in the truck, but it was the same truck, and the same tired people crammed into the small space behind the wall.

"I wish I could see what it is like, outside … *Los Estados Unidos*" The United States.

She said it with reverence. The world beyond the truck walls must be new and beautiful, she thought.

"It is like Mexico," the cold-voiced woman said, smirking. "Dry and dusty like Chihuahua, except the places where the whites live have bigger houses and fancy cars."

"Ah." Inez hissed. "You are a cold bitch, you know that. I hope I don't have to make another crossing cooped up with your vile temperament." She looked at Jacinta. "The countryside here is much like Mexico, but much is different too. You sense it in the air. People do well here. They live and thrive like flowers in black earth."

"It sounds so nice," Jacinta said. "I can't wait for the door to open."

"Soon" Inez put an arm over her shoulder. "Little Jacinta—the little hyacinth, soon you will find your uncle and your new life."

FOURTEEN

Dust

A cloudburst on the horizon filled the air with the scent of rain. Heavy with the fragrances of life, it blew across the plains on a breeze pushed by the distant thunderhead.

Reynaldo 'Sandy' Palmeras touched the four-wheeler's throttle, nudging the speed up over forty-five, fast enough on this dirt road. The machine hummed under him like a cat purring with contentment. He smiled and allowed it to slow without braking, coasting until the four-wheeler rolled to a gentle stop. Sherm Westerfield was going to be happy to have his old buggy back in working order.

He was ten miles out of Creosote on the dirt road that cut across the prairie, west to east. The two men who controlled life in Creosote and along this stretch of Texas brush country lived down this road.

Ten miles to the north Tom Krieg ruled his ranch and everyone who worked for him with an iron hand. An equal distance to the south, Raul Zabala was the lord of everything he could see.

He swung a leg up and rested it on top of the saddle,

leaning forward with an elbow on his knee. The day was hot and clear, except for the thunderstorm in the distance.

He lifted his nose to the breeze. "God, I love that smell."

Sandy spoke to himself and wasn't self-conscious about it. Growing up in Creosote, you talked to yourself a lot, or not at all, and he was too young not to talk at all.

"Looks like it might rain today." His eyes moved from the storm clouds to the horizon and back.

"No, it's headed off to the northeast. Too bad." He shook his head. "Damn, I love the rain. If I ever get away from this place, I'm gonna live where it rains a lot … where it rains every day. That'd be just about perfect for me."

A line of dust appeared, several miles off to the northeast, closer than the storm.

"Some of Krieg's men," he muttered. "I expect they're coming in to join the others at Mazey's."

He was in no hurry to move. He was where he wanted to be and didn't appreciate the interruption coming his way.

With a sigh, he touched the starter. The ATV's engine rumbled to life, and he turned the handlebars and let the idling engine roll him out of the road to the shoulder.

The dust was closer now. He could make out two pickups, moving fast. That wasn't unusual. Fast was the only way to drive when everything was fifty miles away from where you were now. Sandy figured he'd let them pass and then ride on another ten miles or so and enjoy the morning, before turning back to help his mother at the café.

The trucks were a half-mile out now and coming fast. Dust rose behind them, a hundred-foot-high rooster tail, billowing like the smoke from an old locomotive.

Sandy lowered his head, squinted his eyes, and held his breath to keep the dust out. He'd let it settle and then continue on his ride.

"Stop!" A voice shouted from the lead pickup as they passed.

Shit. Sandy knew the voice.

"That's the half breed! What the fuck's he doin' out here?"

The big Dodge 2500 skidded in the dirt. Left without any warning, the truck behind had to veer off the road and slid to a stop in the ditch.

The driver of the second truck got out, pissed off. "What the fuck you doin', Doyle. Tryin' to get us all killed?"

Doyle Krieg got out from behind the wheel of the lead truck and looked at the Krieg ranch foreman, Bud Lawton. "Stopped to talk to my old buddy here." He nodded at Sandy, sitting astride the ATV on the other side of the road. "You remember, *Reynaldo* Palmeras, don't you, Bud?" he sneered. "The half-breed?"

Lawton cast a glance at Sandy, head still down as the dust settled around him. "Doyle, there's no cause to start trouble out here," he tried to reason. "Sandy's just waiting for us to pass."

"Sandy." Doyle threw his head back and laughed. "That's a good one. Use a name like that so he can pretend to be one of us."

"Come on, Doyle. He never picked that name. Everyone calls him that on account of his hair being light and all."

"What do you think, Paco?" Doyle turned to the man who stepped from the passenger side of the Dodge.

"Could be he is not very proud of his Hispanic origins," Paco shrugged. "But it is always that way with half breeds, ain't it? Don't know which way to turn."

"Hey *Reynaldo,*" He called across to Sandy. "I am a proud *Tejan*; my great-grandparents came from Coahuila.

And you, what are you? A half-breed!" Paco grinned and shoved his hands in his jeans' pockets, waiting for Doyle to direct the next move.

Bud Lawton shook his head. Paco González was Doyle's right-hand man and accomplice in stirring up shit whenever the opportunity arose, and Sandy Palmeras on the side of the road presented the perfect opportunity.

Doyle and Sandy had known each other all of their lives, attended school together in Zapata, riding the bus that Tom Krieg provided for the outlying families. From their earliest years, Doyle had held a grudge for Sandy and took to calling him a half breed when they were still in grammar school.

For his part, Sandy accepted it the way a person takes the weight of something you can't change. He was a half breed. He knew it. His white father had deserted his mother of Mexican descent when he was a baby, and she had raised him alone.

For most people, his lineage wouldn't have mattered. There were lots of half Mexicans around. This was Texas, after all.

He figured it mattered to Doyle Krieg because Doyle had to have someone to pick on. Sandy felt sorry for him, growing up on the Krieg ranch with Tom Krieg and a bunch of ranch hands but no mother. The official story was that she had died and was buried on the ranch. The unofficial word, spread around Creosote, in corners where Tom Krieg couldn't hear, was that she found him with another woman, left him, and divorced him.

Sandy didn't know which was true and didn't care. It

didn't change a thing. Doyle Krieg had a bee up his ass when it came to Reynaldo 'Sandy' Palmeras and had been trying to start trouble with him since the first grade.

Sandy stepped off the ATV, folded his arms, leaned against the saddle, and smiled. "Morning, Doyle. How's it going?"

"Hey, that's pretty good English for a half breed." Doyle looked over his shoulder at Paco who grinned. The grin encouraged him to take a step closer to Sandy.

"Come on, Doyle," Bud Lawton put his hands on Doyle's chest. "There's no cause for this. Let's get into Creosote. I'm hungry, and they say Mazey's got some new girls."

Doyle knocked Lawton's hand away. "Get out of my way, Bud. You might be the foreman, but don't forget who I am." He snarled like a petulant lion cub trying to assert itself.

He pushed past Lawton and crossed the narrow dirt road. Sandy stood leaning against the ATV, waiting for what was to come, for what always came.

"Like I was sayin', half-breed." Doyle leaned in close. "You tryin' to be one of us? Give it up. You'll never be nothin' but a half-breed. You know why?"

Sandy waited for it.

"Because," Doyle sneered. "*Tu madre es una puta.*" Your mother is a whore.

Arms still folded across his chest, Sandy's backhanded fist to Doyle's jaw sent him reeling backward. Doyle recovered, pulling himself up straight and the two were on each other like wildcats.

Fists and arms flailed. Dust kicked up around them in a

cloud as they struggled for position and then both were on the ground, rolling over trying to pin the other down to better pummel him with blows to the face.

"Kick his ass, Doyle!" Paco shouted and sauntered across the road to stand over the fray, but just far enough away to not be dragged into it.

"Break it up!" Bud Lawton shouted and reached into the dust cloud to grab a collar.

It was Sandy's collar, and as Lawton pulled him off, Doyle kicked out with his boot, catching Sandy in the face. Lawton released Sandy and grabbed Doyle who moved in to continue stomping his adversary with his boots.

"Enough!" Lawton shoved Doyle, sending him backward to the ground. He pointed a thick finger at him. "You tell your daddy whatever you want, but this fight ends now." He looked at Paco. "Get your ass in the truck. You're driving. I'll follow the two of you, but you get to Creosote. You can go to the café or go to Mazey's. I don't care, but you cause any more trouble, and I'll beat both your asses."

Paco glared at Lawton but got behind the wheel. When Doyle seated himself on the passenger side, Paco gunned the engine and spun the tires, sending a spray of dirt over Sandy who still sat in the road, wiping at the blood dripping from his nose.

Lawton bent over examining the boy's injuries. "Not too bad. Don't look like your nose is broke. Didn't lose any teeth, just busted your lip some." He stood up straight and pulled a bandanna from his back pocket. "Here. It's clean. Wipe your face off with it, then I'd get on back to Creosote if I was you and have Isabella check you over." He started to turn away, stopped and added, "I wouldn't make too much of this, Sandy. You know how Doyle and his daddy can be. It was a fair fight." He smiled. "And you had the best of him until I pulled you off and he managed to cold-cock you with that boot. I'm sorry about that."

Lawton turned and walked to his pickup. He followed the road toward Creosote, pulling away slowly so as not to send any more dust cascading over Sandy.

With the bandanna pressed hard against his nose, Sandy stood and held his head back. It took ten minutes to stop the bleeding.

Once he could lower his head safely without blood dripping from his face to the ground, he beat his shirt and pants with his hands to clean himself off, sending puffs of dust drifting away in the breeze.

"Fucking dust. I swear I'm gonna go live somewhere where it rains every day, and there ain't no goddamned dust."

FIFTEEN

Dreams
_____

The mood was light. Jacinta listened as the others chatted among themselves.

Where are you going?
Who will you stay with?
How will you arrive there?
Is someone going to meet you?
We are going in the same direction.
Can we travel together?
Is someone meeting you?
Could you give me a ride as far as Dallas?

There in the gloom behind the truck's false wall, they spoke among themselves, at ease as if they were going on a holiday trip. Jacinta allowed herself to relax. She was genuinely sleepy for the first time in days. Her head began to drop to her chest, her eyes closed, and her breathing settled into a soft, rhythmic sigh.

"Poor child," Inez said as Jacinta's cheek touched her shoulder, resting there as she fell deeper into sleep. She lifted a hand and stroked the girl's hair, pushing it back away from her face.

"Hmph." As usual, the cold-voiced woman sitting on the other side of the girl was annoyed.

"Why does she bother you so?" Inez shook her head in disgust at the woman's surliness.

"She doesn't belong here."

"And you do?" Inez's eyes flashed at the woman. "Who made you the decider of who should be here and who should not?"

"A girl like that." The woman shook her head. "She could put us all in danger. She is weak."

"Really?" Inez shook her head. "I don't think so. She came from a different life than you or I, yet, she is here, without mother or father or anyone to guide her. She made it here, onto the truck and across the border. She had to figure these things out for herself."

"She had help. The priest, remember."

"True enough." Inez nodded. "Her priest told her about this way of crossing the border and put her in touch with that peacock, Pepe Lopez. Who told you the first time? Who guided you and said here is a way to get over without being caught, or raped or left to die in the desert?"

Inez smirked. "I'm sure whoever it was, it was not a priest. You are just a cold woman and something else." Inez peered into the woman's eyes. "I think you are jealous of her."

"Jealous!" The woman threw her head back. "That's a laugh. Why would I be jealous of *una insignificante*—a pipsqueak—like her?"

"Because she is innocent, and you know you are not." Inez's tone was final, putting the matter to rest.

Exhausted from lack of sleep and the tension of the

trip, Jacinta slept through all of this. She was vaguely aware that they were talking, heard them mention a girl, sensed that they spoke of her, but the voices were too far away from her dreams to force their way into her consciousness.

Instead, the face of her uncle smiled at her. It was the face in the picture her mother had given her. In her dream, it was a sunny day, and he stood smiling under the sun, his arms open as she ran to him.

The truck lurched to a stop. Jacinta's eyes fluttered open. She looked up and realized her head rested against Inez's shoulder.

"I'm sorry." She sat up straight, brushing her hair out of her eyes, blinking to clear away the fog. "I didn't mean to …"

"It's fine, little one." Inez patted her arm. "You must be very tired. This trip has been stressful for you." She smiled. "It is almost over now, and you will be able to relax. Soon, you can sleep for as long as you want at your uncle's house in Houston."

"Yes." Jacinta smiled. "My uncle."

The truck was backing now. They felt it turn and move for several minutes in reverse before it lurched to a stop again. There were voices outside. Then the back door was thrown open.

Jacinta looked around at the others. They sat quietly, waiting.

Men were moving about now in the back of the truck. She heard a machine of some kind, a vehicle that rolled onto the truck and then back off, vibrating the floor and walls.

Finally, the false panel was removed, and they filed out into the back of the truck. The tomatoes were gone. The forklift that had moved the crates into the warehouse sat on the loading dock, but there was no driver.

The only people she saw, other than the passengers that had made the crossing with her, were the two men from the front of the truck and three more standing on the loading dock. One held a board with a paper clipped to it and seemed to be the one in charge.

"I'll call you your name." The man with the paper paused and regarded the faces before him. "You will go to another truck that will take you to your next city."

"Another truck?" Jacinta reached for Inez's hand. "We are not there yet?"

"Relax," Inez reassured her. "It is all very organized. This is the first stop. From here they take us to other places where we can get transportation to our destination. Me, I will be dropped off in Dallas where I will take a bus to Nevada to see my son. "You are going to Houston, so they will take you somewhere to get a bus in that direction." She smiled. "In fact, Houston is in Texas as is this place, so maybe they will take you all the way."

"Do you think so?" Jacinta's eyes were hopeful. The idea of taking a bus alone in a strange country was more than a little intimidating.

"It's possible," Inez reassured her. "But even if not, be strong and remember you will be with your uncle when you arrive."

The man with the board and paper started calling out names. Singly, and in small groups, the passengers separated to the trucks the men indicated.

Inez was called, and she leaned over to give Jacinta a kiss on the cheek. "Be safe little one and be happy at your uncle's house."

Then she was gone. Jacinta looked around. Only five

remained on the dock. One was the cold-voiced woman. Then her name was called, and she walked away, throwing one final scornful glance in Jacinta's direction.

That left four on the dock waiting. The man with the board flipped a page and eyed each of the remaining faces.

"Okay." He nodded. "You four will leave tomorrow. We don't have a truck going in your direction today. *Sigue a esos hombres*," His Spanish was barely understandable Spanish, but he motioned to the two men standing to the side. "Follow them. We have a room with beds and food for you. Then tomorrow you leave."

The four women looked at each other. Jacinta felt her heart rise into her throat. Please, no more delays.

Then one of the women shrugged. She was tall and lean. Jacinta thought she looked like a model in a magazine. "*Vamonos. Un día más no va a doler nada.*" Let's go. One more day isn't going to hurt anything.

The tall woman led off, walking behind the two men. Jacinta and the others followed

As the man had promised, they led them to a room where there were beds, a television, a small refrigerator, and a table with chairs. The women each selected a bed and sat on it, testing the springs. The woman who had led the way went to the television and began searching for a Hispanic station. She found one and sat at the table to watch a popular Mexican soap opera.

Another went to the refrigerator and found soft drinks, milk, and an assortment of meats and vegetables. One pulled out a box of Oreo cookies and smiled.

"These are excellent!" She held one up for the others to see. "I have had these in Monterrey. Eat them with a glass of milk, and you'll see how good they are."

One of the girls joined her at the table to share in the

cookies. Jacinta stretched out on the bed she had selected and closed her eyes. Soon, just one more day, she thought.

Her face relaxed into a smile. She drifted off to sleep and dreamed. Uncle Arturo smiled as in the photograph her mother had given her, his arms open to welcome her to a new life.

SIXTEEN

Paid in Full

He pushed the empty plate across the counter, yawned, arched his back, and stretched his arms out over his head.

"You look tired." Isabella refilled his coffee cup from the pot on the counter.

"No more than usual." Sole smiled and lifted the cup. "Nothing this won't fix."

"Caffeine isn't rest. When was the last time you slept in a bed?"

"Good question." He thought it over for a minute. "Week before last, I guess. Motel outside Abilene, I think it was."

"You think?" Isabella's smile lifted a little to one side, wrinkling her brow in curiosity. She leaned her elbows on the counter in front of Sole. "So, what's driving you, Bill Myers?"

"Nothing's driving me." He was more than a little uncomfortable as she leaned close, staring into his eyes. "Like I told you, I'm taking some time to wander the country, see things."

"Bullshit." It wasn't a curse but a statement of fact. This time her smile twisted into a full smirk. "You don't look like a wanderer. You're a seeker, searching for something ... or someone."

He started to reply, fumbled for something to say, and shut his mouth. A shrug was the best response he could give. It had been a while since a woman could silence and challenge him in one breath and do it with a smile that made him want to linger.

"Well, whatever you're looking for, it's keeping you from getting a good night's sleep. That's plain enough to see."

"I'm fine." He sipped the coffee. "Just needed a good meal."

"She's right," Sherm Westerfield chimed in. "It doesn't take a genius to see you look worn to a frazzle." He shook his head. "None of my business, but you'd profit from a couple of good nights' sleep and some regular meals."

He was surrounded, and they were right. It had been weeks since he'd stayed long enough in one spot to allow his body and mind to recharge. He moved from place to place, almost randomly, but always in the direction of the border, inexorably toward the reckoning that waited. Sooner or later, it would come.

"I've got a room and a bed you can use," Isabella said it without any pretense or flirtation. Her voice made it plain that the offer was a simple one without strings attached or fringe benefits implied.

"No." Sole shook his head. "I need to..."

"Oh, hush." She stood up straight. "I'm not propositioning you. I like my men rested and clean. You don't seem to be either." She eyed him up and down. "I imagine you haven't had a good clean-up or shower since that last night in your Abilene motel."

Weeks of sleeping in his truck and washing up in restroom sinks had left their mark. A glance in the mirror on the wall embarrassed him. He saw what they saw, a disheveled man with tousled hair, dirty clothes, and an aroma that preceded him by several feet.

"I don't know …"

"It's right next door." Isabella was pleasant but persistent. "A couple of the old driller shacks I keep cleaned up and ready. Rent them out to Krieg and Zabala's men and the local drunk cowboys when they can't make it home after a night boozing and whoring."

Sole didn't know what to say. He should move on. He was close to the border now.

It had taken him more than a year to work his way here. Every mile brought him closer to the *Los Salvajes* cartel and the man called Bebé Elizondo. If he found him, he would find the other, the one who had been there that night, the one who had taken everything from him.

"The bed is clean and …" Isabella sniffed the air comically. "There's a shower."

"Alright. Maybe I can stay for a couple of nights." Sole nodded. "What's the rent?"

"Do some odd jobs for me here. Sweep up, wash dishes, change light bulbs, that sort of thing and we'll call even." Lips pursed together, Isabella gave a nod, settling the matter. "Finish breakfast and I'll show you the shack where you can bunk for as long as you like."

The roar of engines speeding into town turned their heads toward the window. The pickups skidded to a stop on the dirt road outside. When the cloud of dust settled around them, the doors to both pushed open. Two men exited the first truck, one from the second.

"That's Doyle Krieg and his asshole sidekick, Paco

González." Sherm gave a sigh. "Things always seem to take a turn for the worse when those banty roosters show up."

"Who's the other?" Sole watched them stand in the middle of the road, scowling for a few seconds while the man in the second truck said something, pointing a finger at the one called Doyle Krieg.

"That's Bud Lawton, foreman out on Tom Krieg's ranch." Sherm gave him an approving nod. "Decent man, loyal to Krieg, but still a good enough sort. Seems to be reading the riot act to Doyle."

"Doyle Krieg? What's his relation to the Krieg who owns the ranch?" Sole watched the trio through the window.

"His son." Sherm shook his head. "Always got a chip on his shoulder. Looks for trouble wherever he can find it, and if there's none to be found, he'll find a way to start some."

"Looks like the lecture is over." Isabella wiped the empty countertop in front of a couple of stools, then turned to head into the back room. "I expect they'll want some breakfast, late as they are."

The door pushed open, and the three men entered taking seats at the counter.

"Morning Isabella," Bud Lawton called toward the sound of pans clanging in the kitchen.

"Morning, Bud," She called back.

Doyle threw a scornful glance in Sherm's direction and looked at Sole. "Who the fuck is this?"

Sole sipped his coffee without comment, in no mood to find more trouble in an out-of-the-way hole like Creosote.

"That's Bill Myers." Sherm looked Doyle up and down. "The bigger question is what the fuck happened to you?"

The bruise on the side of Doyle's face and torn shirt

were signs that he had been in some brawl already this morning. It didn't require much intuition for Sherm to figure that Doyle had been the prime instigator of the problem.

"Mind your own fucking business, old man."

"Man shows up bruised and torn like he got his ass whipped …" Sherm shrugged and grinned as he turned away. "Only natural to ask a question."

"Warnin' you, old man." Doyle turned back to Sole, seated at the end of the counter. "I asked you a question, asshole."

"Yeah, he asked you a question," Paco chimed in.

Sole put the coffee mug on the counter and rested his eyes on the pair. Doyle glared at the newcomer. Paco looked at Doyle, waiting for the next move.

"What was the question?" Sole replied, his eyes fixed on Doyle. If there were to be trouble, it would start there.

"I said, who the fuck are you?"

Sherm started to say something, but Sole gave a shake of his head, indicating he would handle things from this point on. Sherm smiled and looked at his coffee. This should be interesting. He didn't figure Bill Myers was going to have much trouble handling a peacock like Doyle.

"Like he said. Name's Bill Myers."

Doyle stood up and walked around the counter to stand behind Sole. "And what the fuck are you doing in Creosote, smelling up the place like a shithouse."

Sole swiveled on the stool to face Doyle. "Having breakfast. Now you need to go sit down and do the same. There's nothing here you can handle, son."

"Who the fuck you callin', son. I ain't your fucking son."

Isabella came from the kitchen. "Doyle, leave him be.

He hasn't done anything to you, and he's my customer. Set down and eat or get out."

"You talk to me that way?" Doyle raised his brow. "I already did for your half-breed son this morning."

"What?" Isabella stepped toward him. "If you …"

"It's alright," Bud Lawton broke in. "I stopped it. No real damage done to either." He chuckled. "In fact, I'd say Doyle got the worst of it."

"Shut up, Bud!" Doyle turned his stare on Isabella "And you, you *puta*—whore—get your ass back in there and get our breakfast."

Doyle gasped. Sole's right hand flashed out, taking hold of his throat in an iron grip while his left hand went low and applied vice-like pressure to his balls. He pulled. Doyle tiptoed forward, wincing in pain.

"Mind your language."

Doyle's eyes widened, casting a look for help to Paco whose eyes were as wide and surprised as Doyle's. Paco was going to sit this one out. Sole pulled Doyle closer.

"Let him go, mister." Bud Lawton figured it was time to break things up. "You don't want to have his daddy down on your head."

Sole ignored him, his eyes fixed on Doyle's. "Now sit down and eat or get out. Either way, I don't want to hear another word out of your mouth."

He gave a shove and Doyle tumbled backward, hitting the wall and sliding to the floor. Paco rose and ran to his side, helping him to his feet.

"You don't know what you done, you motherfucker!" Doyle shouted and headed to the door.

"Yeah, you motherfucker," Paco repeated, looking over his shoulder as he followed Doyle into the street and across to Mazey's.

Sole turned back to the counter. His eyes met Isabella's.

"I think I will take you up on that offer of a room and bed." He shook his head and smiled. "Lack of sleep must be making me irritable."

"Good." She laughed. "And, for dealing with those two, I'd say the first week's rent is paid in full."

SEVENTEEN

Interesting

"Who is this man?" Benito Diaz peered through the fly-specked window of Rosita's Cantina.

Across the street, a man exited a dirty pickup truck and stood on the curb, lighting a cigarette. He inhaled deeply and let his eyes wander up and down the street as if he were waiting for someone.

"That's Pepe Lopez." Mario Acosta sat wedged between Diaz's two younger sons at a tiny table by the window. There was no hesitation in his response. In fact, he was downright eager to please his captors. Besides, Krieg and Zabala were far away on their Texas ranches, not facing an angry Yaqui.

"And who is Pepe Lopez?" Diaz asked, blowing smoke from a cheap cigar across the table.

"He is like me." Mario shrugged. "A *coyotaje*, working with the *gringos*, Krieg and Zabala."

"You no longer work for them." Diaz's eyes narrowed. "Do not forget this."

"Yes, of course. I understand. I was only answering your

question." Mario spoke rapidly, reminding himself to be more careful with his words.

He had heard that during the days of the revolution, Yaquis cut the tongues from those who offended them. He had no idea if this was true and had no intention of finding out firsthand.

"The man there," Mario continued, "Pepe Lopez works with the *gringos* as I did before meeting you. He has been with them much longer, though."

"Good." Diaz smiled and flicked ash from the cigar onto the tiled floor. "And where has he been?"

"I heard that he had a load that went north yesterday. He must be back from that trip."

"He takes them north for the *gringos* himself?"

"No, no. It doesn't work like that." Mario shook his head. "The *gringos* arrange the transport in their trucks."

"Then where is he returning from?"

"There are stops along the way."

"Stops?" Diaz's eyes flicked in the direction of his oldest son, who nodded.

"Yes, stops. Places where they allow everyone out for water and to relieve themselves," Mario explained. "They treat the travelers well, guarantee they will not be harmed. That is why so many are willing to pay the *gringos* to go north."

"So this Pepe Lopez is coming back from one of the places where they stop? But you don't know where. Is that it?"

"Exactly. He goes to the last stop to give instructions and make sure all is well before the final part of the journey to the border crossing."

"And this is how it always happens?"

"Yes." Mario nodded solemnly. "To my knowledge."

He was nervous. Cramped between the two brothers, his shirt was soaked with perspiration. Worse, they perspired also, their wet clammy bodies pushed against him, preventing him from getting up from his chair. It was clear they had not bathed recently. Their stale body odor even overpowered the stench of the reeking cigar their father smoked.

Diaz was quiet for a minute, watching through the glass. Pepe Lopez finished the cigarette and tossed it in the gutter, lighting another immediately, his eyes moving up and down the street.

"He is waiting," Diaz said.

"Yes." Mario nodded. "It seems so."

"Who does he wait for?"

"How can I know?" Mario shrugged, lifting his hands, palms up. "Not everything is about the business of taking people north."

"No, he waits for business. I can tell by the look on his face, the way he searches up and down the street." Diaz rested his elbows on the table, the cigar clenched between his teeth. "He has just returned from the last stop, as you say, and now he comes back to Torreón and stands in the street smoking, without any purpose, but he is not relaxed and at ease." Diaz shook his head. "No, it must be about this business of taking people north."

"Perhaps." Mario had no way of knowing why Lopez stood smoking in the street, but he figured it was best to agree.

"There." The oldest son pointed out the window. "Someone comes."

"A priest," Diaz muttered. "What can that mean?" He looked at Mario, his heavy brow almost covering his eyes.

"I don't know." Mario watched as the priest stopped to converse with Pepe Lopez. "I have never met him."

"What does he have to do with the business?" Diaz asked.

"I can't say." Mario shook his head slowly side to side. "It could be nothing?"

"No, it is something." Diaz nodded his head, certain. "It is about the business of taking people north."

"I have met this priest," one of the younger sons who had Mario wedged in said.

"You know a priest?" the older son said, laughing.

"I don't know him, but the girl I am with sometimes, she knows him. She made me go to church so she could confess what we were doing to a priest." He nodded to the cleric conversing with Lopez across the street. "That priest ... Father Alfonso."

"A priest and you can even remember his name his name!" The older brother laughed. "This is interesting."

"Leave your brother alone," Diaz ordered. "But you are right. A priest meeting with Lopez who works with the *gringos*. This may be very interesting."

EIGHTEEN

Downright Rude

Isabella was right. He was exhausted, running on adrenalin and coffee for weeks. He hadn't realized until now how exhausted. Sleep was for later he told himself. He could rest after it was done, he had muttered to himself during the long hours on the road.

Now, lying back on the bed in the old driller's shack, John Sole felt the last bit of reserve energy fade away like an overworked engine idling down to a complete stop. He closed his eyes and slept.

The big Dodge 3500-dually rumbled into town. It was more truck than Tom Krieg needed for personal use, but most things Krieg had or did were more than the average person would consider necessary. He lived life large and enjoyed throwing it in the faces of others.

Raul Zabala was cut from a different cloth, a simpler cloth. He lived life for pleasure. When he wasn't rolling on the floor with his children or frolicking in the bedroom with his plump wife, he was out looking for entertainment at Mazey's or cruising the bars of Brownsville or Laredo.

On the surface, they made an odd pair of partners. What made their business relationship work was their mutually ruthless approach to any endeavor involving money. Their business enterprises, legal and illegal, were managed without concern for the consequences to others. And God help the person who deliberately stood in their way.

Krieg brought the Dodge to a stop in front of the café and stepped out. Zabala exited the passenger door. Both men eyed the line of pickups from their respective ranches parked in front of Mazey's.

"Looks like the boys are in full swing." Zabala grinned and took a step in that direction.

"We've got business first." Krieg looked into the truck and motioned. "Let's go."

Stu Pearce shoved open the back door and jumped to the ground. Like Zabala, he cast a longing glance at Mazey's but followed Krieg to the café door.

"That his truck?" Zabala nodded at a dusty Ford pickup parked at the end of the café building.

"Could be," Pearce said. "Didn't get a good look at it. He was parked up towards the highway. We were down by the river."

"Let's find out." Krieg pushed the front door open and stepped inside followed by the others.

"Must be big doings today." Sherm was seated in his usual spot, drinking coffee.

Isabella sat on a stool behind the counter, sipping from her own cup. "What brings the bosses to town?" she asked as Krieg led his party in.

Krieg stopped by the door to survey the small space and then walked to the counter. "Looking for someone."

"Not too many to choose from." Sherm chuckled. "Are they male or female? Take your pick. We got one of each."

"Tell them." Krieg nodded at Stu Pearce.

"Yeah, well right ... so I sent a fella this way earlier. Said he was hungry." Pearce nodded to the street outside. "Could be his truck there."

"Could be," Isabella said. "Yeah, a new face showed up to have breakfast. What of it?"

"Where is he?" Krieg's tone sent the message that cooperation was expected and interference would not be tolerated.

"Not here." Isabella put the coffee cup down on the counter and stood up straight. Her eyes met Krieg's defiantly. "What's he to you?"

"Not your business."

"You come in asking about a customer. I reckon that makes it my business."

Their eyes were locked. "Don't get in my way, Isabella. I won't tolerate it, even from you."

Raul Zabala decided it was time to intervene. "You two, always blowing up at each other. Such a waste between a man and a woman." He shook his head and leaned on the counter. "His truck is outside. That means you either have him in the kitchen washing dishes for his breakfast or he's at Mazey's with the boys." His eyes narrowed, and a grin spread across his face. "Or do you have him hidden away in a bed somewhere ... maybe your bed."

"A man smells like he did, he's not getting in my bed." Isabella's lips pursed in annoyance. "What do you want with him?"

"Like Tom said, none of your damn business." Zabala turned from the counter. "But you told us enough. Come on, Tom, let's check the drill shacks."

Krieg glared into her eyes for a few seconds longer, then turned to follow Zabala. Stu Pearce shuffled from foot to foot for a few seconds, not sure what to do, embarrassed at being the cause of the trouble with Isabella.

"Get your ass out here, Pearce!" Krieg bellowed from outside.

"Sorry about all this," Stu said, turning to the door and hurrying to follow his bosses.

Sherm looked up from his coffee as the door closed. "This could be ugly." He put his cup down. "I think I'll go keep an eye on things. Waking a man up from a deep sleep, bad things can happen, and I don't think Krieg is gonna be gentle about it."

"You're right." Isabella stepped from behind the counter. "I'm coming."

The door burst open sending sunlight blazing across the bed. John Sole's eyes flashed open and then blinked shut in the glare. His right arm lifted holding the Colt pointed at the three forms silhouetted in the doorway.

"Who the fuck are you?" he mumbled as he tried to shake the sleep from his head.

"I was going to ask you the same question." Krieg held his ground as did Zabala.

Stu Pearce eased himself back toward the open door. He had already stood in front of that big-ass Colt once that day and saw no reason to repeat the experience.

Sole sat up in bed, eyes moving over the intruders. No weapons were visible. He lowered the pistol enough to rest it on his knees while keeping an eye on them.

"You always break in on a man like this?"

"I do." Krieg nodded. "When he assaults one of my men for no good reason."

"Oh." Sole nodded and eased his legs over the side of the bed to stand.

His eyes never left the men by the door as he loosened and stretched his neck and shoulders, feeling more awake as the seconds passed. The advantage they held over him when they came through the door had dissipated to a standoff.

"Didn't seem like for no good reason at the time. Seemed like I had plenty of reason."

"Such as?" Krieg snapped back.

Sole had to give him credit. The big man in the doorway wasn't backing down, even with the Colt in his face.

"Well, let's see." Sole smirked. "First off, he woke me up with his firing rounds off so early in the morning. That was impolite. Then I found him shooting at a family of Mexicans across the river. That seemed uncalled for and since they weren't shooting back, also impolite." He shrugged. "Then he threatened to kill me … I think his exact words were I'll cut your fucking heart out." He called to Stu Pearce, visible and huddling just outside the door. "That's about right, isn't it?"

"Uh, well, yes, sir. That's about exactly what Lucky said."

"Seemed like a threat that should be addressed at the time rather than later." Sole shrugged. "So you see, I had plenty of reason."

Krieg and Zabala exchanged glances, and Krieg nodded. "Get dressed and come outside. We'll talk." He nodded at the pistol in Sole's hand. "Bring that along if you want, but there won't be any need for it. Just talk."

It only took a minute for Sole to pull his jeans on and

slide a tee-shirt over his head. He stepped onto the shack's stoop in bare feet.

"What do you want to talk about?" he asked, checking the hands of his visitors for weapons and then tucking the Colt into his waistband.

"You know who we are?" Krieg asked.

"No." Sole shook his head. "Some sort of head bosses around here or something like that."

"Something like that." Krieg allowed a faint smile to cross his face.

Zabala grinned wide. "Goddamned right, something like that. We are *the* head bosses around here."

"Okay. So what do you head bosses want with me?"

"Not many people would dare pull a pistol on us." Krieg stared into Sole's face. "No one, in fact."

"You come crashing into my room while I'm asleep." Sole shrugged. "Seemed like the smart thing to do at the time."

"Still, that took balls. Showed you were ready for whatever happened. We might be able to use a man like you."

"Doing what?"

"Security. We run a fleet of trucks."

"No." Sole shook his head. "I'm just passing through."

"Passing through to where?"

"My business." Sole shook his head. "Not yours."

"Fair enough, but you'll need money wherever you're headed, and we pay pretty good." Krieg persisted, softening his tone a bit. "Best wages you'll find anywhere around here. All you have to do is ride shotgun on our trucks a couple of times a week picking up loads below the border and bringing them back over … you know, keep a lookout for *banditos*."

"Below the border? Mexico?"

"That's what I said." Krieg nodded. "That worry you?"

"Nope. You just hired yourself a security man."

"Good. Get some rest then come out to our depot." He nodded at Isabella and Sherm, watching the exchange from the street. "They can tell you where it is. By the way, what's your name?"

"Bill Myers."

"You have ID that will get you across the border and back? We do things legal."

"I expect so. Driver's license and a passport card."

"That'll do."

Krieg and Zabala turned away. Stu Pearce gave a smile. "Welcome aboard."

"That's the motherfucker!" Doyle Krieg came running down the road from Mazey's. "That's the motherfucker that roughed me up!"

Krieg stopped and looked at his son. "Roughed you up? How?" He turned to Bud Lawton who had followed Doyle into the street. "What happened, Bud?"

"Doyle had a little confrontation with that fella there." He nodded at Sole standing barefooted on the bungalow stoop. "Didn't amount to much."

"Amount to much!" Doyle hollered. "He grabbed me by the neck, nearly choked me and goddammit he took hold of …" Doyle stopped, realizing that the rest of the description was less flattering.

"And what?" Krieg stared at his son whose face reddened. He turned to Lawton. "Bud?"

"Well, he sort of grabbed Doyle by the nuts, and you know … squeezed."

Zabala laughed. Krieg shook his head in disgust.

"Why?" Krieg looked at Sole.

"He used some nasty language to Isabella."

"What did he say?"

"I'd rather not repeat it."

"You put hands on my boy. I expect an answer as to why."

Sole remained silent, his eyes locked on Krieg's.

"He called me *puta*—whore." Isabella stepped forward. "Myers here stepped in at that point, and I appreciate what he did. Doyle had it coming."

Krieg eyed his son for a moment and nodded. "I expect he did."

He turned and led the way back to his pickup. A minute later, the big Dodge headed out of town. Doyle Krieg stood open-mouthed in the road. Bud Lawton shared a grin with Sherm.

"Can I go back to bed now?" Sole turned back to the drill shack, yawning and shaking his head. He grumbled, "All this commotion when a man's trying to sleep ... downright rude where I'm from."

NINETEEN

Work to Do

A lone, desultory fly droned against the windowpane. It didn't seem too unhappy about its captivity inside the air-conditioned office of *Comandante* Enrique Valera of the *Policía Estatal*. Whenever it came into the intense superheated rays of sunlight refracted by the window glass, it buzzed away toward the cooler air blowing from an overhead register

Border Patrol Officer-in-Charge, Emmett Brewer, watched the fly move in lazy arcs around the office, its gauze-like wings barely keeping it aloft. After a minute or two, it would return to the window, driven by some inscrutable fly instinct to seek escape, although not very enthusiastic about the idea.

Brewer was there for the weekly coordination meeting between the local Mexican state police and the Border Patrol agents operating in the adjacent district across the river. The sessions alternated between the *Policía Estatal Comisaría*—State Police Station—and the Border Patrol offices.

This week they met in Reynosa, across the Rio Grande from McAllen, Texas. Brewer waited patiently for Valera to arrive. He had learned during his five years of service in this district that their Mexican counterparts had a more fluid understanding of time. Any suggestion that they should arrive in a more timely fashion invariably led to even longer delays and the inevitable smiling lecture about the *norteamericano* custom of being ruled by the clock in all matters.

He crossed his legs, relaxed in the chair, and watched the fly. Brewer had come to accept the delays and even tended to agree with his Mexican counterpart about unnecessary rushing about. Slavery to the clock was not conducive to good health, Valera had said once. Brewer couldn't argue, and if they wanted to take their time about things, so would he.

Fifteen more minutes passed before *Comandante* Valera arrived. Trim and neat in his sharply pressed black trousers and white uniform shirt bearing his badge of rank, Valera walked briskly to his desk and took a seat. There was no greeting or the usual exchange of pleasantries.

"How are you, Enrique? Well, I hope." Brewer greeted him in fluent Spanish. "You seem a bit agitated."

Valera tossed a brown envelope he held onto the desk. "We must speak of this."

"Alright." Brewer reached for the envelope, lifted the flap, and turned it up for the contents to fall out on the desk. He raised his eyes to Valera. "What's this?"

"A bullet, of course." Valera's eyes narrowed. "You should ask where it came from."

"Okay." Brewer nodded. "I'll play along, Enrique." He lifted the clear plastic bag and examined the bullet inside. "Copper jacketed, about a hundred and fifty grains, but it's a little hard to be exact because of the deformation. It struck something hard. I'd say .30-30 caliber, but I can't be sure." He put the plastic evidence bag back on the desk. "So, where did it come from?"

"It was fired across the Rio Grande from your side, along with many others like it."

"Do you know who fired it?"

"No." Valera shook his head and sat back in his chair, hands folded on the desk, regarding his counterpart. "But I know who it was fired at and why."

"Are you going to tell me?" Brewer's face twisted up in a wry smile. "Or make me guess."

"This is not a laughing matter, Emmett."

"Never said it was, but you're playing the drama without giving me any facts. Tell me what this is about."

"Someone fired this round and others at a family attempting to cross the river."

"A family?"

"Yes." Valera's voice was icy, his eyes fixed on Brewer's. "A family. A father leading his wife and children to cross the river. Some were no more than babies."

"Babies," Brewer whispered and leaned forward to pick up the plastic evidence bag again and peer at the mangled bullet. He wasn't sure he wanted to know the answer to the question, but he asked, "What did it hit?"

"Ah, yes." Valera nodded. "At least that is fortunate. It struck the father, hit him in the leg, and broke his femur. That explains the bullet deformation."

"Yes, it does." Brewer nodded. "The father? He survived?"

"Fortunately, he still lives. It may take him years to recover fully, and the doctors say he will never walk without limping, but yes, he survived."

"That's good." Brewer's mind flipped into investigative

mode. "Did the family get a look at who was shooting at them?"

"We interviewed the father and mother and two of the older children. They could tell he was a white American. There was another with him, but the second did not shoot." He shook his head. "The distance was too far. They couldn't give any more description than that and did not get a good look at their faces."

"But we have this." Brewer held up the evidence bag with the bullet.

"If you can find the rifle that fired it."

"We'll do our best, Enrique."

"You must do better than that, Emmett. We may have a difference of opinion on how to control the border between our countries, but I hope we can agree that shooting at unarmed men and women is not an acceptable practice." Valera leaned over the desk, his eyes hard. "You must control your vigilantes and find the ones who did this." He cast a glance at the bullet. "They must be punished."

"They will be," Brewer said evenly without breaking away from Valera's stare. "But out of respect for our working relationship, keep in mind that the *Policía Estatal* has agreed to patrol your side of the river to prevent people from trying to cross."

"Are you trying to place the blame for this incident on us?" Valera's voice rose in indignation.

"Not at all. Shooting at anyone, on either side of the river is a violation of our laws and yours. You have my word that we will find those responsible and punish them." Brewer raised an eyebrow. "I am only wondering how an entire family, including several small children, escaped undetected by your patrols. Crossing illegally is also a violation of the law, ours and yours. I merely suggest that we both have some investigating to do."

Valera rose, standing at near attention in front of Brewer. "I will await your report on the matter."

"And I, yours." Brewer stood. "Work with us on this, Enrique, not against us. If we want to play the blame game, there is more than enough to go around. Blame is for the politicians. You and I …" Brewer's hand motioned from his chest to Valera's. "We have work to do."

TWENTY

Not so Bad

"Clean this shit up." Tom Krieg walked from the bathroom adjoining his master bedroom in the rambling ranch house and kicked at a pair of women's panties lying on the floor.

"You didn't mind them there last night when you pulled them off my ass." Claire Toussaint stretched on the king bed and peered at Krieg over a mound of rumpled sheets. "In fact, you were in a hurry to drop them there as I recall."

"Clean the place up." Krieg picked up a pair of jeans from the chair where he had dropped them the night before, pushed one leg in then the other. "Not in the mood for your shit this morning."

"You can treat me like your whore. I guess that's what I am, but you don't have to be an asshole about it." Claire lay on one side, her head resting on her hand, watching him. "I could do something and maybe to make you less of an asshole."

Claire leaned back, stroking her curving hip and thigh, letting her hand rest between her legs. She smiled at him and sat up suddenly so that her breasts swayed enticingly. Krieg ignored her and continued dressing.

He found his boots and sat down on the bed to pull them on. Claire put an arm around his waist, her hand finding the zipper on his jeans.

"Stop," Krieg said gruffly, tugging at one boot.

Claire had the zipper down now. Her hand slid inside.

"Stop." His voice was less gruff.

Claire swung her legs over the side of the bed and knelt before him.

"I have to go." Krieg spoke through gritted teeth, angry at himself and at Claire, but unable to deny his arousal.

"Soon," Claire cooed.

He moaned as she lowered her head. His hands clutched at her hair, dark and flowing down over her face as she worked on him. He pulled her head down, thrusting deeper, his head thrown back, eyes closed.

She gagged and choked. Her eyes watered. He held her head, tearing at her hair and ears. She wanted to cry out but couldn't as he forced her head down.

There was no love-making involved, only the satisfaction of an animal need. Claire had known it would be like that when she began tempting him. She didn't care. Keeping him with her, even for this, was all she expected from life.

She had been nothing more than a New Orleans whore when she met Tom Krieg. He was younger then, just graduated from the University of Texas and doing a bachelor tour around the country with his Tex-Mex friend Raul Zabala.

It began as a one night fuck, then another. Soon, he

would find reasons to come to New Orleans to find release with her for the animal raging inside him. Eventually, he brought her to Texas and set her up in an apartment in Laredo.

She was still his whore, bought and paid for, but she had outlasted the wife who had given him a son. The wife had suspected their arrangement and challenged him one day. Krieg laughed at her and admitted it. He could do what he wanted, and she was powerless to stop it. She knew it was true and left. Krieg moved Claire into the guesthouse on the ranch the next day.

She remained there because she put no restrictions on him. She understood a man like Krieg and her place in his world. As for her world, she had none. Her life was bound to his.

Tom Krieg could come and go as he pleased. He could whore around with other women and hear no protest from her. She expected no kind words and never received any. Tenderness was never in his touch. He used her, and being used by Tom Krieg was all the world she knew or expected.

Claire understood being used. She was good at it. Being used was a lifestyle, familiar and comfortable for her. It was the life she had led since being raped by her father's brother at the age of ten. She understood the rules to this life, and perversely, understanding the rules, gave her the only sort of security she had ever found.

Krieg grunted. His hands clenched, pulling her hair until Claire wanted to shriek in pain, but he held her head down, thrusting deeper. He gave final shuddering grunt and pushed her away.

She sat on the floor, gagging, hands at her mouth, looking up at Krieg through watery eyes like a dog hoping to have pleased his master. He pulled on the other boot.

"I've got business today." He stood and stepped around her. "Sleep in the guesthouse tonight. I want to be alone." As he walked down the hall from the bedroom, he shouted over his shoulder, "And get that shit cleaned up!"

Then he was gone.

Claire Toussaint sat on the floor, face red, lips bruised. After a while, she became aware that she was cold and reached up to pull the sheet from the bed to cover her nude body. Wrapped in the sheet, she lay on her side on the floor, her cheek resting on her hand.

A drop of blood seeped from the corner of her lips. She must have bitten her tongue as he used her. She ignored the blood. It would heal. Next time she would be more careful.

TWENTY-ONE

The Devil's Door

At least they were comfortable. The bed was small. The room had no windows. The noise from the air conditioner mounted through the wall over Jacinta's bed was loud and made the wall vibrate when it came on in the night, blowing cold air down on her.

But the sheets on the bed were clean and crisp, and the blanket was warm. Compared to the little room in the house where she had watched over the children, Jacinta was more comfortable than she had been in years. She pulled the blanket tight around her and hugged the pillow, pretending it was her mother, and they were holding each other in the dark room in this new place.

Tomorrow, she thought. Tomorrow they would send her on the other truck to Houston.

No, wait! Not tomorrow! Today! It must be after midnight. They had been in the beds in the room for hours. She would be with her uncle and family today!

Uncle Arturo would be surprised and would take her to

his home. He would tell her stories about her mother about the games they played together as children. They would be like the stories her mother had told her, and she would smile because they were the same stories but a little different because it was Uncle Arturo telling them and not Mama.

Jacinta willed herself to go back to sleep so that the time would pass quickly. Eyes clenched shut, she was like a child waiting for Christmas morning. After a time, her breathing became regular, and she drifted into sleep, a smile spreading across her face.

"*Hola, paisano.*" Raul Zabala looked up from the newspaper he had spread across his desk in the office they shared.

"You gotta talk that Mex shit to me first thing in the morning?" Krieg plopped into the chair behind his desk.

"Gotta keep you practiced up." Zabala grinned. "Noticed you forgetting how to roll your r's."

"Fuck my r's." Krieg poured a cup of coffee from the pot on the credenza behind his desk. He lifted it and nodded at Zabala. "Thanks for making the coffee."

"What you talking about? I always make the coffee." Zabala leaned forward, peering at his partner over the paper. "Besides, you look like shit. Claire must have rode you hard last night." A lurid grin crept across his face. "Or the other way around."

"Claire does what I say," Krieg snapped back.

"Sure, sure." Zabala nodded and went back to his paper, lifting it wide and turning a page then spreading it out on his desk again.

"Why the fuck you still reading a newspaper?" Krieg

eyeballed him, annoyed, still feeling the animal inside raging.

It was different from the earlier sadistically sexual need to possess and ravage Claire. This was a restless, pacing rage, like a tiger roaming from one end of his cage to the other, looking for a place to rest, never satisfied, never at peace.

"*Laredo Morning Times.*" Zabala tapped the paper on his desk. "Have it delivered to the ranch every day. All the news you ever need is right here."

"They make apps for that. Get all the news you want on the phone, or is that something a Mex can't figure out?" Krieg sneered.

Zabala looked up from the paper. He folded his hands on the desk. "You best keep in mind that I'm not your whore or one of the hired hands around here." His eyes narrowed. "And I'm not a Mex. I am a *Tejano*. You know this, so I figure you've got something eating away at you, or you wouldn't go out of your way to insult me and risk me cutting your throat."

"Just restless." Krieg sipped his coffee and then figured he should make peace with his partner. "Sorry."

"I see it building in you. Like a pipe about to bust open." Zabala nodded, accepting the apology. "Seen it happen before. When it does, it's always after dealing with the boy." He stood and walked to a bank of television monitors and hit a control button on the console. "Let's see what we got today. Bet there's something here to take the edge off for you."

The monitors flickered to life. Zabala clicked the selector, and a room appeared on one of the screens. There were eight beds in the room. Four were occupied.

"There." Zabala pointed to one of the beds where a young girl slept, curled on her side. "The priest sends you a present."

"Not a virgin." Krieg shook his head. "Too valuable for resale."

"No, no." Zabala shook his head, a curious expression on his face. "Not a virgin, but, I have never understood the attraction of a virgin. Give me a woman who knows her way around a bed." He laughed. "And one with lots of curves to hold. That's the woman for me."

"You don't have to understand. Our customers want virgins when we can get them and pay a premium for them."

"True enough." Zabala nodded. "And these are not virgins, but the young one there, she will be like a virgin to a man like you." He laughed. "That will take the edge off you for a while so we can all get some work done without you snarling all the time."

"Where are they going?" Krieg leaned back in his chair, his eyes unmoving, focused on the young girl in the bed, sleeping and unaware that the cameras watched.

"They are promised to a buyer in Baton Rouge." Zabala shrugged. "If they get three instead of four, we will make it up next time."

It was a side business and a profitable one. They delivered ninety-nine percent of the people they brought across the border as promised to a place where they could make their way into the interior of the country. An exclusive one percent was reserved for a specialized market.

That one percent brought Krieg and Zabala more revenue than all the others combined. Sold to brothels and human traffickers in and out of the United States, those girls would spend the rest of their lives as prostitutes. Most would not survive a decade. Drugs would take some. Others would succumb to untreated sexually transmitted diseases. Some would take their own lives out of desperation.

The demand grew with every passing year. Zabala had discovered the market for the young girls one night while visiting a strip club in Atlanta.

A drunken conversation with another patron as they paid for lap dances opened his eyes to the possibilities. He had taken on the mission of expanding their business. He moved carefully, making contacts in the dark corners of every major city in the country. It was slow going at first, but once he knew where to look, and they understood his almost limitless source of young women, finding buyers was not difficult.

The four young women in the room were part of the one percent. The future—unknown to them as yet—would be a dark one. In the end, they would be used up and thrown away, to be replaced by others.

Zabala and Krieg were friends only to the minimal extent that either held any real feelings for anyone but themselves. Their relationship was more symbiotic than anything else. They needed each other to survive and prosper.

Now, Krieg was in one of his periodic rages. It was a side of his personality that Zabala accepted, and one for which he had the cure.

"Come." Zabala turned for the door. "Let's go examine the merchandise."

"Wake up, ladies!" The door crashed open, and three men entered the room. "Time to go to your destinations."

The man with the paper had returned. Two others accompanied him. They smiled pleasantly.

"Hurry and dress now, and as promised, we will get you to your destinations." The man with the paper made an act of scanning the document in his hands and looked at three of the women. "You three will go with this man." He pointed to Raul Zabala. "He will see that you arrive at your destination."

"You." He looked at Jacinta. "You will go with this man." He indicated a stern-looking man standing to the side.

"But we do not go together?" Jacinta's eyes widened, suddenly afraid.

"You are going to Houston, correct?"

"Yes, Houston." She nodded.

The man with the paper looked at Tom Krieg. "He will take you to Houston."

He looked at the others. "Now get ready. Wash up. Have something to eat from the refrigerator. In thirty minutes, you go."

The men left the room. The girls exchanged hugs and said goodbye to Jacinta.

"Don't worry," they said. "This is just the last part of the trip. Soon you will be with your uncle in Houston, and we will be with our families."

Thirty minutes later, they left the room. The three girls climbed into a van. Raul Zabala smiled at each and helped them in, saying a few words to each. Then they were gone, and the last three faces from her journey across the border were gone from Jacinta's life.

Zabala directed her to a large pickup truck where the stern-faced man waited. Without a word, he opened the passenger door for her and then closed it firmly behind her.

They drove along dirt roads for almost an hour before he turned the truck onto a long drive that passed through a gate. A large house loomed out of the prairie dust a mile ahead. The man stopped the truck and got out, opened the passenger door and motioned Jacinta out.

"But aren't we going to Houston?" Her voice trembled as she fought to keep the tears from rolling down her face.

Everything had been a lie. She felt herself sinking into an abyss, unable to stop the fall. The world was full of deceit, and there was no one left to trust, especially not this stern-face man.

"Out," Krieg ordered.

She had to jump from the high truck seat to the gravel drive, stumbling to her knees as she landed.

"There." He pointed to the front porch

They mounted the steps, and Jacinta's shoulders began to shake with her sobs. "But this is not Houston. You said you would take me to Houston."

He made no reply. They stood on the porch, and he turned the door handle. The interior of the house loomed open, wide and dark, full of uncertainty and fear.

Her tears were uncontrollable, her sobs becoming a wail as she stood before the dark opening shaking her head.

"No! Father Alfonso promised me a door to a new life." She shook her head in denial as if that would make the man and the door and the house vanish. "Not this. It can't be."

She stood frozen on the porch. Tom Krieg put his hand

in the middle of her back and shoved her through the doorway.

Jacinta toppled forward onto the cold tile floor. She turned and looked up into the face of the man. His eyes were slits, snake eyes, devil eyes. They stared down at her, and she knew now. The door to the new life Father Alfonso had promised was the devil's door, and she had fallen into hell.

TWENTY-TWO

Shake on It
_____

A tousled-haired figure walked in, dressed in the same blue jeans and tee-shirt from the day before.

"Well, Bill Myers. We were wondering if you were going to drag out of bed today." Sherm Westerfield spun on his stool to grin at John Sole.

"Good morning." Sole yawned widely and sat on a stool beside Sherm. "Least, I guess it's morning." A question crossed his eyes. "Did I miss dinner?"

"Son, you missed everything." Sherm laughed. "Had us worried." He leaned toward Sole, lowering his voice to a conspiratorial whisper. "Isabella even sneaked in to check on you when you didn't show out for supper or beers last night."

"She did?"

"Yep. Said you were passed out snoring up a storm, sounded like a freight train roaring through town." Sherm grinned. "Don't worry. She didn't take advantage of you in your weakened and helpless condition."

"I wouldn't remember if she had." Sole smiled. "And that would be a damned shame."

"That it would, son." Sherm slapped his knee, laughing. "That it would!"

"Morning. What you two gabbing about?" Isabella came from the kitchen and poured a cup of coffee, placing it on the counter in front of Sole.

"Just letting Bill here know you didn't have your way with him while he was incapacitated."

"Humph. He'd remember if I had." She turned to Sole, leaning her hip against the counter in the way that was becoming familiar to him and that never failed to catch his attention. "That was a hell of a nap."

"Sorry." A sheepish grin spread across John Sole's face as he reached for the coffee. "Guess I was more tired than I thought."

He sipped the coffee. It was rich and dark and fragrant. "Damn, that's good. I needed it."

"That all you need?"

The words hung in the air. Sole hesitated, then swallowed the coffee, aware of Sherm's grin and crinkled eyes watching from the side.

Isabella laughed. "I mean breakfast. Do you want something to eat?"

Her tone was frank, without flirtatious undercurrents. Nothing was implied or promised, and there was no indication that she expected anything other than an answer to her question.

Sole looked into her brown eyes. They were rich and dark like the coffee, and more satisfying. "For now," he said, lifting the mug. "This will do."

"You missed the party last night," Sherm broke in.

"Party?"

"Yeah, party. Most everybody in fifty miles showed up. Filled the place 'til they were standing in the street."

"What was the attraction?"

"Fiesta for Isabella's son, Sandy." Sherm slapped his knee. "Helluva good time. Young Sandy is gonna be leaving us soon, headed off to Austin or Dallas or somewheres. Old Carl Chaney pulled out his guitar and played and sang, and everyone joined in on the choruses with him and danced with the ones they come with or with someone else's. Even that little snot, Doyle Krieg got to having a good time, dancing with one of Mazey's girls."

"Sounds like I missed something big." Sole looked at Isabella. "Sorry about that. I would have liked to meet your son."

"Oh, you will." She smiled and ran the rag over the counter by Sole's hand for no particular reason. "He hasn't gone anywhere yet. Still saving his money. He'll be around a while yet." She nodded at Westerfield. "Old Sherm organized it for Sandy." She leaned forward, resting her elbows on the counter in front of Sole. "I think it was his way of putting pressure on Sandy to make his move and get out of Creosote."

"Hell, it was my way of having a damn good time," Sherm said. "If it helped young Sandy make up his mind to get out of here, so much the better. Hate seeing that boy waste his life away."

Sole noticed Isabella's smiled turned down. "I take it you don't share the same feelings."

"Oh, no. I agree. He needs to find his way out of here." Isabella nodded, staring at the spot she wiped on the counter in slow circular motions. "I mean, look around. There's nothing here for a young man unless he works for Krieg or Zabala, and that …" She shook her head. "I don't want that for him. There's so much more for him out there, somewhere, anywhere. It's just …"

The prolonged seconds of silence signaled her discomfort in talking about her son's possible, if not pending, departure. Sole made an attempt at changing the subject.

"Anyway, sorry, I missed the party." He smiled. "I think I will have something to eat. What's for breakfast?"

"Same damned thing as every day!" Sherm chimed in with a chuckle. "You can have eggs, bacon, beans, and tortillas, or for a change, there's tortillas with bacon, eggs, and beans. Take your pick."

"Believe I'll take the second. Let's lead off with the carbs." Sole shot a smile at Isabella, letting his eyes linger on hers.

She returned it with one of her own and held his gaze for several seconds longer than necessary. "I'll bring some breakfast out for you." She turned and walked to the kitchen.

"I'll be damned." Sherm watched her go, a curious smile on his face.

"What?" Sole asked, lifting the coffee mug.

"I saw something in her face, I don't recall seeing before, at least not for a long while."

"What? Speak up."

"She's a hard one to read, a real woman, not some gossipy windbag like those city girls. She keeps things down inside, but I been knowing her all of her life, and I believe I saw something in her eyes just now."

Sole put the coffee mug down and turned to Sherm on the stool. "You going to tell me, or not?"

"Yeah, I'll tell you." Sherm focused on Sole's eyes, trying to read them the way he had Isabella's. "What I read in her face was feelings … feelings for you, Bill Myers." His eyes squinted as if peering through a telescope, trying to discern the minutest features on the distant planet of John Sole's face. "But I'm not sure what I read in your face. Some pain, I think ... loneliness ... carrying your own hurts around like her, pushed deep down inside."

"You read a lot in a face, Sherm. Maybe it's not all true, though." Sole felt like squirming.

"Could be." Sherm shrugged. "But enough of it's true. That worries me."

"Why?" Now, Sole's eyes narrowed.

"Hurt, pain, loneliness ... in a man like you ..."

"A man like me?" Sole watched Sherm's face, but the old man held his ground.

"Yes, a man like you." Sherm shook his head. "Those things drive a man like you ... take control of him sometimes ... make him do things to hurt other people, even if he don't intend to."

"I wouldn't hurt Isabella." Sole's voice was quiet, chastened by the words of a man who could see past his shell.

"I hope not," Sherm said. "I don't know anything about you, Bill Myers, except you stood up for Isabella and faced down Doyle Krieg and his daddy. That's something, I'd say, but there's more to a man than that. Something inside is driving you, but you best keep it reined in, son. I'd rather see you dead in a grave than hurt that woman or her boy."

"I will not hurt her. You have my word." Sole nodded. "Besides, I don't think there's as much going on there as you think."

"There is. I can see it, even if you can't ... or don't want to." Sherm picked up his mug and sipped the coffee, thinking things over. "Anyway, I'll take your word that you'll treat her right like she deserves." He extended a leathery hand. "Shake on it, Bill Myers, or whoever you are."

They shook. Sole tried to ignore the 'whoever you are' comment, annoyed that his eyes must have telegraphed to Sherm that he had hit on a truth about his identity. Sherm smiled knowingly.

"Your secret is safe with me." His bushy brows rose as he grinned. "But you treat her right, or this old man will put a hurtin' on your ass you'll remember, and it won't matter what name they call you by."

"I believe it." Sole smiled.

"Breakfast is on." Isabella walked in from the kitchen carrying two plates and placed them in front of Sole.

"What the hell?" Sherm opened his eyes wide in astonishment. "That's a goddamned T-Bone steak!"

"Looks good." Sole picked up the knife and fork, cut a piece of steak, and swirled it through egg yolk.

"All I ever get is beans and bacon with my eggs," Sherm complained.

"You never backed down Lucky Martin and Tom Krieg all in one day, not to mention run that foul-mouthed Doyle Krieg out for his rudeness." Isabella leaned against the counter watching and smiling as Sole ate.

"Well, I woulda," Sherm moaned. "If I'd a known there was a T-bone steak to be had, I sure as hell woulda."

TWENTY-THREE

Savior

The massive oak door swung open, flooding the interior of the church with the sunrise. The darkest corners of the ancient building glowed orange and pink, the statues and shrines casting long shadows across the pews.

Alfonso Alberto Cordoba Maria del Castillo Cabeza looked up from his chair in the small apse that held the shrine to Saint Manuel Moralez. It was a nook really, modest and without the trappings of other shrines. Moralez was only a minor saint, a Roman Catholic layman whose execution was ordered by President Plutarcho Elías Calles for refusing to renounce and deny the Church during Mexico's Cristero Rebellion.

Father Alfonso squinted into the light at the four figures silhouetted in the open doorway. They looked otherworldly, seeming to float above the floor in the glow from the door. Father Alfonso was not a superstitious man, but he made a quick sign of the cross to Saint Manuel.

The figures approached. Father Alfonso rose from the chair where he had been seated reviewing his sermon for the mass he was scheduled to conduct in an hour. The pages dropped from his hands as the apparitions approached, and the faces became clear.

"Priest, you look like you have seen a ghost." Benito Diaz grinned a wide, toothy grin.

"I … I was not expecting anyone so early for mass." Father Alfonso clenched the folds of his clerical vestments, trying to dry the dampness from his hands.

"Mass?" Diaz threw his head back, laughing. "Do we look like superstitious peasants to you, coming here to confess our sins?"

"We are all children of God." Recovering from his surprise, Alfonso made an effort to speak in the modulated tones he employed during sermons. "We all must …"

"*¡Por favor, sacerdote! ¡No llenes mis oídos con tu mierda!.*" Please, Priest! Do not fill my ears with your bullshit!

Alfonso's mouth snapped shut.

Diaz looked at one of the men with him, his youngest son. "The door."

"*Sí*, Papa."

The son went to the still open door and closed it. The sunlight disappeared. Gloom settled inside the church. Ice water flowed through Father Alfonso's veins, chilling him to the bone.

"Please," Alfonso croaked. Alone with Diaz and his sons, all pretense of priestly control vanished. "There is a mass soon. People will be coming."

"Then you must speak quickly." The whites of Diaz's eyes shone brightly in the darkened building, seeming to float in the air, unconnected to the man who stared at Alfonso.

"Speak?" Alfonso shook his head. "But what about? I don't know …"

Diaz's arm came up, backhanding Alfonso across the mouth. Muffled laughter came from the young men standing beside their father.

"I believe you do know what about." Diaz moved closer in the gloom until his face was only inches from Alfonso's. "Do you recognize me?"

"Yes, of course." Wide-eyed, Father Alfonso nodded.

"Then you have heard of my business." He smiled. "It is no secret from Durango to Coahuila."

Alfonso nodded again.

"Then you know what we will speak of." Diaz leaned even closer so that his breath full of peppers and garlic filled Alfonso's nose. "You will provide me the information I want."

"Y-yes. Y-yes, of course," Alfonso stammered. "But what is it you want to know."

The grin was back on Diaz's face. He nodded. "Everything."

An hour later, Diaz nodded, satisfied. "This has been a good conversation." He turned to leave. "We will speak again, Priest."

Father Alfonso wanted desperately to shout, no. No more speaking together in closed churches! Instead, he dabbed with his sleeve at the blood that trickled from his lip where Diaz had backhanded him.

The church's door was thrown open, and Diaz and his sons stepped out. It was full morning now and the first parishioners, mostly old widow women in black were lined up outside, wondering why the great doors had not already been thrown open for them.

Diaz grinned and nodded at them. They lowered their

heads and stepped aside as he and his sons made their way down the steps. They may have wondered what Yaqui pagans like Benito Diaz and his sons were doing in the church so early, but they kept their thoughts to themselves. Perhaps, they came to confess their many sins. If so, that was between them and Father Alfonso.

The widows' eyes opened wide when Alfonso came in to serve the mass. The swollen lip was noticeable. A few, whose eyes were not so old, also spotted the drops of blood on the sleeve of his vestments and nodded knowingly to each other. The Yaquis were pagans after all.

When the mass ended, the widows lit candles and knelt before the Virgin Maria, asking her to protect Father Alfonso from the pagans. Father Alfonso had never hurt anyone. He was a savior to the unfortunate, helping the needy to cross the border safely to the north in search of their families. Surely the *Santa Madre*—Holy Mother— would protect him from the likes of Benito Diaz and his unholy spawn.

TWENTY-FOUR

Friends

The bed moved and bounced as he rose. She remained frozen, turned away from him on her side, curled in a fetal position.

Heavy footsteps thudded across the floor as he made his way to the bathroom. Still, she remained frozen, her eyes squeezed shut.

A long sigh and yawn filtered through the sheet pulled over her head as he relieved himself and scratched. Her hand slid up under the sheet until her thumb rested against her lips like a child seeking the comfort of her mother's breast.

She heard water run in a sink, then the sound of a toothbrush. He spat and gargled and spat again. A minute later, the shower hissed and started. He thumped about the room gathering his clothes while the water ran.

Cowering under the sheet, she curled up on her side and tried to remain completely still. Perhaps he would forget about her, go about his day and leave. Then she could escape, that is if she ever dared peek out from the under the sheet.

He was in the shower now. She could hear him, water splashing, an occasional grunt as he washed his privates and rinsed himself.

Soon, she thought. He would open the door and leave the room. That would be her chance. She tried to visualize where her clothes were scattered about the floor, left where he had pulled them from her before he …

She squeezed her eyes tighter, trying to forget that part. It was different than when the father of the children she watched forced himself on her. This man was rough. There was anger in him, and in the way he handled her body. It was as if she were to blame for some terrible wrong he had suffered.

He was out of the shower now, walking through the room, dressing. Drawers opened. Hangers in the closet tinkled, making an incongruously pleasant sound in the midst of her terror. The bed moved as he sat down to pull on his boots.

He stood, and his booted feet clomped across the room. Keys jingled as he thrust them into his pocket.

Soon. Another minute and he would be ready. He would leave. She would peek out from under the sheet to be sure first. Then, she would scurry about the room and find her clothes and creep out. When no one was watching, she would run down the stairs and out the door.

She had no idea where she was, but she would run into the countryside. Somehow she would find her way to Houston and to Uncle Arturo. The Blessed Virgin would not abandon her. Father Alfonso's promises of a new life would be fulfilled. She had only to escape this devil who had lied to her and taken her.

Soon now. Very soon. She controlled her breathing so that there would be no movement. Just a little breath, then let it out and another very small one. He would forget about her hiding in the bed under the sheet.

"Get up!" Tom Krieg threw the sheet from Jacinta, exposing her nude body.

Reflexively, a hand rose to her breasts and the other between her legs trying to hide what he had already seen and taken from her.

Krieg reached down and took hold of her hair, turning her head back so that she was forced to look into his eyes.

"*¡Levántate! Vístete!*" He spoke Spanish to her. Getup! Put on your clothes!

Head pulled back so that she looked at him through slitted eyes, a tear formed and slid down her cheek. For a second, her eyes darted toward the window. It was a bright day outside.

His lips twisted into a sneer, and he released her hair. "Don't even think about it, girl." He shook his head. "Even if you get out, there is no place to run to."

"But ..." Somehow she managed to force the words through the fear and out of her mouth. "Houston. You said you would take me to Houston and my uncle. You had me, but surely now you can take me to ..."

"Shut up." There was disgust in his voice. "There is no Houston, not for you. There is only here. You belong to me now."

Jacinta began to sob, her bare shoulders shaking as her hands went to her eyes, unconcerned with exposing herself to him now.

"No. This cannot be happening." She shook her head. "After last night, I thought you might ..."

"It is happening." Krieg's voice was blunt, unsympathetic. "You stay here ... especially after last night."

"I would tell no one," she pleaded.

"I know." He nodded. "There will be no one to tell because you will stay here. And at that, you're better off. You'll have food and clothes. You won't want for anything, not like those girls who were with you. They will be sold from man to man until they are used up. You will only have one man ... me." He turned to the door. "Now clean up, get yourself dressed, and come downstairs. There's someone I want you to meet."

The door closed firmly behind him, and she heard him walk heavily down the hallway and then down the long stairs to the main level of the house. Dazed, she sat for several minutes before her body began to do what he had ordered.

Robotically, she gathered her clothes from the floor. The thought of standing in the shower he had used minutes before made her skin crawl, so she washed her body with a rag over the sink and rinsed her mouth with water. She had no brush and used her fingers to smooth her long, tangled hair.

Then, she left the room, closing the door firmly behind to keep the memories from that place from following her. The house was immense, but the sounds from downstairs guided her. People were talking.

She made her way down the stairs and hesitated. The front door stood open. Outside the prairie stretched to the horizon. No other habitation or signs of life were visible. She could leave, but he was right. There was no place to go and no place to hide in that vast, open expanse.

"Shit. What we got here?" Two young men walked through the front door as she stood by the stairs gazing out.

The one who spoke came to her and leaned close. "Hey, baby, you here for a good time? You make my daddy a happy man?"

The man with him laughed.

"Once he's through with you, maybe you can make me a happy man too." Doyle Krieg grinned.

"And me too!" Paco González laughed.

"Get away from her." Tom Krieg walked in from the next room, reached out and took Jacinta roughly by the arm. "Come with me." He pulled her along behind him.

Doyle and Paco watched smirking as Krieg led the girl into his office and closed the door behind them.

"Sit down." Krieg pushed Jacinta toward an oversized, leather chair. She sank into the seat and leaned back, instinctively trying to make herself as small as possible.

A woman laughed. Jacinta turned to the sound. She had not noticed the woman seated in an identical chair. The laughter faded, and the woman smiled. It was not an unpleasant smile, but it held something unspoken, some knowledge that made it less welcoming.

"This is Claire," Krieg said. "Claire will look after you ... show you around. You will be friends."

Their new friendship was not a suggestion or a promise of the relationship to come. It was an order, and both women lowered their heads to acknowledge the command.

TWENTY-FIVE

Which Dumbass

"This is a long ways from proving a damn thing." Salvia County Sheriff, Paul Dermott, tossed the plastic envelope containing the deformed bullet on his desk.

"Look at it again," Emmett Brewer said calmly. He had expected resistance and prepared accordingly, willing to sit there all day if that was what it took.

"What is it you think I'll see, Emmett?" A wry smile crossed Dermott's face. "Or hope I see?"

"Do I really have to lay it out for you?"

"We both know where you're going with this." Dermott leaned back in his chair, propped his boots on the desk, and smiled. "And you know the position I'm in here. There's no federal agency behind me. I won't be transferring out to another post in a couple of years." Dermott shook his head and leaned farther back in his chair, putting distance between himself and the Border Patrol's District OIC. "Nope. I'll be here dealing with the residents and voters of Salvia County."

"You mean dealing with Tom Krieg and Raul Zabala."

"Yes, they are two of the residents of the county. They are entitled to a voice in this office just like everyone else." Dermott nodded. "And a listening ear."

"Why do I get the feeling that you listen a lot closer to them than some of the other voices that come into your office?"

"Careful. I don't care for the implication." Dermott's eyes narrowed, and his posture in the chair stiffened. "We enforce the laws of the state of Texas equally to all. No one gets special treatment."

"I am not questioning your integrity, Paul. I am asking you not to look the other way."

"Sounds like the same thing to me." Dermott sat up straight, elbows on the desk, glaring at Brewer. "You show me a goddamned crime, and I will do what I can to find the perpetrator. But this …" He nodded at the bullet on the desk between them. "This is nothing … proves nothing. You are going to have to give me more than this if you want me to wade into the shit storm with you."

"The bullet came from the leg of a man trying to cross from the Mexican side. He was shot by someone on the Texas side."

"You say." Dermott shook his head and peered at the slug. "To me, it's just a bullet. Could have been found anywhere or pried from a piece of plywood where somebody was taking some target practice."

"It comes from a reliable source. Enrique Valera over in Reynosa. He got it from the doctor who cut it out of the victim's leg."

"Reliable?" A smirk spread across Dermott's face. "That word doesn't mean the same thing on both sides of the Rio Grande."

"That's not fair, and you know it." Brewer's voice took

on a hard edge. "You think you've got problems dealing with the voters in Salvia County? Put yourself in Valera's place. He's under pressure from every corrupt politician and cartel member in northern Mexico. Still, he is working with us to shut down the border crossings, and it's having an effect." Brewer picked up the bag with the bullet. "He gave me this, and I promised to find out where it came from."

"You really think you're going to find the rifle that fired that bullet."

"I'm going to try my damnedest." Brewer peered into the bag. "Winchester .30-30, not the most common rifle around."

"Not uncommon either," Dermott shot back. "Plenty of old cowboy types like to carry Model 94s."

"True enough." Brewer nodded. "That's why I could use your help."

"Did he die?"

"Who?"

"The man the doc pulled that slug from."

"No. He'll recover."

"So, I don't get it." Dermott sighed and shook his head. "If someone is trying to help you control the border, and no one was killed, it seems like you should be welcoming the assistance."

"Shooting innocent civilians is not help. If it were the other way around, you'd be taking raiding parties across the river to find the ones who fired that bullet into one of your citizens. Don't deny it. You would."

Dermott made no reply. The truth of Brewer's words hung in the air between them.

"Valera didn't do that." Brewer shook his head. "He gave the bullet to me, and I promised to handle it on our side. I call that pretty reliable and fair."

"Alright." Dermott gave in. "What do you want from me?"

"I'm going to start by paying Krieg and Zabala a visit. It would help to have another law enforcement witness along, a local one, one that I can trust."

"Trust?" A wry smile crossed Dermott's face. "Even with all of the *voters* I listen to?"

"Never said I didn't trust you, Paul, and I never said I didn't understand your situation here." Brewer grinned. Time to lighten the mood. "I promise not to stir the pot. Just going to ask questions and see where things go. Try and come up with enough to get a warrant to search for the rifle and find which dumbass pulled the trigger."

"Which dumbass, huh?" Dermott allowed himself a smile. "Well, you'll find Krieg and Zabala have no short supply working for them. Narrowing it down to just one dumbass could be kinda tough."

TWENTY-SIX

From the Mouths of Babes

The normalness of the day was pleasing and at the same time, disconcerting. Normalcy had not been a part of John Sole's life since the day everything changed.

He had lingered over breakfast, making small talk with Sherm and Isabella. The topics were mundane, the weather and local gossip, mostly. Sole listened to the gossip, piecing together an image of life in Creosote and the character of these two people who were the closest thing to friends that he had met in a long while.

The little snippets of day-to-day existence in Creosote were filled with a sort of small-town charm, except for the ones that included Tom Krieg and his partner Raul Zabala. Sole sensed a dark side to things when they were the topic of conversation. Even Sherm lowered his voice to a whisper when he mentioned them.

After an hour of small talk, Sherm rose from the counter. "Gotta go." He tossed some cash on the counter and headed for the door. A minute later, he was rolling down the road in his pickup, trailing a cloud of dust.

"Something we said." Sole smiled at Isabella.

"Nope. He heads out every morning after breakfast." She glanced at the clock on the wall. "And at that he's late. Must have been entranced by our riveting conversation."

Sole laughed. "Never considered the weather to be that riveting a topic."

"All depends on the company and who's talking about it." Isabella leaned close across the counter. "There are days when I think my skull might explode if one more cowboy tells me it's a hot one … or a dusty one … or a late spring or early winter or …" She shrugged and smiled. "You get the picture."

"I get the picture." Sole nodded. "Still, I can see how the routine here could be … comforting."

"Routine?" Her face twisted into a lopsided smirk

"Sure. You know, the normalness of everything." He turned and nodded out the window. "Things don't seem to change much in Creosote."

"You got that right!" she laughed. "Not a damn thing changes … ever."

"I can see how that could be comforting. Sometimes things change too much."

His face darkened for a moment, and then he shook it off, but not before Isabella noticed. God only knew what this man was holding inside, but she figured it had to be something terrible to take hold of him like this and not let go.

"Get out. I'm closing up," Isabella said brusquely then ran the rag once more over the counter, took Sole's coffee mug, placed it in the sink, and came around the counter.

"Oh, sorry." He stood, surprised by the sudden change in her demeanor.

"Nothing to be sorry about." She opened the door and waited. "I close every day after breakfast."

He walked out into the morning sunshine. The air still had the fresh morning scent of sage and prairie grass, but the day's heat was building. He looked around, a little embarrassed and not sure what to do next. Isabella laughed.

"Come on. I've got a shady porch at my place, and we can sit … if you want." She reached out and took his arm. "Don't worry. I'm not going to bite, and I don't expect anything. Just nice to have some company and conversation."

"It's just …" He held his ground, standing in the middle of the street.

"I know. There's someone … or was." Her eyes softened. "I won't ask about her. You can talk or not. That's up to you." She grinned. "As long as you don't mind if I talk. Damn if I don't feel about to burst with things to say to someone who hasn't already heard them a thousand times."

"Alright." He relented and allowed her to tug him along down the street.

"Morning." Mazey sat on her stoop, watching, a knowing smile on her face.

"Morning, Mazey," Isabella said as she trudged past holding Sole by the arm.

"Looks like a hot one, don't it Isabella?" The smile on Mazey's face broadened into a grin, and she let loose a resonant laugh that began deep in her belly.

"Yes, it does." Isabella pulled Sole's arm close holding it against the side of her breast and laughed.

He followed along, feeling as awkward as a teenager caught in the back of his daddy's car with the prom queen. The movement of her breast against his arm as they walked had his undivided attention.

They retraced the walk that Isabella took every day on her way to the café, and in a few minutes arrived at her small frame home. As promised, the porch was on the north side and shaded from the sun.

"Sit here." She pushed Sole into a wicker chair and went inside.

He sat, surprised at how comfortable he felt in her presence. He noted the worn, but dust-free porch planks, the small but tidy patch of grass in the yard, a tool shed off to the side, flowers growing in a neat plot beside the porch, and a vegetable garden surrounded by wire fencing in the yard, just at the far edge of the grass.

The screen door squeaked, and Isabella came onto the porch holding two glasses of lemonade. She handed one to Sole and sat in the chair beside him.

"I've got something stronger if you want it."

"No." He shook his head. "This is fine." He sipped the lemonade. "Perfect, in fact."

They were quiet for a minute, sipping lemonade and watching a catbird move through the grass, stalking an earthworm. With a sudden hop, it pounced and poked its head into the grass. The worm dangled and wriggled in its beak as the bird lifted and fluttered to a nearby bush to enjoy its meal.

"What do you suppose the worm feels," Isabella said.

"Interesting question. Guess I've never given much consideration to the feelings of earthworms." He looked to the side and smiled at Isabella. "Callous, huh?"

"No." She shook her head. "I don't know anything about you, Bill Myers, or whoever you are, but I would say that being callous is not in your make-up."

"Why did you say that?"

"Because I can see from your actions that you are not callous."

"Not that. What you said about whoever I am?"

"Oh." She put the lemonade down on the porch and pulled her legs up into the chair, resting her chin on her knees as she thought about it. "I don't know, really." She turned her head toward him. "There are a lot of unspoken things about you. Mystery sounds too dramatic … just things that you don't want people to find out or get close to … maybe your name and who you really are is one of those things." She nodded and put her chin back on her knees. "But I would bet that your name is not really Bill Myers."

There was nothing to say. Lying about it would not convince her otherwise. Besides, she was right, and he was not sure he could lie convincingly to this woman.

After a minute, Isabella broke the silence. "Are you going to do it?"

"What's that?" He was relieved to have something—anything—to talk about.

"Go to work for Tom Krieg?"

"Oh." Suddenly, he was not so relieved. "I might."

"Okay." She said it with a nod, considering his possible employment by Krieg as something she would have to accept as part of knowing him. "I imagine you have your reasons."

"I do."

"Sounds mysterious."

He made no reply. Krieg's offer of employment would get him south of the border. That was all that mattered to him. He would be closer to the men he sought, would have a chance to get the lay of the land and come up with some sort of strategy. He might even figure out a way to survive. There was no way to explain all of this to Isabella.

"Alright then," she said after a minute. "You do what you have to do. If you need a friend while you're here, I'll be your friend. Just one thing." She paused, waiting for him to turn his head in her direction and look at her. "Watch your back with Krieg and his partner Zabala. They will use you up and throw you away. Everyone is expendable to them. If you don't believe me, check with Sherm. He'll be able to lay things out for you better than I can."

"I'll remember that, and I do believe you. Thanks for the warning." He nodded and hesitated. "And thanks for being a friend. Haven't had one of those in a while."

"Well, you've picked up a couple in the last day." She chuckled. "A middle-aged woman and an old man. Keep this up, and we'll have to throw a party and invite all your new friends."

"I'll keep that in mind," he said, smiling. "Haven't had one of those in a while either."

Their banter had a seductive quality, innocent enough on the surface but with the unspoken understanding that she was all but asking him to stay around and see what could become of their relationship. It was all the more tempting because she was more than pretty. Isabella was genuine, smart, and frank, without pretension or flirtation. She said what she thought and let you know what she wanted.

They came from completely different backgrounds, but the similarities between her and Shaye were undeniable. Was that the reason he felt the attraction, the need to find someone like Shaye? In his heart, Sole knew that would be unfair to Isabella. Using her as a surrogate for his dead wife would leave them both empty and searching for something more between them.

The roar of an engine sounded at the far end of town.

An ATV running at full throttle came down the road, sliding sideways into the driveway. A young man in blue jeans and a tee-shirt got off, removed his helmet, and walked to the porch.

"You must be the new guy." He grinned and stepped up on the porch.

"Guess I'm the newest one around." Sole smiled, taking an immediate liking to the boy's straightforward ways.

"Sandy Palmeras." The boy extended his hand.

"Bill Myers," Sole said, casting a momentary side glance at Isabella.

"I want to thank you, Bill, for looking out for my Mom. I heard what you did for her and how you handled Doyle Krieg and his father."

The boy spoke like a man. His grip was firm. His face smooth, bearing the bruises of his fight the day before, but it was a serious face with a dignity beyond his years.

"I didn't do anything you wouldn't have done."

"That's true, but I wasn't there. You were. Thanks for that." Sandy smiled, turned, and pulled the screen door open. "I'll leave you two love birds alone, now."

Sole sat looking straight ahead, not daring to turn toward Isabella as his face reddened.

Isabella laughed at his discomfort, giggling, "From the mouths of babes."

TWENTY-SEVEN

A Chancy Thing

The pickup rolled to a stop in the bare dirt and scrub grass that served as the front yard of the shack. Sherm Westerfield sat behind the wheel, waiting for the dust to settle around the truck before pushing the door open.

"About time you made it home!" The man on the porch was sprawled back on one of the wooden crates that served alternately as a chair, table, or footstool, as the occasion required.

"Reggie!" Sherm plodded through the dirt to the shade of the porch, his feet raising little puffs from the ground with each step. "Haven't seen you in two months, maybe longer." He reached the porch and slapped Reggie on the shoulder. "Want a beer?"

"I'm ahead of you." Reggie lifted the bottle from the porch beside his crate and shook it around to indicate its depleted level. "Looks like I'm dry."

"Here." Sherm opened the old Frigidaire that sat on the porch in all weathers and pulled out two bottles. More dust rose into the air as he slammed it shut again. "Damn stuff gets everywhere, don't it?"

"That it does." Reggie accepted the beer with a smile, twisted the cap off, and raised the bottle. "To Robby."

"To Robby," Sherm replied solemnly.

Both turned the bottles up and drank half down before coming up for air. It was their tradition.

Reginald 'Reggie' Prince was like a son to Sherm Westerfield, which to the casual observer would seem entirely peculiar. Reggie grew up in the Sunnyside district on the south side of Houston where in any given year he had a one in eleven chance of being the victim of a violent crime.

Reggie managed to stay ahead of the odds, but between the ages of fifteen and eighteen, he was the victim of three strong-arm robberies and an assault. The assault by a man with a knife who had just been ejected from a bar for being disorderly left him with a three-inch scar along his left cheek. It wasn't personal. Reggie just happened to be passing by on foot and made a convenient target.

Not long after, Reggie decided that if he was going to be a target, he would do so on his own terms. He enlisted in the Army and was deployed to Afghanistan and then Iraq the following year. It was on his third deployment, back to Afghanistan, that he met Sherm's son Robert. As often happens when individuals from vastly different backgrounds are thrown into close quarters under trying circumstances, they find friendship in unlikely places and with unlikely companions.

The only thing Reggie and Robby shared was the accident of being born in the state of Texas. During a patrol in Taliban held territory, they found something else in common.

When the firefight erupted around them, they were riding through what had seemed to be empty desert a moment before. Triggered by an improvised explosive device that destroyed the command Humvee and the lives of the platoon leader and his driver, the attackers poured fire into the remainder of the platoon.

Snipers concealed two hundred yards away behind a ten-foot-high mound of dirt began taking their toll. The soldiers were forced to keep their heads down or risk a bullet through the brain. As they sought cover, Taliban fighters emerged from nearby camouflaged positions dug into the sand to hammer the column with automatic rifles and grenades.

Reggie and Robby took up position between the wrecked Humvee and an abandoned troop truck. Back to back, they defended each other and the half dozen wounded soldiers sheltering with them.

An eternity later—twenty-two minutes according to the official Army log—help arrived, and the Taliban fled. Reggie and Robby were the only members of the platoon not wounded or killed in the fight.

The other survivors credited them with saving their lives. Both were awarded the Bronze Star.

Their friendship blossomed during the ensuing months. Promises were made to stay in touch. With three weeks remaining in their deployment, they came under fire once more. This time the odds were better, and the Taliban left over a hundred dead fighters on the field. The American soldiers suffered only four wounded and one killed—Robby Westerfield.

When his enlistment ended, Reggie came to the Texas brush country to find Robby's father and pay his respects. He had only planned to stay for a few hours. He remained there for a month, and the two bonded, held together by the memory of a dead son and friend.

Eventually, he left and returned to his home in Houston, such as it was. His mother had passed away during his second deployment. He thought of returning to the Army, but the fire was gone for him. He found other ways to survive, street ways.

Sherm never asked much about his life. Reggie came and went, doing whatever he did when he was away. Sherm was reasonably sure it wasn't entirely legal and probably had something to do with drugs, but he but never asked questions. It didn't matter.

Reggie was Robby's friend, and by extension, Sherm's friend and the only connection remaining to his dead son. As unlikely as the paring was—a young inner-city African American and a curmudgeonly old west Texas cowboy—Reggie began to look at Sherm as a sort of father figure. The feeling was mutual, and Sherm had found another son to ease the pain of the loss of his boy.

They sat on the crates, sipping their beers. A dust devil rose out of the prairie a mile away, swirling into the sky. Reggie laughed.

"What's so funny?" Sherm asked.

"That whirlwind out there makes me think of all the ways we grew up different, Robby and me. Never see something like that around the city, but I'll bet Robby saw it a thousand times … ten thousand."

Sherm nodded. "I reckon he did."

"Just makes me realize how chancy life is," Reggie mused. "One born in a city, one out here, different lives, seeing different things, smelling different smells."

"Yep, I suppose it could have been that way. Like you say, life is a chancy thing."

"One thing I know, though." Reggie's voice lowered, thoughtful as he watched the whirling dust move away in the distance.

"What's that?"

"Wouldn't have mattered ... me here and Robby in the city ... wouldn't have changed a thing. Robby would still be the best friend and best man I ever knew."

Sherm nodded and wiped at a tear.

TWENTY-EIGHT

The Most Beautiful Prison

"This is your home?" Jacinta stood before the guesthouse situated a hundred yards from the main house.

"It's where I stay. This is where you will stay, as well." Claire smirked. "Nothing around here is mine ... or yours. Everything belongs to Krieg."

"He gives this house to you as a place to live?" Jacinta was incredulous. She stared wide-eyed at the structure. "Where I come from, this is the house of a person of wealth. And he gives this to you to live in for free?"

"Nothing is free here. I pay." Claire's eyes met Jacinta's. "You will pay."

Jacinta nodded her understanding. She had already begun paying. They mounted the steps to the porch side by side. Claire pointed to two cushioned chairs, upholstered in floral print slipcovers.

"Sit. We'll talk."

A live-oak shaded the porch. Sprinklers hissed out in the open yard, sending sprays of water over the lawns and flowers and making tiny moving rainbows from the refracted sunlight. Jacinta had only seen such grandeur and extravagance in public buildings in Mexico, never in a private home. Even the family whose children she had tended and who were considered wealthy in Culiacán never had such a place as this to call home.

"There are some things you must understand." Claire waited for Jacinta to turn her head in her direction. "These are things he will expect that you understand. If you do, you will be treated well. If not …" Claire shrugged. "You must learn these things."

"I should not be here," Jacinta said softly, shaking her head. "This is a mistake. I should be on my way to Houston to my uncle's home."

"And I should be a lady in a palace." Claire laughed. "But I am not, and you are not on your way to Houston. You are here." She leaned toward Jacinta. "And at that, you should be grateful. You will live well here, plenty of food, clothes, a house to share with me, and even a good bed to sleep in when he does not want you."

"I don't want to be here."

"Want has nothing to do with things. You and I …" Claire touched her breast and motioned to Jacinta's. "We are the same. We were not born for our own pleasure, but for others. That is not such a bad thing when you come to understand it. Most of all, don't resist it. Accept it. Enjoy the life you will have here and forget the life you wish you had but never did … and never will."

Tears glistened in Jacinta's eyes. Claire's words were not spoken in anger. They were not full of hate. They were not outwardly threatening. They were merely hopeless, and that made them terrible to hear.

Claire explained the conditions under which Jacinta would live from this time forward. It was a life without choice or other possibilities. Dreams and hopes of anything else were futile. Jacinta was crushed.

When she finished explaining things, Claire waited while Jacinta stared out into the yard, seeing nothing, drying her eyes with her sleeve from time to time. It would take time she knew, for the young woman to accept the reality of her new life. They had plenty of time.

Minutes passed before Jacinta turned to Claire. "How long have you been here? Is there really no hope?"

"Eighteen years." Claire watched the horror spread across Jacinta's face.

"So long?"

"Yes." Claire nodded and reached to pat Jacinta's hand. "Yes, so long to live a life that is good for me." She rose from the chair. "Come. I'll show you your new home. We can talk, have something to eat. If you need to cry some more, we can sit together, and I will put my arms around you and let you use my shoulder for your tears."

Claire took Jacinta by the hand and led her into the house. It was beautiful, spacious, every room clean and fresh with flowers from the garden in the vases and sparkling glass in the windows. It was the most beautiful prison, Jacinta could have imagined.

TWENTY-NINE

Everything Returned to Normal

"What the fuck!" It was an exclamation of panic, not a question.

The van veered toward the truck from the oncoming lane. Marty Slocum jerked the wheel hard to the right, sending the K and Z truck careening into the roadside ditch on its side. Screams and cries rose from the passengers concealed behind the interior walls.

Sliding sideways across the highway to block the road, the approaching van skidded to a halt. Figures dressed in dark clothes and face shields jumped from the van and fanned out around the truck lying on its side now, wheels spinning and engine revving.

"Get off me!" Chesty Miller, the security man for this trip, was pinned down in the passenger seat by Slocum who had fallen onto him as the truck turned over on its right side.

Slocum shook the cobwebs from his head and took his foot off the accelerator. The engine quieted, although the muffled cries of pain and terror coming from the back of the truck remained audible in the night air.

"Get the fuck off me!" Miller could see the men outside surrounding the truck, moving into firing positions. Pinned under Slocum's weight, the Remington 870 twelve-gauge shotgun still clenched in Miller's fists was useless. He thought of taking a shot through the windshield to scatter the attackers, but he couldn't bring it up in the cramped space.

Slocum took hold of the steering wheel and pulled himself up. First one hand and then the other found the open driver's window. He pulled himself up and pushed his head out.

From twenty feet away, a man lifted an automatic rifle and pointed the muzzle at his face. The rifle jerked three times in the man's arms, and three rounds crashed into Slocum's head and neck. It happened so quickly, and the range was so near that Slocum never heard the shots and never knew he had been killed. He dropped back through the open window to land on top of his companion.

Chesty Miller had the unpleasant fortune to see everything that was happening as he struggled to find a way to use the shotgun. Head swiveling from side to side at the figures just feet away outside the truck now, the frustrating futility of his predicament became apparent.

He made one final, massive effort to bring the shotgun up to defend himself and the cargo he was paid to protect. The roar of the shotgun inside the confined space of the truck was deafening. The result was a hole blown through the roof of the truck cab, sending the 00 buckshot harmlessly into the roadside ditch. The man outside laughed and slid the charging bolt back on the rifle.

Miller could only watch as he approached, the grin

visible through the cloth shield covering his face. Their eyes met for an instant. The rifle bucked, and thirty .762 rounds crashed through the window, riddling Miller's body. Unlike Slocum, he survived for several seconds, dimly aware that he was dying and that the man outside didn't care enough to even finish the job with a single bullet to the head to put him out of his misery.

"Quick. Move!" Benito Diaz stood at the back of the truck while two of his sons worked to open the truck's rear cargo door.

It took several minutes to move the load of avocados out of the way. Two men climbed in and began throwing the crates toward the door. Two others outside grabbed them and threw them to the side of the road. When they had cleared a path to the panel door concealing the passengers, they all climbed aboard.

Panic-stricken wails from the back had continued throughout the attack on the truck and unloading the crates. Now, as the panel was pulled off, the cries ceased. One by one, the hidden passengers emerged, wide-eyed and terror-stricken. They had heard the shots that eliminated the driver and security guard.

They whispered among themselves, supposing that they were next. All expected to be lined up beside the road and gunned down, their bodies left in the ditch for the vultures and coyotes. Several collapsed to their knees in the dirt, crossed themselves, and began praying. Others, men and women, sobbed and looked into the eyes of Benito Diaz, pleading for their lives.

The men with the guns gathered around. The passengers were lined up in two rows along the side of the road. Another truck approached and stopped alongside the gathering in the road. Prodding and shoving with the muzzles of their rifles, Diaz's men forced them into the truck.

A minute later, the truck disappeared with the passengers in a cloud of dust. Benito Diaz turned with his sons to the van and departed in the opposite direction.

Silence ensued. The creeping, living things of the desert made their way to the wrecked truck and began feeding on the carcasses of the dead Americans. Everything returned to normal.

THIRTY

Be the Hawk

The sun jumped up over the horizon with enthusiasm, climbing eagerly into the morning sky. In a moment, the Texas brush land was awash in its orange-pink glow. John Sole smiled and thought the words that always came to him at moments like this.

Shaye would have loved this ... and the children. Don't forget Samantha and Bobby.

He clung to the thought, letting it rest in his mind as the sunlight washed over his face. He could feel her hand in his, her head on his shoulder as she snuggled close, see the smiles on the faces of his children. It was a family moment, except there was no family any longer. There was only John Sole.

He sat on the hood of his pickup and stretched back, leaning against the windshield and watched the world around him awake. It was his third sunrise since coming to southwest Texas and Creosote, but only the first he had witnessed.

Gunfire on the Rio Grande had interrupted his sleep

the first day and any interest he might have had in the rising sun. He slept through the second and taken a late breakfast with Isabella and Sherm and then spent the day on Isabella's porch sipping lemonade and talking.

Today, he had risen early, while it was still dark outside. There was something he wanted to do—had to do—but before that, he had to think. He drove ten miles along the dirt road out of Creosote. There was no hurry. He let the truck roll along just barely above idling speed.

Once, his headlights picked up three coyotes on the side of the road. They looked like a mating pair with a juvenile, probably a yearling pup. The big male stood his ground and took up position in the middle of the road staring into the headlights. The female crossed the road and waited for the juvenile to follow. When they were safely in the brush on the other side, she gave out a yip, and the male backed away. His family safe and rear guard duties completed, he trotted off after them and disappeared into the prairie grass. Sole took his foot off the brake, letting the truck roll forward again.

As the eastern sky lightened, and the sunrise approached, he found a hunters' turnout, a simple gravel trail disappearing in a straight line into the brush. A quarter-mile off the dirt road, he came to a small knoll. Blackened rocks circled to create fire rings marked the old hunt camp. He stopped the pickup, got out, and took a seat on the hood to watch the sunrise.

Now, as the brief, fiery sunrise turned into full day, he considered what he was doing. For the first time, he questioned his motives and wondered why he questioned them.

For more than a year he had moved in this direction, his mission clear, the end inevitable. But now, there was Isabella, and he hesitated.

Three days ago, she had been nothing to him. Today she was—what?

The image of her face came to him, her legs stretched out in the wicker chair beside him on the porch, her laugh, the straightforward way she had of speaking, letting him know that she sensed something between them but was not putting any requirements or expectations on him. She would let things happen naturally or not at all.

Something inside stirred. He tried to push the feeling away, force it deep down because along with it came that other feeling—guilt.

He had a mission. There was no time for stirrings, for feelings. There was Shaye and the children.

We are gone.

The voice whispered inside him. He sat up straight on the hood of the truck, and the guilt returned.

We are gone, the voice repeated.

No! He had a mission. He would see it through, or everything was wrong, out of balance. Without it, there was nothing, no purpose. Without it, everything became senseless loss and waste.

That can't be what the universe intended, indiscriminate, irrevocable loss, and waste. The mission—justice—gave everything purpose, made sense of things. Without that he would go mad. Perhaps, he was mad, he considered as the voice came back to him.

We are gone. She could make you happy.

The memory of Shaye's voice whispered to him, reasoning.

If things were reversed, how would you want us to live without you? Miserable, alone, unhappy for the rest of our lives?

No. It's not the same, he argued back. I should have

been there. It should have been me, not you. That's why. You were innocent.

We are gone. Nothing you do will change that. This justice you seek is an empty thing. It will not make you happy.

Happy? I don't even know what that means anymore.

Stop feeling sorry for yourself! Nothing is hurting us now. Be happy. Forget the past.

I can't. He shook his head and tears slid from the corners of his eyes across his face. Wiping at them with the back of his arm, he jumped to the ground.

John, please.

He shook his head. No. Maybe after, I will be able to do what you want but not yet.

The voice was no more than a sigh now, whispering sadly in his ears.

I'll be here if you need to talk.

I know. Because your voice comes from me, from every memory of you that fills my dreams. I will never escape your voice because I can't escape my dreams. I don't want to escape them.

As you say.

The voice faded away. He had won the argument, an argument with a memory. He shook his head. Admit it. You are insane.

Overhead, a hawk circled in the sunlight. Sole squinted up at it, watching it bank and plunge toward the earth, focused on its prey, intent and undeterred by the presence of this puny human in the vast prairie.

He climbed into the pickup and started the engine. Be the hawk, he told himself.

THIRTY-ONE

Call it a Hunch

They bumped off the asphalt onto the gravel lot at Krieg and Zabala Trucking and Imports. A reluctant Sheriff Paul Dermott drove. Seated on the passenger side, Emmett Brewer looked over the dozen trucks scattered around the lot. A few were backed up to the loading dock where crates of various Mexican produce were stacked.

He'd seen the company's trucks at border crossings on their trips out and back to the Mexican farms that supplied them with produce for their customers. The drivers were always cooperative and submitted willingly to the required vehicle inspection. The Border Patrol K-9 operators had never once detected narcotics or a whiff of explosives.

Dermott steered for the office wing attached to the main warehouse. Two men standing beside one of the trucks eyed them as they passed. One held a shotgun. Brewer's head swiveled to maintain visual contact with them.

"What?" Dermott asked, noting Brewer's scrutiny. "The one with the shotgun? Lots of people have shotguns. Probably showing it off to his friend, or trying to sell it. No law against that."

"Not, the shotgun," Brewer replied. "The way they eyeballed us as we passed."

"What about it?"

"I've been in law enforcement long enough to get a feeling for when someone is nervous about my presence."

"You mean a hunch?" Dermott laughed. "Hang on. I'll pull out my crystal ball and see if I can get a quick reading on them."

Hunches are the stuff of Hollywood, and cops know it. Unless of course, it's their own personal hunch, in which case it becomes a sound, rational, cognitive theory, based on, experienced, deductive police work. Courts, however, are not impressed with hunches, and no law enforcement officer wants to stand in front of a judge and base his testimony on a hunch.

Brewer understood Dermott's skepticism. He'd been on the receiving end of a tirade from a judge once who made the point that police hunches were about as useful in proving a case as two farmers arguing about which sow's teat gave the most milk. Forget the teat. The proof was in the fattest piglet.

Dermott was right. The stares of the two men meant nothing … yet.

Brewer accepted the jibe. "Maybe a hunch, but they were eyeballing us pretty hard."

"Just not used to seeing a sheriff department cruiser pull in."

"I expect not," Brewer agreed.

Brewer knew that Krieg and Zabala ruled their little Texas empire with a strong, hand. They kept it gloved mostly, but when pushed, they had a reputation for taking the glove off and using their iron fist to put down their competitors and critics hard and fast.

It was clear that Dermott and the rest of the Salvia County Sheriff's Department gave them a wide berth and for obvious reasons. They were voters, after all, and no doubt controlled, or at least heavily influenced, the voting decisions of a good many others around the county.

Consequently, Brewer didn't expect much assistance from Dermott in getting to the bottom of the shooting along the Rio Grande, but having him accompany him on the visit was a small victory in itself. It wasn't that Dermott was a bad man or an incompetent sheriff. He was merely a politician, concerned, as most are, with being reelected. Brewer's eyes were open to this fact and assumed that Dermott would sit back and watch while he handled the questioning and follow-up investigation.

The sheriff slowed to a stop in front of the office, and they stepped out, conscious of more eyes—on the dock, in the lot, in the office—watching them. Dermott led the way through the door into the small reception room. A graying, smiling woman looked up.

"Hello, Sheriff. Didn't expect to see you here today."

"Ella." Dermott nodded and leaned over the small reception counter, smiling. "Nice to see you." He looked around. "Are they here?"

He knew they were. Their pickups were in the lot outside, but it was the courteous thing to say.

"They surely are. Shall I get them for you?"

"Please, Ella." Dermott turned, leaning his rump against the counter and smiled at Brewer. "Should just be a minute, while Ella rounds them up."

"That's fine." Brewer sat in one of the undersized chairs lining the wall to wait.

They heard Ella on the phone. "Visitors to see you." There was a pause, and then she said, "Yes, sir."

She looked up at Dermott, who twisted his head around toward her. "They'll be just a moment, Sheriff."

"Thanks, Ella." Dermott began whistling a favorite country tune by a new artist out of Austin.

Brewer examined the small space. Everything seemed normal. Men at work in the lot and on the dock. Ella tapping a keyboard on her desk. Dermott whistling. Krieg and Zabala's empire exuded peace, tranquility, and business as usual.

Zabala's eyes narrowed as had Krieg's when Ella spoke the words, "Visitors to see you."

It was a code, a warning for them to be on the alert because there might be a problem. Otherwise, she would have just announced the name of the visitor. Ella was a valuable employee and always received a nice Christmas bonus.

They turned from the monitor showing the room where their overnight guests were accommodated. All the beds were occupied. Eight young women sat on them chatting, munching food from the refrigerator, waiting for the next leg of their journey.

Zabala pushed a button for another camera view and the reception lobby popped onto the screen.

"Goddammit," Krieg whispered.

"Yeah," Zabala concurred. "I was afraid this would happen." He tried to put a positive spin on the view of the sheriff and Border Patrol agent waiting patiently in their lobby. "They don't have warrants, or they'd be back here already. There's nothing to worry about. Whatever it is …

whatever they want or questions they ask ... we don't know anything."

"You know exactly what it is and what they are going to ask."

"Yes, and we don't know anything, *amigo*," Zabala reinforced. "Just don't go losing that razor-edged temper of yours."

Krieg glared at the counsel from his partner but did not argue. He punched the intercom button on his desk phone. "Bring them in, Ella."

"This way." Ella smiled and rose, leading them through a door at the back of the reception office, down a short hallway, and into another office.

Krieg and Zabala rose from their desks as they entered. Zabala smiled and put out his hand to Dermott.

"Sheriff! Damned good to see you!"

"Raul," Dermott said, taking his hand and giving it a friendly shake.

Brewer took note of the fact that they were on a first-name basis.

Dermott shook Krieg's hand with more formality but with the same congeniality. "Tom, thanks for giving us some time." He turned to Brewer and made the introductions. "This is Emmett Brewer, U.S. Border Patrol. He's the OIC in the district. Has a few questions for you."

Introductions complete and duty fulfilled, Dermott stepped to the side and sat in a chair across from the desks.

"Questions, huh?" Zabala smiled. "From the Border Patrol." He threw his hands up in mock panic. "Don't arrest me, sir. I'm legal. Been here all my life. See my back's not even wet."

Dermott laughed. Krieg watched the exchange without emotion. He had seen the Zabala show before.

Brewer smiled to match Zabala's. "I'm very familiar with your history and family Mr. Zabala. Everyone around here is." He turned to Krieg. "And your family's as well, Mr. Krieg."

"Please," Zabala interjected. "Call me Raul and this surly individual is my partner, Tom."

"Thanks, Raul."

"Sit, please." Zabala indicated a chair beside the one Dermott had taken. "Now what can we do for you?" he asked once Brewer was seated.

"I can tell you're busy, so I suppose I should get right to the point."

"I suppose you should." They were the first words that Krieg had spoken. Unlike Zabala, there was no attempt to conceal his annoyance under a cloak of good humor.

"Alright." Brewer nodded, smiling, and fixing his eyes on Krieg's. "There has been some shooting."

"So?" Krieg replied, irritated. "Lots of guns around here. A lot of people shoot them."

"Someone has been shooting at people trying to cross the border … trying to keep them on the other side of the river."

"Hmph," Krieg smirked. "Sounds like someone's been doing you a favor." His eyes narrowed. "You might even say they were doing your job for you."

"We don't shoot illegals crossing." Brewer shook his head. "We apprehend them. Send them back."

"Well, if you don't mind my saying so." Krieg gave a mean little smile. "That's a crock of shit. We know all about catch and release and the asylum loopholes."

Brewer's face showed no reaction. He'd known men like

Krieg, powerful, arrogant assholes. Unlike Zabala who sugar-coated his power with a heavy sprinkling of amiability, Krieg liked to throw it in your face, challenging you to respond. Brewer wasn't sure which one was more dangerous, but for the moment, he was dealing with Krieg.

"Yes, there are loopholes." Brewer nodded. "We are waiting for Congress to fix them. Until then, we enforce the law as it stands. We catch, detain, and deport as the law allows." Now his eyes narrowed to match Krieg's. "We do not shoot them."

"We don't shoot people either. Why are you here?"

"Because *somebody is* shooting people. It's not a secret that you have been very vocal about stopping illegal immigration. Both of you."

"So? We're not the only ones who think the Border Patrol is doing a piss poor job at the one thing they are supposed to do. If I had my way, I'd fire the whole lot of you and start over" He smirked "I imagine that's the real reason you're here. To take a jab at your detractors."

Brewer pulled a photo from his breast pocket, and tossed it on the desk.

"What the hell is this?" Krieg stared at the image without touching it.

"That is a bullet, a .30-30. Ballistics show it was probably fired by a Winchester Model 94 or a similar model." He had promised to get to the point, so he did. "We would like to find the rifle that fired it ... and the owner of that rifle."

"I don't own a Winchester 94." Krieg looked at Zabala. "You?"

"Nope." Zabala shook his head. "Never liked the .30-30 ... not enough knockdown power for big game." He grinned. "And I only hunt big game."

Brewer was sure that was the case. Asshole and disingenuous that they might be, they were not stupid. Whatever their feelings about immigration, Brewer was reasonably sure there was no way either would risk their own hides by shooting at an unarmed, illegal border crosser.

"I thought as much. Still ..." Brewer smiled into Krieg's glaring face. "Someone around here might have one ... could be someone who works for you."

"How would we know what kind of rifles our people own?"

"Because they are your people, as you call them," Brewer threw back at him. "And I hear it's a close-knit group."

"I can tell you," Zabala interrupted, the smile wider than ever on his face. "We don't have any idea who might own the rifle that fired that bullet. Probably a lot of those rifles in Salvia County ... hundreds of them."

"Probably so," Brewer agreed. "That's why we thought we'd try to narrow things down some. Any of your people ever talk about hunting with a .30-30, or target shooting with one, or a Winchester handed down from grandpa? Anything like that might help us find the rifle?"

"Nope. Not to my knowledge," Zabala said, smiling. "How about you, Tom?"

"No."

Zabala shrugged. "Sorry, we can't help you, Agent Brewer." He rose from his chair, ending the conversation. "If there is nothing else, we need to get some work done around here."

He clapped silent Sheriff Dermott on the shoulder who took the cue and stood. Brewer was slower to rise, never breaking his eyes away from Krieg's face.

"If you happen to think of something or remember

someone who owns a .30-30 caliber rifle, give us a call," Brewer said. He mustered up a friendly smile, mostly to annoy Krieg. "We'd appreciate it."

Krieg glared.

Zabala stepped in between Brewer and Krieg's desk. "Absolutely. You'll be the first person we call." He escorted them down the hall to the reception area.

"Thanks for stopping by," Zabala said as they went through the reception office door. "Give my best to your wife and family, Paul."

"Will do, Raul, and the same to yours."

A minute later, he rejoined Krieg in their office and shook his head.

"Do you think you could have been a little more of an asshole?" Zabala asked with a sarcastic smirk.

"What's it matter?" Krieg was still fuming. "Like you said. He doesn't know anything."

"Well, he didn't before he got here, but after your little performance I'm not so sure."

Krieg took a deep calming breath. After a few seconds, he said. "We need to make a call."

"Yeah." Zabala nodded. "Guess it has to go down like that."

"It does." Krieg pulled out his cell phone and punched a number. When the call was answered, the message was simple. "We have something for you to do."

Dermott backed the county car away from the building and pulled through the lot to the road. The same pairs of eyes followed them until they were out of sight.

"See, I told you," he said when they were a mile down the road.

"You told me." Brewer nodded.

Dermott turned toward him a curious look on his face. "You still don't believe it though, do you? You still think they have something to do with shooting at people along the border."

"Don't you think Krieg was a little too snarly for a man who knew nothing when I asked about the bullet?"

"That?" Dermott laughed. "You have to understand Tom Krieg. He's always pissed off about something, and he for sure doesn't like being asked questions about his business. That doesn't make him the ring leader of a bunch of vigilantes taking shots at illegals."

"So, you're saying he was pissed off because that's his nature."

"I'm saying exactly that." Dermott nodded his head to show that was emphatically what he meant.

Brewer shook his head. "I'm not convinced." He shrugged and smiled. "Call it a hunch."

THIRTY-TWO

A Little Less Like an Asshole

"Well, looks like we got company!" Sherm shouted from the shade of the porch.

Sole thrust an arm out the window and lifted it in greeting as he let the pickup roll to a slow stop in the yard, careful not to kick up the dust. He got out and walked to the porch.

"Morning."

"Morning back, Bill Myers."

"Morning," Reggie Prince said, eyeing the newcomer. "Sherm told me there was a new face in town."

"I'm Bill ... Myers," Sole said, mounting the steps.

"Reggie ... Reggie Prince." Reggie grinned. "And before you ask, yeah, that's my real name."

"Wouldn't have thought otherwise," Sole said smiling.

Their eyes met. The mutual but friendly appraisal lasted several seconds before Sherm figured they'd had enough get acquainted time.

"Pull up a seat, Bill."

Sole turned a spare crate around and sat so that he faced both men.

"Want a beer?" Sherm nodded at the old Frigidaire. "It's all cheap, but it's cold, and it's free."

Sole craned his neck out from under the porch overhang to check the sun's position in the sky. "Must be about ten o'clock. I'd say that's late enough."

Sherm and Reggie laughed. Sole pulled the old fridge door open and grabbed one of the generic no-name beers that Sherm bought by the case in McAllen.

He popped the tab and lifted the can. "Cheers."

"Back at you," Sherm said, and all three turned their cans up and sucked down half before lowering them and wiping their mouths.

"Good beer," Sole said.

"Bullshit." Sherm laughed. "It's cheap horse piss, but it's beer and to tell the truth, I've never been all that picky about beer."

"Works for me." Sole turned the can up and downed the last of it.

"Grab another," Sherm said.

"Believe I will." Sole snagged another from the fridge. "I'll pay you for the beer."

"The hell you will. That'd be a goddamned insult."

"He means it," Reggie threw in. "You're a guest. Guests don't pay."

"Okay." Sole nodded. "No offense meant, and I appreciate the beer. I suppose I better slow down then."

"You do, and you'll get left behind," Sherm grinned and said as an aside to Reggie. "Go easy on him, son. He's still learning our godforsaken ways."

"I see that." Reggie nodded. "So, Bill Myers …" He said the name slowly, pronouncing each of the three syllables distinctly as if he was trying it out in his mouth to see if the name matched the face in front of him. "How did you end up drinking beer on Sherm's front porch?"

Sole was beginning to wonder why everyone in Creosote was so quick to perceive that his Bill Myers identity was a fraud. Probably because he was not the only one around using an assumed name. Liars can always spot another liar.

"Long story," Sole said in answer to Reggie's question, and then turned the tables, smiling. "How about you?"

Reggie chuckled, sending the message they both knew the other was full of shit. "Same here ... long story."

"So what made you stop by for a visit, Bill?" Sherm watched the exchange, oblivious to the subtle assessments passing between the two. "Get bored with Isabella's company?"

"Not sure that would be possible," he said with respect.

"That's for damned sure."

"In fact, she suggested that I stop by and visit with you before ..."

"Before you go off working for that Tom Krieg, right?" Sherm interjected and smiled, knowing he had hit on the reason. "Yep, she probably warned you about him then said check with me about the situation before you do anything rash."

"Something like that." Sole nodded, letting the old man talk now that his tongue was loosened.

"Alright." Sherm leaned forward, elbows on his knees, the beer cradled in his leathery hands. "It's not complicated." He looked into Sole's eyes. "He's a mean son of a bitch, and this partner Raul Zabala is one and the same, he just hides it better. So, if you're going to work for them, you better understand they are going to expect you to be as mean as they are, do things the way they would do them … hurt people the way they hurt them."

"Hurt people? I was told they import vegetables and fruit from Mexico. I'll just be along as security to protect the cargo."

"True enough, at least that's what they told you, and I don't know for certain it isn't true." Sherm's eyes narrowed. "But what I do know is true is they will use you up and then throw you away. They did it to my son."

"Your son? I wasn't aware you had…" Sole looked around the house and yard.

"Oh, he's not here." Sherm shook his head. "Won't never be here again."

"Sorry, Sherm. He got hurt working for Krieg and Zabala?"

"He did." Sherm nodded. "Oh, not physical in some way you could see the hurt." He shook his head. "No, it was a hurt inside him. He never talked about it, but there was something that happened, something about doing the job for them that hurt him inside, made him feel bad … guilty even. That's why he left and headed off to the Army."

Sherm's eyes filled with water. "That's why I won't never see him again."

Sole listened without speaking. He had experienced enough of his own pain to understand that there was nothing he could say to make it easier.

"But," Sherm said, looking up, smiling at Reggie. "I gained another son from it all. Reggie and Robby were best friends. Reggie was there when …"

Sherm stopped talking. Sole felt like an asshole for intruding on his memories and opening old wounds. Reggie put a hand on the old man's shoulders.

"I'm not sure what Isabella expected me to say to you."

Sherm looked into Sole's eyes. "A man like you … you know your own mind, and you have your reasons for working for those men. Be careful and understand the hurt they bring to whatever they touch. That's all I have to say."

They sat without speaking for a long while. As noon approached, Sherm reached for another beer and passed cans around to the others. He waited while they popped the tabs then lifted his up in a toast.

"To Robby."

"To Robby, my best friend," Reggie echoed.

They turned to Sole. Sherm nodded, inviting him to join them.

"To Robby," Sole repeated respectfully, feeling a little less like an asshole.

THIRTY-THREE

A Brave Smile

"You seem happy."

Sandy came in from his work shed at the side of the café and found Isabella whistling softly as she went about readying the afternoon meal for her customers. A socket wrench in his hand, he went behind the counter, took a glass from the pyramid stack by the beer tap, and plunged it into the ice bin. He eyed her reaction as he crunched the ice without adding water.

"Do I?" Isabella looked up and smiled, wiping at the mist of perspiration on her forehead with the back of her hand. She shrugged. "I'm happy enough, I guess."

"More than that, I'd say. It's good to see."

"You talk like I'm miserable most days."

"Well …" He grinned. "I wouldn't say miserable. Subdued might be a better word."

"Subdued? Aren't you the student of human behavior all of a sudden?"

Actually, it wasn't sudden. Sandy had been a keen observer of life as long as she could remember. Older and wiser for his years than most others imagined, he saw things no one else saw.

Mazey and a few of the more superstitious local cowboys swore he must have visions because he could tell them so much about themselves by merely watching. Sandy found the idea hilarious and scoffed at the thought of anything so supernatural.

To Sandy, it was simple. He paid attention—to everything.

It became a game to occupy him. He observed and then said things to make them gawk. The mystery in their eyes made him laugh

Isabella was accustomed to his serious nature and somber eyes examining everything and everyone, including her. She understood why Mazey and the others looked at him as someone with particular aptitudes, maybe psychic ones. His ability to unravel the thoughts and secrets and motives of others could be disconcerting, especially if they were trying to hide something.

Even as a toddler, he would sit quietly and watch her as she worked, making her feel that somewhere in his three-year-old brain, he was assessing her. Sometimes she would turn and catch him watching and feel suddenly uncertain of herself. What did he see? What was he thinking? What did he understand about her that she didn't know herself?

That was when he was a baby, though. She was too familiar with his look of concentration to worry much about it anymore. Others might squirm under the microscope of his examination, some even took offense, but it was only Sandy being Sandy.

It was a diversion for him, something to occupy his

mind. Creosote offered little in the way of distraction for a growing boy. Mazey's whores would have been happy to have him visit, would have even given it to him for free to have the bragging rights to say they were his first. Isabella politely kept him away from them, making it clear to them that he was off-limits.

A few times, when some drunk cowboy or K and Z driver had taken offense at his prying ways, she had cautioned him to be more circumspect when engaging his habit of studying people. A couple of times at school, he had learned the lesson the hard way and tussled in the parking lot when classes were done for the day.

These days, most people had no idea they were being scrutinized, evaluated, and filed away somewhere in his mind as data to be recalled if needed in the future. Isabella could see it though.

"Is he going to stay?" A sly smile crept across Sandy's face.

"Who?" she said, innocently, and then laughed because they both knew who he meant. She shrugged. "I don't know."

Now she looked into her son's eyes evaluating and assessing. "Does it matter?"

"It might … to you." He turned the glass up and munched some ice. "I wouldn't mind either."

"Why?" She was more than a little interested in his assessment of Bill Myers.

"I like him." Sandy shrugged to show it was nothing more complicated than that, then he smiled. "If having him around makes you happy, I like him more."

She leaned against the counter and thought it over while he sucked on the ice. "He's different," she said.

"Yes, he is." Sandy looked at his mother. "You want to talk about it … about him?"

"That's why I asked."

"Okay." He nodded. "So, to be honest, I haven't figured him out much. He's harder than most to study."

That was what Sandy called it when evaluating a subject, whether it was a person, a bird in the yard, or the clouds on the horizon. It was his study. Isabella waited for him to continue.

"So, there's not much." He looked up and stared at the ceiling tiles, considering what to say about Bill Myers. "First of all, that isn't his real name, but I guess you figured that out already."

"I guessed as much." Isabella nodded. "Man shows up here out of nowhere, but he's not your typical drifter. He's smart, had some education at least, chances are he's running from something, so he wouldn't use his real name."

"Running to something, not from," Sandy corrected her. "If he was running from something or someone, I wouldn't be so happy about him being with you. Running from means, he's in trouble, and trouble could follow along behind and suck you into it, whatever it is."

He shook his head. "No, he's running to something, like he has an appointment, or is trying to find someone or discover something. He's restless, always looking into the distance, but there's no fear there like a person on the run. He's thinking, planning something. I don't understand his reasons for not using his real name, but whatever they are, it's serious, and that makes me worry about you a little, but as long as he runs toward whatever it is and doesn't bring it this way, I suppose things will be alright. Besides, I like seeing you happy."

He paused and considered his next words. "He has feelings for you, but something is keeping him from letting you in too deep to whatever he is feeling. I'm guessing something happened to someone he cares about ... a woman maybe."

He watched his mother's face. She smiled.

"I already figured that out."

"Those feelings for the other person are strong. It's in the way he looks at you, and then a shadow crosses his face like he is reminding himself about the other person." He smiled. "But then he looks at you again, and I see the feelings there. It must be like something pulling him in different directions inside."

He hesitated, not sure if he should say the rest.

"Go on," Isabella encouraged. "I can take it."

"I don't think he will stay long. Creosote is just a stopover for him. This appointment or meeting or whatever it is he is running to is stronger than anything else ... stronger than the feelings for you." He looked into her eyes, his voice gentle. "Mom, he will leave one day ... maybe soon."

She tried not to show any reaction. She failed. Her son saw through the stone face she threw up as a defense.

"Of course, he will move on," She said, cynically. "Why the hell would anyone but me stay in a place like Creosote, with whores for neighbors and drunks for companions?"

She picked up the dishrag and began wiping the counter in circles the way she always did when preoccupied with her thoughts. Sandy had confirmed much of what she already knew about Bill Myers. In her heart, she hoped that he would have discerned something different about the man.

"Guess I'll just have to make the most of things until he runs off to that appointment you say he has and does whatever he is planning."

She put on a brave smile for her son. It was a fake, and he knew it. It didn't require any special powers of observation to see the sadness in her face and the tear that she brushed away when she thought he wasn't looking. She changed the subject.

"So what do you have going today?"

"Headed out to Krieg's place with those four ranch ATVs he had me work on." Sandy popped a chunk of ice in his mouth and headed for the door. "Matter of fact, I better get moving. I'd like to get paid before next month." He shook his head and grinned. "For a man with as much money as he's got, he sure can dodge a bill if you let him see it coming. Gotta sort of sneak up on him."

"Good luck." Isabella laughed. "Watch out for that Doyle Krieg. He's liable to be lurking around somewhere dodging any real work."

"Don't worry about Doyle. I can handle him," Sandy grinned and touched the bruise on his face from their last encounter. "Besides, I'm a peace lover."

She watched from the counter as he pulled his old pickup from around the side of the building, towing a trailer loaded with the four ATVs.

He was a good boy, she thought. No, not a boy—a man. Bill Myers had seen it in him, shaken hands with him the way a man does, spoken to him the way one man speaks to another.

As she watched him leave, she wondered when manhood would drag him away from her and send him out into the world. Part of her dreaded the thought, but another wished it would happen soon. Take him far away from this place where the future held only a pain that he did not suspect.

It had to be. Sandy had to leave her as surely as Bill Myers would one day decide to move on. Only she would remain in Creosote until the Texas wind dried her out like the dust and blew her away.

The brave smile was back on her face, but she did not feel very brave. The loneliness hovering over the horizon made her heart shrink in despair.

THIRTY-FOUR

Job Interview

"There's a Bill Myers here to see you, Mr. Krieg." Ella announced the visitor without giving the coded warning. There didn't seem to be anything threatening about a drifter looking for work, and she'd seen worse specimens. "Says you told him to come by for a job."

"Send him back."

"Mr. Krieg said to go on back." She eyed the scruffy newcomer, doubtfully. "Through the door and down the hall on the right."

"Thanks." Sole went through the door from the reception area to the hallway.

Ella shrugged. Mr. Krieg must have his reasons for telling a drifter to stop by. Maybe he needs someone to wash trucks.

Krieg sat upright, elbows on the desk as Sole came to the office door. Zabala assumed his usual posture, leaning back in his chair, hands behind his head, eyes half-closed, but it was Zabala who spoke first.

"Come in." He regarded Sole from under his partially

closed eyelids and nodded to a chair between and equidistant from both desks. "Have a seat."

Sole sat without speaking, his posture erect but not formal. He met Krieg's unblinking stare with one of his own.

"I expected you yesterday." Krieg's words were clipped, his displeasure at the delay in the new man's arrival evident.

"Had some things to take care of." Sole ignored the Krieg's tone.

"You said you wanted this job." Krieg stared at him, trying to intimidate him in the way he did most men.

Sole remained unintimidated. He nodded. "I do."

"I expect my men to show up when they're told."

"I said I'd take the job. I never said when. I'm here now." Sole gave a sigh and moved his legs under the chair, preparing to stand. "You still want me to work for you or not? I can leave just as easy as I came."

The respect and fearful deference of virtually everyone in Salvia County had made Krieg unaccustomed to being challenged. This man's entire demeanor challenged him. There was no deference in him and damned little respect.

Raul Zabala watched the interaction with interest and repressed a smile at his partner's discomfiture. In his mind, they had a choice. Tell this drifter to get the fuck out and keep going, or make use of the same traits that Krieg had identified in him when they met. The time had come to lead the discussion in a different direction.

"What's your name again?" Zabala asked although he remembered. It was his way of telling the newcomer not to feel so special that they should remember his name or anything else about him.

"Bill Myers," Sole said and turned calmly toward Zabala.

He understood the change in tactics and repressed a smile. He might have used the same method in that other life when questioning people, probing their weaknesses, and searching for answers had been part of his daily life. The difference was that Zabala did it clumsily.

"Bill Myers, do you still want to work for us?"

"Like I said, I'm here now." He nodded. "I want the job."

"Good." Zabala sat up straight in his chair. "Let's have a job interview then."

"Fair enough." Sole nodded.

"First off, is Bill Myers your real name?" Zabala's eyes narrowed, watching for any reaction on Sole's face.

"It is my name," Sole said evenly and without reaction

It was a comfortable lie because for now, it was true. He had taken the name when he paid the counterfeiter in New Orleans for the ID and had used it continuously since. As far as he was concerned, Bill Myers was the only name he had now or planned to have in the future.

Zabala could ask some follow-up questions that might make it more difficult to conceal the truth. How long have you been Bill Myers? Where did you get the identification that you carry now? Who was your mother? Where did you go to school? What was your last address?

He asked none of these questions because he really didn't want the answers, didn't need the answers, and Sole knew it. His next question got to the specifics of the work they expected him to do.

"Have you ever killed anyone?"

"I have."

His reply came without hesitation. Zabala and Krieg exchanged a look. Now Krieg spoke.

"Who?"

Sole smiled. "You know I won't tell you that."

"In the military?" Krieg asked.

Sole nodded and told the truth. "I served in the military."

"What branch?"

"It doesn't matter."

"If we search for discharge papers, a DD-214, for Bill Myers, will we find one?"

"I'm sure you will."

It was one of the reasons he had picked a common name. William Myers, Bill Myers, Willie Myers, all could be found in the records of every state's DMV and in every branch of the military.

"You're not being very cooperative here." Krieg's level of annoyance edged up again. "You say you've killed and you want us to give you a job."

"You wouldn't ask that question unless it was a job qualification." Sole allowed his smile to spread a little wider. "You want someone who will stand up to whatever it is that threatens your business. That might mean killing to protect your interests. That's the kind of security you want."

"And you'll do that? Stand up to any threats against our business?" Zabala asked, watching his face.

"If it comes to that, yes. I wouldn't be here if I had a weak stomach about it." He felt no obligation to elaborate that he would only kill in self-defense.

Zabala leaned back in the chair again and smiled. "I think that concludes the job interview." He looked at Krieg. "What do you say?"

Seconds ticked by as Krieg and Sole locked eyes again. It was juvenile, Krieg trying to intimidate him with a stare, while Sole concealed his amusement.

Sherm's warning about the hurt his son had experienced rang in his ears. Krieg was a bully and an asshole, pure and simple. Zabala was more accommodating, but that only made him a more dangerous asshole in the long run.

It didn't matter. This job, no matter what it involved, would get him below the border on a regular basis, and without a lot of questions being asked. He had business in Mexico, and if he hadn't blown the job interview, turning it down was not an option. He'd been intentionally brash, figuring that was the type of personality they wanted to see. He was beginning to think he had misplayed his hand when Krieg finally spoke.

"Okay. You start tomorrow. Seven in the morning. Be here on time. No more strutting in whenever you feel like it."

"See you then." Sole rose and left the office without another word.

Zabala watched their new employee walk through the reception office on the video monitor. He nodded at Ella as he left the building, and Zabala couldn't help wondering if they had just been played by a pro. No one could be as sure of himself and unintimidated as Bill Myers appeared to be. He looked at Krieg.

"I think we should go slow with this one. Let's see how he does on some dry runs, strictly legitimate stuff, before we bring him into the full operation."

"Arrogant asshole," Krieg muttered and nodded. "You're right. If he's as tough as he appears, he could be of service. If not …" He shrugged. "We make him go away."

THIRTY-FIVE

News

An engine roared behind him. Pepe Lopez stepped up from the dirt onto the narrow walk along the side of the alley. He turned as the Dodge Ram pickup bearing the marking of the *Policía Estatal* skidded to a halt, and two men jumped out. The driver stood by the open door. The other approached. Lopez stood his ground.

"I have news." *Sargento* Miguel Garcia tugged at his pants and adjusted his belt under his protruding belly as he approached Lopez. "There is a problem."

"What would that be?" Lopez eyed the fat state police sergeant. "I already paid you this week."

"If you had answered your phone, you would know the problem." Garcia gave a smug grin wide enough to expose a gold tooth, a molar that had cracked and been replaced thanks to the payoffs he received from Pepe Lopez and his *gringo* employers. "No doubt you were with your whore."

"Where I was is not your affair."

"Maybe it should be. Then I could know where to find you when there is important information to share." He smiled. "The sort of information you would want to hear before your n*orteamericanos* find out."

"*Cortar la mierda. Basta del misterio.*" Cut the shit. Enough of the mystery. Lopez was losing patience. "Give me your news, Garcia. I have business elsewhere."

"No." Garcia shook his head. "I think your business is with me today." He turned his head and gave a dramatic look up and down the alley. "Your last shipment has been hijacked."

"What do you mean, hijacked?" Sour acid rose up from Pepe's belly into his throat. "That cannot be. The driver and security man would call and tell me if there was a problem. There would be some word …" His mouth closed and panic replaced the impatience.

"There is no word from them because they are dead." Garcia reached into his shirt pocket and pulled out a pack of cigarettes. He offered one to Lopez who accepted with trembling fingers.

"Dead?" Lopez looked up as he leaned over to accept the light from Garcia.

"Yes, dead … on the road near Monclova." Garcia lit and inhaled his cigarette until the end burned cherry red even in the bright daylight.

"I must …" What, Lopez wondered. What must he do to stay alive when Krieg and Zabala received the news of the hijacking?

"Don't worry, at least not yet. I stationed men there, blocking the road, keeping others away. I did not report this up the chain of command, and the farmer who found the truck is in our custody where he will stay until you decide what we should do with him." Garcia inhaled and blew a great plume of smoke that encircled them. "But you must come with me to see and decide how we handle this. I can't keep this under wraps forever. Sooner or later it will get out, and we don't want Enrique Valera, that asshole *comandante* from Reynosa, hearing about it and nosing around."

"Take me there."

"Very good." The grin spread across Garcia's fleshy face again. "That's what I have been saying. We must go."

The drive took an hour. Garcia had taken the initiative to station men a mile in each direction from the scene of the attack, closing the road to all traffic. They passed by the roadblock, and the sergeant gave a limp-wristed salute as his men outside stiffened to attention.

Pinned in the narrow expanded cab space behind Garcia and his driver, Lopez thought they would never arrive. When they did, he wanted to puke out his breakfast.

The smell of death was in the air. Marty Slocum and Chesty Miller lay in a crumpled heap, tangled together in the cab of the overturned truck. Slocum's face was down between his knees. Chesty's eyes stared blankly through the bullet holes in the windshield.

Carrion seekers had already made their way into the truck. The soft flesh around the mouths and noses had been torn away. One of Chesty's eyes protruded from the socket where some small creature had considered his eyelid to be an especially tasty delicacy.

The bile rose in Pepe Lopez's throat again. He turned away, his brain trying to process it all.

Garcia was calm. No matter the outcome, he and his men would be paid—had been paid. For them, this was an entertaining interlude, a bit of drama in their otherwise drab existence.

Think! Pepe looked again at the truck and the bodies of the men he had seen just the day before, alive and well.

The bodies. There was nothing to do about them. They were dead.

The truck. Trucks get hijacked sometimes, especially trucks from the other side of the border.

The cargo. He scanned the side of the road, taking in the scattered and broken crates of avocados. A plan began to take shape.

"Alright." He turned to Garcia. "There has been a hijacking. That is what you will tell your superiors."

"Of course." Garcia nodded and shook his head to indicate this was not news. "I must report the hijacking." He sighed as he tried to explain the real problem to Lopez. "My superiors are not fools. They will want to know why it was selected and attacked. They will want to know the motive." He looked around at the scattered crates and shrugged. "As you can see, the cargo of avocados remains. The real cargo is gone. A motive will be difficult to explain."

"Not so difficult, if you listen to what I say." Lopez spoke with more confidence now, recovering from his initial shock. He realized there was a reason that he paid Garcia and not the other way around. "You will say that it may have been a competing truck company, one from Mexico perhaps, unhappy about the competition from the north."

"That's it? A competitor?" Garcia shook his head.

"No, that is one theory you will offer. You will show them that you are a thinking man." Lopez smirked. "You might even get a promotion from this."

"A promotion?" Garcia's eyes narrowed. "How?"

"You will show that you are leaving no stone unturned in the investigation and will offer the second possible motive."

Garcia's brow furrowed, a sign that his labored brain was making every effort to follow Lopez's reasoning.

"You will also explain in your report that the attackers could be from one of the drug cartels who attacked because they thought the truck carried drugs and not avocados."

"But the truck did not carry drugs." The glimmer in Garcia's eyes brightened a little. "So, the avocados were of no importance to the cartel attackers, and they left them."

"Correct," Lopez continued. "Then they killed the men in the truck to eliminate witnesses. This will give them two reasonable avenues to investigate."

Lopez looked around as Garcia soaked in his instructions. He peered into the back of the truck and nodded, satisfied. It would work.

"Now, get your men to work and put the panel to the hidden space back in its place. Then throw the crates in. You can leave a few scattered around the ground, that would be expected, but most of them should be overturned inside the truck. Once the panel is in and the avocado crates are scattered about inside, no one will suspect there was any other cargo."

"And the farmer who reported this to us?" Garcia asked.

Lopez thought it over for all of two seconds. It was regrettable. The farmer was on the wrong road at the wrong time. Sometimes life is like that.

"He must disappear ... no trace of him left behind. You understand that there can be no witness who can undermine your story of what happened." He watched Garcia's beefy face for some sign of reluctance. "Will disposing of the farmer be a problem for you?"

"For me?" Garcia's broad shoulders shrugged, tightening the uniform shirt across his belly. "One farmer, more or less, is of no consequence." He laughed. "There are plenty to go around. Of course, there will be a search when his family reports him missing, but …" He smiled and shook his head. "He will not be found."

"Good. Now let's get it done."

"Okay." Garcia nodded, his face a mask of concentration as he began reviewing the instructions in his mind. He looked at the men standing around smoking cigarettes, waiting for orders, and shouted, "*¡A trabajar!*" To work!

Pepe Lopez watched as two men of the *Policía Estatal* worked inside the truck's cargo department to replace the panel. While they worked, others tossed the crates inside in a haphazard fashion as would be expected when the truck rolled into the ditch.

Lopez surveyed their work and nodded, satisfied. Garcia stood to one side, his lips moving silently, trying to commit the story to memory so that it would stand up under questioning from his superiors. The other state police officers gawked at the bodies in the cab. One pinched his nose shut with his finger and pointed, saying something that made the others laugh.

The plan was coming together. Now it was time for the most challenging part.

Lopez reached into his pocket, pulled out his cell phone, took a deep breath, punched in the number, and waited. It was answered on the third ring.

"Yes."

Lopez swallowed once to ease the tightening in his throat. "I have news."

THIRTY-SIX

The Hog Was Out of His Sty

The café door opened with a thump as the door banged against the wall. The man standing there grinned at her. He always grinned, and it always annoyed her.

Isabella looked up from the newspaper spread before her on the counter. "You're letting the dust in, Claude."

Salvia County Deputy, Claude Brainerd, shuffled through the door, hitching his pants and Sam Brown belt up over his belly as he walked, slamming the door behind him. He was a disagreeable sort, and having him around, generally put everyone else in a disagreeable mood as well. Usually, locals went the other way, if they could, the way they might try to get away from the smell of an outhouse when the wind changes directions. Isabella couldn't go anywhere.

"What brings you to Creosote?" she said with a sigh, folding the newspaper for later.

The morning had been slow, and the lunch crowd light. Even Mazey's business was off across the street. Having

Claude Brainerd in town was not going to improve things. Isabella had been enjoying the quiet—until now.

"Just passin' through, Isabella. Always have to come by and have one of the best pieces of meat around." His mouth opened in a leering, gap-toothed grin. "I mean one of your famous hamburgers."

He plopped on a stool directly in front of her. She backed away to try and avoid the chronic halitosis and stale body odor that preceded Brainerd's bulk wherever he went.

"Hmph." She motioned with her head at the empty counter. "Not much trade today. Already turned the grill off and cleaned up."

"I'll wait." Brainerd rested a sweaty arm on the counter. "Won't take much to clean up after one burger." He nodded at the cooler behind her. "And I'll take a beer while I wait."

"Aren't you on duty?"

"You gonna report me?" He shook his head. "Naw, I don't think you'd do that to a friend."

Claude Brainerd was no friend, but he was right. If she reported him for having a beer, it would only bring more trouble. Brainerd would find something to stick his fat nose into, stirring shit up just for the hell of it. When he got like that, getting rid of him was like trying to dig a tick out of the crack of your ass with a bowie knife. He's happy where he is, and if you get too aggressive about it, you might cut off more than you bargained for.

It was best just to let him have what he wanted and move on as quickly as possible. She opened the cooler, twisted the cap off the beer, and thumped in front of Brainerd.

"I'll get your burger." Isabella turned toward the kitchen without any further comment.

"Rare," he called after her. "Extra onions and throw some jalapenos on it."

The clang of pans and utensils from the kitchen signaled her annoyance. Brainerd grinned and gulped the beer in one long chug then went around the end of the counter to the cooler and grabbed another one.

When she came out with the burger a few minutes later, she found him turned with his back to the counter, looking out the window. His Sam Brown belt holding the service weapon, taser, and portable radio, was laid out on the counter beside him. She marveled at the length of the belt required to circle the deputy's gut.

"Here." She clunked the plate holding the burger and a mound of fries in front of Brainerd, put the mustard and ketchup bottles in front of him, and stood back.

He spun on the stool, and his immense, red face lit up. His shirttails were out, and he scratched underneath with both hands as he surveyed the food.

"Damned belt irritates the shit out of my skin." He lifted the shirt to display a red band of mottled flesh over his belly.

Isabella grimaced in disgust.

"Looks good." Brainerd finished scratching and grabbed the mustard and ketchup, drenching the entire affair in both.

Isabella watched as he opened his mouth and shoved the burger nearly half in on the first bit. Four bites later he was finished and began working on the fries.

"Beer," he said through a burp that caused him to gasp and exhale sending the reek of onions, jalapenos, and tooth decay in her direction.

She noted the two already on the counter and got him another without comment, wondering if Mazey was preparing one of the girls for a visit from the deputy. They ran for cover whenever Brainerd showed up and drew straws to decide who would have to service him. Denying him was out of the question.

After cramming the last of the fries into his mouth, he turned the bottle of beer up and washed it all down. With an echoing belch that would have eliminated all competition at the state fair's annual burping contest, he slammed the bottle down, pulled a wad of crumpled bills from his pocket, and tossed them beside the bottle.

"Here. This ought to cover it."

Brainerd grabbed the Sam Brown belt and slung it over his shoulder and headed for the door. His shirttails were still out, and Isabella was grateful she didn't have to stare at his ass crack that would undoubtedly be visible if not for the shirt.

Outside, he stopped for a moment and looked longingly across the road to Mazey's. None of the girls were in sight, and the usually open door was closed tight. That didn't mean anything, and he knew it. If he wanted one of them now, they'd open up for him.

He pushed the lust back down into his groin and shook his head. Maybe later, after. For now, he had work to do, an assignment from Tom Krieg himself.

Isabella watched him go and then looked at the wadded cash on the counter. She could swear it looked sweat-stained, or worse. The thought of touching the money made her cringe, and she pulled out a pair of disposable latex glove she kept in a box to wear when cleaning the restroom.

Delicately, she unwadded and straightened the bills out, side by side—a five and two ones. Seven dollars on a tab of thirteen dollars and fifty cents.

She tossed the bills in the sink and soaked them with disinfectant spray then laid them out on a towel to dry. Outside the window, the county pickup rolled slowly down the road and out of town.

Good. The hog was out of his sty today, but at least he was going to root around somewhere else.

THIRTY-SEVEN

First Things First

"You're late, and your shipment is late. Why?"

There was no hint of a threat in the voice that vibrated into Pepe Lopez's ear. Tom Krieg didn't believe in hints. The menace in his tone was clear and unmistakable.

"There has been a problem." Pepe Lopez tried to control the trembling in his hand that threatened to send the cell phone tumbling to the ground.

The silence that ensued was even more menacing. Lopez looked around to see *Sargento* Garcia watching, a small smile evident on his lips. Fuck you, he thought. If I go down, so do you.

"Are you going to tell us about your ... *problem*?" Krieg's voice rumbled at him like distant thunder, warning of the destroying winds that follow.

"Y-yes, yes, of course," Lopez stammered. "Except it is not my problem. It is our problem."

"Speak, goddammit!" Krieg roared, and the thunder surrounded Lopez.

"Amigo, calmarse y nos dice lo que es el problema." Friend, calm down and tell us what the problem is.

There was no thunder in Zabala's voice. It was serene even. Serene like the hiss of the snake that bites when you aren't looking, Lopez thought.

Best to just say it. That would be the worst of it. After, if they had not sentenced him to death, perhaps he could find a way to survive. He looked at Garcia, still watching like a vulture, ready to pick up the scraps. He walked several paces away so that the police sergeant could not hear what Krieg and Zabala shouted at him over the phone.

"We have been attacked." He spoke quietly into the phone, deliberately using the word we to demonstrate that he was as much a victim as they were.

"Attacked?" The rage still thundered in the background, muted as Krieg considered what the words meant. "What are our losses?"

"Everything. It happened on the road to Monclova. The truck was wrecked, Slocum and Miller dead ... both shot."

"The cargo!" The sharpness was back in Krieg's voice. "What about the cargo?"

Lopez knew he wasn't referring to the avocados. "Gone. No sign of them. Apparently taken onto another vehicle. We checked the area and didn't find any of them dead or on foot."

"How many?"

"A big load, twenty-eight." Lopez spoke rapidly, trying to move the conversation as far as possible from the initial thunder. "Seventeen women, the rest men."

"Who?" Now Krieg's voice was quiet, and somehow that made it even more threatening.

"We haven't determined that yet."

Once again, Lopez intentionally used the third person

plural pronoun—we. He'd be damned if he was going to go down alone. If Krieg and Zabala decided to take their wrath out on someone, Lopez had no doubt that he was the most natural target. A little company might make him less vulnerable. The time had come to include Garcia and the *Policía Estatal* goons that worked for him.

"Garcia and his men are searching the wreckage for clues."

"Where were they when this happened?" Zabala asked. "Why did they not know something was going to happen on the road we pay them to protect?"

"Valid questions," Lopez agreed, happy to deflect some of the attention. "I will find out why and make sure the ones who failed to do their job pay for their mistakes."

He nodded to Garcia who continued to eye him from a distance, the annoying smile still on his fat face. He gave the sergeant a palm down signal to indicate he was trying to calm things down with his superiors.

"Fucking find out who!" Krieg shouted. "I want the name of the person behind the attack!"

"Yes, yes, of course. We are working on that as we speak. It must be one of our competitors ... other *coyotajes*."

Lopez shot a disgusted glance at Garcia and his men, gathered around the truck gawking at the bodies of Slocum and Miller. Fat chance he was going to have finding the attackers with this group of clowns.

"Pepe, speak to me."

Zabala spoke, probably thinking his calm voice would reassure Lopez and elicit more information than Krieg's rage. It sent a chill up Lopez's spine, giving him the sensation that someone was creeping up behind him in the dark.

"Yes, Raul," Lopez responded. "I am trying. It's just that

we have very little information now … for the moment … we will find out more, of course, but it will take time."

"I understand," Zabala said. "Is there a competitor that you would suspect?"

A reasonable question instead of rage. That, at least, was refreshing but changed nothing.

"All of them, *jefe*." He tried reasoning. "That is the problem."

"Yes, of course." In the air-conditioned office, Zabala looked at Krieg and shook his head, which meant that he should not interrupt. Zabala would handle the conversation from this point until Krieg reigned in his fury. "So start with your contacts in the villages and cities and barrios. Someone who knew of this shipment informed those who attacked. They had advance knowledge. Begin there."

"Yes." Lopez nodded. He had already decided to seek out the person who had the most intimate knowledge of this shipment, although that person seemed an unlikely traitor.

"Take care when you speak to them," Zabala continued. "Do not let the informer know that he is suspected. Make him think all is well between you and him."

"If I find him, I will kill him."

"No. You mustn't, at least not yet." Zabala spoke like a coach instructing his team on the next play. "We will use this informer and devise a way to eliminate those who attacked us. Only then will he die." Zabala paused, waiting for Lopez to acknowledge his instructions.

"I understand." Lopez wondered if the informer and attackers would be the only ones targeted for elimination.

As if he read his mind, Zabala offered some words of reassurance. "And you, Pepe Lopez, will have the pleasure of killing the informer when the time comes."

Lopez was not reassured. He imagined Krieg standing

behind him, ready to put a hole in his head once the informer had been eliminated. For now, though, he could only do what they expected.

"I will find the informer," he said.

"Good!" Zabala beamed at him over the phone. "Contact us every day, morning and evening, and as soon as you have information. Now go and find the informer."

"I will, *Jefe*."

The call ended, and Zabala resumed his customary position in the chair, leaned back, hands behind his head.

"Don't look so smug," Krieg shot at him. "We've got a problem. We are going to war across the border, and we don't even know who it is we are fighting."

"I am aware of the problem." Zabala smiled. "But there is opportunity here too."

"Opportunity. What the fuck do …" Krieg's eyes narrowed as he considered Zabala's words. "I see your point."

"Yes. We didn't ask for the war, but with careful planning, we can make use of it and eliminate our competition. Instead of being one of many who provide our special services, we will be the one and only."

"Yes." Krieg nodded. "And our inventory for our other market will also increase."

"Correct. Now you get the picture. More pretty faces to choose from gives us the chance to boost sales and improve our product line."

"But first, we have to fight a war." Krieg returned to the business at hand.

"Yes," Zabala agreed. "But we must do more than that. We must win it."

Five hours away by car, on the road to Monclova, Pepe Lopez considered the task at hand. He would survive, at least until he could discover the identity of the informer. Until then, he had to make sure that there were others to blame if there were any other attacks.

"Garcia, come here," he called to the sergeant.

"Yes." Garcia strolled over, lighting a cigarette as he walked.

"There may be other attacks planned. Have your men on patrol. Cover all our routes."

"That will require my men to work around the clock."

"I don't care."

"Then they must be paid."

"No more shipments can be lost." Lopez leaned toward Garcia and tapped his chest with a forefinger. "As for pay, your men should consider that there will be no pay at all if another shipment is lost."

Lopez became aware that the sergeant's men were watching. Garcia turned his head to the gathering of state police officers and shook his head, meaning for them to remain where they were, then he turned back to Lopez.

"Be very careful, Pepe." He leaned close enough for Lopez to feel his breath on his face. "We have had a long relationship in this business, but remember that you are not the only ... how is it the *norteamericanos* say?" His eyes widened, and he smiled. "Ah yes, you are not the only game in town, and your employers in Texas should remember this also."

Garcia slapped Lopez on the shoulder to demonstrate to his watching officers that all was well between them. "Now we will get to work and try to protect your shipments, and I know that when this affair is over, you will compensate my men for the many extra hours they will have served you.

You will do this because my men will expect it and you know that they can find you wherever you are."

Garcia walked away and shouted to his men to give them their orders. Pepe Lopez stood in the road, sweating under the sun. He now had two problems, find the informer, and deal with Garcia who vastly overestimated his importance to the business.

First things first. He could deal with Garcia later. Finding the informer was a matter of critical importance if he wanted to avoid a bullet in the head.

THIRTY-EIGHT

The Music

"Hey, girl!" Doyle Krieg grabbed the crotch of his jeans and ground his hips.

"Don't forget me!" Paco González aped Doyle's movements and leered at the girl on the porch of the guesthouse.

"Ignore them. They are pigs, but they can't hurt you." Claire reached out and patted Jacinta's arm. "They wouldn't dare. His father would beat them."

They sat side by side in the chairs on the guesthouse porch, sipping coffee. Tom Krieg had not called for either of them in the night. Jacinta gave a prayer of thanks for that, although Claire warned her that one day soon he would call for her again.

Her sleep had been fitful. At one point she must have cried out in the night because she woke to find Claire in bed with her holding her head against her breast and patting her shoulder the way one caressed a sick, feverish child.

"There, there, little one. It will pass."

The words were even almost the same ones Jacinta had

used with the children she had tended in Mexico. She blocked the thought of the night and Krieg and the promise that he would call for her again soon. Blocking everything out was the only way to remain sane.

"I know you want some of this, girl!" Doyle grinned and stroked the front of his pants.

He and Paco were closer now, standing on the lawn twenty feet from the porch. Jacinta looked away.

"Go away, little boy!" Claire called out. "Before your father finds out what you are doing."

"How's he gonna find out? You gonna tell him?" Doyle came closer and rested a boot on the porch steps.

"You know," Paco leered at Claire. "For an old whore, you don't look so bad. How about it ... you and me ... we go have a little fun inside?"

"In your dreams," Claire smirked. "And I'll bet they're wet sticky dreams when you think of me."

"I'll bet she's right about that!" Doyle laughed.

"*Puta* ... whore, bitch," Paco snarled.

"Run along now, boys. Come back when you're grown men." Claire lifted a cup from the side table and sipped the coffee that had now become cold.

"You should watch that mouth, whore."

Claire put the cup down and leaned forward, glaring into Doyle's eyes. "No, you should be more careful with your mouth. If I tell your father about this, it will be bad for you."

The reaction was immediate. Paco took a step back, deciding retreat might be the better part of valor, or at least the best way to avoid an ass-kicking by Tom Krieg.

The threat only made Doyle angrier.

"He might give me the back of his hand. I've had that

before." Doyle's eyes narrowed into mean snake-like slits. "You'll get a hell of a lot worse, don't forget it."

She never forgot it. She didn't care. Over the years, Tom Krieg had beaten the caring out of her. Their eyes remained locked together, a cobra and a mongoose, each searching for precisely the right moment to strike and survive the encounter.

Seconds passed. The silent battle might have continued if not for the crunch of gravel under tires in the drive.

Paco turned toward the sound. "We got company."

Doyle looked over his shoulder. "Son of a bitch."

Sandy Palmeras drove slowly along the drive. He'd been to the Krieg place before, had worked on vehicles for the ranch many times, but it always seemed a little surreal, coming out of the brush country into the landscaped gardens and lawns.

He brought the pickup to a stop and hopped to the ground. Doyle and his asshole buddy Paco were fifty yards away at the guesthouse porch, no doubt harassing Claire and another girl seated with her on the porch.

He knew Claire. Everyone knew Claire. Tom Krieg's mistress was a fixture in the county, although no one ever called her his mistress in his presence. She was always referred to as Claire or Miss Claire, or Miss Toussaint on more formal occasions.

He didn't recognize the other woman, but she looked younger. Maybe a relative of Claire's he thought. He called to Doyle.

"You boys want to give me a hand here?"

"Do your own fucking work." Doyle turned back to the women and said something that made Paco laugh.

Claire didn't laugh though, and the girl beside her lowered her head. His mother's words rang in his ear.

Watch out for Doyle Krieg. Well, he was watching him now, could see him over there plain as day. He shrugged and walked toward the guesthouse.

"Miss Claire." He nodded in greeting as he approached the porch.

"Sandy." Claire smiled. "It is good to see you. You haven't been around for a while."

"Been busy." Sandy's eyes moved to Jacinta. "And this is?"

"This is Jacinta," Claire said. "A ... friend."

There was just the slightest hesitation, but Sandy caught it. A friend? A friend of whose, he wondered but didn't ask.

"Hello, Jacinta ... *Hola Jacinta*. That's a pretty name."

He spoke in semi-fluent Spanish. Everyone in southwest Texas spoke at least a little Spanish and Sandy's was better than most, certainly better than Doyle's.

"Jacinta," he continued. "That's a flower, isn't it? In English, we call it hyacinth."

"Yes, a flower. *El jacinto*, but for a girl, it is Jacinta."

Jacinta smiled for the first time since arriving at the Krieg estate. The smile was not lost on Claire, who was happy to see the girl relax for a moment and forget her situation. She saw that Doyle also noticed the smile and his eyes darkened. They must be cautious. Jacinta's pleasant conversation with Sandy could have disagreeable, even dangerous, consequences.

"It's a beautiful name." Sandy took a step up on the porch, bent over, and extended a hand. "I am Reynaldo Palmeras, but everyone calls me Sandy because of this." He took his other hand and lifted a few strands of his hair.

Jacinta's smile broke into a laugh. There, standing on the guesthouse porch, on a day like any other when he expected nothing exceptional to happen, Sandy heard the most beautiful music he had ever heard in her laughter.

He looked into Jacinta's dark eyes and something inside him changed. Without knowing it, he had taken another step into manhood.

Claire saw it, and her face darkened with concern. "Don't let us keep you from your work, Sandy. Mr. Krieg will want his machines unloaded and in the barn before he gets home."

"You're right." Sandy nodded and looked at Doyle. "You gonna help?"

"Fuck off." Doyle and Paco smirked and strolled away from the porch and any possibility that they might have to do some work.

He turned back to Jacinta. "Maybe I can come visit you again."

"I would like that." She knew Claire's worried eyes bored into her but said it anyway.

After losing so much, she thought, what else could she lose? The boy's face was open and honest. His eyes pierced into hers, studying them as if he saw things that others did not.

The devil called Krieg, who had stolen her life from her, might not be happy, but she didn't care. This moment was theirs, between her and this boy called Sandy. He had no power to steal this tiny moment of happiness from her.

"Good." Sandy turned toward the truck and went to work.

When he had the ATVs unloaded and in the barn, he stopped at the porch. "*Adiós por ahora.*" Goodbye for now.

"Goodbye for now." Jacinta smiled and held his gaze until Claire broke in.

"Goodbye now, Sandy. Go home safely," Claire said,

taking Jacinta by the hand to coax her into the house while she looked over a shoulder at the smiling young man.

The miles back to Creosote passed without Sandy remembering how he got there. His ears still rang with Jacinta's laugh, the music that had changed him, the music he had to hear again.

THIRTY-NINE

Some Mex Gonna be Happy

"Why the fuck we gotta meet here?" Lucky Martin slammed the door on the rusted pickup.

"Why the fuck do you think?" Deputy Claude Brainerd leaned against his county truck, smoking a cigarette, his belt and holster laid out across the truck's hood.

On temporary leave from K and Z Trucking, while things settled down over the shooting at the river, Martin had driven his personal truck. He resented having to burn his own gas to come to this meeting. After all, the whole thing was being blown out of proportion.

All he did was take a few shots at a bunch of Mexicans trying to cross the river illegally and by, God, he stopped them. So, one got nicked in the process—so fucking what? If they hadn't tried to cross, they wouldn't have been hurt. Everyone was acting like he had done something wrong just for doing what they paid him to do.

Not to mention, he got his ass beat by some drifter in the process. Now, the word was going around that they were going to hire the drifter because he was such a fucking tough guy. It was bullshit.

As far as he was concerned, that drifter better watch his back. It was just a matter of time before Lucky Martin found a way to even things up with him.

"Goddammit, Claude. I don't like being here."

Martin looked around. He was parked in nearly the same place along the river bank he had been on the day of the shooting. He touched his hand tenderly to the still swollen jaw the medics in Brownsville had wired partially shut until the fracture healed. Unable to open his mouth fully, his voice had a curious hissing quality as the words passed over what was left of his teeth.

"Damned if you don't sound like a hair-lipped rattler." Brainerd laughed. "Did you bring it?"

"Yeah, I got it."

"Where?"

"In my truck."

"Let's see it."

"Shit."

Martin turned around and walked back to his truck. Brainerd followed, tugging his pants up under his belly as he walked.

"Here."

Martin tugged the squealing door open, reached behind the seat, and pulled out a Winchester Model 94. He handed it to Brainerd who immediately levered open the chamber.

"It's unloaded," Martin sneered. "No way I'd hand you a loaded rifle."

"Good thinking." Brainerd smiled. "Better safe than sorry, though. That's what my daddy always said."

He turned and pointed down the bank toward the river.

"Show me exactly where you were and what happened over there."

"What the hell is this all about?"

"I'm supposed to follow up. Seems you started a shit storm, putting a slug in that Mex. They want me to make sure everything's cleaned up … no loose ends lying around."

"Goddammit! I already explained everything to Krieg and Zabala. They're the ones that told me to stay out of sight for a while. You know them, right? The ones that pay you your kickback for being their boy."

"Yeah, I know them." Brainerd's small pig eyes narrowed in his fat face. "And you best watch your mouth … boy."

Their eyes were only locked for a second before Martin backed off, not feeling all that lucky. "Okay," he said. "Sorry, Claude. I suppose you're just doin' your job the way I was when I shot near them Mex people tryin' to swim the river."

"Show me where you were."

"Alright. This way."

Lucky Martin led the way along the bank fifty yards or so to a point where the clearing across the river and the small stand of bushes were visible.

"They was over there." He pointed. "Me and Stu, we was here."

Brainerd looked down at the ground.

"You won't find nothin'," Lucky snapped. "Me and Stu cleaned up the brass if that's what you're thinkin' … me injured and all, in pain … I still done my job." He nodded at Brainerd. "You tell them that."

"I will." Brainerd walked toward the river. "Shit, Lucky.

Can't be more than a hundred yards or so away. How the hell did you miss."

"I didn't fucking miss."

"Well, you told Krieg and Zabala that you wasn't aiming at nobody, yet you managed to put a round in that Mex." Brainerd turned and grinned. "Sounds like a miss to me."

"I didn't miss." Lucky hissed through the wires holding his jaw in place. "Look."

He stepped forward, pointing at the far bank. "See that clump of brush over there."

"Yeah, I see it."

"They was in there, all of them. I just put a couple of rounds nearby to sort of warn them to go back the way they come. Next thing I know, that damned Mex is out crawling around, so I put some rounds in the dirt near him."

"That don't explain how you managed to hit him."

"Because, goddammit, the Mex started jumpin' around like a monkey. He jumped hisself right into one of my bullets. That's all they was to it."

"You're sayin', you shot him by accident."

"Damned right it was by accident. There's no way …"

Lucky Martin never saw the pistol. Brainerd reached into the pocket of his trousers and pulled the small .32 caliber semiautomatic. While Martin pointed across the Rio Grande to the clump of bushes where the Mexican family had taken refuge from his bullets, Brainerd pulled the trigger three times in rapid succession.

Fired from a distance two feet, all three slugs penetrated the back of Lucky's skull. It took less than an ounce of lead to snuff out his unpleasant existence.

Lucky Martin dropped where he stood. The only sound was the lifeless thud when his body hit the dirt. Brainerd looked down at him for a moment, searching for signs of life. There were none. Then he scanned the distance to the water and cursed.

"Fuck. Shoulda got him closer first."

It took the deputy a couple of minutes to drag the corpse to the water's edge and roll it in. He tossed the rifle in behind him.

For a moment, he thought about tossing the pistol in the river with the rifle. It was just a Saturday night special, a cheap piece of steel like a million others. He'd taken it off a drunk Mexican he locked up one night and then hung onto it for use in some special occasion. Putting holes in Lucky Martin's head was special enough he figured.

An untraceable weapon was a handy thing to have, especially the way things were heating up with Krieg and Zabala lately. You never knew. He might be called on to use it again. He decided to hold onto the pistol.

"Some Mex over there gonna be happy when old Lucky's body bobs up somewheres along the bank." Brainerd pushed the pistol back in his pocket and made his way up the slope, panting and muttering.

He stopped to wipe the sweat from his face with the back of his arm. "Least I won't be the one pullin' him out."

FORTY

La Guerra

Mario Acosta did not want to be there. The blast furnace of the noon sun beat down on the top of his head until he thought his brain would roast inside his skull. Worse than the sun, though, was the stench.

Twenty men stood in a circle baking under the sun outside Benito Diaz's shack. In the center of the circle was a wire enclosure. Inside the pen were twenty-eight men and women. A few of the girls looked to be no older thirteen of fourteen. The terrified prisoners inside the wire eyed the stone-faced men on the outside. Many wept, certain their departure from this world was imminent.

The captives lined the wire praying for deliverance. The center of the enclosure had become a cesspool, the only place they could relieve themselves. Puddles of urine and the watery bowel movements of those overcome with fear steamed under the sun and released their noxious fumes, making it difficult to breath.

Acosta had never experienced anything so foul. The

stench of human excrement, sweat, and fear filled the air. He gagged and feared he might add to the smells by puking his guts out on the ground. He could only wonder at how much more terrible it must be for those crowded together inside the pen.

He had arrived in the back of the same van that brought him the day they abducted him from Torreón. Over his objections, they warned him that the *jefe*, Benito Diaz, expected his presence. Acosta had nodded and climbed into the van. Resisting was pointless. On arrival at the shack, he was ordered to join the men standing in the dusty yard. Diaz was nowhere to be seen.

A few minutes later, another van arrived, holding another reluctant visitor. The priest he had seen with Pepe Lopez the day he and Diaz spied on them emerged from the back. He looked even more unhappy to be present at the gathering than Acosta. He too joined the group and was directed to stand beside Acosta.

The wait seemed interminable. The fiery ball blazing in the sky did not discriminate. It beat down on the heads of those inside and outside the wire with equal intensity. Acosta thought he might pass out. A few of those inside the pen did, and others bent over to wave their hands and try to revive them. At one point, the priest standing beside him swayed and bumped against Acosta's shoulder.

At the moment when it seemed no one could withstand the heat and smell another minute, Diaz, flanked by his sons emerged from the shack. They crossed the bare ground to the circle of men, their shoes kicking up puffs of dust as they walked.

Two men parted as they passed through the circle and then closed up again until their shoulders touched. Diaz turned around, looking into the face of each man standing outside the enclosure. With the exception of Acosta and the priest, their high cheekbones and brown faces marked them as native descendants of some distant tribe. Though Acosta had taken to thinking of Diaz as a Yaqui, he had no proof of his parentage. Still, the dark faces surrounding him made him feel uncomfortable, an outsider not of the tribe.

After a minute, Diaz turned to the wire pen and spoke.

"You are here because you chose poorly. You were lured into doing business with the *gringos*." He gave an understanding smile. "Now, I know that they made you many promises. You have heard that they would guarantee your safe arrival across the border. But as you can see …"

A saintly smile on his face, he lifted his arms and spread them wide to indicate the people inside the wire. They hung on every word he spoke, well aware that he held their fate in his hands.

"But as you can see," he continued, shaking his head. "There are no guarantees. They could not protect you even here in your own land. There is a lesson to be learned from this." He waited while every eye lifted and every ear turned to hear the lesson. They would gladly accept it if only they could leave this terrible place.

"The lesson is this. You must never do business with them again. If you wish to cross the border, you will come to me and no others. This must be clearly understood by everyone here." He paused, looking from face to face behind the wire. "Do you understand?"

The heads of every man woman and child inside the enclosure nodded emphatically. Hope shone in their eyes and replaced the dread on their faces.

"Good." Diaz smiled. "This is very good. There is one more thing. Every lesson requires some reminder, so the lesson is not forgotten."

The hope faded. The dread returned, and their faces paled under the burning sun.

"One must be sacrificed to teach the lesson."

The whimpers and sobs that had run as an undercurrent to his words rose in volume until they became a mournful wail. They huddled together, averting their gaze from the man who held their fate in their hands, crossing themselves and praying that some other would be chosen to be the example.

"Why do you weep so?" He asked, clearly enjoying the moment and the power he held over his captives. "This is a natural thing, a lesson we even take from the Holy Church. Did not a loving Father sacrifice a son for His other children, to teach them the lessons He left with them?"

A self-satisfied grin spread across Diaz's face, pleased with his warped use of the theology these peasants bowed before. "So you see, it is only natural ... ordained by God even." He lifted a finger to point at the sky. "One of you must be sacrificed to teach this lesson. That way, you will spread the word and always remember that you must never again try to do business with the *gringos*."

Diaz gave a final nod to emphasize the logic of it and that the decision was made, then turned away from the wire. His eyes met those of Father Alfonso.

"You, Priest. You will pick."

"Excuse me?" Alfonso's eyes widened. His head moved slowly from side to side. "No ... I can't be the one."

"Yes, you can." Diaz lifted his head up to the sky, an amused smile spreading across his face. "You will do this, Priest, or there will be consequences, unpleasant ones."

"How can I?" Alfonso turned to those huddling behind the wire. They looked away, fearing that making eye contact would prompt him to select them for the sacrifice. He shook his head. "I can't. Please don't insist."

"Insist! I can do more than insist. This is not some confessional discussion with one of your church widows!" Diaz's voice thundered. He withdrew the knife he carried tucked in his belt and held it before Alfonso's eyes. "Choose, or I will." He looked at the people cringing before him in the enclosure. "Should it be this little one?" He pointed the blade at a weeping girl of thirteen. "Or that woman who is carrying a child inside her to be born in another month?" He looked into Alfonso's eyes. "Or should you be the sacrifice. That might be more fitting after all, but then I need you, so no, you cannot be the sacrifice." He tapped the knifepoint on Alfonso's chest. "Choose now, Priest."

Mario Acosta, stared at the ground, silently praying that Diaz would not single him out and make him part of the horror playing out. Standing pressed together in the circle with Alfonso at his side, he could feel the priest tremble. He was terrified, and Mario wondered which the priest feared more, his own death, or the eternal damnation that would follow if he selected one of these people to be butchered by Diaz and his men.

Alfonso could do nothing but weep, tears rolling down his cheeks to fall and disappear in the dust. His eyes swept the crowded mass of bodies inside the wire, each terrified to meet his gaze. Close your eyes and point, he thought. Let God determine who would be the sacrifice.

Yes, that was the way. The thought was a revelation. It took the burden from him and placed it squarely on God.

Let God decide, God who knows who the sinners are and who should be the sacrifice. He closed his eyes, lifted an arm to point so that God, or fate, or the devil could choose who was to die under the burning sun.

"Take me."

Alfonso's eyes opened in shock. The old man pushed his way through the throng to stand before Diaz on the other side of the wire.

"Take me," repeated.

"It is not your decision, old man. It is the priest's. If he chooses you, so be it. Otherwise, it will be another." Diaz jerked his head, motioning at Alfonso. "What do you say, Priest?"

The old man turned to the priest and nodded. "Pick me. Let these others go." He smiled in an attempt to set Alfonso's mind at ease. "It's alright. My wife died five years ago, and I miss her."

Alfonso was speechless. He looked into the old man's eyes, ashamed of his own fear but thankful that God had provided a sacrifice and saved him from choosing. "Yes." He nodded and looked at Diaz. "This man. Take him for your sacrifice."

"As you say." Diaz nodded, and two men pulled the wire gate open for the old man to come out.

He stood calmly before Diaz and his men. There was nothing he could do, even if he had wanted to fight. The men stepped back from him in a show of respect.

"*¿Cuál es tu nombre, Abuelo?*" What is your name, grandfather? Diaz stepped forward and put his hands on the man's thin shoulders.

"Manuel," the old man replied.

Diaz turned to the others still inside the wire. "Remember this man, Manuel, in your prayers tonight. Because of him, you will live."

Diaz turned, nodding to the man standing to Mario Acosta's right. The man pulled a long-barreled revolver from his belt and thrust it toward Mario.

"Kill him," Diaz said.

"What?"

"Take this pistol, put it to Manuel's head, and pull the trigger." Diaz shrugged. "It is a simple thing to do."

"But I can't be the one." Mario's eyes were now as wide as Alfonso's had been a moment before.

"Enough! Kill him, or you will take his place."

Diaz nodded and led Manuel, the old man, to a place in the dust ten yards from the wire enclosure. Diaz's men stepped away, allowing everyone behind the wire to see the drama being played out.

"Now," Diaz said, his eyes boring into Mario's.

There was nothing to be done about it. Mario had no illusions about his own courage. He had none, and the fact did not shame him.

He had watched Father Alfonso's moral crisis with curious interest. Now that he was drawn into the midst of the drama, he felt nothing beyond the instinct to preserve his own life at all costs.

He took five steps toward Manuel. Their eyes met. Mario dared not look away for fear of missing the shot. The old man smiled, and Mario squeezed the trigger.

The .44 caliber bullet plowed through the old man's skull and flew off into the desert behind him. When it was done, his body lay on his side. Blood trickled from the hole in his forehead across his face and dripped onto the parched earth.

"Very good!" Benito Diaz came up behind Mario and removed the pistol from his trembling hand. "You are one of us now." He turned to Father Alfonso. "You too, Priest. You are one of us, part of our army."

Mario Acosta no longer felt like a spectator among these tribesmen. He had become like them—a murderer. He stared down at the body of Manuel, the old man, and felt his soul tremble inside, already lost and on its way to hell.

Diaz took a step away to face his gang of armed thugs that he called an army. He lifted the revolver in the air. "*Guerra con los gringos.*" War with the *gringos*!

"*La guerra!*" the gang shouted back.

FORTY-ONE

Recon

At six forty-five in the morning, Sole pulled off the two-lane road into the lot at K and Z Trucking. Fifteen trucks bearing the company logo were lined up in the gravel with fifty or so men hovering in groups around them.

He pulled to the side of the lot, wheeling in beside a line of personal vehicles, and stepped out to survey the scene. It reminded him of an early morning muster before an operation during his Marine Corps service.

"How ya doin'? Looks like we're gonna be partnered up today." Stu Pearce walked up, sipping coffee from a styrofoam cup. "Remember me?"

"I remember." Sole nodded at the coffee. "Any more of that around."

"Yep. Over in the garage." Stu turned and led the way. "I'll show you."

Another half-dozen men were inside the garage, gathered around a coffee maker set up on a folding table. Sole nodded at the men standing around as he reached for the pot and filled a cup.

"This normal?"

"Normal?" Stu laughed. "Not sure what normal is around here."

"I counted fifteen trucks outside," Sole pressed. "Driver and security man in each truck adds up to thirty men." He looked out the bay door to the lot. "Must be fifty out there."

"Yeah, well this isn't exactly a normal workday." Stu nodded, a serious look in his eyes.

"Why is that?"

"Don't really know for sure. There's a truck missing … shoulda been back last night. Marty Slocum and Chesty Miller. They're good men. Hope they're alright. Marty's got a daughter gettin' married in a month, and Chesty's son just gave him his third grandbaby." Stu jerked his head toward the men outside. "I expect them being here has something to do with that."

"Looks like all hands on deck."

"Yep. When the call comes, we come runnin'." Stu grinned. "That's how it is at K and Z."

"Hey, you're the fella that laid out ole Lucky Martin, ain't you?" A tall man whose weathered face, lean frame, and dusty clothes made him look like a character out of a Larry McMurtry novel stepped over to the coffee table.

Sole looked him over and sipped his coffee without replying. He figured it wouldn't do to make too much of putting down one of the K and Z men without knowing who his friends were and how many might be standing around.

"This is the one," Stu chimed in for him, grinning and clapping Sole on the back like he had known him all his life. "Put that loud-mouthed pecker-head on the ground like there was nothin' to it."

"Well, hell." The tall newcomer put his hand out.

"Pleased to meet you then. I'm Sid Culper." Sid leaned forward and snickered, "Nobody likes that son of a bitch, Martin anyway. You're among friends."

"Bill Myers." Sole introduced himself and shook Sid's hand. "Good to meet you, Sid."

"Just call me Shorts." Sid grinned. "Everybody does."

Sole eyed him up and down. Measuring people was a lifelong habit, and Sole knew this man stood at least six foot five.

"Shorts? Seems a strange name for a man of your stature."

"Oh, it ain't got nothin' to do with how tall he is," Stu beamed. "It's 'cause he's always walkin' around pullin' his shorts out of the crack of his skinny ass."

Others in the room had gathered around to hear the exchange and admire the man who had done for the universally disliked Lucky Martin. They nodded and laughed at Stu's explanation. Sid—Shorts—laughed too.

Across the lot, Tom Krieg and Raul Zabala came out of the warehouse office.

"Time to go to work," Stu said and led the way to join the other men gathered by the trucks.

It had the feel of a pre-ops briefing without the usual weapons and gear in sight. Tom Krieg did the talking.

"We had some trouble yesterday. Load from Coahuila was hit."

There were murmurs among the men.

"Listen up," Krieg continued in his best George S. Patton voice. "We won't be backing down from this. We will push forward ... double up and triple up on security where necessary ... meet force with force. You know what that means. That's why we've called in the extra hands." He paused, hands on his hips surveying his troops. "Any questions?"

"Any word on Slocum and Miller," Stu Pearce called out.

"No." Krieg glared at Stu. "Consider them casualties, probably dead." Krieg eyed the rest of the group. "That means you don't take chances. Do your jobs."

"What about the police down in Mexico? Have they been advised?" Sole asked.

Laughter rippled through the group. Even Stu Pearce slapped his thigh and chuckled, shaking his head. "That's a good one, Bill … damned good one … police down in Mexico … hah."

Krieg eyed Sole. "Well, Bill Myers. Glad you could make it today, and on time too. I'll chalk your question up to inexperience. Won't take long for you to understand why they're laughing." He looked around the gathering. "Alright, let's go to work. Zabala has your assignments."

The men filed up to Raul Zabala and received their assignments. Each truck had a driver and a security person assigned. Additional security personnel climbed into the rear of some of the vehicles.

"What's that all about?" Sole asked Pearce as they stood in line waiting to get their assignment.

"Trucks heading out where Slocum and Miller were lost. They get more security today."

"So what's the SOP for more security?"

"Yeah, well that's something they'll have to clue you in on some time."

"How about now?"

"Nope." Stu shook his head and gave a nervous laugh. "Not my place to be talkin' about it with you." He nodded at Krieg and Zabala, standing at the front of the line of men receiving their assignments. "They'll fill you in when the time comes."

"When will that be?"

"I reckon when they trust you. That shouldn't be too long though." Stu smiled, trying to get Sole to lighten up on the questions. "I mean, after all, you are the one that beat the shit out of Lucky Martin."

It was their turn to receive an assignment from Zabala. He handed Stu a pickup order for tomatoes from a farm south of Monterrey.

"You drive." He looked at Sole. "You're security."

Stu accepted the paperwork and turned to walk away. Sole remained in front of Zabala.

"Okay," Sole nodded. "So, explain to me what that means. I have no weapons, and I don't see any around. If someone tries to waylay the load, what do I do? Politely say, please don't?"

"Pearce will tell you about weapons." Zabala smiled in his usual affable way that reminded Sole of Wile E. Coyote leering at Road Runner. "Don't worry. You'll have what you need if it comes to that."

Krieg stepped forward. To this point, he had remained to the side, letting Zabala handle the assignments.

"When we get an idea about what you're made of, you'll have all the details. For now, your employment is strictly on a trial basis," Krieg snapped.

"Fair enough." Sole nodded and turned to follow Stu Pearce.

"Best to keep the questions to a minimum," Stu said, leading the way to their truck. "Too many questions and they're apt to think there might be more to you than just a drifter looking for work."

"I hear you." Sole nodded. "Now, what about weapons?"

"Follow me."

Stu led the way to the truck they would be driving and climbed up on the passenger side. "It works like this." He turned to make sure Sole was paying attention and pulled down the sun visor to reveal a seam in the overhead fabric. "Once we're across the border, you pull this flap down and … voila."

A tug on the seam, and the fabric peeled away from its Velcro closure to reveal a shotgun and an automatic rifle secured with clamps screwed into the overhead steel. The additional two-and-a-half inches of fabric and padding in the headliner of the truck cab were unnoticeable. Sole nodded his approval.

"These stay out of sight until we are in Mexico and at least five miles away from the border crossing." Stu's tone indicated the seriousness of the instructions he was giving. "We get caught transporting weapons south of the border, and we'll end up sweating out ten years in a Mexican prison, and Krieg and Zabala will swear they knew nothing about the guns." He shook his head; his eyes locked on Sole's "Believe me. You do not want that to happen."

"I believe you," Sole said.

"Good." Stu resealed the seam that hid the overhead arsenal. His usual, easy smile returned to his face. "Now let's hit the road."

An hour later, they had crossed the border at McAllen and were headed south on Highway 97 out of Reynosa. Sole retrieved the shotgun from the overhead and rested the butt on the floor between his feet.

He was happy to be assigned to the milk run with Stu. Mixing things up with hijackers on behalf of K and Z

Trucking was not in his plans. This was a recon patrol, nothing more.

He was a Georgia boy. Ask him about the Appalachian Mountains near Dahlonega, the black water swamp along the Florida line, or the barrier islands off the Atlantic coast, and he could provide an accurate assessment of conditions, but you couldn't fill a thimble with what he knew about Mexico.

He needed to understand the lay of the land down below the border. The job with K and Z was the perfect cover.

With any luck, he figured to have things scoped out and a plan in place after a few runs south. Until then, Stu was decent company and a useful tour guide.

FORTY-TWO

So Many Secrets

The walk back to her house seemed lonelier than usual. Isabella moved absently past the bungalows and assorted residents sitting on their stoops to get some air before the heat of the day set in. Most lifted a hand in greeting or nodded at her passing.

"Mornin', Isabella."
"Mornin', Mae."
"Mornin', Isabella."
"Mornin', Uncle Charlie."
"Mornin', Isabella."
"Mornin', Rose."

And so on.

Before Bill Myers' arrival in Creosote, she passed them every day after the breakfast crowd left the café. Lately, she stayed open a while longer, hoping for a chance to talk to the new drifter who had taken up residence in the old driller's shack. Sometimes she stayed all the way through until the lunch crowd came in.

Most of the locals winked and nodded and were happy for her, though some had reservations about this Bill Myers fella who nobody knew a damned thing about. Who the hell was he to drift into town and then take up with their Isabella like he belonged here? Their protective instincts were natural. Isabella had grown up around them, had been partly raised by some of them after her father died.

Still, they wanted her to be happy. There wasn't a soul in town who didn't feel a pull in their heart when she strode past their bungalows four times a day. Twice going to the café and twice heading home. It wasn't any sort of life for a woman with the fire to live that burned in their Isabella.

So, they waved as she passed and held their thoughts to themselves. The religious ones whispered a prayer for her that this Bill Myers person, whoever he was, could make her happy, and if he didn't, well he would have to answer to them.

Tires crunched the gravel behind her. She stepped to the side as Sandy drove up in his pickup.

"Hey, Mom. What's up?"

"Just headed back to the house before the lunch crowd comes in."

"I see." He smiled. "No Bill Myers around to keep you preoccupied, huh?"

"What makes you think I'm preoccupied?"

"Oh, I don't know." Sandy grinned and flipped the hair off his forehead with a finger. "Maybe the way you sit there at the counter all moony-eyed, waiting for him to show up every day."

"Is that what you think? That I'm moony-eyed?"

"Sure looks that way."

"Well, for the record. I sit there because after all these years ... my whole life ... in Creosote, there is finally someone I can have a conversation with about something other than cows, fishing, hunting, or how the dust worked its way into the crack of their ass."

"Okay." Sandy nodded, laughing. "We'll go with that. You're just happy to have someone around with conversational skills equal to your own."

"Sums it up, pretty well," she said, laughing with him. "And where are you off to? Somebody need some work on their car?"

"Going to McAllen to pick up some parts, then a stop." He leaned out the window and lowered his voice so that the neighbors on the stoops wouldn't hear what he had to say. " Going to visit someone ... a girl."

Isabella's jaw dropped open, and then she smiled. Her son was at the age when he should have a girlfriend, even several girlfriends. He was smart, made people laugh, easy-mannered, and she didn't mind saying so herself, he was a good-looking young man.

"I'm so happy," she whispered, leaning toward him so that his secret would be between them. "Anyone I know?"

"No. Not likely anyway. I met her at Krieg's place when I took the ATVs back."

The smile faded from her face. "Krieg's place?"

"Yes." He grinned, remembering the exact moment he laid eyes on Jacinta. "She was on the guesthouse porch with Claire Toussaint." His smile widened as hers faded, and for once, his powers of perception failed him in the excitement of telling her about the girl he had met. "She is beautiful, Mom. Long brown hair, almost black really. Brown eyes that make me think I could get lost in them." He shook his head as if searching for the words to describe Jacinta. "And her laugh is like music ... the most beautiful music I've ever heard."

It had seemed like such an empty prayer, all the times she had prayed that her son would find someone—a girl, a woman, to go away with and become a man, have a family, do the things that other young men do. And now, when the answer to the prayer finally arrived, dread filled her chest. If this was how God answered prayers, it was clear he had a mean streak in him.

"That's wonderful, son." It took all of her effort to keep the smile on her face.

Shit! How could she tell him that the girl of his dreams belonged to Tom Krieg and would become one of his whores, no doubt, already was one of them.

"Relax," Sandy said, seeing the concern in her eyes. "I know I have to be careful around Krieg. I won't do anything rash. I'm just going to call on her, maybe see if she wants to go to a movie down in Brownsville or have something to eat." He smiled. "I'd like you to meet her."

"That would be nice," Isabella whispered, her heart breaking over the pain she saw in her son's future. "Do you know who she is? Where she came from?"

"Probably a relative of Claire's. That's why I have to get a move on. Who knows how long she'll be staying here before heading back to school or wherever she came from." He looked into his mother's eyes. "I can't let the chance to meet her slip away without trying."

"Okay." Isabella nodded, torn between spoiling his excitement over his first love and telling him the truth about the girl's status in Tom Krieg's world. In the end, she did not have the heart to ruin the moment for him. "I'll look forward to meeting her."

"Good." Sandy put the truck in gear. "Now I'm going to go see ... oh, I never told you her name, did I?" He grinned. "It's Jacinta ... beautiful, isn't it?"

He rolled away, careful not to kick up dust on Isabella. At the end of the road, he gunned the engine, honked the horn, and sped away, the dust churning up across the prairie.

"Looks like Sandy is excited about something," Charlie Faust called from his stoop, hoping to get the inside information from Isabella.

"I guess it does." Isabella forced herself to smile and continued walking to her house at the edge of town.

Her mind whirled. There were so many secrets, so much that he didn't understand, so much she couldn't tell him. She had resigned herself to the fact that some secrets were hers to carry for life.

FORTY-THREE

Rats

"Get in."

The rust spotted Chevy El Camino could have been a classic north of the border, restored and tricked out for display, making the rounds of car shows around the country. Here it was just another nondescript, dusty work vehicle that did not draw attention.

Pepe Lopez leaned across the seat toward the open passenger window and repeated his command, smiling this time.

"Get in. I'm putting together a load. I need your help."

Father Alfonso hesitated. They were on a side street a block off the Boulevard Francisco Madero, a busy part of Torreón. It would not do for a parishioner to see him get into a car with a known *coyotaje* like Pepe Lopez.

"Get in," Lopez encouraged with a smile. "I can see the street. No one is watching."

"Yes ... but it's just that ..." Alfonso's head turned, his eyes searching the street for someone who might come along.

His encounter with Benito Diaz made him more than a little suspicious of Lopez's motives. Their usual manner of communication was through the confessional. Lopez would pay a young man to go to confession. A message would be whispered to him through the grill, giving him a time and place to meet, a private place, away from prying eyes. Always, Lopez stayed out of sight and was careful not to have them spotted together

Did Lopez know of his involvement with Diaz and the hijacked shipment? Was that the reason for stopping him on the street like this? No, he thought. He could not know. He had only been away from his parish for a few hours, and Lopez was nowhere around then, probably out cleaning up the mess at the scene of the hijacking.

He gathered up his courage. Lopez was here for some other reason, probably to tell him of the hijacking and to warn him to be careful in arranging the next shipment. He looked down at him through the open car window.

"Whatever the reason, Pepe, it is not good to break protocol like this. It is dangerous. Send your boy to confession and give me a place and time. I will meet you there."

"You speak very reasonably for a man who is sweating so much." Lopez smiled. "Get in." He lifted a nine-millimeter pistol from the seat and pointed it at Alfonso. "Now."

Hands trembling, Father Alfonso pulled open the El Camino's door and sat in the passenger seat. He stared straight ahead, afraid to look at Lopez and the pistol pointed at his face.

"Put these on." Lopez held out a pair of handcuffs. The good *Sargento* Garcia had provided him with several sets over the years of their association, for use in special situations.

"But ... why?" Alfonso paled as Lopez dangled the cuffs

in front of his face. "Pepe, what is wrong that I should put these on?"

"Maybe nothing." Lopez shrugged. "Maybe something. Until I find out, put these on, one around your wrist and one through the armrest on the door." He lifted the pistol and pointed it at Alfonso's face. "I won't say it again."

The priest complied, and Lopez wound his way through the city streets until they were out in the country. For over an hour, he drove into the hills, passing through several small villages. As they exited the last one, Lopez pulled onto a dirt road that was barely more than two tire tracks and drove another hour. When he stopped, they were as far from civilization as was possible in this region of Mexico.

Alfonso said nothing, though the sound of his weeping rose in volume the farther they drove. It was the incessant sobbing that convinced Lopez that Alfonso was the traitor, as he had suspected. He might have complained about being taken away in such a manner, shouted for help, or cursed Lopez for daring to molest a priest. Instead, he wept like a woman from the moment the handcuffs ratcheted closed on his wrist.

Lopez braked at the crest of a hill and got out. The pistol was tucked in his belt. Alfonso watched through the spotted windshield as he lit a cigarette, leaning against the fender smoking calmly as if they were on a picnic outing.

When he was finished, he flicked the butt into the brush and came to the passenger door. Lopez yanked the door open, and Father Alfonso tumbled out onto the ground, his arm still cuffed to the armrest.

"Here." Lopez tossed the handcuff key into the dirt beside Alfonso. "Release yourself."

"No ... please don't ... no." Alfonso was blubbering

now, tears streaking his dusty face. He begged, "Please don't kill me. I am a priest."

"Hah," Lopez sneered in disgust. "I don't give a shit who you are. Priest or saint, it makes no difference to me. We are going to speak together. After that, we will see. Now, take the handcuffs off and stand up like a man for once."

It took several tries for Alfonso's trembling fingers to guide the key into the lock on the cuffs. Finally, he stood up and faced Lopez, his sobbing reduced now to an occasional tearful gasp.

"I know you were the one," Lopez began.

"No." Alfonso shook his head rapidly, on the brink of breaking into tears again.

"No? Then why haven't you asked me what I mean?" Lopez smiled. "There is only one reasonable explanation for this. You already understand because you are the traitor who gave someone the information about the last shipment."

"No ... please, Pepe. I would never betray you."

"Really?" Lopez snorted a disgusted laugh. "Like you would never betray the young women who came to you for help, only to send them to the *gringos* to be sold. Don't make me laugh, Priest."

Alfonso lowered his head, his shoulders shaking again with his sobs. "Please don't kill me." He whispered, barely able to make the words leave his throat.

"Whether I kill you or not, is up to you."

Alfonso lifted his head, the slightest glimmer of hope in his eyes. "What is it I must do?"

"You will tell me who you are working with. Leave nothing out."

Alfonso spoke for half an hour, recounting his encounter with Benito Diaz in the church, the plans for the hijacking, the gathering at the shack in the desert, the old man who gave up his life for the others.

"So, you see, Pepe. They came to me ... threatened me ... I did not seek to betray you." He held his hands out, palms up to demonstrate that he had merely surrendered to the inevitable. "I had no choice."

"Yes. I see." Lopez lit another cigarette and considered Alfonso's story. A thought came to him. "You say this man Diaz forced another to pull the trigger and kill the old man."

"Yes, another." Alfonso nodded. "After, Diaz said we were one with them. It was a terrible thing to see."

"And this other, what was his name?"

"I never heard his last name, but Diaz called him Mario."

"Mario." Lopez's eyes narrowed. He knew of only one Mario who worked with Krieg and Zabala. "You may yet live a little longer, Priest. Get in the car."

They retraced the route back to Torreón. On reaching the outskirts of the city, Lopez slowed and told Alfonso to get out.

"If you speak to anyone about our meeting, you will die, and it will be slow. I will cut your heart out while you live for you to see."

"I swear to you, Pepe. No one will know."

Lopez drove away. Alfonso walked the streets toward his parish.

People passing wondered at the priest who walked and sobbed. "He must weep for our sins," someone said. Others nodded and remarked that Father Alfonso truly was a man of God.

As he drove, Pepe wondered how Krieg and Zabala would take the news that there were two traitors in their organization. In the back of his mind, he also wondered what he would have done if Diaz had taken him first instead of Mario Acosta and Father Alfonso.

For all his threats to cut out the priest's heart, he knew the answer. He was no better than they, no more loyal to Krieg and Zabala.

The money he made from their business was excellent, but he was most loyal to breathing and remaining alive. If the others were rats, he was one too, he admitted, and like all rats, he would do whatever was necessary to survive.

FORTY-FOUR

Close
───────

"Relax." Stu Pearce leaned against the shady side of the truck, using his pocketknife to quarter a tomato he had taken from one of the crates the farmhands were loading in the back.

Sole paced the ground around the farm shed where Stu had parked the truck for loading. Shotgun under his arm, he eyed the surrounding fields and hills.

"Thought I was supposed to be the security man on this run."

"You are, but nothin' is gonna happen here." Pearce shrugged. "Or anywhere else, for that matter. This run is a piece of cake. I'm tellin' you, there's nothin' to worry about."

"No?" Sole turned from watching the road leading to the farm. "Why?"

"It just ain't. That's not the way they operate … those that might want what we're hauling."

"They hit a load of avocados, right? So avocados get

hijacked but not tomatoes. Didn't realize hijackers were so particular."

"Hmm," Stu said without commenting further and popped a juicy section of tomato into his mouth like candy. "Nothing like fresh 'maters," he said, changing the subject. "Reminds me of the ones my mama grew in the garden when I was a tyke."

"Don't you worry about getting some bug in your gut down here eating unwashed produce?" Sole asked as Stu chewed and smiled.

"Used to," Stu said, using the back of his hand to wipe a trickle of juice from the side of his mouth. "The Montezuma revenge got me a few times when I first started comin' down here. Not anymore." He shrugged and focused on cutting another section of tomato.

"Didn't know you could be immune to the shits."

"Look around, and you'll see them Mexes drinkin' the water and eatin' the food off the vine just like this. Don't seem to bother them. Reckon they worked up an immunity early on. Me too, I guess." He laughed. "But I hear the young'uns make some nasty diapers for their *mamacita's* before they get to the immune stage."

"Well, if you say there's nothing to worry about, I guess I'll just wander a bit and scope things out."

"Suit yourself." Stu cut another section of tomato, disinclined to leave the shade of the truck.

They were backed up to a rickety shed where a half dozen, brown-skinned farmworkers loaded crates of tomatoes onto the truck. The workers ignored the *gringo* with the shotgun, apparently accustomed to the Krieg and Zabala security methods.

On the side of the shed, Sole found a dozen more workers, sitting in a patch of shade. A familiar aroma filled the air, and he moved closer.

"*¡Hola!*." He called out as he approached.

"*Hola, señor.*" One of the group responded, older than the others.

Sole wasn't sure exactly how to strike up a conversation. He'd been trying to pick up as much Spanish as he could for the last year, knowing he would need it. But the most words he'd strung together were to tell the family at the river to go away and get medical attention. This would be his first attempt to have a real conversation.

"How goes it?" he said, halting at first, but a little more confident that they seemed to understand him.

"It goes well," the man responded. "And you? Everything in order?" He nodded at the shotgun, still tucked under Sole's arm.

"Oh, this ..." Sole put the butt of the gun on the ground and leaned the barrel against the shed, near enough to reach if he needed it. He smiled. "Yes, everything is in order. *Mi compañero* says I worry too much."

The workers laughed.

"Yes," the senior man said. "There is nothing to be concerned about here. No *banditos*."

At that, the others laughed again, louder this time. "*Sí, no banditos,*" they echoed.

"I see you're taking a break. It must be hard work here on a farm."

"Yes. The men work very hard, and now they get a break and a little food. I am Rafael, and these are the workers I supervise for the owner of the farm."

Sole eyed the man's hand.

Rafael held out his arm. "You want some?"

"Sure."

Sole took the joint from Rafael's hand, inhaled and then coughed. The men laughed but nodded their approval.

Most were seated in the shade, smoking marijuana. The few who weren't munched tortillas or leaned back against the shed to doze before going back to work.

"Good," Sole nodded, handing the joint back to Rafael.

"Yes," Rafael agreed. "Excellent marijuana is grown here." He leaned forward and winked. "When I was younger, I worked on a farm that grows it." Rafael laughed and slapped his knee. "We were always high."

"It is not against the law in Mexico?" Sole asked.

"It was. Now, not so much. The Supreme Court is making changes here." Rafael shrugged, and the smile spread across his face again. "It wouldn't matter either way. We smoke it. What are the *policía* going to do? They smoke it too."

Heads nodded, and more laughter rippled through the group.

"If I wanted something more than this? Can you tell me who I would talk to about it?"

"More than this?" Rafael held the joint in front of his eyes and then smiled. "You mean *cocaína*."

"Yes, cocaine. Is it for sale around here?"

"For cocaine, you would have to go to a city. You could get some in Monterrey, but it is hazardous for a *norteamericano*. Probably, the dealer would rob you, and you would not get the cocaine. They might even kill you."

Rafael thought about it for a moment and added, "But you are from north of the border, yes?"

"Yes."

"Then why don't you just get *cocaína* from a dealer there in one of the cities. It would be safer, and they get their cocaine from the same place … from the cartels."

It was the word he had refrained from using, not wanting to arouse suspicion about his motives, but Rafael had used it. "Are the cartels here?"

"They are everywhere, but it is very dangerous for you to try and speak with them directly. It is better to go to someone ... a dealer you can trust, right?" Rafael nodded. "Go to one that you trust and ask for cocaine up north on the other side of the border. That would be the safest thing for you to do."

The others had followed the conversation with interest. Now they nodded their heads in agreement. "Yes, that would be much safer," several said.

"Can you tell me which cartel supplies the cocaine?" Sole persisted.

"Ah, there are several, but the biggest is *Los Salvajes*." Rafael looked into his eyes. "Their name, The Savages, should tell you how dangerous they are, *señor*. You should not try to make contact with them."

"What if I wanted to meet them for business reasons?"

"Business reasons?" Rafael started to laugh, and then the smile vanished from his face. "You mean to sell cocaine for them?"

"Maybe." Sole shrugged. "If I can make a deal with them."

"This I know nothing about." Rafael stood abruptly. "It is time for us to get back to work."

The others followed. Sole heard murmured comments as they trailed off into the fields.

"Crazy *gringo*."

"Gonna get himself killed."

"Better him than us. Stay away from this one if he comes back alive."

"If *Los Salvajes* find out, he was asking questions there will be trouble."

"As long as the trouble is for the *gringo* and not us."

"If *Los Salvajes* is around, they bring trouble for everyone."

He turned to walk back to the truck.

"Hey, *señor!*" A farmhand trotted away from the group headed to the field and hurried after Sole.

"*¿Que pasa?*" What's up? Sole turned to face him.

"Maybe I help you." The man, he was not much more than a boy, still bearing the scars of pimples across his forehead.

"How's that?"

"You ask about *Los Salvajes*, yes? To maybe sell cocaine for them."

"Yes." Sole nodded. "If I can make contact with them. What's your name?"

"Juan Galdo."

"How can you help me, Juan?"

"My cousin …" He paused, scanning in all directions to make sure no one was within listening distance. "He is with *Los Salvajes*. I can tell him of your wish to sell *cocaína* for the cartel. If you pay me."

"I'll pay you." Sole stared into the man's eyes. "How much?"

The look on the field hand's face showed that the question took him by surprise. He thought for a second "A hundred …" when there was no reaction from Sole, he said, "No, I mean five hundred U.S. dollars. I think it is worth that much."

"You have a deal." Sole nodded at the fields where the others were already bent over picking tomatoes by hand. "If your cousin is with the cartel, why are you here?"

"Oh, Rafael is correct. It is hazardous to work with them, *señor*." He nodded at the fields. "Here, the work is very hard, but I go home and sleep, and no one comes with a gun to wake me from my sleep in the night to shoot holes in me."

"But you figure telling your cousin about me is safe enough … for five hundred dollars."

Juan smiled. "*Sí*, for five hundred, it is only a little dangerous."

"Alright." Sole nodded, admiring Juan Galdo's notions about risk and reward. "You tell your cousin I would like to meet him and see about selling cocaine for *Los Salvajes*."

"I will do that. Do you have a phone? I can give the number to my cousin, and he will call you."

"No phones." Sole shook his head. "You contact your cousin and set things up. I will contact you for directions. Where can I reach you, in person?"

"There is a small village near the farm, Correlia. You passed through it coming here. My house is on the south edge of the town." Juan thought for a second, trying to determine how to make his house stand out from all of the other shacks in the village. After a few seconds, he smiled and said, "When you come, there will be a blue blanket on a rope in the yard. My mother hangs clothes to dry there. I will make sure she leaves the blanket there until you come."

"Fair enough." Sole nodded.

"And the five hundred dollars, *señor*?"

"When you take me to see your cousin, you will have the money."

"That is very good." Juan grinned.

"When?" Sole asked.

"It may take a little time. My cousin is very busy with his work for the cartel, and I cannot always leave to go to

Monterrey. I will contact him. The trucks come often for tomatoes. You come again with them, and I will say when we can meet my cousin."

"Good." Sole nodded. "I'll be back."

Juan grinned, then wiped the smile off his face and trotted out to the field to join the others. Sole turned toward the truck.

Just like that, it happened. The cartels are everywhere, Rafael had said. What had seemed so remote, suddenly, became real, imminent, a thing he could plan for and see through to the end.

The air seemed to crackle electrically around him. His senses twitched. He was close, closer than he had ever been.

FORTY-FIVE

It Doesn't Matter

The lights were off at the café by the time Sole drove down the street in Creosote. He let the pickup idle slowly through town without headlights, not wanting to attract attention.

For a moment, he thought of driving through to the other end of town. She might still be up. He shook the idea away. So what if she was up?

Isabella had made it clear that she welcomed his company, but there hadn't been anything more than that between them. Denying that he was attracted to her was impossible. She reminded him so much of Shaye. Maybe that was the problem.

Independent, self-confident, poised, a mixture of outward toughness that concealed something softer under the surface, he found his thoughts dwelling on her more and more. She could laugh at him and not make him feel small. Instead, it seemed she was letting him in on a joke without turning him into the joke.

Stop! There had been no invitations extended to come knocking on her door at two in the morning.

He pulled up in front of his shack, opened the pickup's door as quietly as possible, and stepped up on the stoop.

"How'd the first day on the job go?"

He hadn't seen her. Peering into the shadows by the café, he could make out one of her long legs propped up on the post that held up the awning over the entrance.

"Went okay." He walked toward her and looked up and down the street. "You out here alone?"

"Alone as can be." She laughed. "And you seem surprised."

"I guess I am. Thought everyone, including the unofficial town mayor, would be tucked in by now."

"Hah. I'm not the mayor, unofficial or otherwise. I'm just one of the survivors like everyone else stuck here."

"I was trying not to wake anyone."

"Yep. I saw how you crept down the street. Not much reason to though. The drunks are passed out, and the ones that aren't drunk don't sleep … like me."

"You don't sleep?"

He stepped into the shadows where she sat on an old aluminum lawn chair and looked down, seeing her clearly now. She wore shorts and a halter top, her usual attire, but she made it seem like more, not a woman putting her body on display. She was comfortable in her own skin, and that gave her a simple elegance regardless of her dress. His eyes moved over her body, and his breath caught in his chest.

"No, I don't sleep, not much anyway," she said.

"Why?" He wondered if she knew he stared at her in the dark, committing the image of her to memory.

"Now that's a damned good question, Bill Myers. Got a day or two? We could talk it over. You'd be my analyst."

"Don't think I'd be much good at that."

"Well, we could just talk and keep on talking for as long

as you want." She smiled, her teeth catching the moonlight. "Or whatever you want to do."

There it was. The invitation was in the open, clearly stated, and clearly understood. Isabella was not flirting with him or propositioning him. It was a simple statement, one adult, to another, one lonely person to another, offering comfort and companionship.

"No, I can't …" he started. The voice from his memories whispered in his ear.

Yes, John. You can. I want you to.

"Alright." His voice was barely audible, the word caught in his throat like a man opening a valve, slowly to prevent a flood from pouring out.

"Good." Isabella rose from the chair and reached for his hand.

They walked through the town without speaking. Her hand was warm and firm in his, and when she twined her fingers between his, stirrings rose inside that he thought were dead.

She led the way to her house. This time, they did not sit in the wicker chairs on the porch. She opened the door, stepped in, and turned, smiling, waiting for him to follow. He hesitated, and then stepped through the door.

Isabella held out her hand to guide him to the bedroom. She stood there before him, looking into his eyes, giving him time to become comfortable.

They were close. He could feel her breath on his face. Her scent engulfed him as if she had her arms around him. Then she did.

She stepped forward, rose on her toes, and put her arms around his neck, letting her lips brush his lightly. His arms wrapped around her waist. The kiss deepened, filled with fervor driven by their mutual need to end the loneliness.

They stood like that in her bedroom, embracing, not wanting to separate. Time passed—minutes, hours, John Sole didn't know, didn't care.

She stepped away and loosened the halter top and let it fall. His eyes were locked on her, unable to look away.

Her shorts dropped to the floor. She stepped out of them, and reached up to loosen his clothing, button by button. When they stood naked before each other, she came close again to embrace and continue the kiss.

Pressed together, their passion rose, their breath coming fast in gasps of pleasure and desire. He lifted her from the floor and carried her to the bed.

They made love, desperate for each other at first, then slowing to savor each caress. Every touch was electric. They tried to prolong the moments, not wanting to lose any of it by hurrying. When they came, each heart beating against the other, they remained locked in the embrace that had begun their lovemaking.

As the glow settled over them, she rested her head on his chest, his arms still wrapped around her.

"I won't try to be her," Isabella said.

He started to speak, and she put a finger on his lips to silence him. "I only want you to know. I am not trying to be the one you lost. That wouldn't be fair to either of us. I'm Isabella, and I am happy being me. I have just one question."

"Yes?"

"How long will you be here?"

It was plain what she wanted—a companion, someone to share life, to make a life together. They were the things he wanted, but Isabella had more courage than he and wasn't afraid to say them out loud.

How could he tell her his reasons for being there? How

could he make a promise or guess how long or where he would be in a month, a week or even tomorrow? He might not even be alive in another week.

He answered honestly. "I don't know, Isabella."

She nodded, and her hair moved against his skin, soft and sensual. A tear rolled across her cheek and onto his chest, warm at first, and then cool. She brushed it away, annoyed with herself.

They had the moment. That was all she had ever had, the present. Why would she demand more of him? How could she? The tears dried.

She nestled closer, put a leg over his hip, her lips brushing against his chest. She whispered her own honest reply. "It doesn't matter."

FORTY-SIX

Interlude
___

They settled into a comfortable routine. Sole sat with Isabella and helped in the café most days when he wasn't on a run for K and Z.

Evenings they would sit on her porch watch the sunset, or walk down the road hand in hand and chat with the locals out on their front stoops, or take a ride out into the brush country and watch the night come on until the sky blazed with stars. For a while, the world seemed to pass them by and they found peace.

Neither questioned the other about their past. Now and again a little snippet of their history would slip out in conversation. They would look it over as if they just stumbled on an interesting rock, or bird, or insect on one of their walks. Then they would move on and leave it behind.

The past wasn't important. What was important was the peace they both felt being together, and for the moment, neither wanted to upset the delicate balance that might send it away.

Two or three times a week, Sole would leave early in the morning to make a run into Mexico to pick up vegetables for K and Z. He told them he wanted to make the runs to pick up tomatoes at the farm south of Monterrey, and there didn't seem to be any reason not to give him the assignment with Stu Pearce on a regular basis. They made a good team, and Krieg and Zabala had Pearce keeping an eye on him.

Sole knew that one day the farmhand, Juan Galdo, would have information for him about meeting his cousin, the cartel drug dealer. He went dutifully to see him on every visit to the farm, but the longer he was with Isabella, the less he wanted to receive the information.

What he wanted was to spend every moment he could with Isabella and for nothing to change. At first, he felt guilty and reminded himself that he had a mission, but as the days passed, holding her at night, listening to her voice, hearing her laugh, he felt less guilty, and the mission faded to the background. What mattered was the present with Isabella.

While he was gone on the runs for Krieg and Zabala, Isabella discovered a new emotion. She was lonely.

Living in Creosote, she had always lived on her own but had never felt lonely. There had been no one to be lonely for.

Now there was, and she waited up late until Sole returned from the Mexico trips. She would greet him with supper and a beer, and they would sit together and talk about where he had gone that day, or the gossip making the rounds in the café, or nothing at all. When they were together, the loneliness went away.

She decided it was good not to be lonely, and one day

she told Sole. He agreed and kissed her, but that night as she slept by his side, a chill went through him. He had something to lose again.

Sandy's days seemed interminably long when he could not visit Jacinta. Ranchers and cowhands regularly stopped by his shed at the café to drop off various pieces of ranch machinery and vehicles for repair. At any other time, he would be grateful for the work. Every dollar he earned was going into a bank account in Laredo. One day, he would use the money to make his way out of Creosote and take his mother with him if he could pry her away from the café.

And he would take Jacinta. He would convince her to come with him. He wondered if she was a traditional Mexican girl. Would he have to ask for permission in the old world way? Who would he ask? Tom Krieg?

There were still many questions surrounding their relationship. He had managed a couple of times to steal away for a quick visit to the Krieg ranch. Always, she seemed delighted to see him, but they couldn't really talk much with Claire Toussaint constantly hovering in the background.

Once he asked if he could come by in the evening so they could take a ride. Claire had been about to say something, but Jacinta motioned her away and then turned to Sandy and declined firmly, saying that she was busy most evenings. She was grateful for the invitation, but it would not be possible.

His obvious disappointment tugged at her heart, and she added quickly, "But you can come to visit in the day sometimes, like this. I want you to come by whenever you are able."

Sandy's face brightened a little at that. He was about to ask if it was because there was another she was seeing, but he thought better of it.

Soon, he thought, he would come for a real visit. Spend a day with her. Then they would get to know each other, and she would be able to trust him.

Teamed with Stu Pearce, Sole made the rounds of the farms in north-central Mexico and became familiar with the locals. In particular, they always made the run to the farm south of Monterrey where Sole always found a moment to chat with Juan Galdo.

It was a training and assessment period to determine if he could be trusted to handle K and Z's most precious and profitable cargo. Unknown to him, Pearce was required to sit with Krieg and Zabala in their office every time they returned and report on his conduct. They fired questions at him.

"When will he be ready?"

"Soon, I think."

"How soon?"

"Hard to say. He don't talk much," Pearce would reply.

"So why do you say he will be ready soon?"

"Because he don't talk much." Pearce had shrugged. "He don't blabber on about things, and he seems to be pretty solid. Makes himself at home among the farmers. They respect him, and if it matters," Pearce summarized. "I'd trust him in a fight."

Krieg and Zabala exchanged a nod and dismissed Pearce. The question was, could they trust him in their fight. Eventually, Zabala suggested they keep him on the farm runs and save him for the big operation that was coming.

Krieg agreed, and they spent their days planning their counterattack on Diaz. A great deal of time was consumed putting together the trap that would end his threat permanently. Bill Myers would get his baptism by fire when they sprung the trap. If he didn't work out, he'd be just one more body in the road.

The weeks passed quietly. The interlude was an end to loneliness and a time of peace for Sole and Isabella; a time of anxious love and stolen moments for Sandy and Jacinta; a time of preparation for Tom Krieg and Raul Zabala.

Then the interlude came to an end, and the world changed for everybody.

FORTY-SEVEN

Still Breathing

"The reason for your visit to the United States?"

The Border Patrol agent spoke perfect Mexican Spanish, an indication of his heritage and not education.

"Just here to visit my sister and her family in McAllen."

"Address?"

Pepe Lopez gave his sister's street address in McAllen and handed his Border Crossing Card issued by the State Department along with his Mexican driver's license out the window. The card served as a temporary visa and allowed Mexican nationals to enter the United States legally.

The agent gave it a perfunctory glance. Of greater interest was the database readout on his computer screen that let him know that the vehicle made frequent trips back and forth across the border, never overstayed the legally authorized time, and Pepe Lopez had never been involved in any known criminal activity. He handed the card back.

"Can't stay any longer than seventy-two hours and no farther than twenty-five miles from the border."

"I know." Pepe smiled.

He had no intention of staying any longer than he had to, although his visit would take him more than thirty miles from the *Puente Internacional Anzalduas*—Anzalduas International Bridge. But then, he knew from experience that the border agents would have no way of knowing this.

After a brief visual inspection of the old El Camino, he was waved through. The crossing was routine for people living and working on both sides of the border. As long as they followed the rules, Mexicans with business or family in the States made the crossing without problems, in the same way, Americans going in the other direction visited Mexico.

It was the illegals who created the concerns for the *norteamericanos*. Pepe smiled. They were also the ones making him a wealthy man.

The drive to the K and Z warehouse took a little over half an hour. On arrival, he parked outside the office building and entered. Ella, the receptionist, looked up and smiled.

"Pepe, haven't seen you here in a while. It's not time for the count, is it?"

"No, no." He shook his head and leaned on the counter that served has her small desk. "I have some business with Tom and Raul. I called and told them I was coming."

"Well, it's good to see you." She picked up the phone and punched the intercom for their office. "Pepe Lopez here to see you. Right." She nodded and hung up.

"They said to come on back. You know where it is, down the hall."

"Thanks, Ella."

Pepe walked down the short hall to the office, wishing it was longer. He was not at all sure how this meeting would play out, and a knot was forming in his stomach with every step. When he stood in the door, Krieg looked up and waved him in without speaking.

"Sit down, Pepe," Raul Zabala said.

"What do you have?" Krieg was not in the mood for Zabala's usual pleasantries.

"I found the traitor."

"Who is it?"

"Alfonso."

"The fucking priest!" Krieg roared.

"Are you sure of this?" Zabala asked calmly. "This is a serious matter, and to accuse a priest, we must be certain."

Pepe fought to keep a look of incredulity from creeping across his face. Was Zabala serious about his surprise that it was the priest? Did he really think this supposed man of God who was willing to sell young girls into a life of slavery was above becoming a traitor to preserve his own life simply because he wore a cleric's collar?

He kept his thoughts to himself and replied simply, "I am certain."

"Start talking," Krieg snapped.

Pepe recounted his meeting with Alfonso and the confession he forced from him then added, "There is another."

"Who?" Krieg and Zabala spoke in unison.

"The new one ... Acosta."

"Son of a bitch!" Krieg's fist slammed down on his desk. "I want him dead! I want them both dead!"

"Patience," Zabala said mildly. "We want our enemies dead, right?"

"Goddamned right!"

"Then we must use the traitors to our advantage." Zabala leaned back in his chair, hands behind his head in his usual relaxed position. "I have an idea."

Another hour passed as they discussed Zabala's plan. As they went through the details, Krieg calmed himself and focused his mind on the revenge he would take on Benito Diaz.

"You understand what to do?" Zabala asked Pepe when the discussion ended.

"I understand, but you should understand that it may take some time until they fall into the trap."

"As long as they fall in." Zabala smiled. He stood to indicate the meeting was at an end. "What are your plans for the evening, Pepe?"

"A quick visit to my sister in McAllen, in case the Border Patrol sends someone to check. Then drive home in the morning."

"Give my best to your sister." Zabala sat, and Pepe took the cue to leave the office.

"Leaving so soon?" Ella said as he passed by the reception desk.

"Yes. Only time for a quick visit."

"Well, get home safe, Pepe. See you next time."

"Next time."

Pepe smiled and walked out to his car. It had been a successful meeting. He was still breathing.

FORTY-EIGHT

More Disagreeable Dead than Alive

"Looks like the carp have been having a feast." Sheriff Paul Dermott squatted on the bank of the Rio Grande peering into the shallow water and reeds along the shore.

"How long do you think?" Emmett Brewer stood behind him, staring down at the body of Lucky Martin.

"Not long," Dermott said. "Judging by the decomposition just a couple of days. Most of the damage is from the fish feeding on soft tissues."

"Yeah, that and the bullet holes in his head."

"Yeah, there's that." Dermott gave a wry smile and looked at Deputy Brainerd, standing a few feet away. "Better fish him out, Claude."

"Okay, Sheriff." Brainerd signaled to two junior deputies who grimaced and moved toward the water.

They wore waders and latex gloves, and their faces showed that they were none too pleased to have the assignment to go in after the body. Even in death, Lucky Martin had a way of pissing people off.

With Brainerd standing nearby, ready to do the sheriff's

bidding without actually doing any work, Dermott and Brewer scanned up and down the riverbank for signs of human life on either side. There weren't any, only the usual waterfowls and nesting birds feeding and foraging along the water. If they were aware of the dead man, it was because the decaying body had provided an abundance of tasty morsels in the way of suckerfish, larva, and insects.

"You thinking what I'm thinking?" Brewer asked.

"Probably, but you go first."

Dermott climbed higher up on the bank to get away from the body and the cocktail of gasses filling the air as the deputies turned and tugged at the corpse. The mix of hydrogen sulfide, carbon dioxide, methane, ammonia, sulfur dioxide, and hydrogen created a stench no human ever got accustomed to, although to the scavengers feeding on it, the aroma was like steaks on the grill. Every carrion-eater in scenting distance would be on their way to grab their share of the buffet.

"Alright, I'll go first." Brewer nodded. "This is about the same spot where the shots were fired across the river at the Mexican family."

"It is," Dermott agreed.

"Any idea if Lucky Martin owned a Winchester?"

"He did." Dermott nodded. "Used to compete in the Sheriff's Annual Turkey Shoot with it. Never won but always made a big deal about the sights being off or some other bullshit excuse. But …." Dermott paused to emphasize that he was not going to just buy into Brewer's theory. "Most everyone around here has one, or a similar firearm, and a lot of them are .30-30 caliber. It's a handy multipurpose round."

"True enough, but most everyone isn't floating face down in the Rio Grande with a bullet in his head."

"Actually, it's three bullets." The deputies had dragged the body onto the bank. Dermott pointed at the back of Lucky's skull. "Three holes ... three bullets."

"I stand corrected," Brewer said. "Three bullets in the back of the head which can only mean one thing."

"Yep," Dermott agreed. "Someone wanted Lucky dead."

"Yep. So we're on the same page on."

"Depends on what page you're on, Emmett. Did someone want Martin dead? Sure as hell looks that way. That's where the page stops for me ... at least, for now."

"Fair enough. Mind if I add my two cents worth?"

Brewer understood that Dermott, despite any political connections that went along with his job, was also a good law enforcement officer. He wouldn't be hurried into drawing a conclusion until he had some evidence to go on and would not allow any relationships he had with the locals to influence the way he did his job, once he got to doing it.

"Don't mind at all," Dermott said. "Fire away. Just don't expect me to buy into any theories just yet."

"Way I see it, there's only two reasons someone would want Martin executed like this."

"Go on." Dermott listened while his deputies began the process of photographing and collecting what evidence they could find on the corpse.

"It might be a revenge killing. Someone getting even for the Mexican who was shot."

"Maybe," Dermott nodded his agreement and pointed at one of the deputies standing beside the body. "Check his pants pockets."

The deputy's grimace was discernible through the surgical mask coated with Vicks VapoRub he wore to kill the stench.

"The second possibility," Brewer continued, "is that someone put Lucky up to the shooting and now wants to make sure he can't talk about it."

"Uh-huh, that's definitely a possibility," Dermott said and turned from the body to face Brewer. "But there are a couple of other possibilities, Emmett."

"Alright, my turn to listen." Brewer crossed his arms and waited, his posture sending the message that he would not be easily convinced that he was wrong.

"There's always the possibility," Dermott began, "that on the day in question, ole Lucky was the unluckiest son of a bitch in Salvia County and came down to the river to fish, or scout out a hunting spot and happened on someone who was up to no good. Might have been border crossers or drug smugglers or poachers, who knows, but it might have absolutely nothing to do with the Mexican who was shot."

"That would be highly coincidental, and as you said, it would make Martin the unluckiest son of a bitch around. What's the other possibility?"

"Whether he was unlucky or not, we know for a fact that Lucky Martin was definitely the meanest son of a bitch around. He had enemies … a lot of them. Could be that one of his enemies lured him down to the river, or tracked him down here, and ended his pathetic life for personal reasons … again, unrelated to shooting at the Mexicans."

"Hmph." Brewer was unconvinced, and his arms remained crossed over his chest.

"Take it easy, Emmett." Dermott smiled. "I'm not saying you're wrong, only that we have a lot of investigating to do before we get to a conclusion."

"Fair enough." Dermott was right, of course, and Brewer knew it. "Mind if I stay in the loop on the investigation."

"Wouldn't have it any other way," Dermott said, his nose wrinkling as the deputies rolled the body over on his back and decomposition gasses hissed from his open mouth, adding to the foulness of the air. "Damn! Who would have thought Lucky Martin could be more disagreeable dead than alive?"

FORTY-NINE

She Wept for the Girl

The truck raced along the gravel drive and slid to a stop in front of the main house. A cloud of dust swirled, hiding it from view. Tom Krieg came into view, striding across the lawn, eyes blazing, emerging from the dusty haze like Satan from the smokes of hell.

Claire turned from the window, concern in her eyes. "He is coming."

Jacinta's face flushed red. The look in Krieg's eyes meant that he would want one of them tonight, and lately Jacinta had been the focus of his attention.

"No matter what he says or does, you must remember this," Claire said, taking hold of Jacinta's arms and turning her until she looked into her eyes. "You must say nothing about the boy, Sandy."

"But …"

"Nothing!" Claire hissed her eyes blazing. "You must understand. As bad as you think your life is now, it can be much worse. If he finds out that that boy has been visiting … that he was talking with you as if …"

"As if what?" Jacinta shook her head. "We did nothing wrong. We talked. Talking is not wrong. How can he be upset that we …"

"Listen to me!" Claire was desperate. Krieg was approaching, almost at the steps to the porch. "Do not mention the boy or what he said. Only trouble can come from that."

"But I like him." Jacinta shook her head. "I don't want to be here."

"Shut up!" Claire's desperation turned to anger. "You belong to Krieg now. You must accept this. Life will be better when you do, but you must never tell him about the visits from the boy. If you do, it will be bad … for both of us." She shook her head wishing that Sandy Palmeras had never come to the ranch. "Promise me!"

"I promise." Jacinta nodded.

It had been a shitty week. The visit from Pepe Lopez. Discovering that the priest and Mario Acosta were working with Benito Diaz. Planning a way to stop Diaz. Having Claude Brainerd deal with Lucky Martin. And the shit kept piling up.

Unlike Raul Zabala, Tom Krieg did not possess the ability to accept and adapt to rapid change in an almost lackadaisical way. Each deviation from the norms in his life was a pinprick, and the accumulation of pinpricks had driven him into a rage.

But he knew how to take the edge off his rage. He strode across the lawn to the guest house, feeling the aching urge rising in his loins. Each thrust, every slap, would be a bit of salve to ease the day's maddening stings.

"She had a visitor today." Doyle Krieg came around the side of the guest house as his father reached the porch.

"What?" Krieg stared at his son, annoyed that he had interrupted his thoughts of pain and pleasure. "What did you say?"

"A visitor … the new girl had a visitor."

"Who?" Krieg's eyes blazed.

"The half-breed … Sandy Palmeras." Doyle smiled at the rage rising in his father' eyes. "He's been around a few times."

"A few times and you're just telling me!" Krieg faced his son, fists balled and Doyle took a step back. "What did he want?"

"He sat with her." Doyle smiled and nodded at the chairs on the porch. "They talked together … looked like a couple of lovebirds."

Tom Krieg pushed past his son and mounted the steps. His work finished, Doyle retreated around the side of the house.

Inside, Claire heard them speak through the window. She grabbed Jacinta by the shoulders frantic to give her a final warning.

"Whatever he does, do not fight him. If you fight, it will only be worse. Please, little one, you must understand this." She pulled Jacinta close in a hug.

There was a crash. Tom Krieg stood in the door, a towering, glaring monster, ready to destroy whatever and whoever defied his will. Without speaking, he stepped into the room and pulled Jacinta away from Claire's clinging embrace.

His hand clamped around her arm, he dragged the girl across the lawn to the main house. When she tripped and fell, he continued dragging her over the ground, ignoring her cries of pain.

Claire sat by the window, her hands clenched in her lap, watching, afraid to move or speak. When Jacinta hesitated before the door, Krieg physically threw her into the house, slamming the door behind. From her chair, Claire could see the windows of the house rattle and shake. She tried not to think of what was happening behind the closed door.

"I tried to warn her," Claire whispered. "I tried."

Then she wept for the girl.

FIFTY

Cut!

"You're up." Isabella shuffled into the kitchen, wearing only a tee shirt. She yawned and stretched and blinked her eyes at him, smiling. "I smell coffee."

"I was up early." Sole sat at the kitchen table sipping coffee, taking in her tousled, sexy beauty. "Coffee isn't as good as yours, I'm afraid."

"I'm sure it's fine." She shook her head, yawned and leaned over to plant a kiss on his lips, then took his head between her hands and looked into his eyes. "Thank you for being here with me now."

"Thank you for letting me be here. These last weeks have been ..." He paused searching for the right word. "Special."

"Special for me too," Isabella said, pouring coffee into a cup and taking a sip. Her face wrinkled. "You're right. Not as good as mine."

They laughed together. He looked at her, and the guilt crept over his face. Isabella saw it.

"What?" She put the coffee cup down and sat across the kitchen table from him.

"There's something I have to do." He looked down at the table.

"What? Spit it out, mister." She tried to smile, but it wasn't a very good effort. She sensed that things were about to change. Whatever followed him from his past had finally caught up.

"Never mind." She reached out and put a finger over his lips. "I know you have to go away and do something today. That's why you're up early. I heard you get up … expected you to be gone." She smiled. "But you're not gone."

"I'm not gone. I was waiting for you." He nodded. "I wanted to thank you for everything you've done for me. I feel human again, thanks to you." A cloud came over his face. "It's just that …"

"I said hush … no explanations. You have something to do today. I don't require an explanation, and I won't pry. Just one question."

"What?" He looked up from the table.

"Will you be back when you're done?"

"Yes." He said the word, looking into her eyes, meaning it and hoping it was true.

"Good then." Her smile broadened. She leaned over to give him another kiss. He turned his head up, and her tongue lingered against his lips.

Then she walked from the room, calling over her shoulder, "I'll be here when you get back."

He had been back to the tomato farm three times. On the first two visits, Juan Galdo said that his drug-dealing, cartel cousin was busy but that he was going to set things up for them to meet as soon as possible. Sole had decided it was a dead-end, and he wasn't as close to making contact with *Los Salvajes* as he had initially hoped.

On the third trip that changed. Juan excitedly told him that his cousin Bernardo was willing to meet with him and see if they could make a business arrangement. They set a date and time for the meeting, and Juan reminded him to bring the five hundred U.S. dollars. Today was the day.

He drove and tried to focus on the mission, but thoughts of Isabella filled his mind. Her shape, the touch of her leg against his in the night, the kiss at the table over coffee, every sensation filled his memory, and he found himself smiling.

The little voice from his memory spoke and giggled.

Someone is happy today

He had to admit it. He was happy.

The remote border crossing at a dusty village on the Rio Grande appeared ahead. He had to force himself out of his happy reverie. It was time to get to work.

"What is your reason for visiting Mexico?" The Mexican border guard leaned over, comparing the image on his passport card to his face. "Mr. William Myers?"

"Business. Going to check on some tomatoes south of Monterrey."

The guard squinted at him. "I know you. You have crossed here before, in one of the trucks from Krieg and Zabala." The guard handed his ID back and smiled. "You go to check on tomatoes for Krieg and Zabala, yes?"

"Yes." Sole nodded.

"There are always tomatoes south of Monterrey." The

guard laughed. "I hope you will tell your *jefes* that I have been helpful." He pointed to the name tag on his shirt. "Border Agent Luis Vida has helped you on your crossing today, right?"

"That's right. I'll be sure and tell them."

"*Excelente!*"

Sole took the passport card, and Agent Vida stepped back, smiling broadly.

"*Buen día señor!*" Vida called after him.

Sole put an arm out of the window, waved as he pulled away, and settled back for the three-hour drive to Monterrey. Winding along a back road, he passed through a few dusty villages where locals raised their heads curiously at the North American driving by then looked away. His presence there might be innocent, a tourist risking the drive alone through the Mexican backcountry or he might have other reasons for being there. Either way, centuries of experience had passed on the sound tradition of minding their own business.

Eventually, he came to Mexican Federal Highway Number 54 and made the turn to the south. The route took him through the Monterrey suburb of Ciudad Apodaca.

This was a scouting mission, in advance of his meeting that night with Juan Galdo's cousin, and Sole paid close attention to his surroundings. He had no idea where the meeting was to take place, other than somewhere in the vicinity of Monterrey. It seemed prudent to see the lay of the land ahead of time.

He watched the people on the street. Did they appear safe? Did they hurry along, avoiding communication with others or with strangers like an American from across the border? Were the streets deserted? Did gang members huddle on corners as they often did in cities north of the border?

The answers to these questions varied depending on the neighborhood or *colonia* he explored. By Mexican standards, the risk of being the victim of violent crime in the Monterrey area was only average, but an average risk in Mexico did not necessarily mean the same thing as in the United States.

Sole knew that every city has its dangerous sections. Wander into the wrong parts of Detroit, or Cleveland, or Atlanta for that matter, and the results could be devastating. The problem in Mexico was the difference between safety and imminent danger was a relative thing and often a matter of chance and not always location.

He wound through the side streets, assuming that wherever the meeting took place, it would be in one of the shadier neighborhoods. With one hand, he retrieved his Colt from under the seat where he had hidden it while crossing the border and tucked it into his rear waistband under his shirttail. It wasn't the most comfortable place to carry a weapon while seated, but it was instantly available if required, and that was what mattered most at the moment.

From Ciudad Apodaca, he moved deeper into the heart of Monterrey, noting the touristy safer areas before seeking out the seedier *barrios*. If things went the wrong way, he would need an escape route and would not have time to pull out a map. For several hours, he crisscrossed the city's *colonias*, exploring and making mental notes of the quickest way to the highways leading out of the Monterrey and back to the relative safety of the U.S. border.

In the afternoon, he drove south out of the city on Highway 85. There wasn't much left to do now except meet

Juan and bring him back to Monterrey to make contact with his cousin.

He drove through an area surrounded by green mountains. His mind wandered. A sense of the surreal overcame him as images flashed through his brain.

The face of the informant, Luis Acero. The investigation into a drug-smuggling operation. Shrimp boats on the Atlantic. A helicopter ride. A nervous senator.

The bodies of his wife and children.

He shook his head. The images kept flashing through his mind like the frames in a film, and he was just an actor playing his part. At any moment, a director might shout "Cut!"

He wanted to hear the word, but there was no director, and there was no moving on from the images. John Sole might be one of the actors in this personal drama, but he was also writing the script as he went. The ending would come when he said it was finished, or someone else ended it for him.

FIFTY-ONE

No Expression at All

It was a chance meeting. Either could have been on a different road or passed by on the same one at a different time of day, and things might have turned out differently for both.

As it was, Tom Krieg spotted Emmett Brewer's Border Patrol pickup parked under a mesquite tree not far from the spot along the Rio Grande where Lucky Martin's corpse had been found. He pulled off the road, got out, and looked around. There was no sign of Brewer.

Krieg walked toward the river, feeling the rage building inside. As far as he was concerned, this was his personal stretch of river and part of his domain.

The Border Patrol officer insisted on putting his nose into matters that did not concern him. Now he had the sheriff poking into things.

As Krieg neared the river, he found Brewer kneeling by the bank, examining the mud.

"Heard you were still nosing around on that Mexican shooting."

Brewer turned his head. "That what you call it? The Mexican shooting?"

"That's what it was."

"Two shootings now." Brewer rose to face Krieg. "The Mexican and now your man, Lucky Martin."

"Not my man." Krieg shook his head. "Fired his ass for troublemaking."

"Really? When did that happen?"

"Few weeks ago, and it's none of your goddamned business." Krieg turned his head to spit on the ground and then stared into Brewer's eyes. "You think you can question me?"

"I can ask. Answer or not as you please." Brewer shrugged and smiled. "Thing is Krieg, we'll get to the bottom of things sooner or later."

"We?" Krieg sneered. "You're nothing but a security guard with a title and a fancy uniform."

"If you mean I have no jurisdiction to investigate a murder in Salvia County, you're right." Brewer remained unruffled. "But Paul Dermott has enough jurisdiction for both of us. He'll get it all put together."

Krieg remained silent, the rage inside rising once again.

Brewer smiled. "Don't you ever watch television? No one gets away with this sort of thing … covering up murders. There's always something … some bit of evidence that gets overlooked by the perp. Try as they might to cover things up, they leave something behind, and that something is all it takes to land their ass in jail."

"You saying you found that something?"

"Not saying anything. Figured I'd do some checking on my own." Brewer gave a wry smile. "Just a security guard trying to be a good citizen."

"Fuck you." Krieg spun and made his way up the bank and away from the river.

When he reached his pickup, he extended his hands and leaned forward against the hood, head down staring at the ground. He sucked in deep breaths to extinguish the burning inside, but the fire only grew hotter.

Folklore assigns colors to emotions—green for envy, yellow for cowardice, red for anger. Tom Krieg saw no colors. In his mind, he could only see the face of Emmett Brewer and the confident, mocking smile on his face.

He stood up straight, reached into the truck, and walked back toward the river. His breathing had calmed now.

"Brewer!" Krieg called out from fifty yards away.

Emmett Brewer was kneeling again by the river. He looked over his shoulder and stood. "What the …"

There was no smile on his face now. There was no expression at all, just an exploding ball of red as the 150 grain .30-06 slug slammed into his head.

Krieg turned and walked briskly back to his pickup, pushed the Remington 700 back behind the seat, and pulled away, spinning the truck's tires in the dirt.

He punched the Bluetooth button on the truck's steering wheel, gave a command to make a call, and waited as it rang. When it was answered, he said, "I need to see you … now."

FIFTY-TWO

Nothing Could Change That

"Don't go out there." Claire Toussaint peered through the sheer drapes hanging over the bank of windows that looked out over the yard.

Sandy Palmeras parked the pickup in the gravel drive and got out. He was walking toward the guesthouse.

"I want to see him." Jacinta stood beside her.

"You can't." Claire shook her head and turned to Jacinta's, worry in her eyes. "Nothing good can come of it. You must understand what has happened to you … who you are now."

"You mean who I belong to." Jacinta shook her head. "I am not you, Claire. He may own my body, but he doesn't own what's in here." She tapped her chest. "I cannot live like that for the rest of my life."

"What do you know of life?"

"I know that it is more than this, being used by a man. I know that what he is doing to me is wrong." Jacinta's tone was harsh. "And what he is doing to you is wrong."

"And what makes you think you are the judge of what is

right or wrong?" Claire motioned around the interior of the house with one hand as she held Jacinta with the other. "Look around. Is this so wrong? We have food, a beautiful place to live in." Her eyes were dark and somber. "I know what it is to live without these things, to live in the gutter with no hope for anything better."

"He treats you as his whore. And now, I am his whore."

"And so? You think those women who live in fine houses with their husbands aren't whores?" Claire hissed. "They are even worse because they deny it."

"How sad. You can't see love, compassion, how two people can be together because they care for each other, how a woman can want to give herself to a man without the promise of a fine house or clothes, only the promise of love." Jacinta shook her head. "I feel sorry for you."

"You are a child. You have no idea …"

"Yes, I do." Jacinta cut her off, sharply. "Don't lecture me. I am not a child. I have been the whore of two men now. One day I would like it to be different."

Sandy mounted the steps to the porch and knocked softly at the door.

"I'm going to see him." Jacinta walked to the door and opened it, a smile wiping away her argument with Claire.

"Hello, Jacinta." Sandy grinned, his eyes showing his delight that she had opened the door. He had half expected that she would be gone, or that Claire Toussaint would shoo him away.

"Hello, Reynaldo." Jacinta plucked up her courage and added softly. "I am happy to see you."

Sandy's smile widened at the sound of his given name spoken by her. "Can we talk for a while?"

"Yes. I would like that."

Jacinta opened the door and came out onto the porch

and directed him to one of the cushioned chairs. "What shall we speak about?" She asked and gave a nervous laugh.

The music filled the air again for Sandy. He looked into her eyes, unable to think of anything to say. She laughed again.

When his smile lingered without any words, she asked, "*¿Te comieron la lengua los ratones?*" Did the rats eat your tongue?

Sandy laughed.

"What?" Jacinta smiled. "Did I say something funny?"

"No. It's just the expression you used. In English, we would say, has the cat got your tongue?"

"Oh." Jacinta nodded, and now she laughed. "I like your way better." She made a face and shivered. "It is the way we say it in Mexico, but I hate rats."

"Me too." A serious look crossed his face, and he wondered if he should ask his question, then decided to press forward. "Do you mind if I ask how long you will be here?" The smile was back on his face. "I would like to get to know you better."

Darkness fluttered across Jacinta's face. The change was not lost on Sandy.

"What's wrong? Did I say something I shouldn't?"

Huddled by the window, Claire listened, her stomach churning with concern. Say the wrong thing now, and they would both be punished—Jacinta to teach her to hold her tongue and Claire because she had not controlled Jacinta and allowed her to speak with this boy.

Jacinta looked up, and the smile was back on her face. She spoke softly. "I will be here for a while, staying with Claire."

Claire breathed a sigh of relief that she had not said any more than that. Seated in her chair sipping coffee, she listened to them chatting through the open window, muddling along with Sandy's semi-fluent Spanish and Jacinta's broken English.

It was innocuous chatter, the sort of talk young people make when they are nervous and drawn to each other, not sure what to say or how to proceed. She began to relax. Later, when Sandy was gone, she would have another heart to heart talk with Jacinta. Somehow she would make her understand that she must be cautious, that life here can be good, happy even at times, but that she must never forget her place.

"What the fuck are you doing here?"

The shout came from across the yard. Claire's heart sank. Doyle Krieg followed by his shadow, Paco, walked across the lawn toward the guesthouse.

Sandy made no reply. Jacinta reached out and put a hand on his arm, and for that instant, he felt his life was complete, no matter what trouble Doyle tried to stir up.

"I said what the fuck you doing here, Palmeras?"

"Watch your language," Sandy warned.

"My language!" Doyle let out a harsh laugh. "Because of her? My dad's whore? Are you out of your fucking mind?"

Jacinta moved her hand away from Sandy's arm. He turned his head, a question in his eyes. She looked down, and the shame on her face told him the truth.

Doyle saw it and laughed. "You dumb son of a bitch! You didn't know, did you?" A wide, taunting grin spread across his face. "That's right. She's Tom Krieg's whore." He looked at Jacinta. "How many times has he fucked you now? Five … six … a dozen?"

Claire bounded from her chair and out onto the porch. "Get away from here, Doyle Krieg! Go now!"

"Told you before. Don't forget your place around here, whore." Doyle shot a dismissive glance in Claire's direction and focused on the drama playing out between Sandy and Jacinta.

Sandy made up his mind about something and spoke. "It doesn't matter."

Jacinta looked up, tears streaming down her face. "Yes, it does."

"No." Sandy shook his head. "I don't care about what has happened in the past. I only care about now and how much I want to be with you."

"You don't know me." She shook her head. "He's right. I have become a whore."

"No. I'll take you away from here."

Doyle laughed. Claire shouted.

"No!" Claire reached down and pulled Jacinta up from the chair. "You must go now, Sandy. Do not come back to visit. You don't understand what you're saying."

Sandy rose and looked from Doyle to Claire, then let his eyes rest on Jacinta's face. "I will take you away from here."

"Sandy, stop!" Claire was panicked now. Things were completely out of control. She shook her head, the truth spilling out with her words. "You cannot do this. Jacinta is here. She must stay here."

"I don't understand." Sandy's eyes narrowed, not wanting to grasp Claire's meaning, but understanding it entirely now. "You mean she is a prisoner? I'll go to the sheriff. Tell him what's going on!"

"You can't! You must not!" Claire grabbed his arm, the panic in her eyes turning to real terror. "What do you think will happen to her if he finds out?" She shook her head. "If you care about her, you can say nothing ... not to anyone."

Sandy reached out and took Jacinta's hand. When she

would not look into his eyes, he lifted her chin with his finger. "Come with me."

"I cannot," she shook her head, shame in her eyes. "Claire is right. You don't understand. You must say nothing. It is dangerous for you here. I should not have encouraged you. I was selfish."

"No, not selfish." He waited for her to look up. "You feel it too, what there is between us. I won't let that go. I'll be back." He turned and stepped from the porch, brushing by Doyle.

"You really are one dumb fuck," Doyle said, laughing harder now. "I can't believe how fucking …"

Sandy's fist crashed into Doyle Krieg's open mouth, splitting his lip against his teeth. He doubled over, holding his hand to his mouth, blood dripping between his fingers.

"I told you to watch your language." Sandy glared at him, waiting for some retaliation from the boy who had been tormenting him his entire life. When none was forthcoming, he turned and walked to his pickup.

"You'll pay for that you son of a bitch," Doyle shouted when Sandy was safely out of striking range.

"You know where to find me." Sandy climbed into his pickup, gunned the engine, and roared down the drive, gravel kicking out from under the tires.

Claire pulled Jacinta from the porch into the house. They stood in the living room, surrounded by the plush furnishings Tom Krieg provided for their prison. Claire held Jacinta close, her head against her shoulder.

"*No llores niña. Todo estará bien.*" Don't cry, little one. All will be well.

She spoke the words, knowing they were a lie.

Sandy drove like a man lost in a trance, wandering the

Texas back roads as if the miles would make things clearer. They didn't.

How could he have lived here all of his life and not known what was happening under his nose? Did his mother know? The others in Creosote?

Everything was a contradiction. Nothing made sense, and the only thing that became clear was that there was now one inescapable truth left in his life. He loved Jacinta.

Nothing could change that. He wouldn't let them change it.

FIFTY-THREE

Good Cheer

"It is about time you showed up."

Pepe Lopez sat at a small table at the back of the cantina. Two others were already at the table with him. A bottle of tequila sat in the middle, surrounded by four empty glasses. They had been waiting for the fourth member of their party for over an hour.

"I had business to attend to," *Sargento* Miguel Garcia said, hitching his pants up over his belly as he walked to the table.

"I am your business," Lopez scowled. "You would do well to remember that."

"I have many men." Garcia sat opposite Lopez. "They require my attention. The work of a senior official of the *Policía Estatal* is very demanding."

"Senior official," Lopez sneered. "A sergeant is not so senior."

"More senior than you, *coyotaje*," Garcia replied calmly. He shrugged. "At any rate, I am here now. Why the need for this meeting?" He glanced at the two others seated at the table. "And who are these *cabróns*?"

"These are my associates." Lopez nodded at Father Alfonso, dressed in civilian garb, and Mario Acosta. "Their names are not important for you to know."

"As you wish." Garcia shrugged. "You are right, of course. Their names are of no importance. What is important is the reason for this meeting that you said was most urgent. Please get to the point. I have other business this evening."

"I'm sure you do," Lopez smirked. "No doubt with some *puta* in a back alley."

"If you called me here for insults …" Garcia placed his chubby hands on the table, ready to push his bulk up and walk away. "I don't have to stay and listen to them."

"Sit down." Lopez's eyes narrowed. "You will listen. You live well as a sergeant because you are paid by me, not because of the pittance the State of Coahuila doles out to you. If you want to continue to live well, sit your fat ass down, and pay attention."

"There is no need to speak to me in this manner." Red-faced, Garcia relaxed his arms and folded his hands on the table. "I only meant for you to get to the point of meeting like this." He nodded apologetically. The threat of losing his side income from Lopez had his attention. "You are correct. I should have been here earlier. I was delayed by my captain, who was asking questions about the hijacking near Monclova."

"And?" Lopez asked sharply.

"Oh, all is well." Garcia grinned, to show his good nature had returned. "I have given them the report, as you and I discussed."

"Good." Lopez nodded. "Now to our business." He

looked around the table at the other faces. "Our employers across the border want us to put together a large shipment … three trucks."

"Three?" Mario Acosta raised his eyebrows. "Won't that attract attention?"

"Perhaps, but the *gringos* feel that there is greater security in larger numbers. Trucks alone on the road are more vulnerable to attack." He shrugged. "So they say to me at least."

"When?" Mario asked, his eyes darting to the side where Alfonso sat.

"Two days from now." The sidelong glance at Acosta's partner in treason was not lost on Lopez. He held back the smile that threatened to spread across his face. "I have already arranged the shipment. The trucks will leave the avocado farms and converge on Torreón. Questions?"

There were none.

"Good. It's a very simple plan … security in numbers." Lopez permitted himself a smile now. "And one more thing."

"What's that?" Acosta asked, anxious to gather all the information he could for his new partner, Benito Diaz.

"We will all be along."

"What?"

"We will be along." Lopez nodded at Alfonso and Acosta. "Both of you and me, we will each be in a truck as part of the security."

"I don't think I can." Mario shook his head.

"You will be there. These are the orders from Krieg and Zabala. Each of us is in charge of one of the trucks. They expect us to get them safely across the border."

Garcia had watched the exchange, a grin on his fat face.

He laughed, mocking Mario. "What's the matter, little boy? Are you afraid?"

"And you," Lopez said, scowling at the police sergeant. "You will be along as well, you and your men."

"Me?" Garcia shook his head. "But I can't be involved …"

"You already are involved," Lopez snapped. "You will be there, or your life of luxury will cease." Lopez grinned. "Even more, you will no longer be a police sergeant. Someone will make a call to your superiors and let them know about your activities in working with a *coyotaje*."

"You wouldn't do that."

"Yes, I would," Lopez said matter-of-factly. "We are in dangerous times, a war even. In war, we do things we would not do otherwise. You will drive your police vehicle ahead of the caravan of trucks, making sure the road is clear.

The others at the table were silent. Lopez looked into each of their faces. "Do this," he said. "Let's end this war quickly for Krieg and Zabala so we can return to doing business as usual."

Lopez poured tequila from the bottle on the table into the glasses that had remained empty until now. "To business."

"To business," the others said and lifted the glasses, downing the tequila in a gulp.

"Now, I must go." Mario Acosta rose. "I will need to make some preparations at home to explain my sudden departure."

"If you need to go, go." Lopez shrugged and poured more tequila for himself.

"And I too must go," Garcia said, rising. "There are many arrangements to make if my men are to be in place to follow the trucks."

"Make your arrangements, *Sargento*," Lopez said, sipping the tequila. When they had both departed, he turned to Father Alfonso. "So, will he tell Diaz?"

"Yes." Alfonso nodded. "He may already be on the phone with him."

"And you?"

"I will do as you instructed and follow up with a call of my own to Diaz."

"Will he fall into our trap?"

"It is likely," Alfonso said, nodding and remembering the crazed look in the Yaqui's eyes when he declared war on the *gringos*. "Diaz is a greedy man ... more than that, though, he is proud, and thinks that he can do anything. He will take the idea of the three trucks together for security reasons as a challenge to him. His pride will force him to accept the challenge."

"Good. You can go now. We meet in Torreón in two days."

"I'll be there."

Alfonso stood and walked from the cantina. Outside, he wiped the perspiration from his brow with the back of his arm, wondering at the predicament his greed had brought him to.

It occurred to the priest that this was his penance, helping one gangster fight another. If he survived, perhaps he could go to confession and be forgiven for the wrongs he had committed, for taking money for the young girls he sold to the *gringos*. After all, over the years, had he not forgiven many sinners in the confessional? He would find another priest to forgive him.

Inside the cantina, alone now at the table, Pepe Lopez sipped the tequila then poured another. The plans were made, the pieces in place. The warm tequila glow in his belly flushed his face red with good cheer.

FIFTY-FOUR

Someplace Safe

"Did you know?" Sandy stood in the doorway of the café, glaring at his mother.

"I knew."

Isabella looked up into her son's eyes. They were harsh, cold, and angry. His icy stare made her shudder. There had always been warmth and tenderness between them, and now, she wondered if that was lost forever because she had not been able to bring herself to tell her son the truth.

"You knew that Krieg keeps girls as prisoners ... turns them into his whores?" He regarded his mother as if seeing her for the first time. "And you said nothing? You accepted it ... never reported it to the sheriff ... never said a damned word about it to anyone ... to me!"

Each word was a sledgehammer blow, crashing into her chest. Isabella lowered her head, avoiding the anger in his eyes.

"You don't understand." She fought to control the tears that threatened to cascade down her face.

"Understand! What the hell is there to understand?"

Sandy pounded a fist on the counter in front of her. "He takes women, rapes them, and keeps them prisoner."

"It's complicated, son."

"Don't call me that." He looked at her. "I don't even know you right now. How could you turn a blind eye to what he is doing? He should be in prison!" There was a catch in his throat as he fought back his own tears. "And Jacinta ... she's just a girl, my age. I love her, and she's ..." His voice trailed off, unable to say the words.

"What are you going to do?" Isabella whispered without looking up, dreading the answer.

"I've been driving around in circles, asking myself that question. Jacinta is terrified that I will say something."

"And?"

"I have to. Krieg can't be allowed to get away with this. I'm going to Sheriff Dermott. I'll tell him everything, at least everything I know. It should be enough to start an investigation. Krieg won't be able to hide everything. He can't pay off everybody."

"He can." Isabella raised her head, her eyes pleading with her son. "He will pay off anyone who knows anything. They'll take the money. No one will stand against him. If they try ..." She shook her head. "They won't try."

"Jacinta is there now! Claire Toussaint is there now. I heard what Doyle Krieg said. I'm a witness."

"If you go to the sheriff, you'll never see her again."

"What does that mean? Krieg will do something to Jacinta?"

"Krieg will do whatever it takes to protect himself ... to protect what he is and what he has."

"You mean he will kill Jacinta?" He shook his head. "I can't believe that."

"I mean he will do whatever it takes and Jacinta, Claire,

you … anyone he feels is a threat … will never be seen again."

"I won't let him get away with it." A disgusted snarl twisted his lips. "And I can't believe you have let him get away with it."

He turned and disappeared through the door. Isabella sank to her knees behind the counter and let the tears come, her sobs shaking her frame.

Tires spinning in the gravel, Sandy roared out of Creosote, the dust billowing out behind his truck. As far as he was concerned, dust could swallow up the place, burying it and all its secrets. He was finished with it.

He couldn't go to the sheriff. He couldn't tell anyone. There was only one thing to do. He pressed the accelerator to the floor.

When he arrived at the Krieg ranch, he pulled up the service road that led to the cattle pens behind the barn. Stepping from the pickup, he stood for a moment looking for activity. There was none. The ranch hands were out working the cattle or handling chores. Doyle Krieg and Paco weren't around, but that could change at any moment.

He made his way around one of the pens and started across an open lot that led to the guesthouse's backyard. He stopped and knelt by a hydrangea bush, glancing around to make sure no one was in sight. Running across the yard now, he went to the back porch and peered through a window. There was no sign of Claire and Jacinta.

He tried the back door, found it unlocked, and pushed it open. He walked in as quietly as he could and came around a corner into a hallway. Halfway down the hall, a door opened, and he came face to face with Claire Toussaint.

"What are you doing here?" Claire's eyes were wide with fear. She craned her head to see around Sandy, expecting to find Tom Krieg's hulk bearing down on them.

"I'm taking her with me."

Sandy pushed by Claire. She grabbed his arm.

"You can't. You don't understand what you're saying."

He pushed open the door Claire had come through and stopped for an instant shocked by what he saw, then ran to the bed. Jacinta lay on her back, one side of her face swollen, one eye completely closed. Blood had dried on her bruised lips.

"Jacinta!" Sandy knelt by the bed, taking her hand in his.

Her eyes fluttered open. "Reynaldo," she managed to whisper. "I knew you would come."

"Who?" Sandy turned to glare at Claire. "Krieg?"

"He came home, not long after you left. I watched from the window. There was already anger on his face. I could see it even from here. Then I saw Doyle stop him and speak to him. He pointed here to the guesthouse. The next thing, Krieg came across the yard and …" Claire nodded at Jacinta and closed her eyes, her voice a whisper. "This is what happened. I tried to warn you."

"I'm taking you with me." Sandy put an arm under Jacinta to help her from the bed.

Claire pulled at him from behind. "Sandy, you can't. You must go. He said he would be back. If he finds out you were here …"

"What?" Sandy stood to face her. "He'll beat me too?"

"No." Claire shook her head. "He will kill you." She

nodded at Jacinta. "And her. Please go before you make things worse."

"Stay out of my way, Claire. I'm taking her with me." A thought occurred to him and the same look of disgust he had shown his mother crossed his face. "You are part of this, aren't you? You help him."

"There are things you don't understand."

"Stop!" His shout startled Claire to silence. "My mother said the same thing! I understand she is a prisoner here." He shook his head. "She is coming with me."

"Don't be angry with your mother, Sandy. She was trying to protect you."

"From what?"

Claire started to speak and then shook her head, uncertain what he had heard from Isabella. "Whatever you think now, your mother loves you. She has tried to protect you all these years."

"Protect me?" he hissed. "From the truth?" He shook his head. "Get away from me."

Pulling the blanket from the bed, he reached down to touch Jacinta's arm. "Can you walk?"

"Yes." She nodded. "Not fast, though."

She could barely stand. The look of hopeless terror in Jacinta's eyes overwhelmed Claire, and for one moment, she was ashamed enough to put aside her own fears. "Yes. Take her away from here, but go now and go quickly. If he finds you, he will kill you both."

Sandy turned to her and found her face changed, the fear replaced by resolve. "And you? What will he do to you?"

"I will tell him you forced your way in, and I could not resist. But you must go quickly. He left but he will be back at any time."

Together they eased Jacinta up from the bed. With an arm around, her Sandy walked her to the back door.

"Where is your truck?" Claire asked.

"Behind the cattle pens."

"Go get it. Drive across the back lawn and bring it to the rear of the guesthouse. It will be quicker that way. She cannot walk fast, and if someone sees you, they will stop you."

He hesitated. Jacinta patted his arm. "Do as she says. She is right. I cannot walk fast." She nodded. "I trust her."

Sandy raced from the guesthouse back porch to his pickup. A minute later, he was roaring across the lawn, tearing out clumps of grass as he slid to a stop.

Claire helped Jacinta down the steps. They stood for a moment beside the truck, and Claire held her close, whispering in her ear, "*Ten cuidado, pequeña.*" Be safe, little one.

Sandy came around the truck to lift Jacinta into the passenger seat then turned to Claire. He looked into her eyes, searching for the secrets that she and his mother had kept from him.

"Thank you, Claire."

"Don't thank me. Go!" She stood on her toes and kissed his cheek. "Go away fast, before he comes back."

Sandy climbed in beside Jacinta, threw the truck in gear and sped away across the lawn and out to the county road. He worried they would never get off the Krieg ranch before being spotted. With a jerk of the wheel, he skidded onto a dirt trail that led off into the hills.

When they were out of sight from the main road, he slowed and reached for Jacinta's hand. Her fingers curled gently around his, and he turned his head. Bruised and swollen as she was, she managed a smile.

"Thank you, Reynaldo."

He lifted her hand and brushed her fingers with his lips. "I won't let them do anything to you."

"I believe you." Her smile seemed brighter for an instant. "Where will we go?

"Someplace safe."

FIFTY-FIVE

Enough was Enough

"What's' up?" Claude Brainerd pulled up beside Tom Krieg's pickup. He looked around and then back at Krieg, curious. "And why the hell did you want me to meet you out here?"

They sat at on the shoulder of a gravel path five miles off the county road. It ran alongside the barbed wire enclosing the range where Krieg pastured his cattle. Several steers jostled for position around a nearby galvanized stock watering tank fed by a well pump.

Krieg watched them and ignored Brainerd's question, the ferocity still smoldering in his eyes. Piled on top of everything else going on, Brewer digging into his business, and then Isabella's bastard trying to take what was his, Tom Krieg was a volcano on the verge of erupting.

He'd taken care of Brewer's smug self-assurance. Now, he had a job for Brainerd. After, he would go back and finish what he started with the girl.

Brainerd waited. When Krieg was like this, he was dangerous. He was as likely to vent his anger on the deputy as anyone else. Minutes passed before the fury subsided enough for him to speak through gritted teeth.

"I need you to take care of something for me."

"Sure." Brainerd grinned. Taking care of business for Krieg had been a profitable sideline for him over the years. The grin faded as Krieg told him what he wanted.

"You have to be kidding." Brainerd shook his head. "I can't …"

"You will," Krieg said. "You will, or you'll spend the rest of your life in prison."

Krieg ticked off the crimes that would cost Brainerd his freedom. "Fraud, accepting kickbacks, aiding and abetting in numerous crimes, including kidnapping and human trafficking. Then there's the small matter of the murder of Lucky Martin. I'll bet you stood there beside Dermott, looking pure as the driven snow when they pulled his body from the river."

"But I …"

"Shut up." A sneer crossed Krieg's face. "You played the game, now you pay the price."

Brainerd swallowed nervously, his face pale. Krieg was right. He was trapped. He had played with the devil, without considering the hellfire. Now, when things were getting hot, he had no choice but to keep playing.

His oversized head nodded slowly, the flabby jowls beneath protruding in rolls of fat. "Okay."

"Let me know when it's done." Krieg put his truck in gear and sped away.

Brainerd sat in his truck as the dust settled around him, wondering how handcuffs would feel on his fat wrists. He shook the thought off. Just get it over with, he told himself.

He drove slowly. Maybe Krieg would change his mind

and tell him to call it off. It was an idle hope, and he knew it.

He arrived at the point along the Rio Grande that Krieg had described. Half waddling and half crawling, he made his way gingerly down the bank to the water's edge. Emmett Brewer's body lay exactly where Krieg said it would be.

Brainerd couldn't help gawking at what he found. Krieg had neglected to mention the fist-sized hole the rifle round had punched out of the back of Brewer's skull. Flies were already buzzing around it, depositing their maggot eggs in any wet, fleshy crevice they found.

The deputy peered up and down the bank and across the water. No one was in sight on either side.

As instructed, he took the .32 pistol from his pocket and pointed it at what was left of Brewer's head. Eight sharp cracks sounded as Brainerd squeezed the trigger sending all eight bullets into Brewer's already-shattered skull.

Krieg wanted to cover the fact that Brewer had been killed by a .30-06 round. Brainerd regarded the mangled mess that had been Brewer's head. The eight small-caliber rounds could not disguise the fact that something larger had ended the Border Patrol officer's life. The rifle bullet had passed through the skull and ended up somewhere on the opposite bank of the river and would never be recovered, but the light .32 caliber slugs would be.

Brainerd looked at the pistol in his hand. He still wanted to hold on to it, but this was too much.

He tossed it into the water then looked down at Brewer's body. Krieg wanted it rolled into the water. Brainerd hesitated.

He'd followed Krieg's instructions to this point, but whether the body was recovered in the water or on the bank seemed irrelevant. He knew from experience that the risk of leaving behind some incriminating evidence would increase dramatically if he touched and attempted to drag the body to the water. Fibers, body fluid transferal, a footprint he forgot to cover up, and a thousand other tiny bits of evidence could send him to prison as part of a conspiracy to murder a federal agent.

He shook his head, pleased with his analysis of the situation and made an executive decision. Enough was enough.

FIFTY-SIX

Raging Maniac

The door crashed open. Tom Krieg stomped through the guesthouse to the bedroom in the hallway. He felt as if the walls were closing in on him. The beast inside demanded its release.

He wanted the girl, needed her, now. A moment later, he reemerged from the bedroom, eyes blazing. He sprang toward Claire, huddled against the far end of the sofa trying to make herself as small a target as possible.

"Where is she?" Krieg thundered.

"Gone," Claire whispered, terrified at what was to come. "I couldn't stop him."

She cowered on the sofa, pulling her knees up and lowering her head to cover her face.

"Who?" Krieg's fist flashed out and caught her in the side of the head.

He reached down and grabbed her hair, pulling her up so that her face was inches from his, his hand wrapped around her throat. The purple lump on the side of her face grew as she dangled before him, half suspended in the air by his grip on her throat. She was buying time for them and was paying the price. Krieg's hold on her throat tightened.

"He forced his way in … went into the bedroom …" She shook her head, choking the words out. "I couldn't stop him."

"Who!"

Krieg's grip tightened, and she was afraid she might pass out. Part of her prayed that she would. The questions would end then, at least for a while. She clung to consciousness, trying this once to do the right thing. The young couple needed time to put as much distance between them and the hell Krieg had created. The more he questioned her, the farther away they ran.

Claire's eyes fluttered closed as if she might faint. She gasped, delaying the inevitable a little longer. Her youth had been stolen by this evil man. She could not allow it to happen again to Jacinta. Perhaps this was the penance God required for the life she had lived. Her own life was the price of forgiveness.

It didn't matter anymore. Krieg had beaten her before, and Claire had no doubt that he would beat her again. Desperately, she fought to hold onto consciousness. Krieg threw her back onto the sofa and backhanded her across the mouth, opening a gash in her tongue and lip.

"It doesn't matter. I know who." He towered over her, glaring down.

She gasped for air and held her hand to her mouth to stem the blood flowing down her chin.

"You'll pay for this." He turned and stormed from the guesthouse.

Claire Toussaint sobbed. She'd been paying for it all her life.

The drive to Creosote at seventy miles an hour on the back roads took twenty minutes. Krieg's pickup roared through town, sliding to a stop in front of Isabella's home. He stomped to the porch, took hold of the doorknob, found it locked, and kicked the door open.

He stood in the doorway, backlit by the sun low on the horizon, a dark, hulking shape. Isabella sat with Sherm Westerfield at the kitchen table across the room. Eyes red and wet, she looked up.

"Get out," she said. There was no reason to ask what he wanted.

"Where are they?" Krieg stepped through the door, his hulk moving menacingly toward Isabella.

Sherm rose to stand between them. Isabella remained seated, unflinching. Nothing Tom Krieg did to her could be worse than the look of disgust she had seen on her son's face.

"You don't belong here." Sherm moved closer.

"Get out of the way old man, before you get hurt."

"I'm not moving anywhere." Sherm's eyes burned with anger. "Never liked you, Krieg … always thought you were an asshole, but now …" Sherm shook his head. "Now it all makes sense."

Krieg looked past him to Isabella. "What did you tell him?" he hissed.

"Everything." She rose to stand beside Sherm. "He knows it all."

"You stupid bitch. You don't have any idea what you've done."

"I know I lost my son … maybe for good … because of you … because of the secrets I've kept." She shook her head. "No more secrets."

"That's right, Krieg. No more secrets." Sherm moved in

front of Isabella, his face inches from Krieg's. "Your little business ... what do they call it, human trafficking? Taking girls, raping them, selling them, keeping them as prisoners. It's done. I'll see to that."

"You do, and you'll die, like your son."

A cloud passed over Sherm's face. He nodded as if a great mystery had been revealed to him. "That's right. Robby found out what you were up to. I didn't know what it was then, but he couldn't stomach it, so he walked away from it and left to protect me. He knew what I would do if I found out about it. Now he's dead, killed in Afghanistan." Sherm's eyes narrowed. "But you're responsible for it. You killed my boy. I won't shut up."

"That pissant son of yours kept his mouth shut because he knew what would happen if he didn't. You should follow his example." Krieg nodded at Isabella. "Like her."

"He was a boy," Sherm said, his eyes filling with tears. "Confused by what he discovered, not sure how to deal with it, worried about me. I wish he had come to me and told me."

"If he had, you'd both be dead now." Krieg looked at Isabella. "You tell him the rest? That your bastard boy is mine."

"She told me." Sherm nodded.

"You were just another whore, even in high school." Krieg sneered. "You weren't even very good at that. Got knocked up in the back of my pickup and wouldn't get rid of it." He looked at Sherm. "That's the real secret she kept all these years. Her son is mine. I own him, like everything else in the county."

"You don't own shit," Sherm growled back. "You use people to get what you want. Those days are over."

"He took what belongs to me."

"That girl doesn't belong to you, and neither does Sandy." Isabella's tears had dried, replaced by cold anger.

"He took what's mine!" Kreig's voice boomed at them like thunder, ready to hurl lightning into their faces. "Anything happens to him, you have yourself to blame. Now, where is he?"

"You think I would tell you, even if I knew." A look of disgust covered her face. "You're not only a bully. You're a fool."

He stepped forward, pushing Sherm back into Isabella so that he could reach her. Sherm's struck one feeble blow against the bigger man's shoulder before Kreig's fist crashed into his jaw and sent him to the floor. Kreig reached for Isabella, holding her by one arm as he backhanded her across the mouth.

"Make you feel big?" she spat at him through a split lip. "Beating an old man and a woman makes you feel like you're in control." She shook her head. "You don't control anything anymore. The secrets are out. Your power is gone."

"We'll see about that."

With a shove, he sent her to the floor, her head banging against the kitchen table. Kreig turned and disappeared through the door. Isabella reached out to Sherm and helped him sit up. He shook his head to get rid of the cobwebs and looked around.

"Is he gone?"

"He's gone." Isabella nodded.

"I have to go too. I need to get the sheriff on this." Sherm tried to pull himself up from the floor and then sat back down.

"You need to sit here and rest for a bit. We need to think this through. I'm not sure who we can trust."

"You think Sheriff Dermott is in on this?" Sherm was incredulous.

"I can't say, but Robby must not have been sure either, so he did what he thought was best for both of you. He left and stayed quiet to protect you. There had to be a reason he didn't come to you … a reason he was afraid for you and didn't go to the sheriff." She shook her head, trying to think things through. "All I'm saying is that for now, we don't know who to trust."

"Alright." Sherm nodded and managed to climb into a chair. He sat for a moment, breathing deeply and gathering his thoughts. "But there is someone I do trust, and someone you can trust, I believe." He looked at her. "Is he coming back?"

"He said he would be back tonight." She nodded. "He wouldn't say it unless he meant it, and you're right, I do trust him."

"Me too." Sherm nodded. "You wait here for Myers. I'm going to go round up Reggie Prince. That'll give us two we can trust. Then we can make a plan."

She watched him shuffle to the door and out into the twilight. Alone in the house, her bravado began to fade. She trembled for her son. Tom Krieg was a raging maniac.

FIFTY-SEVEN

The Innocent

A series of back roads, some nothing more than dry washes, led them from the Krieg ranch and away from Salvia County. When Sandy made it to Highway 83, he turned northwest and followed the Rio Grande for an hour. As the sun lowered in the sky, he leaned forward, peering through the windshield.

"What are you looking for?" Jacinta asked.

They had driven mostly without speaking. Sandy was tense, feeling the need to put miles between them and Krieg.

"We need to get off the road for the night. There's a place I know where we will be safe."

"Should we not drive on as far as we can go?" Jacinta's face reflected her concern at stopping their escape so soon. She would have preferred to put another thousand miles between them and the devil called Krieg.

Sandy spoke gently, trying to reassure her.

"I would keep going if we could, but we will need money. I know where to get all we need, but there isn't enough time to get there today. Tomorrow morning we will move on and have all the money we need. Then we will go and keep going. I promise."

Jacinta nodded and smiled bravely. "I trust you, Reynaldo. If you say we should stop for now, then so be it. It is only that if you hadn't come for me, I don't know …" Tears welled up in her eyes, and she lowered her head.

"I won't let anything happen to you, Jacinta." Sandy took her hand and lifted it to his lips briefly. "I promise."

They traveled another mile or so before he slowed. "Here," he said and turned onto a narrow dirt track that led off to the east.

The trail wound through scrub brush and down into shallow valleys between low, hills. A couple of miles in, he turned onto a second trail, this one even smaller and narrower than the first. The pickup bumped along a rocky stream bed for a mile or so then climbed back out onto level ground. Undergrowth crowded in from the sides so that at times Sandy had to slow to make sure he was still following the path.

"We're here." The trail came to an abrupt end.

"Where?" Jacinta looked around, her eyes puzzled.

They were surrounded by thick brush as tall as the pickup. Beyond the brush were trees she could not identify.

"Right there. That's our home for the night."

She leaned forward. "Where? That tree?"

Sandy laughed. "Come with me."

He got out and helped Jacinta down from the passenger side. Holding her hand, he led her toward a dark mass that did, in fact, appear to be a tree in the dusky gloom. As they got closer, Jacinta saw that it was a small hut.

"Oh," she said, smiling with surprise. "A house. *Qué sorpresa!*" What a surprise!

She laughed with delight, and the music came, filling him as it had the first time they met.

"Not exactly a house," he said. "But for tonight it will keep us safe."

He pulled at the wood plank door. The hinges were rusty, and the door sagged, dragging on the ground. He pulled harder and led the way inside.

"What is this place? Is this your home?"

"No." Now Sandy laughed. "Not home, but a place I have visited many times with a friend. Don't worry. We're safe here."

The hut was Sherm Westerfield's backcountry cabin. Over the years, he had taken Sandy there on annual hunts for whitetail deer.

Hunting was really just an excuse to get away. Mostly they talked, sat around a campfire that Sherm would build in the clearing near the door, and ate steaks that Sherm packed in. When Sandy was sixteen, he had his first beer there, after Sherm made him swear that he would not tell Isabella who he was sure would brain them both him with a frying pan if she found out.

Sandy laughed and took the beer. It was a strange taste, and he wasn't sure he liked it. Sherm said that was a good thing and not to become too fond of beer, although he sat back and enjoyed several more while Sandy sipped the one in his hand.

Sandy found the kerosene lantern Sherm kept on a shelf by the door. He shook it and was thankful there was still fuel inside. He lit the wick and then looked around for the bedding they left sealed up in plastic bags in case the place ever leaked while they were away.

It only took a minute to spread the blankets and make a serviceable pallet on the floor. He found an old hemp gunny sack that once held potatoes and stuffed it with crumpled newspaper Sherm kept around as fire starter. This he placed on one side of their sleeping pallet as a pillow for Jacinta.

When he was done, he surveyed his work and turned to her. "It's not much. I wish it was better."

"The walls and roof are good." She smiled and thumped her hand on the wall, and a cloud of dust puffed into the air around them. They laughed. "This will be a good place for us. The bed is wonderful, and I am sure you will keep me warm if the night is too cool."

Sandy blushed and nervously changed the subject, reminding her, "It's only for the night. Tomorrow, with the money I'll get, we can drive far away. Then you can have a nice motel room."

"Motel?"

"Motel ... like a hotel except ..." He shrugged and realized that motel or hotel would be all the same to her. "We'll get a nice hotel room far away from here."

He helped ease her sore body down on the blankets and then took a galvanized pail hanging from a nail in the wall. In the back of the room, Sherm kept gallon milk jugs full of water that he purified with a drop of chlorine bleach and then resealed. He always said they were for emergency use in case they ever got stranded there by a flash flood in the stream. Sandy figured that Sherm would agree that this qualified as an emergency.

He opened one and sniffed. The faint odor of chlorine was no worse than some city tap water he'd tasted before, and he figured it was safe.

Pouring two jugs into the pail, he brought it to Jacinta. "You probably want to wash up. You can use this. We have more water for the night."

"Thank you."

She spent some time cleaning her hands and face in the pail while Sandy went outside. She heard him moving things around. When he came back, she had finished washing. He smiled down at her, and then an embarrassed look came over his face.

"I … uh … it's probably been a while since you … well, since you …"

"I have not relieved myself in a long while," she said to make things easier for him. "How do I do that here?"

"I'll show you." He reached out a hand and helped her to her feet. "When it's just Sherm and me, there's no problem. We go out into the brush with a roll of paper and take care of business."

He took a roll of toilet paper from a shelf by the door and led her outside and around the side of the cabin. "I rigged this for you."

He pointed to two old milk crates with two planks separated by a gap across the top to form a seat. "You just sit there, and … well, do what you have to do. See here, I dug a hole under the planks. When we leave, I'll fill it in." He was proud of his handiwork. "Everything goes back to nature."

Jacinta grinned. "I have never had anyone build a toilet for me, and such a very fine one too."

She laughed again, and Sandy was becoming addicted to the music it made.

"If you don't mind, I would like to use it now," Jacinta hinted with a twinkle in her eye.

"Oh, right. Sorry." He placed the paper on the plank and went around the side of the cabin to wait by the front door.

After a few minutes, Jacinta hobbled around the corner. "Thank you, Reynaldo. You are very thoughtful."

As the night came on, Sandy retrieved all the food he had in the truck, which consisted of two bags of potato chips and half a package of snack cakes. He laid the provisions on the blankets in front of Jacinta.

"Sorry. Things happened so fast I didn't have time to get any real food."

"This will be fine." She smiled. "We have warm blankets, a roof, water, and dinner. What more could we want?"

He sat beside her on the blankets and they munched the potato chips and drank chlorine purified water like they were sipping fine wine. The snack cakes served as dessert.

Sandy turned the lantern flame down until it sputtered out and pitch blackness descended around them. Jacinta came close to him, resting her head against his chest. He put his arm around her, and held her, careful not to move suddenly and cause her pain.

They whispered in the dark, speaking of where they might go, what places they could see together. It was the dream talk of young lovers, the kind of innocent talk that made everything seem possible. After a while, they slept and the dreams became real for a time.

FIFTY-EIGHT

Foolish
___

As the day wore on, Sole left Monterrey and headed south on the back roads, winding towards Juan Galdo's village near the tomato farm. Late in the afternoon, he entered the narrow lane lined by small shacks and adobe structures. He slowed, eyeing each yard as he passed.

As Juan had promised, a blue blanket hung on a rope in the yard of a shack on the south end of the village's single lane. Juan ran out of the hut, grinning and waving as Sole halted his pickup.

"*Señor!* I knew you would come. I said this very thing to my cousin." Juan pulled the door open and climbed into the passenger seat. "He seems excited to meet you." Juan leaned toward him and grinned. "And to do business with you. You have the money ... the five hundred U.S. dollars?"

"I have the money. You get it after I meet with him. Where do we go?" Sole asked.

"There is a cantina in Monterrey ... a place he goes to a lot. He will be there. Don't worry, though. It is a public place. Many come to drink and eat there. Nothing bad can happen there in front of so many people." Juan nodded, tapping the side of his head with a finger. "My cousin is very smart. He said you would not want to be in a private place since you don't know if there should be trust between you. He was right, no?"

"He was right." Sole nodded.

Juan chattered nonstop on the way back to Monterrey. Here and there he pointed out some landmark or a village where he knew a girl or a place where you could buy cheap tequila or the best marijuana.

The sun was setting as they came into Monterrey. Juan directed him through the winding streets. Sole made a mental note of every turn.

"It is just here." Juan pointed ahead. "At the end of the block. You see that building with the little red lighted sign in the window that says Victoria. That means they sell Victoria beer there." He nodded enthusiastically. "It is the best beer in Mexico. I hear that you *norteamericanos* drink Corona." He wrinkled his nose in a scowl and shook his head. "Not good ... piss water. Take it from your friend Juan Galdo. Victoria is the best beer in Mexico."

"I take your word." Sole let the pickup roll slowly toward the end of the street. "Where do I park?"

"Just there. Right in front. My cousin has a man there already to keep the space open. You park, and he will watch your truck for you." Juan smiled. "My cousin is an important man, you see."

"I see."

Sole stopped in front of the cantina that had no other marking except the neon Victoria beer sign in the window. A heavyset man wearing a floral shirt and who looked like he had just stepped off a plane from Maui pointed to the curb, indicating that he should stop there.

Juan pushed the door open and grinned at the heavyset man.

"Gustavo! *Qué pasa!*"

Gustavo ignored him and kept his eyes riveted on the *gringo*. As Sole stepped out of the pickup, Gustavo put his hand out. "Keys."

Sole shook his head. "Nope. They stay with me."

A moment of confusion fluttered across Gustavo's beefy face. "Keys or you don't go in."

Sole shrugged. "Okay, I don't go in." He started to get back into the truck.

"*Espera un minuto por* favor!" Wait a minute, please! Juan was desperate.

In an instant, he saw his five hundred dollars floating away. He looked at Gustavo, desperately reasoning.

"Gustavo, please. It is only natural. My friend comes here because I bring him, but he does not know yet that he can trust you, as I do." He leaned closer and lowered his voice. "He has much money and wants to do business. Do you want to be the one to turn him away? Are you going to tell my cousin that you turned him away without letting them meet and hear what he has to say?"

Gustavo was unmoved by Juan's pleas, but after several seconds of staring into Sole's expressionless face, he said, "Okay. You go in, but I go with you."

"Suit yourself." Sole shrugged and followed Juan toward the cantina door with Gustavo hovering behind.

"Wait," Gustavo said as Juan was pulling the door open.

"Now what?"

"Do you have a gun?"

"Yes, and it stays with me too." Sole smiled. "Do you have a gun?"

"Yes." Gustavo nodded seriously. "More guns than you, I think."

"So looks like you got the upper hand. We going in or not?"

"We go in."

Inside, Juan pushed through the crowded, smoke-filled space toward a table at the rear. Heads turned to eye the gringo walking into a place so far off the usual streets where the tourists frolicked in relative safety.

"Bernardo, my cousin!" Juan stopped in front of a table where a thin man with a scruffy mustache sat with his back to the wall, reading a newspaper.

Bernardo looked up. "Cousin, Juan. I assume this is the n*orteamericano* you spoke of."

"Yes, yes." Juan's head bobbed up and down. "This is him … from the United States."

"What is his name?"

"His name?" A sheepish grin spread across Juan's face. "I never asked."

"Bill Myers," Sole said.

"Bill Myers, from the United States." Bernardo nodded at a chair across from him. "Have a seat."

Sole sat, aware that Gustavo continued to hover over him. The room was crowded with locals, but a few left, apparently unsure of what was happening, and not wanting any part of the trouble that might ensue.

Bernardo lifted a hand and called out to a heavyset man behind the bar. "A beer for my friend here … Victoria."

The bartender nodded and turned to the back room.

"Where are you going?" Bernardo was annoyed.

"You drink all my good beer. I have to go open another case," the bartender called over his shoulder.

Bernardo turned to Sole. "So, you want to do business with me."

"If we can work things out." Sole nodded at Juan, who beamed proudly that he had brought these two businessmen together. "Your cousin tells me you are connected to the cartel … *Los Salvajes*."

"My cousin says too much sometimes." Bernardo's eyes narrowed, shooting an annoyed look at Juan.

The beaming smile faded from Juan's face. "I was only trying to be helpful, Bernardo."

"Shut up." Bernardo scowled. "You always were the dumb one in the family."

Sole could almost feel Gustavo's Fat belly rubbing on the back of his neck. It was time to get down to business or get out of town.

"Are we going to do business or not?" he asked and placed his hands on the table as if he would push himself up and leave.

"That depends," Gustavo said, smiling. "Do you have any experience in selling cocaine in the United States?"

"Some." Sole nodded. "But I can learn more … from you."

"It is interesting that you say that. I would have thought there was much we could learn from you" Bernardo tossed the newspaper he had been reading on the table and opened it up. Inside was a crinkled photograph from a different newspaper, taken the day that John Sole buried his wife and children. "This is you, is it not? A police detective from Atlanta in the United States?"

It might have been that Bernardo had counted on shock to immobilize John Sole. It could have been that seated at his favorite table in his favorite cantina surrounded by people who knew and feared him, he was overconfident. It could have been that he expected the hulking presence of Gustavo to cowl the American.

Those assumptions were wrong, and the moment of hesitation they created provided the opportunity for Sole to act first. He rocked his chair to the left and toppled to the floor, coming up with the Colt in his hand.

People scattered. Sole ignored them and Gustavo who was fumbling with the shirt under his protruding belly to retrieve his pistol. Bernardo was the most significant threat, and as the drug dealer lifted a large revolver from his lap and turned, Sole pulled the trigger twice. Both bullets struck Bernardo in the chest, and he slumped in his chair.

"No!" Juan screamed. "What have you done?"

Sole swiveled toward Gustavo the second threat. The big man was just freeing his weapon from under the tight waist of his jeans.

"Don't do it." Sole shook his head.

Gustavo hesitated and then relaxed his hand.

"Hold it by the barrel and put it on the table."

With two stubby fingers, Gustavo held the Glock's barrel and gently placed it on the table in front of Bernardo's blood-spattered body, then stepped back. Everyone else in the cantina was either on the floor, behind the bar, or had fled through the door when the shots thundered through the room.

Sole lifted the Glock, pressed the magazine release button, and pulled the slide to eject the round in the chamber. Then he picked up the revolver from the floor where Bernardo had dropped it, opened the cylinder, and emptied the rounds, letting them scatter on the floor. He motioned with the Colt.

"Sit down."

Gustavo sat in the chair beside Bernardo, his eyes focused on the pistol in Sole's hand.

"Don't move until I'm gone." Sole nodded. "I will kill you. You believe that?"

Gustavo nodded.

"Good."

Sole backed away at an angle that allowed him to scan for threats behind him. Everyone who remained in the cantina was on the floor or hiding behind the bar. This wasn't their fight.

Outside, he climbed into the pickup and gunned the engine, backing down the block to the main cross street. Juan ran from the cantina, waving his arms and shouting words that Sole could not make out over the engine noise. Then he made the turn onto the cross street and worked his way out to one of the main arteries leading to the north and away from Monterrey.

Frustrated, he pounded his fist on the steering wheel one time and then forced himself to relax and think things through.

Because of his carelessness, everything had turned to shit. The photograph, taken as he sat beside the open graves of his wife and children, had been featured prominently in the Atlanta Journal-Constitution on the evening of the funeral. It was there for anyone to find and use to identify him.

He shook his head. It was more than a careless mistake. He had been foolish. He could not allow that to happen again.

FIFTY-NINE

An Advantage

"There has been word from Monterrey."

"Word? Please be more specific, Alejandro." Juan Manuel—Bebé—Elizondo flicked ash from the end of his cigar.

His lieutenant, Alejandro Garza, stepped onto the hacienda veranda.

"We have a man there, not a senior man, but one who helps arrange shipments and maintains our contacts with the *Policía Estatal*, that sort of thing."

Elizondo eyed Garza curiously. "It is not like you to avoid coming directly to the point, Alejandro. I assume this means the word you bring is not news that will be pleasant company here on my veranda as I watch the sunset over the Pacific."

"Our man has been killed," Garza said, returning to his usual blunt method of imparting information. He waited a moment for Bebé to absorb the news and added as a point of clarification, "By a *norteamericano*."

Elizondo puffed the cigar until the end glowed cherry

red, held the smoke in his mouth for several seconds then let it drift up and away into the as he considered the implications.

"So, you think the one who killed our man is the one we have been waiting for?"

"I cannot be certain yet." Garza nodded. "But the man who did this matches the description."

Garza took a folded piece of paper from the breast pocket of his jacket and placed it on the table beside Elizondo. The picture of the American police officer, John Sole, had been downloaded from a story shortly after the murder of his wife and partner in Atlanta more than a year earlier.

Elizondo took the picture in his hand and stared into the eyes. The police officer looked haggard, worn with care and grief. The photo image had been captured by a newspaper photographer as he left the funeral of his wife and children.

"After so much time." Elizondo looked from the picture to Garza. "You still think he seeks a way to have his revenge for the loss of his family."

"Time is of no consequence to a man like this." Garza knew this because placed in the same circumstances he would have reacted identically and would be just as unstoppable. He shook his head. "And it is not revenge he seeks."

"What then?" Bebé looked up, curious as always to hear the thoughts of his enigmatic friend and partner.

"*Un ajuste de cuentas … justicia.*" A settling of accounts … justice.

"You think it is simply to balance the scales, a banker making sure that all the debits and credits are in their proper order and the bank account is in balance." Now Bebé shook his head. "That seems so passionless."

"No, not without passion," Garza corrected. "Justice is

his passion. It is what molded him. He served in the U.S. Military, fought in a war, and was a police officer. All of these parts of his life molded him, leaving him to believe in only one idea."

"And that idea is justice, not vengeance driven by remorse, agony over the loss of his wife and children?" Bebé's voice showed that for once, he doubted Garza's assessment of the situation. "It is an interesting theory, Alejandro."

"It is important to understand our enemy," Garza explained. "Vengeance is hot-blooded, thoughtless, and careless."

"And this man is not."

"He is not." Garza's eyes were intense as he tried to convey the seriousness of the point he was making. "His need for justice was brought on by his loss, but he will not be careless or rash. He made a mistake today, allowing himself to be identified and then killing our man, but he will not repeat it. I have known men like this. His planning will be cold and calculating. When he finally comes to us, he will be dangerous, perhaps the most dangerous enemy we have faced."

"I see." Bebé Elizondo settled back in his chair as the sun dipped below the horizon, casting a final flash of orange across the water. He looked at Garza. "What are your plans?"

"I am making inquiries. We must find him and take the initiative, and we must be equally calculating in our preparations."

Elizondo ran the lighter's flame over the tip of the cigar that had gone cold as they spoke. "As always I leave these matters in your hands, Alejandro. Now sit here with me and enjoy the final afterglow of the sunset. After that, we will have some wine. Tomorrow you can determine how you will deal with our calculating seeker of justice."

Garza took the chair beside Elizondo's, but he was not waiting for tomorrow to plan. He was already considering their options as Elizondo admired the sunset.

A man driven by the need for justice would also be guided by a moral code, a sense of right and wrong. Garza's only concern was to eliminate the threat at all costs no matter who might be harmed in the process. Right and wrong did not enter into his planning.

If their enemy was calculating and cold, Garza was ruthless and unconstrained by any code of morality. In his mind, he had the advantage.

SIXTY

No One Would Ever Know

Sole had kicked in enough doors to recognize forced entry when he saw it. Isabella's door hung half off its hinges, the frame shattered around the lock. His hand moved to the .45 still in his waistband.

Pistol out in front of him in a two-handed combat posture, he nudged the door out of the way with his boot and advanced into the living room. He took a quick look to either side for threats and walked the few feet into the kitchen. Other than a chair turned over and the table pushed across the room, nothing seemed out of place, except the blood on the floor.

Sole knelt and examined the blood. It was fresh, still damp to the touch. He rose and advanced into the hallway that led to the bedrooms. The first was empty. He moved to the door at the end of the hall and pivoted quickly into the room crouching, ready to face the intruder.

"Thank God you're here." Isabella turned from the dresser where she was dabbing with a tissue at the blood still dripping from her lip.

Sole thumbed the safety, tucked the pistol in his waistband, and crossed the room. She came into his arms and buried her head against his chest.

"Isabella, what happened?" He wrapped his arms around her.

"He's gone," she sobbed.

"Who? The person who broke in?"

"Yes," she nodded. "But that's not what I mean. Sandy's gone."

"Gone? Where? Why?"

He pushed her away, holding her shoulders at arm's length. "Tell me what happened. All of it."

There was a lot to tell, and for the next ten minutes, she bared her soul. Gradually, he pieced together the story and had a reasonably clear picture of what had happened and what had to be done.

Sandy was in love with a girl named Jacinta, an illegal immigrant. Tom Krieg smuggled illegals in his trucks and had brought her over to be used and then sold. Sandy found out and went to take Jacinta away. Krieg wanted her back and was in a rage. He broke into the house, beat Sherm Westerfield, and slapped Isabella around. Then he stormed out.

"Any idea where Sandy would have gone?"

"No." She shook her head and sobbed. "He hates me, but there's something else you should know."

The time for secrets was over. She was dragging him into a quagmire, and he had a right to hear everything before he decided to wade in or not.

She took a deep breath. This was the hardest part. "Krieg is Sandy's father. We were in high school. I was stupid, got in his truck with him one night, and we did what kids do. I got pregnant. He wanted me to get rid of the baby, but I wouldn't. Since then, he has threatened to take Sandy away from me to keep me quiet about things."

"Take him away, how? Courts don't usually take a child away from its mother. Even Tom Krieg would have a hard time trying to prove you weren't a fit mother."

"Courts wouldn't have anything to do with it." Her eyes watered and the tears began falling again. "He said he would do what I should have done before he was born … get rid of him. He swore I would never see Sandy again. I know him. He would do it." She shook her head, her lip trembling. "I didn't want to lose my son, so I kept quiet about everything."

Sole held her close. "You did what you had to do, Isabella. It may take time, but Sandy will understand that."

She buried her face in her hands. "I'm so ashamed." She shook her head, sobs shaking her body. "So many people hurt. God knows how many … girls like Jacinta. I said nothing, and now, I've lost my son anyway."

Suddenly, she sagged against him as if telling him the truth had sapped the last bit of strength from her.

"Stop blaming yourself. You're one of Krieg's victims. We'll find Sandy. He'll understand."

"You'll stay then?" She looked up at him.

"Not going anywhere." He leaned down and kissed her cheek, careful to avoid the bruised lip.

A thought occurred to him, and he lifted his head up to look into her eyes. "Where's Sherm?"

"He left. Told Krieg that he wasn't going to let him get away with it, that he would report everything to the sheriff, except we didn't know who to trust, only you and Reggie Prince. I waited here for you, and he left to find Reggie Prince."

"We have to go." Sole spun abruptly and led her from the room.

Sherm Westerfield arrived at his shack, hoping to see Reggie's car there, but he was nowhere in sight. That wasn't unusual. Reggie came and went as he pleased, but he'd been around a lot lately. Sherm figured it was because of some trouble with the law back in Houston.

Reggie never talked about it, and Sherm never asked, but it was pretty clear that Reggie lived on the dark side of things when he wasn't around the shack. He didn't begrudge him that and never pried, but he did offer a prayer for him now and again, especially when he hadn't been around in a while.

"Probably gone into Brownsville for some fun," Sherm said as he stopped the truck in the dirt yard and got out.

He stomped the dust off his boots on the porch and went inside for a cold rag and ice to hold against his swollen jaw, then headed back out to sit on a crate, drink a beer, and wait for Reggie. When he got there, they would go find Isabella and Bill Myers and try to come up with some sort of plan and figure which law enforcement officer or agency, if any, hadn't been bought by Krieg. Then they could report things and end his smuggling operation and get help finding Sandy and the girl, Jacinta.

When he returned to the porch, he found another vehicle pulled up in the yard. Sherm realized it must have rolled in slow over the dirt trail with the headlights off so he couldn't see it approach.

"Who's that?" He said, leaning forward to peer into the dark.

A dark figure stepped from behind Sherm's truck.

"Damn, you're a big fella," Sherm called out. "Come closer so I can see you clear."

"Close enough," a deep voice replied in a rumbling voice.

Sherm had no time to comprehend what happened next. Moving at twelve hundred feet per second, the nine 00 buckshot pellets from the shotgun peppered his face and chest before his brain registered the sound. It's possible the exploding flash from the muzzle, moving at the speed of light, sparked a neuron or two somewhere down deep in his subconscious, but no one would ever know. Sherm Westerfield was dead.

SIXTY-ONE

Focused

A helicopter landing in such a small, out of the way village would typically have been an event of immense curiosity to the locals. Tonight the residents of Correlia huddled in their homes behind doors and windows they covered with blankets and sheets. No one wanted to see the visitor, or more correctly, no one wanted to be seen catching a glimpse of the person arriving on the helicopter.

Prying into cartel business was unhealthy. Whatever was happening in the shack where Juan Galdo lived with his mother was between them and their cartel visitor.

The rotor continued to spin overhead as the engines wound down. Alejandro Garza stepped out and walked calmly to the man waiting beside a car at the edge of the landing field. Two others, one large and bulky, the other lean and muscular, both in floral shirts, followed him out and took up positions on either side. Each held an automatic rifle and had a pistol tucked in their waistband.

"He's waiting for us," The man said and opened the passenger door to the car he had driven.

Garza said nothing and took a seat. The men with him glared at the man who had driven the car and then climbed into the rear seat. When they were in, the driver scurried around to the other side and climbed behind the wheel.

It was a short drive, and no one spoke. They covered the mile from the field to the little house at the other end of the village in a few minutes. When they arrived at the shack, a police officer from Monterrey, off-duty but in full uniform, met them by the door.

"He is inside, waiting for you." The officer smiled politely and nodded.

Garza nodded at the two security men. "Wait here." He looked at the police officer and added, "You too."

The officer's face showed his disappointment, but he remained stationed by the front door. The security men moved to either side of the shack, weapons in their hands, peering out into the night.

Garza nodded for the driver to open the door and lead the way inside. Juan Galdo sat at a small table by the wood stove in the main room that served as living room, kitchen, and his bedroom. Across from him was Gustavo, the fumble-fingered security man who had not been able to protect Bernardo from the North American.

"Are we alone?" Garza asked the driver.

"*Si señor, absolutamente.*"

"And his mother?"

"She is with a friend at another home in the village. No one else is here."

Satisfied, Garza nodded and reached into the breast pocket of his jacket, removed a piece of paper and unfolded it. He placed it on the table in front of Juan.

"Is this the man?"

Juan stared down at the image on the paper. It was the same image Bernardo had shown at the cantina.

"*Sí, sí*. That's the fucking *gringo* that killed my cousin." Juan looked up to see Garza watching him and then looked away again, muttering, "I thought he was going to kill me too."

"Did he threaten you? Shoot at you?"

"No, no, nothing like that, *señor*."

"What did he say?"

"That he wanted to sell *cocaína* for *Los Salvajes*." Juan was becoming nervous. He had to swallow hard to get the words out. "You must understand, sir. I thought he was serious. I thought this would be a good thing for Bernardo ... and for you."

"Don't be afraid. You acted correctly. The fault is with those who should have stopped him."

Garza turned to Gustavo whose perpetually red face was almost purple. "And you? Is this the man who came to the cantina?"

Gustavo extended a trembling finger and turned the picture toward him as if it might bite him. "Yes, sir. That is the man who came to the cantina."

Garza reached down, picked up the paper, and nodded. "Very well." He placed an envelope on the table in front of Juan. "Open it."

Juan opened the flap and peered inside then looked up stunned. "*Gracias, señor. Muchas gracias.*"

"There are twenty thousand Mexican pesos in that envelope, the equivalent of a thousand US dollars. Pesos will be easier for you and your mother to spend. If I gave you dollars, someone would cheat you out of their value. Do you understand?"

"*Sí señor. Esto es muy excelente! Gracias, gracias.*" Yes, sir. This is very excellent!

"You understand what this means?" Garza nodded at the envelope.

"Yes, I think." Juan was leery.

"It means you work for us now, and that you will not speak of our meeting, of what happened in Monterrey, you will not say a word to anyone, no matter who asks."

"Yes, yes." Juan nodded fervently. "I understand."

"Good." Garza turned to the door. Over his shoulder, he called to Gustavo, "You come with us."

The blood drained from the bumbling security man's face, changing it from purple to white. He rose and moved numbly to the door, giving a desperate backward glance at Juan, who ignored him as he cradled the envelope to his breast.

Outside, Garza handed another, smaller envelope to the police officer who thanked him profusely and extended his hopes that he could be of service in the future. Then he walked to the car.

The back seat was crowded, with fat Gustavo seated between Garza's oversized security men, but the drive was short. As they exited the car, one of the security men led Gustavo to the waiting chopper where the rotor was spinning and the engine warming up.

Garza asked a final question of the driver. "He will be there?"

"Yes." The driver nodded. "Everyone is to be there. Those are the orders."

"Good."

Garza turned to the helicopter without another word. As it lifted from the field, the driver squinted into the whirling dust cloud it left behind. A smile played across his face in the dark. He envisioned a prosperous future, with more envelopes, much larger than the one Garza had given to Juan, stacked in neat piles in front of him.

Alejandro Garza sat quietly in the helicopter, scanning his phone for messages and making meticulous notes on his calendar. Somewhere over the Sierra Madre Oriental, the two guards stood up, opened the side door, and tossed a pleading Gustavo out.

"Shoot me!" he begged. "I don't want to die like this! Shoot me!"

They didn't, and his last screams faded away in the rotor wash as he disappeared into the black. Focused on other matters, Garza never looked up.

SIXTY-TWO

I Expect You Know About These Things

The headlights lit up the bloody spectacle on the porch like a spotlight on a stage. Reggie Prince sat on the planks, his back against the wall of the shack, his face buried in one hand while the other rested gently on Sherm's lifeless chest. He looked up into the light, his eyes glistening with his tears.

Isabella sat in stunned horror. Sole was out of the truck instantly, the .45 in his hand as he moved to the porch, scanning the area for threats. Satisfied that there were none, he approached Reggie. Isabella exited the pickup and followed.

"They killed him." Reggie shook his head as if that might make it not true. "He was like a father to me, and they shot him down."

He leaned over and stared at Sherm's chest, looking, hoping for some sign of life. His hand clenched at the front of the dead man's shirt. He trembled with anguish.

"I should have been here," Reggie said through his tears. "Should have stopped them from hurting him."

"It's not your fault," Isabella said. "You didn't know what was happening."

Reggie raised his eyes, a puzzled look on his face.

"But you knew? That's why you're here. You came here because you were worried about Sherm," he said, putting things together in his mind as he spoke. "You figured something was going to happen to him."

"We weren't sure." Sole shook his head. "But yes, we were worried about him."

"Why?" Reggie glared at them. "Did you do something to cause this?"

Isabella began sobbing again. "I didn't mean to."

"What does that mean?" Reggie shouted. "Who did this?"

"I have a good idea," Sole said. "Or at least an idea about who is behind it." He looked at Isabella. "Tell him."

She nodded and recounted the events of the day. When she got to the end, Reggie pounded a fist against the shack's wall.

"Krieg! I'll kill the son of a bitch!"

"Slow down." Sole nodded and looked into Reggie's eyes. "We want the same thing."

"No." Reggie shook his head. "No, we don't."

Sole mounted the step and reached out to touch Reggie on the shoulder. "You should move away from the body. This is a crime scene now. There may be evidence."

"Krieg owns the law around here. Krieg is going to pay for this ... my way."

"He'll pay. I promise."

Reggie looked up. "You're a cop, aren't you? Or at least you were."

"I'm a man, like you," Sole replied.

"I knew it the first time we met. The way you looked at me, saw things with those cop eyes, trying to see what's underneath, what's behind everything. And now, talking about this being a crime scene." Reggie's face twisted into a sneer. "Yeah, you're a cop."

"Whatever I was before, this is who I am now, Sherm's friend … and yours if you want a friend."

"Sherm liked you." Reggie pushed himself up straight and ran the back of his arm over his face to wipe away the tears. "He trusted you." He laughed. "Except that name … Bill Myers … he said you shoulda picked a better name than that."

Isabella was on the porch with them now. She reached down and took Reggie's arm. He stood, and she wrapped her arms around him in an embrace, letting her own tears fall on his shoulder.

After a minute, she lifted her head and looked at Sole. "We have to tell someone … the sheriff?"

"No." He shook his head. "That's what Sherm said he was going to do, and this is what happened."

"So we do nothing?" she asked.

"I didn't say that."

Reggie was overcoming his shock, anger pushing the pain to the background. His eyes went from one to the other. "I want Krieg dead, not in jail."

"If you want justice for Sherm, so do I," Sole said. "And for all the others."

"I don't care about the others," Reggie said bluntly.

"I would have thought that slavery was something you would care about."

"Careful what you say, white man, using a word like that to me. You don't know anything about it?"

About slavery?" Sole shook his head. "True enough. Never been a slave and none of my ancestors were slaves to my knowledge, but I know it when I see it and those girls, kidnapped, abused, sold off like property he owned ... that's slavery."

Reggie was quiet for a moment, then nodded. "Fair enough. So what do we do, *Bill the cop?*"

Reggie threw the name at him like a dirty word. Sole looked from Reggie to Isabella. It was time for truth, or at least a part of it.

"Call me, John."

"John," Reggie said simply. "That's a start, I suppose."

Isabella put a hand on Sole's arm. "What do we do ... John?"

"Sooner or later, the sheriff will get involved. This is a murder, and they will start looking for suspects among those closest to Sherm." He paused to let that sink in.

"You mean us," Reggie said.

"That's where they will start. If they're any good at investigating, they'll figure things out and move on ... unless they're on Krieg's payroll."

"So we're back to square one. Who do we trust?" Isabella asked.

"For now, just us," Sole said.

"Told you, I'm not waiting for the law," Reggie growled. "One thing is sure. I don't trust any law around here."

"Neither do I," Sole agreed. "But if you want justice for Sherm, we have to move fast and do what has to be done before the law is involved, whether we want them here or not."

"So what do we do?" Reggie asked.

"We find the person Krieg wants, and we'll find Krieg."

"Sandy," Isabella said, and her eyes widened with concern. "And the girl, Jacinta. You think they're in danger." She shook her head. "I was hoping if they got away, they'd be safe."

"They won't be safe until Krieg is gone."

"Gone? You mean …" She looked from Sole to Reggie.

Their eyes said it all. It wasn't just Reggie. Neither was inclined to see Tom Krieg make it to prison.

She wondered what that said about the man who had come into her life so unexpectedly. She nodded, accepting their sense of justice as her own and wondered what that said about her.

"Did Sandy have money?" Sole asked Isabella.

"A little. A few hundred dollars in cash, maybe."

"That won't get them far. Can he get more?"

"Yes." Isabella nodded. Her son did not do things halfway and did not act rashly. He would think things through and make a plan. "There is more money."

"Where?" Sole and Reggie spoke in unison.

"In a bank in Laredo." She paused and shook her head. "There wouldn't have been enough time for him to get there to make a withdrawal today."

"That means they're holed up somewhere, a place they feel safe." Sole looked out into the night. "Big country … any idea where they might go … someplace Sandy knows."

"It could be anywhere," Isabella shook her head. "He knows this country like the back of his hand, every nook and cranny. If he wants to hide, he'd have no problem staying out of sight."

"But he has Jacinta with him. He might be more selective about his hiding place with her to take care of."

"There's a place," Reggie interjected. "It's where he used to go sometimes with Sherm. I was there with them a few times. A little hunt cabin in the backcountry." He looked from one to the other and nodded. "It's a place with good memories. If I was hiding out, it's where I would go."

"How far?" Sole asked.

"Couple of hours," Reggie said.

"Let's go." Sole looked at Isabella. "You come with us. You're not safe with Krieg on a rampage."

"I had no intention of letting you leave without me." She brushed past him moving toward the pickup. "That's my son out there."

"What about Sherm?" Reggie asked, looking down at the old man's mangled body.

"Leave him where he is." Sole put a hand on his shoulder. "It's hard, but we can't move him. If we try, there will be signs. It'll look like we were involved in his death, trying to cover it up in some way. It's best to leave him and let someone else discover the body."

"Alright, *John-the-cop*," Reggie said. "I expect you know about these things."

"I do."

SIXTY-THREE

Time to Go

Sunrise was hours away when Sandy stirred and sat up. He moved slowly, gently taking his arm from under Jacinta's head and looked down at her sleeping form. After the horrors she had experienced, she seemed at peace in her dreams.

Could he really do this—take her away, escape Tom Krieg and his money and influence? In his anger the day before, everything seemed possible. Now, he felt far less sure of himself.

Jacinta turned, and her eyes fluttered open. A smile crossed her face, and she lifted a hand to touch his face.

"You're still here," she said, her fingers running along his cheek. "I was afraid it was a dream … that I would wake and you would be gone, and I would still be back in that house."

She shuddered. He leaned down and let his lips brush against her cheek. "I'm here."

And like that, his courage and confidence returned. He pushed himself up and stretched, arching his back and lifting his arms high over his head, finishing with a giant yawn and a shake of his head.

Jacinta laughed. "You look like a shaggy monkey when you do that."

"And you look beautiful," he said, smiling down at her.

"I don't feel beautiful, only dirty and bruised."

"I'll get you some water to wash," he said, reaching for the pail again to empty one of the water jugs into it. "We'll be leaving soon."

"So soon?" She squinted into the dark toward the crack around the door. "It's still night outside."

"Yes, I'm sorry, but we can't stay here long. We have another three-hour drive to Laredo where the bank is. That's where I can get money. I have an account there. I've been saving for years, and my mother put money in too. I'll take my share, and we'll have all we need, at least for a while, but I want to be there when the bank opens so we can get away as soon as possible."

He lit the lantern and then filled the pail as he spoke, placing it in front of her. "Here, let me help you up."

She washed using a piece of a bar of soap he gave her and drying with a towel. He turned away to give her privacy.

"Are you always going to do that? Turn away?"

"I just thought …"

"That I am a shy school girl?" She laughed. "No, there is no school girl here. Not anymore. I want you to see me as I am."

He turned, and his heart leaped into his throat. Her clothes lay on the floor. The marks of the beating Krieg had given her were visible, but they could not dim the vision before him.

"You are beautiful, Jacinta."

She smiled and extended her hand to him. He stepped forward into her arms. She stroked the side of his face with her fingertips as they kissed, and he thought his knees might buckle under him.

After a minute, she broke away and lowered herself onto the blankets. She held a hand up to him.

"We don't have to," he managed to croak out, breathless at the vision before him. "I don't want to hurt you."

"You won't. I know you'll be gentle." She took his hand and pulled him down to her.

He wasn't sure what to do. She pulled him closer on the blankets, their lips touching, her body warm and full against him.

"Reynaldo, I have been taken by men." She shook her head. "But I have never been loved by a man. I want you to love me … to make love to me, Reynaldo."

They lay together with the lantern light casting their flickering shadows against the wall. Their lovemaking had a dreamlike quality to it. Every touch, every caress bound them together, not just for the moment, but for the future, whatever that might bring.

As their passion ebbed, they lay side by side, her head nestled against his chest. Sandy—Reynaldo—wondered about that future. In a few minutes, they would leave this place. As shabby as the cabin was, it was a home for them, but they couldn't stay. They had no supplies, and it was just a matter of time before Krieg found them.

He pondered where they should go and what to do next. There were so many questions. Yes, he had money in the bank, but eventually, they would have to settle down somewhere. What would he do to support them? How would they get Jacinta into the country legally?

Then, there was his mother. She had kept a terrible

secret from him, but already, his anger was fading. Whatever else she was, whatever else she had done, she had brought him into the world and loved him and provided for him in the best way she could. If she was flawed, so was he. Would she be safe with them on the run, or would Krieg threaten her, harm her in some way as a weapon to draw them home?

He had no answers. Jacinta murmured as she dozed and he held her closer. He was sure about only one thing. They had to get moving and keep moving until they were somewhere where Krieg would never find them. After that, there would be time to come up with answers to the other questions.

He stirred and touched Jacinta's face with his fingers. Her eyes opened, and she smiled.

"It's time to go," he said as he helped her up to face the day.

SIXTY-FOUR

More Important Business

"Any idea where we're going?" Isabella stared out into the dark through the passenger window.

"No," Sole said. "Following Reggie to Sherm's cabin. I take it you were never there."

"No." She shook her head. "Sandy would go with him during hunting season. It was their man-time." She smiled at the memory of her son coming back excited and full of stories about the cabin and hunting and sneaking his first beer without Mom around. "Male bonding. I was never invited. Sherm looked after Sandy."

"He was a good man." Sole nodded.

"Yes, the kind of man Sandy needed in his life," she agreed. "If I could only have been as good a mother."

"Stop blaming yourself." He reached out to put his hand over hers. "Sandy is a fine young man. He's that way because of you, not because of the asshole sperm donor who got you pregnant."

"I lied to him." She shook her head and turned back to the window. "All those years, I lied to him."

"You protected him. Look at me, Isabella."

She turned her head toward him. The dashboard lights revealed the tears in her eyes.

"You are the victim, Isabella."

"You keep saying that." She shook her head. "I'm not so sure."

"Well, I am. I have some experience in dealing with victims, people who have been bullied and controlled by others. Many never realize they are victims until some traumatic event crashes into their lives."

"Experience." She said the word slowly and looked at him. "So, Reggie is right. You were a cop … a police officer … weren't you, John."

He hesitated for a second but realized there was no reason to deny the truth. He nodded. "Yes."

"But you're not one now, right?"

"Right."

"Mind if I ask why?"

"Personal reasons." It was a shitty answer, and he knew it. She deserved to know more, but knowing more was dangerous. The truth was he might never be able to explain everything or that he would even be alive to share his past with her.

She remained silent for a long while. Finally, she said, "Okay, John. I won't pry. I'm smart enough to see that there was someone else once and that your reasons for keeping things to yourself have something to do with her. I suppose I can live with that for now." She laughed wryly. "Seems I have no choice."

He felt like an ass, but telling her more would only put her in danger. Putting other people in danger seemed to be his area of expertise, and he was determined that this time the person he cared about would not be hurt.

"One more question," she said, turning to him.

"Yes?"

"Is John your real name?"

He laughed. "It is."

Up ahead, the tail lights of Reggie's truck turned and disappeared off the dirt trail they had been following for an hour. Sole followed and pulled up in a small clearing. Reggie was already out, advancing toward a small cabin. Sole and Isabella followed.

"This is it," Reggie said, pulling the door open.

They followed him into the dark interior. He fumbled with something by the door and a moment later light from a lantern cast a glow around the two small rooms. Reggie moved through to the next room.

"They've been here." He lifted a galvanized pail. "It's still damp inside. They poured water into it." He pointed at a corner. "There are the empty water jugs Sherm kept here."

Isabella held up a plastic bag. "Sandy was definitely here. Potato chip and snack cake wrappers in the bag."

"How long do you think they've been gone?" Sole asked.

"Hard to say," Reggie said. "They must have been in a hurry to move on to leave in the middle of the night.

"Trying to put as much distance between them and Krieg." Sole nodded. "Smart, staying off the roads in daylight and moving at night." He looked at Isabella. "What about that bank, in Laredo?"

"They'll need money. I think that's where he would head."

"Alright then, let's get on the road."

He led the way from the cabin, and a minute later, they were backtracking along the trail to the main county road.

As they drove, Sole's cell phone chimed. He recognized the number.

"Who's that?" Isabella asked.

"Looks like K and Z Trucking are trying to contact me," he said and put the phone on the console.

"What about?" Isabella's brow furrowed in concern. "About this ... about Sandy?"

"I doubt it," he said reassuringly. "Krieg doesn't know I'm out here with you. Probably work-related ... one of their all-hands-on-deck calls to get everyone there."

"You going to answer?"

"Nope. They can leave a message. I've got more important business."

SIXTY-FIVE

Words Were Cheap

"What the hell is he doing here?" Raul Zabala squinted under the security lights that lit the K and Z lot at night.

A pickup he recognized pulled off the main road and stopped on the far side of the lot. It was after midnight, and their crew had a busy day ahead. They didn't need any distractions.

Tom Krieg turned to stare in the direction of Claude Brainerd's personal vehicle and scowled. "He's here to see me ... personal business."

"What sort of personal business?"

"Not your affair." Krieg shot a warning look in Zabala's direction. "Stay out of it."

"If it affects what we do here, it is my business." For once, Zabala put aside his easy-going façade and met Krieg's domineering defiance with his own. "Brainerd here, today, when we have a shit storm about to hit, and it makes me think something is going on I should know about."

"There's nothing that concerns you."

"Bullshit." Zabala nodded at the line of men standing in

front of a row of assorted unmarked pickups, SUVs, and vans. "In case you forgot, we're going to war today."

Krieg glared but said nothing. Zabala turned to the men.

"Alright. Everyone listen up." Zabala eyed the men up and down the line. "We have good information that today's the day. You know your job. When Diaz shows his hand, you come in and end things. Put them down hard and fast. Any questions?"

Zabala waited, watching the faces before him. There were no questions.

"Good." He nodded. "This ends today. When it's done, there's a five thousand dollar bonus in it for each of you."

Zabala turned to Krieg who stood staring at him. They had not discussed the bonus money in advance. Tough shit, Zabala thought. Krieg's preoccupation with his personal affairs had left Zabala to make decisions about the operation, and he made this one, knowing Krieg would be pissed.

"Anything you want to add?" he asked his partner.

Krieg shook his head, working to control his temper in front of the men.

"Everyone accounted for?" Zabala asked the team leaders, Stu Pearce and Sid 'Shorts' Culper.

"Everyone except Myers," Stu responded.

"He get the call?"

"Everyone got the call." Stu nodded. "He never answered. Left him a voice mail but no response."

Zabala shot Krieg an annoyed look. No doubt, Myers' absence was related to whatever personal business was on Krieg's mind.

"Alright. He just lost his job. If we can't rely on him today, we can't rely on him ever. Besides, one less gun won't matter. You boys have all the firepower you need." Zabala grinned at the men. "Tequila and beer on me when you get back. Now, get it done."

They loaded quickly, jostling each other, joking and making cracks about the bonus. That was something they had not expected. The bosses must really want this done right, and done right meant they wanted Diaz and his sons dead. They had every intention of doing things right and earning their bonuses.

The vehicles pulled away, and Zabala turned to his partner. "Let's hear it."

Krieg stiffened, unaccustomed to being challenged, even by Zabala. "Mind your tongue, Raul."

Zabala was not backing down. "I'll mind my tongue when you put your dick back in your pants and tell me what's going on." He smirked. "That's right. I know about the girl. Heard the rumors that Sandy Palmeras came and took her away. Doyle's been talking to some of the boys."

"I said it's none of your business," Krieg said through gritted teeth.

"It is absolutely my business. Your whoring around with one of the girls is one thing. You going on a rampage is something else." Zabala jerked a thumb toward Brainerd who waited by his pickup, intent on the body language between the two men. "What did you have him do? I want to know now. If we have to fix things, I'm the one with the cool head, not you."

Zabala motioned to Brainerd to wave him over. The deputy shuffled in their direction, unsure about what was happening or whether he wanted any part of it.

When Brainerd stopped a few feet away in a weak attempt to avoid the line of fire, Zabala looked at him. "You're going to tell me everything."

Brainerd looked at Krieg and swallowed. "I, uh …" He hesitated to say more.

"Fuck it," Krieg said suddenly. "Tell him. What's done is done. Best he knows anyway."

The deputy reviewed the recent assignments he had received from Krieg. Zabala had approved, along with Krieg, the murder of Lucky Martin, so that information came as no surprise. Brewer was another matter.

"You killed a Border Patrol agent?" Zabala's face was incredulous. "Are you insane?"

"Don't say that." Krieg stiffened. "Don't ever say that. He was onto us. Found him prowling around down by the river. It seemed pretty clear that he knew we were involved in getting rid of Martin and shooting the Mexican. It was just a matter of time before he proved it. Evidence always turns up. I had to make sure he didn't find it."

"You mean couldn't find it, so you added another body for them to investigate. How does that make things better?" Zabala shook his head. "You *are insane*."

"I said, don't say that."

Zabala ignored him and turned to Brainerd. "What else?"

The deputy looked at Krieg, confusion and fear on his face. He had never seen Krieg and Zabala at odds like this. He felt like a child walking in on a fistfight between his parents, not knowing which side to take or who would win.

"I'll tell him," Krieg said, disgusted. He faced Zabala defiantly. "I had him kill Sherm Westerfield."

"What?" Zabala reached out and grabbed the front of Krieg's shirt.

"Get your hands off me!" Krieg's fist came up and knocked his hands away. "No one touches me like that, not even you." He thumped Zabala in the chest with a forefinger. "Had to be done. He found out about our operation. Said he was going to the sheriff. If we had waited, it would be too late."

Raul Zabala stood open-mouthed, shoulders sagging under the building's security lights. He looked up into the sky and took a deep breath, staring at a distant cloud sailing past the moon, then lowered his head and looked at Krieg.

"You couldn't just fuck her and send her off like the others, could you? You made it personal. Your ego got us into this mess." Zabala shook his head in disgust. "I'll handle the fight with Diaz today. You take care of your *personal business* … all of it. You know what that means.

"I know." Krieg scowled. "Don't worry about my end of things."

There were three more witnesses, Isabella, the girl Jacinta, and Sandy Palmeras. All were a threat if they talked, and they surely would at some point. He stared into Krieg's eyes.

"Can you do it?"

"I said I'd take care of business, and I will." Krieg stared back.

"I'm sure you will." Zabala shook his head. "You are one cold motherfucker, Tom Krieg."

He turned and walked across the lot to the office building. Ella wouldn't be in for hours to make the day's coffee, but he had a bottle of tequila in his desk drawer and could use a nip now. "One more thing," Zabala called over his shoulder.

"What's that?" Krieg stood motionless, fists clenched at his side.

"Start thinking about how you want to divide up the company. Once this business with Diaz is settled, and you clear up your *personal affairs*, we're done."

As Zabala walked through the office door, Krieg stepped closer to Brainerd. "I know where they'll go. You get there first, find them, bring them to me, and there's another twenty thousand in it for you."

Claude Brainerd was no runner, but he moved across the gravel lot to his pickup like a galloping hippo and roared off into the night. Tom Krieg followed, driving away from the business he had built with Raul Zabala. His partner's words echoed in his ears. "We're done."

Words were cheap. It was what you did that counted, and Tom Krieg would do anything to hold on to what was his. Of all people, Zabala should have understood that.

SIXTY-SIX

The Streets of Laredo

It was just after five AM when they arrived in Laredo. Sandy drove by the bank to check the opening hours. The sign on the door read nine AM to four PM. He planned to be long gone by closing time.

"*¿Dónde estamos?*" Jacinta said, yawning—where are we?

She looked around, stretched, and sat up straight. "Is this the bank with the money?"

"It is, but we have time to kill."

"Killing time … that is a funny expression." She smiled and leaned over to kiss his cheek. "I should be practicing my English."

"Your English is good, getting better all the time. Are you hungry?"

"Yes, very."

"Good. We passed an all-night diner on the way into town. I'll backtrack, and we can grab some greasy bacon and eggs—*tocino grasiento y huevos*."

"*Perfecto*," she grinned.

Sandy made a u-turn in the bank parking lot and pulled onto Guadalupe Street. The diner was several miles back at the point where Highway 83 comes out of the backcountry and enters the city limits.

Traffic was light this early in the morning. Laredo is a good-sized city of a quarter-million people, but the pace of life is slower than in the Texas megalopolis regions of Dallas and Houston. Most locals were just waking up to sip their morning coffee.

Except for three cars belonging to the night cook, a waitress, and a lone customer, the diner lot was empty. Sandy pulled in and opted for a parking space across the lot from the building so that he could watch the activity inside without being seen.

A customer sat at a table in a corner away from the door, drinking coffee and reading a newspaper. The waitress leaned against the counter, chatting with the cook.

"Looks good." He pushed his door open. "Let's go. I'm hungry."

Claude Brainerd let out a long, howling yawn followed by a belch and a fart, both of which came from deep within his expansive gut and bowels. He lifted his ass and tugged at his shorts to straighten things out and make sure he hadn't shit his pants.

His gut had been rumbling for two days. The work Krieg had him doing was upsetting his system and regularity. At some point, he was going to have to find a place to take a dump. What then?

He'd been staring at the bank from the parking lot of a

closed office building across Guadalupe Street since three AM. Focus, he told himself. There is no way you can tell Krieg you missed them because you had to take a shit.

He looked around the interior of his truck for something he might use as a bedpan if it came to that. There was nothing, just some old papers strewn on the passenger side floor. He eyed them only for a moment. There was no way his fat ass was going to squat on some papers in his truck and drop a load.

He shook his head. Focus.

When they pulled into the bank lot, he almost thought he was dreaming, watching through one eye and slumped back in the seat. That lasted a second before he sat bolt upright, leaning over the steering wheel.

"Son of a bitch," muttered. "They're here."

Krieg had told him they would come here, that Sandy had money in a bank in Laredo and would go for it if he had any brains. He had no idea how Krieg had that piece of information, but he didn't argue with him. The promise of an extra twenty thousand dollars provided all the motivation Brainerd needed.

The ride from the K and Z lot was an easy drive, if monotonous. Highway 83 paralleled the Rio Grande from McAllen to Laredo. Traffic at that time of night had been almost nonexistent. He arrived at the bank three hours later after leaving Krieg.

He was familiar with Sandy Palmeras' pickup, had even stopped it a couple of times to warn the kid to slow it down. In the early morning dusk, he couldn't make out the occupants, but there was no mistaking the pickup.

After a few minutes, the truck rolled through the bank lot, turned around and pulled back onto Guadalupe Street, heading back the way they had come. Now what?

He might catch a break. If they went back to Salvia County, he could wait until they were back in his territory and get some help from Krieg before stopping them. The worry was what if they didn't stop?

How would he stop them here in Laredo? It was one thing for Krieg to give orders and tell him to bring them to him. It was something altogether different to find a way to take two people into custody, on his own and acting without legal authority. As it turned out, they made it easy for him.

"Looks good." Sandy pushed his door open. "Let's go. I'm hungry."

He barely had time to recognize Claude Brainerd. The deputy roared up beside them. His window was down. Sandy's eyes widened for a moment when he saw the taser in Brainerd's hand pointing at him from just a few feet through the window.

The darts flew into Sandy's chest. He collapsed in the open door of his pickup.

Jacinta screamed. The Brainerd sent the taser's backup shot into her stomach. She writhed in pain on the seat.

Unlike the department-issued tasers that had a charge limit of five seconds to prevent abuse, the private version offered a thirty-second charge. Fifty thousand volts for that length of time was more than enough to put down the baddest, meanest son of a bitch. Brainerd used all thirty seconds on both of them until they were nothing more than quivering masses of human ectoplasm.

He moved quickly, checking the diner window. No one was paying attention to the parking lot. After handcuffing both, hand and foot, he grabbed Sandy by the back of his pants and shirt and tossed him into the crew cab of his pickup. A few seconds later, he did the same to Jacinta. She landed on top of Sandy who had just begun to recover enough of his faculties to struggle against the shackles.

After closing the door on Sandy's truck so it would not attract attention from the diner patrons or a patrolling cop, Brainerd climbed behind the wheel of his own pickup. In the back, Jacinta moaned. Sandy began to stir, kicking his feet against the door.

"I wouldn't do that," Brainerd said over his shoulder. "Settle down, or the girl will pay the price. I'll let her ride the lightning again. How about that? Another taste of fifty thousand volts for her. You want that? You just lay there still until I say you can move."

"Let us go you son of a bitch." Sandy could barely speak, his voice strained and breathless, still feeling the effects of the taser.

"You know that's not gonna happen," Brainerd said matter-of-factly. "You've got an appointment."

"With who?"

"I always thought you were a smart boy. Who do you think?"

Sandy settled down on the floor with Jacinta lying half on top of him. Shackled hand and foot, he was trapped. Anything he did to escape would be too slow to prevent Brainerd from stopping the truck and kicking his head in, or Jacinta's.

He wanted to shriek out his anger, but the effort would be pointless. He had to remain calm. Think, analyze, assess, he told himself, and wait for that one small instant when Brainerd was careless. Then be ready to act.

In the front, Claude Brainerd sang a classic old western song off-key.

"As I walked out on the streets of Laredo, as I walked out on Laredo one day. I spied a poor cowboy wrapped in white linen, wrapped in white linen as cold as the clay …"

SIXTY-SEVEN

Possibilities

They arrived in the city limits as Laredo was stirring about and beginning its day. On the outskirts of town, they passed near an all-night diner where a confrontation had taken place not an hour earlier. They never saw the large man in a dark corner of the diner's lot struggling to load two heavy bundles into the back of his crew cab.

Isabella directed Sole to the bank on Guadalupe Street. They pulled into a parking lot across the street, followed by Reggie Prince. It was almost the exact spot where Claude Brainerd had waited and watched the bank.

Sole, Isabella, and Reggie pushed their doors open, stepped out, and stretched. Then they gathered between the two trucks.

"What now?" Reggie craned his head to look over the top of his truck to the bank lot.

"We wait," Sole said.

"For how long?"

"That's a good question." Sole gave a wry smile. "I

don't have a good answer." He looked at Isabella. "How about you?"

"The bank opens at nine. Knowing Sandy, he won't just wait there in plain view. They're probably somewhere in the area, planning to come back at opening time."

"Okay." Sole nodded. "So we wait until the bank opens."

The next two hours passed in excruciating slow motion. Isabella walked across the lot to a nearby convenience store and brought back cups of black coffee. It tasted terrible, but it was black and hot and helped wash the fatigue from their brains.

As the bank opened and customers began to come and go with no sign of Sandy, they became restless. Forty-five minutes after the opening, they were standing between the trucks again.

"What do we do now?" Reggie asked.

"I could have been wrong," Isabella said. "Maybe he decided not to come for the money."

Sole was quiet, thinking through their options. After a minute, he said, "The way I see it, they had two options. If they didn't chance coming here, Sandy might have figured he could earn money along the way."

"So they could be anywhere." Isabella said.

"Right."

"Like finding a needle in a haystack, or worse," Reggie added.

"Worse," Sole agreed.

"What's the second option?" Isabella asked, not willing to accept the possibility that her son and Jacinta were gone.

"Number two is not good." Sole's voice was somber. "They may not have come to the bank because someone stopped them."

Isabella's face paled. "You mean Krieg found them."

"Just a possibility," Sole tried to reassure her. "We don't know where they are."

"So that brings me back to my question," Reggie said. "What do we do?"

"At this point, I think we have to follow the possibility that gives us the best odds."

"What does that mean?" Isabella's brow furrowed with concern.

"The odds against finding them out on the highway are astronomical," Sole explained. "There's too much country for them to disappear into. If they hopped on Interstate 35, they could be two states away by now. The more time that passes, the farther away they are and the slimmer our chances of finding them. On the other hand …"

"What?" Isabella asked.

"If Krieg intercepted them, we know exactly where they are." He looked from one to the other. "And that's also where they will be in the most immediate danger."

"So we go to Krieg," Isabella interjected. The concern on her face morphed into outright fear.

"Yes," Reggie whispered, the memory of Sherm's mangled body on the porch vivid in his mind. "We go to Krieg."

SIXTY-EIGHT

Rat Trap

The convoy wound through the narrow back streets of Torreón. Stu Pearce, in the front pickup, put a hand out the window and the procession came to a halt, lining up along the curb of an alley near the Nuevo México district, a neighborhood controlled by rifle-toting cartel gang members.

Pearce got out of the pickup while the driver kept the engine running, peering nervously around at the surrounding shacks and houses. This was enemy territory for *gringos*.

"Relax," Stu said. "Everyone's in bed, and if anyone is awake and wondering what a line of vehicles loaded with armed men are doing outside their house, trust me. They aren't going to come out nosing around."

He walked toward the rear of the procession and met Shorts Culper getting out of the van he was in five cars back. As the leaders of the K and Z expeditionary force, it had been deemed best for them to travel in separate vehicles.

"You sure this is the right spot?" Shorts asked, looking around at the darkened houses.

"Yep." Stu nodded. "Came through here a couple of times with Lopez. That's why we picked it. Won't be no *policía* snooping around in this neighborhood."

"Okay." Shorts stretched and yawned. "I could use some coffee to wake me up."

"Sorry. Already drank what I brought with me. I expect you'll be awake enough when the bullets start flying."

"I expect so," Shorts agreed with a nod, wishing he'd brought a second thermos of his wife's coffee. "Sure would like to get this done and get back across the border. Feel like I'm on another planet."

"I reckon we are the aliens here. Kind of comical ain't it. We're the illegals on the wrong side of the Rio Grande." Stu laughed. "That's what they call ironical. Just keep thinking about that bonus Zabala promised. That'll make the time pass quick enough."

A rooster crowed from a nearby house. Shorts turned to study the surrounding neighborhood.

Both men were tired, as were the twenty others in the vehicles with them. It had taken coordination for all to cross the border at different points and times to avoid raising suspicions about their purpose. That ate up a good part of the night, and the drive to Torreón had used up the rest.

"What time you got?" Shorts asked.

Stu looked at the glowing dial on his old Timex. "Just after five."

"Soon," Shorts said, relieved.

"Soon," Stu agreed and took out his cell phone.

"Here. Take this." Pepe Lopez held out a nine-millimeter pistol to Father Alfonso.

"A gun?" The priest shook his head. "I can't do that ... carry a gun ... use it to harm another. Whatever else I am, whatever else I have done, I am still a priest."

"That is not going to keep the bullets from putting holes in your head. You may need to defend yourself when Diaz realizes he has been deceived into attacking our little caravan."

Alfonso stared at the pistol.

"Your choice." Pepe shrugged and started to lower it. "Your life."

Alfonso reached out suddenly and took the gun. "Show me how to use it."

Pepe gave him a five-minute briefing on how to release the safety, aim, and squeeze the trigger. When he was done, he looked into the priest's sweating face and figured that he would be a dead man before the day was through.

"And you?" Pepe turned to Mario Acosta. "Are you armed?"

"Yes, of course." Mario lifted his shirt to reveal a military version Beretta Model 92F.

"Careful. That big *pistola* is gonna pull your pants down." Pepe laughed. "Or shoot your balls off."

"Let's just get moving."

"Soon," Pepe said.

Alfonso took a cell phone from his pocket and looked at the time display. "It's five fifteen."

The words had barely left his mouth when Pepe's phone chimed. He answered, nodded, and said, *"Bueno."* The others waited expectantly. "Let's get moving," he said.

They climbed into the three K and Z trucks that had

been stationed in the city. They were empty, carrying no produce and no border crossers behind their false walls.

Sargento Miguel Garcia had assigned an off-duty officer to each of the trucks as the driver. Pepe climbed into the lead truck, and Mario took the rear. Alfonso nervously boarded the middle vehicle of the caravan, missing the step and striking his forehead against the door. The driver laughed as the priest pulled himself up into the cab rubbing his head with one hand.

Engines roared to life, and the trucks began to move through the darkened streets of Torreón, headed toward the outskirts of the city in the direction of Monclova. Passing an intersection in a rundown neighborhood, Pepe leaned out the passenger window and blinked a flashlight beam three times.

"There they are." Stu hurried back to the lead pickup, and the line of vehicles loaded with K and Z men moved to follow.

Thirty minutes later, they were well out of the city and away from prying eyes. Pepe's lead truck turned down a dirt trail toward a farming village several miles off the main road. After another half mile, it rocked to a stop, and the brakes creaked on the following vehicles as they slowed in unison.

There was no time to waste, and the loading went quickly. The K and Z assault team climbed out of the six vehicles that had brought them across the border and loaded into the rear of the marked K and Z trucks, six armed fighters to each truck. Stu Pearce led a team into Pepe Lopez's truck in the front of the convoy, and Shorts Culper climbed into the rear truck where Mario Acosta watched in frightened awe.

As the traitor, he was the only one present who had

been kept out of the plan to trap Diaz. It dawned on him at once that there would be a fight, and the chances were excellent that he would end up in the crossfire, both sides considering him an enemy.

Pepe Lopez walked back to his truck, smiling. "Give me your gun." His pistol was pointed at Mario's face."

"But I …"

"Hand it over."

Mario handed the Beretta out the window.

"Good. You should have remembered which side you are on." Pepe took the pistol from his trembling hand. "If you try to run away, Garcia's men have orders to shoot you down. Play your role, and there is a chance that you may survive this day."

Pepe turned without saying more, went to the front of the procession, and climbed in his truck. Mario was frozen in his seat, terrified. Diaz would think he betrayed him. Krieg and Zabala already knew he had betrayed them.

The three K and Z trucks proceeded toward Monclova. Mario Acosta watched dazed as the lead vehicle bumped along the dirt road. Both sides had set a trap for the rats, and he was the first rat caught.

SIXTY-NINE

A Lie

"Where do you want them?" Claude Brainerd checked on his passengers in the rearview mirror as he spoke on his cell phone.

"Bring them to the barn," Krieg replied. "This could get messy."

"Right." Brainerd disconnected and spoke over his shoulder, smiling. "Won't be long now."

"You bastard," Sandy snarled, straining at the shackles.

"That's funny, coming from you." Brainerd chuckled as he made the final turn onto the drive to the Krieg ranch.

They passed the house and went to the back lot where Brainerd drove his truck through the barn's wide bay door. Tom Krieg waited inside, standing in the center of the immense space.

"Packages delivered," Brainerd said, grinning as he climbed out of the pickup.

If he was expecting a word of appreciation or a pat on the back for a job well done, none was forthcoming. Krieg ignored him glowering through the truck windows at Jacinta. For the moment, he ignored Sandy.

"Get them out," he ordered.

Brainerd opened the crew cab door and pulled Sandy out by the collar, letting him land with a thud on the concrete. He reached for Jacinta, and she tried to kick at him with her shackled feet.

"Bitch," he growled and took her by the hair, dragging her out head first.

"Leave her alone, you son of a bitch!" Sandy shouted and struggled against the shackles, desperate to find a way to protect her.

Tom Krieg stood over the two prostrate figures twisted side by side on the floor. Sandy glared up at him, fury burning in his eyes. Jacinta saw the devil she had escaped towering over her and wept.

"You can go," Krieg said without looking at Brainerd.

"Uh, there's the …" Brainerd hesitated. "I mean, you promised …"

"The bonus?" Krieg's head pivoted toward the deputy, annoyance on his face. "You figure I keep twenty thousand in cash lying around?" He shook his head, smirking as if to say, you really are a dumb son of a bitch. "I promised you a bonus, and you'll get it. Have I ever shorted you?"

"No," Brainerd replied meekly.

"I'll call you in a couple of days. The money will be deposited in an offshore account with a passcode that I'll give you. You'll be able to withdraw it there."

"But, I thought …"

"Leave the thinking to me. You're not very good at it." As always, Krieg was feeling mean and took it out on the person who had loyally followed his orders.

Brainerd's face flushed.

Krieg sighed, realizing he might need the deputy's assistance again soon. "Look any withdrawal over ten thousand dollars is reported to the Feds. So, I make a few smaller withdrawals for business purposes, and no one asks questions. Then I deposit the smaller amounts into the offshore account."

Brainerd's brow furrowed trying to comprehend the complexities of banking law. Krieg's patience was at an end.

"Get out … now."

Claude Brainerd nodded and climbed behind the wheel of his pickup. His visions of newfound riches were overshadowed by the mystery of offshore accounts and federal banking rules.

He looked in the rearview mirror as he drove down the entry ramp to the yard. Krieg stood, fists balled on his hips, glaring down at his captives.

"I wouldn't want to be them," Brainerd whispered, accelerating away from the barn and whatever horror Krieg had in mind.

"Let us go. You don't have any right …" Sandy shouted.

"Shut up." Krieg's boot caught him in the ribs. "I should have seen to it that your mother taught you some manners."

"Fuck you!" Sandy managed to hiss at him through clenched teeth.

"You should treat your father with more respect."

There, he had said it. The great secret was out, and Tom Krieg relished the look it left on Sandy's face. Today was the day to take care of loose ends, and the boy had been a loose end since the day Isabella told him she would not abort her baby.

"What?" Sandy's mouth opened then closed, and he shook his head, denying the possibility.

"It's true, boy. I'm your dear old daddy," Krieg sneered.

"Bullshit."

"Yeah, that's what I said when your mama told me." Krieg shrugged, enjoying the boy's torment.

"I don't give a fuck who you are. Let us go!"

"Nope. That's not on the agenda today." Krieg laughed.

"What are you going to do?"

"Well, to quote the old joke." Krieg was feeling powerful and in control. "I brought you into this world, and I can take you out."

"Look do what you want to me, but leave her alone." Sandy twisted, trying to get closer to Jacinta and somehow protect her from this monster.

"She is a separate matter. What happens to her would happen whether you had ever met her or not. Forget her."

"No!" Sandy roared.

The boot flashed out again, catching him in the chest and knocking the wind from him. "Shut up."

Krieg reached for Jacinta and dragged her to her feet. She stood for a moment before her shaky knees buckled. She fell, hitting her head hard on the concrete.

"I'll kill you," Sandy seethed.

Krieg ignored him and took hold of the shackles around Jacinta's ankles and dragged her unconscious body across the concrete and into a windowless storeroom. He slammed the door and turned back to Sandy.

"Let's talk, son," he said, a nasty grin on his face.

"I'm not your son."

"You are, boy. There's no doubt about it. I fucked your mother in the back of my pickup when she was about your age." He smirked. "She was a whore even then."

"I don't believe it."

"Accept the truth or not. I don't give a shit, but part of me is in you." Krieg smiled.

"I'm not anything like you!" Sandy shouted, trying to drown out the truth of Krieg's words.

"You are. That's why you're here. Taking the girl was the kind of thing I would do. It took balls." Krieg shook his head. "Problem is you got in the middle of my business. Now I have to make a decision."

"What decision?"

"Whether a boy from Creosote disappears alone … or his mother goes with him."

"Leave my mother out of this," Sandy strained, red-faced at the steel restraints.

"No." Krieg shook his head. "She's part of everything. I told her to get rid of you, abort you, but she wouldn't. I warned her what would happen to you if she ever spoke about my affairs."

"Affairs!" Sandy said scornfully. "You make it sound like some sort of real business."

"It is business." Krieg grinned. "And pleasure."

"You're a fucking maniac."

Krieg's boot flashed out again, catching Sandy in the ribs. He rolled over in pain.

"Don't say that … ever."

Sandy gasped for air. Krieg took a breath and picked up where he left off.

"Anyway, she believed me and stayed silent to protect you. In return, I gave her money to keep the café afloat when business sagged, even helped out putting money for you in that bank account in Laredo." He smiled. "I knew you'd go there. That was too much to leave behind. Like I said you're just like me."

Sandy shook his head in denial. Could it be true? His

mother had never been happy in Creosote. Often, they talked of moving somewhere else, but always, she encouraged him to get away on his own. She would never leave.

Sandy kicked and jerked on the floor in frustration. "I'll kill you."

"Now you're talking like your old man." Krieg grinned. "Just hold on to that thought. Let it bake inside you for a while. You'll see we are not so different, after all. I want you to know it in your heart before I do what I've been waiting to do all your life."

Krieg turned and walked from the barn. The big bay door rolled closed, and Sandy was left in the gloom. He turned on his side and squirmed toward the storeroom. He called through the door.

"Jacinta."

"I hear you, Reynaldo."

"Thank God. I was afraid he …"

"My head hurts, that's all."

He moved closer to the closed door, pushing his back up against it to be as near to her as possible. He felt a thump against the door and knew she had done the same.

"I'm so sorry I got you into this," he said softly.

"You have done nothing to be sorry for. This man is an evil one."

Evil. It was the only description that fit Tom Krieg, father or not.

"What do we do?" Jacinta asked through the door, and the tremor in her voice told him that she was afraid of the answer.

"I'll think of something," he replied, knowing it was a lie.

SEVENTY

Settling Scores

Benito Diaz stood in the shade of an overhanging rock scanning the valley below through a pair of binoculars. In the distance, three trucks appeared and took the turnoff from Highway 30 onto a back road to Monclova. As they drew closer, he could make out the K and Z markings on the side.

A few minutes earlier, three cars of the *Policía Estatal* had made the turn and proceeded slowly down through the pass. The *gringos* thought they would keep them safe. Diaz laughed and spit on the ground. "*Putos polis.*" Fucking cops.

They would pay for their arrogance. The route had been selected carefully, electing to leave the main highway and take this secluded mountain pass, while the *policía* on their payroll checked the way ahead. They thought they could deceive him, that he would not discover their location. Diaz laughed.

"They're on time," He said, focusing on the trucks now. "The priest and that weakling, Acosta, have done their work." He smiled and nodded to his sons, gathered behind him. "Go to your stations. Have your men ready. Remember, they all die. No prisoners and no mercy. We send a message today. This is our country and our business."

"And the priest and Acosta?" his oldest son looked at his father.

"Everyone," Diaz said firmly.

His sons nodded their understanding and moved off to gather the men and prepare the ambush. Diaz watched the trucks, approaching closer. In another ten minutes, they would be at the bend in the road selected for the attack.

Pepe Lopez watched the road ahead, comparing the terrain to the map in his lap. He didn't have the faith that Father Alonso pretended to have, but he offered a silent prayer that Diaz had not changed the ambush site at the last minute. It went something like, *Dear God, please make sure everything stays the same so we can kill the motherfuckers.*

"There." He pointed, and the driver slowed. "Up ahead. That is the spot. They'll be just around that bend in the road."

The driver brought the lead truck to a stop, and the others followed suit. In the rear, the doors popped open, and the K and Z assault teams jumped out. Stu Pearce led his team up the slopes on the right. Shorts Culper led his men to the left. The third team from the middle truck would follow along the road and wait for the attack to begin then come in from behind and provide the final crushing blow to Diaz's hijackers.

When the assault teams were concealed on the slopes and moving forward, the trucks on the road began easing their way around the bend. Everyone knew what to expect, but that didn't make it easier to sit in the truck like a target.

There wasn't much else they could do. Their plan relied on the speed and marksmanship of the shooters to take out the Diaz attackers before they were able to pour fire into the trucks.

They were almost at the turn now. Pepe Lopez looked up the slopes to make sure the K and Z men were moving forward and ready. He figured it wouldn't hurt to offer another, slightly modified prayer. *Dear God, make sure these gringos can shoot straight and kill these motherfuckers.*

In the center truck's cab, Father Alfonso had been praying out loud since they turned off the main highway. This greatly concerned his police driver. Priests weren't supposed to be afraid to die, were they?

Mario Acosta, bringing up the rear fought to control his bladder. His bowels, on the other hand, were well under control. His sphincter had tightened to the point that you couldn't drive a nail up his asshole with a sledgehammer.

The lead truck came around the bend, followed by the others. Pepe Lopez braced himself. Ahead, a van was pulled across the road, and armed men formed a line to each side. Behind the rear truck, another group of Diaz men rushed from concealment in the ditches and behind boulders.

Pepe Lopez was ready, his hand on the door handle. His police driver was already pushing his door open.

"Wait," Lopez ordered. "Wait for our men take out the lead shooters."

It was too much for the driver, and he jumped to the ground, his pistol in his hand. Diaz's men in front shot him down and took aim on Lopez still in the truck.

From his vantage point high above, Benito Diaz saw the trucks stop and the armed men exit from the rear. He knew instantly what was happening. Instead of falling into the trap he had set so carefully for them, the *gringos* had set a trap of their own.

"*¡Mierda!*" he screamed and waved frantically to his sons and their men already taking up positions on the road below.

The distance was too great for them to hear. His youngest son looked up and saw his father waving from the summit above.

He laughed and called to his brothers, "Papa is wishing us good success."

They all waved back and then made themselves ready to murder the *gringos*.

Gunfire cracked and thundered from the slopes. Diaz's men began falling one by one.

Taken completely by surprise and unsure where the fire came from, they milled about, crouched in the middle of the road, fired wildly up the slopes. Some stood up straight, searching for their attackers.

They made themselves easy targets for Pearce, Culper, and their men. The third team advanced along the road around the bend. They moved from body to body methodically putting a bullet in each head.

When it was done, Diaz's sons and twenty of their men lay dead in the dirt. In addition to the dead *policía* in Lopez's truck, the K and Z assault teams had suffered only three minor wounds from the wild shots Diaz's men fired up the slopes.

It was an enormous victory. They gathered in the road congratulating each other and slapping backs. Someone began chanting, "USA, USA, USA," as if the ambush had been a sporting event.

"Where's Lopez?" Stu Pearce looked at Alfonso.

The priest shrugged. "I haven't seen him since the shooting began."

"You?" Pearce swiveled his head toward Mario Acosta.

"I saw him jump into the ditch when the first shots were fired. After that …" He shrugged. "He must have run away like a little coward," he added with bluster, hoping no one would notice the wet stain on the crotch of his blue jeans.

On the summit above, Benito Diaz wept for his sons, murdered by the fucking *gringos*. His grief was short-lived, followed by another emotion.

A helicopter rose over an adjacent hill. The side door was open, and a man sat there. Surprise replaced his grief for a moment, and Diaz squinted at him wondering who would fly a helicopter into this remote valley.

His final emotion was fear. The man had a rifle. Diaz lifted the Tec-9 machine pistol he carried to swagger about with in front of his men. It would have been useless at this range against the helicopter, but it didn't matter.

Before he could squeeze the trigger, a .30-06 round plowed through his chest, and he sank to the ground. A second round shattered his skull for good measure.

The roar of the rifle shots startled the K and Z men. Their celebration came to a halt as they watched the helicopter swoop down into the valley. Several lifted their rifles. Others gave a shout of triumph.

"It's Krieg and Zabala!"

"Fuck, yeah! They came to finish off that old bandit Diaz."

"Leave it to them to come in like the fucking cavalry."

The rifles lowered. All eyes were focused on the chopper. Most expected it to land and for the bosses to step out and congratulate each of them. There might even be another bonus.

The helicopter moved slowly toward the men in the road. At a distance of two hundred yards, it hovered. They felt the rotor wash in their face as they gazed up at it.

Slowly, it rotated on its axis to reveal the open side door.

"What the fuck." Stu Pearce lifted his rifle, and the others did the same.

It was too late. Firing at a rate of five thousand rounds a minute, the M134 minigun clamped to the chopper's door frame buzz-sawed through the compact body of men showering the surrounding ground with blood and bone fragments.

Within a minute, every man who had exited the trucks to spring their trap on Diaz was dead or dying. The minigun's electric motor ceased its deadly whirring, and the six barrels stopped spinning.

The helicopter settled onto the road, the engine idling so that rotor continued to spin overhead. The blades cast a blurred circular shadow on the road and surrounding hillsides.

Alejandro Garza stepped out holding the rifle he had used to kill Benito Diaz. His two guards who had manned the minigun followed, each armed with an AK-47. Bebé Elizondo made sure that the *Los Salvajes* cartel was never short of firepower.

Garza's men began searching for survivors. There were only two.

Father Alfonso and Mario Acosta had crouched behind

the others just as the firing began. Both were severely wounded but breathing.

Garza's men dragged them away from the rest of the bodies. Alfonso moaned. Mario stared wide-eyed at the hard-eyed men standing over him, too weak to beg for mercy. Both received a bullet through the brain.

"It went as planned, did it not?" Pepe Lopez scrambled, smiling down the hillside where he had hidden during the killing.

"We'll see." Garza turned to his security men. "Find him."

One by one, they pulled the bodies out of the heap and laid them out on the road. As they worked, *Sargento* Garcia and his *policías* returned to the scene. They stood meekly by the side of the road, ignored by Garza.

"All is well, no?" Garcia said to Lopez.

"Shut up." The more they prowled through the bodies, the more Lopez's nerves tensed.

Surely he was there, the *norteamericano*. They would drag his bloody corpse out, and the trouble would be over.

Lopez watched, and each time a body was rolled over, and Garza shook his head, the knot in his stomach grew. He had been with Garza the night before, driven him through the village to Juan Galdo's home where he showed the picture of the American. Galdo had been adamant that it, it was him, and that he was the one who killed his cousin Bernardo.

Lopez had arranged the trap, emphasizing to Krieg and Zabala the number and ferocity of Diaz's fighters. As expected, they were more than willing to send all their men to the fight.

The rest was simple. The K and Z men would ambush Diaz's unsuspecting fighters. Then Garza would show up and kill the K and Z men just as they were flushed with their victory. The one Garza hunted, John Sole who had been working with Stu Pearce, would be killed as well. Except, there was a problem.

"He is not here." Garza walked to Lopez.

"But …"

"He is not here," Garza repeated.

"But he should be … he must be … they would have sent everyone to take out Diaz. They would not take chances on not having enough men."

"He is not there." Garza's voice was controlled, indifferent almost as if they were discussing the weather. "We had a business arrangement. You provide the American, and we eliminate the others so that you control their business." He shook his head. "We fulfilled our agreement. You did not."

Lopez's mind was reeling. The penalty for failing in an agreement with *Los Salvajes* was well known.

How many seconds would Garza wait before having his men put a bullet in his head? Or, he might choose to do it himself. Behind him, Garcia and his *policías* stepped away, making sure they were not in the line of fire.

"I … I think I know where he may be." Pepe spoke rapidly, rushing as many words as possible through his mouth before the bullet tore through his brain.

"Do not trifle with me." Garza's eyes narrowed threateningly. "What is to happen will only be worse for you."

"I swear," Lopez pleaded. "I am not trifling. I do know where he might be … a small town across the border."

"And how can I believe you?"

"Do you think I would have brought you here if I had known he would not be in the trucks?" Lopez shook his head, adamantly. "No! I knew what would happen if the plan failed. I believed he would be here. I would not try to deceive you. If the *gringo* is not here, it is because he did not act as expected, but I know where he must be."

"How do you know this?"

"Because they told me." He motioned at the dead K and Z men lined up on the ground. "They told me. You must believe me."

Garza was silent for several seconds. There was some truth in Lopez's words. He was far too great a coward to attempt to deceive *Los Salvajes*.

He nodded. "Alright. Have your police sergeant take you to Monterrey. Meet tonight at my hotel and we will make one more plan." Garza shook his head. "The last one."

Lopez exhaled a slow breath, thankful that he had not been ordered to get into the helicopter. He had no illusions about Gustavo's fate the night before.

Garza added a word of warning. "Come to the hotel. Do not try to run away. If you do, your end will be much worse than a bullet in the head."

"I will be there. You have my word."

"Your word?" Garza's cold eyes almost twinkled with mirth. "The word of a man who has betrayed everyone who trusted him? You almost make me laugh."

Garza turned, motioned to his men, and boarded the helicopter. A moment later, it lifted, following the road as it gained altitude until it disappeared over the hills. Pepe Lopez could breathe again. The blood surged back into his face. He would live, at least for a few more hours.

"It seems your partner is not very pleased with you." *Sargento* Miguel Garcia's fleshy face spread into a taunting grin. "You should know, Pepe, that a man like that always settles his scores."

"You think I don't know that." Lopez turned from staring after the departing helicopter to face Garcia. "*Saco inútil de mierda.*" You useless sack of shit.

Garcia's face flushed, but he remained silent. He might be the *Sargento* and have the power of command, but Lopez had the money. Garcia had no illusions about which would hold his men's loyalty if he challenged Lopez.

"Get out of my sight," Lopez said.

Garcia nodded without speaking and withdrew to his police vehicle. Pepe Lopez stared into the sky where the helicopter had disappeared over the summit and prayed yet again. The multitude of prayers he had flung to the heavens that day were his personal best record for devotion.

Dear God, Don't let that asshole motherfucker Garza kill me.

SEVENTY-ONE

Justice

It seemed the drive back to Salvia County would never end. Isabella's thoughts were knotted with contradictions. She desperately wanted to find Sandy and Jacinta safe and bring them home. At the same time she fervently prayed that they had not been intercepted by Tom Krieg. But then, if he didn't have them, as John pointed out, they could be anywhere, and they might never find them.

Five miles out from the Krieg ranch, Sole took a dirt road and headed out into the prairie. Reggie followed. When they were well off the main county road and out of sight, he pulled over. They needed a plan.

"We need a back way in," he said as Isabella and Reggie gathered close. "If we find them, we'll want the vehicles nearby so we can load up and get away quickly. That means we have to find an access point near the ranch where we can, conceal the vehicles, and move forward on foot. Stealth and speed are our friends. Any suggestions?"

"Stealth and speed." Reggie had suspected as much. "You were a cop and military too, right?"

"Marine Corps."

"Action?"

"Desert Storm. You?"

"Army. Afghanistan …three deployments."

"That's some shit," Sole said. "Hooah, Army."

"Oorah, Marine." Reggie managed a smile, something he hadn't done since finding Sherm on his porch. "I think I have an answer to our tactical need for stealth and speed."

"I'm all ears."

Isabella watched the exchange, wondering what else there was to know about this man. A cop … a Marine … what else? It didn't matter. For now, she just wanted her son back.

They talked over their plan, and Reggie led the way, following the side road for several more miles. Then he pulled off and headed out through the scrub brush and grass with Sole following.

They stayed below the rises, weaving their way through the washes and valleys toward the Krieg ranch. Finally, Reggie stopped and got out.

"Should be about here," He said and started up a small hill, just high enough to conceal their vehicles.

Sole and Isabella crouched and followed.

At the top, Reggie lay prone in the grass peering down the slope. Below them, not more than two hundred yards away, sat the Krieg ranch estate. The main house was to their right, the guest house across from it to the left. Farther on was the barn and beyond it the corrals and livestock pens.

"That's some damn fine navigating," Sole said, admiringly.

"Wish I could get us closer, but this is the best I can do,"

Reggie said. "If I had a map, there might be a better spot, but …" he shrugged.

"This'll do just fine," Sole said sizing things up. "Wish it was dark, though."

"Yeah, the night is our friend," Reggie said. "A nice moonless one would be good."

"And some NVGs," Sole added, referring to standard military helmet-mounted night vision goggles.

"We're not waiting for the night are we?" Isabella was concerned. If Sandy was down there, she wanted him out now.

"No." Sole shook his head and looked at Reggie, who nodded agreement. "If Krieg has them, waiting until dark is not an option. If he doesn't …" He shrugged. "Won't much matter. They might lock us up for trespassing."

"Or shoot us on sight," Reggie muttered.

"True enough, but I don't see that we have any other options."

"Agreed."

Sole rolled on his side and pulled the .45 from his waistband. "What are you carrying?"

There was no question that Reggie was armed. Sole had noted the bulge under his shirt while he was sitting on Sherm's porch the night before.

"Glock 19," Reggie said, taking the pistol from his belt behind his back.

"Okay. The way I see it, we move fast down the hill. You take the rear of the main house, I'll take the front. Check windows for anyone inside. There might be an alarm system, so stay away from doors for now."

"Roger that."

"If you spot them inside, wait for me, and we'll figure

out how to get them out." Sole looked at Isabella. "You wait here."

"Not fucking likely," she snarled, causing him to recoil for an instant. "I'm going with you. If no one's there, it won't matter. If someone is, they might hesitate shooting you if there's a woman around ... maybe."

Sole looked at Reggie. "You've known her a lot longer than me. Talk some sense into her."

"Nope." Reggie shook his head. "Not me."

"Alright," Sole sighed. "Stay close."

He rose, and they moved down the slope toward the main house. Reggie split off toward the rear, Sole with Isabella behind him heading for the front.

There was no sign of life visible through any of the windows. They made their way around the sides and back to regroup near the front porch.

"Do we go in and clear it room by room, to make sure?" Reggie asked.

"I think so. It's a shitty plan, but if he has them in there, we don't have time to waste."

"Window?"

"Front door," Sole said. "Stealth and speed, remember. Opening a window and climbing through will make noise and alert anyone inside. Assume we are danger close. We go through the front, as fast and quiet as possible."

Sole moved carefully onto the porch steps, hoping there were no creaky loose boards. Reggie followed, instinctively watching their rear for threats.

"No," Isabella whispered. "There."

Sole and Reggie froze in place. They turned their heads to follow her pointing finger.

Claire Toussaint stood on the guesthouse porch. Head

swiveling from side to side to make sure no one was watching, she lifted a hand and waved them over.

"Who's that?" Sole asked.

"A friend ... I think. Her name's Claire Toussaint. She belongs to Krieg." Isabella began moving across the yard toward the guesthouse.

"Wait," Sole whispered. "Could be a trap."

Isabella ignored the warning and trotted toward the guesthouse.

"Shit."

Sole looked at Reggie. They gave each other a shrug and followed, running to take up protective positions on either side of Isabella.

As they came to the guesthouse, Claire receded into the shadow of the doorway. Her eyes darted back and forth, nervously searching the yard for people or vehicles approaching.

"The barn. They're in the barn."

"Are you sure?" Isabella asked.

"Yes. You must hurry. Krieg left, but he will be back."

Sole watched, trying to get a read on the woman, looking for some indication that she was lying. He'd never met her, but if Krieg was around, she might be sending them into an ambush.

"Let's go." Isabella turned and headed around to the side of guesthouse toward the barn.

"Wait." This time Sole took her by the arm and forced her to stop.

"Let me go." She struggled to pull her arm from his grasp.

"I will, Isabella, but you need to stop." He released his grip on her. "You go storming into that barn like this and

Krieg might …" He hesitated. "Well, we want Sandy and Jacinta out alive. We don't want to force his hand."

"He's right," Reggie said. "Let us handle this. If Sandy and the girl are there, we'll get them out."

"Alright." She nodded and took a deep breath. "Just hurry, before it's too late."

They moved around the side of the guesthouse toward the corrals that ran parallel to the side yard. Crouching behind the steel rails for as much concealment as possible, they trotted toward the barn. Sole took the lead, Reggie watching the rear with Isabella between them. The last fifty yards were in the open.

Sole stopped to assess the situation. The large bay door on the front of the barn was closed. Trying to roll it open would take time and attract attention. A walk-through door on the side wall was also closed, but opening it would be easier. The rear and far sides of the barn were not visible from their vantage point.

"I'll take the walk-through door." Sole turned to Reggie. "You take the far side or rear. There's probably another door or a window. Watch it. If he's there, we don't want Krieg getting away out the back with them when I make entry."

"You got it." Reggie nodded.

Sole looked at Isabella and started to speak.

"Don't even think it." She shook her head. "I'm going with you."

"Alright." He sighed. "Stay low and stay behind me."

As they crossed the open space to the barn, Reggie peeled off to move around the far side. Sole and Isabella wasted no time going directly to the walk-through door.

The door had a lever handle. Sole pushed it down

slowly with his left hand, the Colt in his right hand. He eased the door open, and Isabella gasped.

Sandy lay on the floor against a storeroom door on the far side. He was shackled hand and foot, and even from a distance, they could see that his face was swollen and bruised. Blood stained the surrounding concrete.

Isabella ran to him. Sole stood by the door, scanning the interior from one end to the other for threats. None appeared, and he advanced, holding the pistol in a combat-ready posture.

Isabella knelt at Sandy's side, tears falling as she tried to find a way to unlock the cuffs on his wrists and ankles. Sole stood over her, eyeing the barn's vast interior. There were too many places of concealment. Equipment, machinery, storage rooms, workbenches.

"No, no." Sandy shook his head and thumped it against the storeroom door behind him. "Jacinta. She's in there. Get her out."

Isabella looked up at Sole. He tried the door handle. It was locked.

With a final look around the barn, he pushed the pistol back in his waistband and trotted to a workbench against the adjacent wall. After rummaging around for a few seconds, he came back holding a crowbar.

He pulled Sandy out of the way and said, "Stand back."

Placing the end of the bar where the door and latch meet, he pulled hard. On the third pull, the door popped open.

The young girl lay on the floor in the center of the room, bloody but not as badly hurt as Sandy. She was shackled in the same manner, though, and Sole bent to lift her into his arms and carry her out. He stepped through the door and placed her gently on the floor beside Sandy.

"Jacinta," Sandy murmured through his bruised mouth.

"Reynaldo." She smiled, tears filling her eyes at the sight of his battered face. "What has he done to you?"

"We have to get them out of here … carry them if necessary. I'll find Reggie."

He turned to the walk-through door and stopped. Claire Toussaint stood there. Behind her, Tom Krieg held a shotgun at her back and prodded her forward.

"I'm sorry," Claire sobbed. "He said he would kill me … cut me in pieces." She shook her head. "I'm so sorry."

"So, this is why you missed the call-out last night." Krieg looked at Sole and shook his head, laughing. "I guess you figured out you're fired." He motioned with the shotgun to Sole's midriff. "Put your pistol on the floor."

Sole reached into his waistband and retrieved the Colt, holding the butt between his thumb and forefinger. It was a damned rookie mistake, he thought with disgust. He had allowed himself to get caught up in the drama before securing the scene. Shit! He placed the pistol on the floor and stood to face Krieg.

"I've been waiting for you. I knew you'd come." Krieg eyed Isabella, a smirk on his face. "And that you'd do anything to save your boy."

"He's your son too," Isabella said.

"You think so? What's that they say?" Krieg laughed. "Being a sperm donor doesn't make you a father. Well, I guess we're living proof of that. No, he doesn't mean any more to me than the coffee I pissed down the toilet this morning. Body fluids, that's all."

"You have me. Let him go!"

"You don't seem to understand." Krieg shook his head. "I had to get you here to tie up all the loose ends at the same time."

He turned his head toward Sole. "You too, Bill Myers or whatever your name is. She tell you I fucked her?" Krieg was enjoying the moment. He laughed. "You're a bonus. No witnesses. With all of you disappearing at the same time, I imagine the sheriff will figure you did away with them and took off."

Sole knew he was right. He was the newcomer, the unknown factor and by default would be the person of most interest in the disappearance and suspected murders of the others. It didn't really matter because he would be in the same grave with the others if Krieg had his way.

Krieg gave Claire a shove. She stumbled to the floor, trembling and holding her hands over her face. There was no mistaking what he meant. No witnesses.

He lifted the shotgun to sight along the barrel at Sole's face.

"Lower your weapon Krieg." Reggie Prince stepped into the barn from the walk-through door.

Krieg froze. Careful not to make any sudden moves, he lowered the barrel until it pointed at the floor.

"All the way. On the floor and step away from it."

Krieg knelt and placed the shotgun on the concrete, then rose to face Reggie. "You?"

"Yeah, me."

"Took your damned sweet time about it," Sole said, retrieving the Colt from the floor.

"Sorry about that. Only found one back window, and it had a security screen over it. Had to make my way all the way around." Reggie smiled. "You got a big ass barn here, Krieg."

Isabella stepped forward. "What do we do with him?"

"First things first," Sole said. "The keys to the shackles, Krieg."

"In my pocket." Krieg looked from Reggie to Sole, both men pointing their weapons in his direction.

"Hand them over."

Krieg reached into his pocket and slowly pulled the keys out. Sole took them and handed them to Isabella.

"Take their shackles off." He turned back to Reggie. "What's your call?"

"Seems like a pretty clear-cut case." Reggie's eyes narrowed. "First, there's what he did to these young people. No doubt, he was going to kill them."

"And us," Sole agreed. "No doubt."

"Next, I expect there's a reason you go around using names that ain't yours."

"There is." Sole nodded. "And I expect there's a reason you disappear and then hide out with Sherm from time to time."

"There is."

"So, we both have reasons not to leave someone behind who can ID us and raise suspicions with the law."

"Not to mention what he's done to all those other girls," Reggie added.

"True enough. That's not a habit he's going to give up. There'll be more if he has his way."

"You're full of shit, and I don't scare that easy." Krieg glared from one to the other. "Take your whores and that little bastard and get off my property."

"We're getting to that," Sole replied calmly. He looked at Reggie. "Then there's what happened to Sherm."

"I never touched the old man," Krieg said.

"No, but that buckshot you sent his way did," Reggie said. "Whether you pulled the trigger or someone did it for you, it's all the same."

"That's right," Sole added. "You said you were eliminating all the witnesses. Sherm Westerfield was the first."

"Yeah, there's that." Reggie nodded, his eyes fixed on Krieg's.

"Seems like a clear call." Sole nodded. "Take a vote. I say, do it."

"Agreed. It's unanimous."

"What about us? Our vote?" Isabella spoke up.

"Do it," Sandy said.

"No, you don't vote on this, Sandy." Sole shook his head and looked at Isabella and Jacinta. "None of you vote. This is our decision. We carry the burden for what happens, not you. For the record, nothing you say will change it, and nothing we do now is your responsibility."

The trial was over. In a court of law, a good lawyer might have gotten Krieg off. There were no lawyers here, and no appeals to a higher authority. Tom Krieg's sentence had been handed down. There would be no appeals.

He looked at Reggie and nodded. "Do it."

Reggie motioned with the Glock toward the storeroom door. "In there, Krieg. Move."

"You're full of shit." Krieg sneered. "You don't have the balls. It's murder."

"Not murder," Sole said. "Justice."

Reggie's pistol caught Krieg across the jaw, opening a bloody gash. "Move."

Reggie prodded Krieg in the chest with the barrel of the Glock, backing him to the storeroom door. "Inside."

"You don't know what you're doing." Confusion replaced the usual fierceness in Krieg's eyes. "You can't do this."

Reggie pushed him through the door and closed it behind him.

"I'll make you a rich man," Krieg pleaded, fear replacing the confusion. "You don't have to do this."

"I do," Reggie said.

As they unshackled Sandy and Jacinta and helped them to their feet, three sharp cracks sounded through the closed storeroom door. A moment later, Reggie stepped from the room, closing the door firmly behind him.

"It's done."

"Let's get everyone out of here." Sole looked at Claire. "You too. Get up."

They helped Sandy and Jacinta across the yards and lawns, up the hill and back to their vehicles where they managed to climb into Sole's pickup. Claire rode with Reggie.

"Don't go back to Sherm's place," Sole said leaning in to speak to Reggie. "If they've found him, they'll drag you into the investigation."

"I know. Don't worry. I got someplace I can go. Won't nobody come looking for me there." Reggie looked at Claire in the seat beside him. "What about her?"

"Here's some money." Sole pulled out the roll of bills he carried. "Use it to get her on her way or settled somewhere. Sorry to put that on you, but ..." He looked at the others waiting in his truck. "I've got other things to take care of."

"Understood, brother." Reggie held his hand out, gripping Sole's firmly. "You take care, Marine."

"You too, Army."

The two trucks bounced their way across the prairie and over the back roads until they hit the county road. Reggie headed north, Sole turned toward Creosote.

Isabella had said little since finding her son alive. She was awed and a bit fearful of the man she now called John. In the space of a few hours, he'd rescued her son and

Jacinta, decided the fate of Tom Krieg, and given his assent to his execution.

He was an enigma. The words he said to Krieg rang in her ears.

Not murder. Justice.

SEVENTY-TWO

Odds

"Who found him?" Sheriff Paul Dermott knelt beside the body of Emmett Brewer, sprawled in the mud along the Rio Grande.

"Couple of boys out fishing."

The deputy responding to the call nodded in the direction of two sixteen-year-olds who had figured today was a good day to cut class and cast a line into the river. They stood watching the deputies do their work, securing the crime scene, and gathering evidence. Dermott walked over to them.

"Tell me what you saw boys."

Dermott noted that both were pale and green around the gills. Decomposition was well underway, and Brewer's body bore the signs of scavengers feasting on tender morsels they pulled from his eyes and mouth.

The taller and paler of the boys spoke first. "Not really anything, Sheriff. Just out walkin' the bank, lookin' for a place to set and fish, we come on the …" The boy hesitated, searching for a polite word for a corpse. "We come on him ... the dead man ... and called you right off."

"See anyone else around?"

"No, sir, not a soul."

"Touch anything? Touch him?"

"Oh, hell no." The boy looked like he might gag at the idea of touching a dead man. "I mean, no sir, we didn't touch nothing."

"How close did you get to the body?" Dermott surveyed the surrounding ground for footprints.

"Not too close. Say about ten feet or so, just close enough so we could tell it was a dead ... I mean it was the smell that got our attention right off."

"Yeah, it's an aroma you won't ever forget, son." He nodded at the boys' feet. "Let me see the soles of your shoes."

They lifted their shoes. Dermott waved a deputy over. "Photos of their shoes top and bottom."

"Right." The deputy nodded and took the pictures with a digital camera.

"What's that for," the boy asked nervously. "You think we done somethin'?"

"Nothing to worry about," Dermott replied. "Just pictures so we can tell whose footprints are whose. You say you were about ten feet away, so we can eliminate any prints that match your shoes farther than ten feet out."

"Eliminate?"

"Yes. We want to find the killer, and he might have left footprints around here somewhere. If he did, we might be able to track him down from the type of shoe." He smiled. "Of course, we need to eliminate yours right off, don't we?"

Dermott left out the part about verifying their proximity

to the body and that while, for the moment, they weren't suspects, that could change.

"Oh." The boy nodded at the explanation, but the expression on his face showed he doubted the reason.

"Okay." Dermott nodded and looked at the other boy. "How about you? See anyone? Touch anything?"

"No, sir." The boy shook his head solemnly.

"Okay. The deputy here is going to take your names and addresses and write up your statement."

Dermott turned away.

"Sheriff?" the shorter boy called out.

"Yes, son?"

"We gonna be in trouble for cuttin' class? My Dad'll beat the hell out of me if he finds out."

Dermott repressed a smile. "We can keep it between us for now, as long you're telling me the truth."

"Oh, yessir, it's the truth for sure."

Dermott walked back to the river bank and gazed down at the Border Patrol agent who had been his friend and colleague. He didn't have time to grieve. That would come later.

"What were you doing here, Emmett?" He scanned up and down the bank. "What did you find?"

His portable radio crackled. "Dispatch to unit one."

"Go ahead, Sally," he responded.

"Sheriff, have another report of a dead body, possible homicide."

"What?" Dermott stared in disbelief at the radio in his hand. A murder a year in Salvia County would have been an increase in the homicide rate, by a wide margin. Now they had three in a matter of weeks—Lucky Martin, Emmett Brewer, and now ... who? He lifted the radio and asked, not sure he wanted to know and asked, "Do you have an ID on the possible homicide?"

"Tom Krieg. The report came from his son Doyle." Sally the dispatcher's voice was breathless.

This sort of drama didn't pop up every day in this backwater county, and now here she sat at her console, smack dab in the middle of it all. Wait until her sister Agnes in Tulsa heard. She'd pee herself.

Dermott stood speechless for a moment. Tom Krieg, the county's preeminent citizen, a homicide victim? It seemed too incredible to believe.

"I'll be en-route to the Krieg place," he said. "What unit is responding?"

"Unit four, Brainerd."

"Alright, tell Claude I'm on my way and to secure the scene but don't touch anything."

He trotted to his vehicle, calling over his shoulder to the three deputies gathering evidence, "Take care of the scene here. I'll be back."

His mind whirled. He figured the odds against three people being murdered in such a short period in Salvia County were a million to one, but the plain fact was, they had three homicides. By his estimation, the odds the murders were not connected in some way were about as likely as a meteor crashing through the roof of his truck and crushing his ass—at this exact moment.

He gave a quick glance at the sky and satisfied himself that no meteors were headed in his direction. He gritted his teeth and nodded. No, the murders were related in some way, and by God, he was going to get to the bottom of it.

SEVENTY-THREE

Plans

Sole pulled his truck all the way around the house to the back door. After checking to make sure no residents of Creosote were out snooping around the yard, he and Isabella helped Sandy and Jacinta into the house.

They sat at the kitchen table behind closed blinds, speaking quietly as the sun sank below the horizon. Sandy was battered, though somewhat better since being freed from the shackles. Jacinta sat beside him holding his hand, not quite as bruised, but still sore from her ordeal.

Isabella sat across from them with Sole seated beside her. If there had been any doubt before, he was part of the family now. Without him, Isabella shuddered to think what might have happened to her son and Jacinta.

"It should have been me," Sandy said.

"What are you talking about?" Isabella asked.

"I should have been the one to kill the son of a bitch."

"Don't say that," Isabella leaned forward and took his hand. "Don't ever say that."

"Why? Because he was my father?" He looked into her eyes and saw the confirmation. It was true.

"I ... I should have told you. I wanted to tell you. I just couldn't find a way." She shook her head. "So many things I should have done to protect you, and I failed."

"You didn't fail." Sandy shook his head, and his eyes softened. He reached over and squeezed Isabella's hand. "You were trapped. Krieg was good at trapping people, using them. That's why I should have done it ... killed him to even the score for you." He put an arm around Jacinta. "And for her ... for all the others."

"No." Sole shook his head. "It's an easy thing to say, but not so simple to do. You don't need to carry that burden for the rest of your life. Trust me. It never gets lighter."

Sandy didn't argue, but the fire of hate for the man who had abused his mother and Jacinta burned in his eyes. Sole understood.

"There are plans to make," Isabella said, smiling to change the subject from murder. "Are you two planning to marry?"

"Well ... I ... actually ... We didn't really spend any time talking about that." Sandy sat quietly for a moment. "We were planning to run away, to get away from Krieg. The word married never came up. It was just about being together." He nodded. "But yes, married is what we should be, I think." He turned to Jacinta. "Are we planning to marry?"

"Are you asking me to marry you, Reynaldo?" Jacinta smiled and winked at Isabella.

"I ... well, yes, I am asking you to marry me. Will you?"

"Yes." She leaned over to kiss his cheek. "I will, Reynaldo."

"I like that name," Sandy said, looking at his mother

and John. "I suppose Krieg didn't like it … too Mexican for him, even for his illegitimate son. That's why you called me Sandy, to appease him?"

"That's why." Isabella nodded, embarrassed. "Would you like me to call you Reynaldo, instead?"

"No." He shook his head. "I'm used to Sandy, been called that by everyone I've ever known. You're Mom, and I'm Sandy. Always been that way, and that's how it should stay." He squeezed Jacinta's hand. "But I like it when you call me, Reynaldo. I'm Sandy to everyone else but Reynaldo to you."

"I'm sorry," Isabella said, feeling chastened and guilty. "One more thing I kept from you."

"Don't be sorry," Sandy interrupted firmly. "But from now on, no more secrets or hiding who we are."

"Fair enough." Isabella put on a smile. "Now let's plan a wedding."

"There is something to discuss before the wedding," John interjected.

The others turned toward him.

"Some loose ends to tie up." He looked across the table. "Where is your truck, Sandy?"

"In a diner parking lot outside Laredo. That's where Brainerd nabbed us."

"Okay. You two will stay here, and your mother and I will drive to Laredo and back during the night. We need to hide the pickup in the shed before the town is awake in the morning."

Isabella nodded.

"The next loose end is Brainerd. How much does he know?"

"Everything," Sandy said. "Not who killed Krieg, but he knows we were the last ones with him."

"I'll figure out something to do about that."

"What?" Isabella asked, her brow furrowed, concerned.

"I'll think about it and let you know."

Sole avoided her gaze, but she let it go. If whatever he was planning protected Sandy and Jacinta, she had no objections.

"Last," he continued. "Jacinta's status in the United States. She's an illegal immigrant, undocumented. She will need a Green Card to stay here."

"Won't marriage solve that?" Isabella asked.

"Probably," John said. "But the longer we wait, the harder it is to get the approval. Immigration takes a dim view of marriages for the purposes of entering the country. Still, marrying sooner than later and applying for permanent residency will make things easier than waiting. Also, we need a plausible reason that Jacinta crossed the border."

"I came to be with my uncle in Houston," she said. "The devil Krieg stopped me."

"To be with your uncle is a good reason." Sole nodded. "For the sake of your residency application, we should avoid any reference to what happened with Krieg."

"You mean what he did does not get investigated?" Sandy asked, surprised, and uneasy with the idea.

"No. It will be investigated. Somebody will find his body, possibly already have, and will start putting things together. The K and Z smuggling operation will be shut down, and everyone involved will be found out. ICE, Border Patrol, Homeland Security ... they're all good at what they do. They will figure things out. For now, let's get Jacinta on the path to legal residency and citizenship."

"Agreed," Isabella said.

"One more thing," Sole said. "You two stay out of sight

and heal up. We don't want people seeing your condition and asking a lot of questions."

There was no argument. Heads nodded. Fatigue was settling into their bones.

"We have to get on the road to Laredo," Sole said to Isabella.

"Do we really need to go tonight? I'm dead tired."

"Yes. Tonight if we want to secure Sandy's truck before someone reports it abandoned and has it towed. That would leave a paper trail that could blow our story. We'll bring it back here and hide it in the shed, but we have to get it done before daylight."

"Alright," she said, and once again, she wondered about his past and the ease with which he knew how to cover their tracks. "You drive. I'll sleep on the way."

Sole stood. "You two get some sleep. Stay out of sight. If anyone comes to the door, stay quiet and don't answer." He looked at Isabella. "If we leave now, we can make it back before daylight and grab a couple of hours of sleep for ourselves."

SEVENTY-FOUR

You're an Idiot

Claude Brainerd was standing with Doyle Krieg when Sheriff Dermott pulled up beside the barn.

"Where is he?" Dermott asked, walking past them to the barn.

"Inside. There's a storeroom on the far side."

"I'll take a look." Dermott looked at Doyle. "You stay here."

"It's my father. You can't tell me to …"

"Stay here," Dermott said and turned away. "Come with me, Claude."

They entered the barn and stopped. Dermott stood by the walk-through door, scanning the scene from one end to the other. He took out his phone and snapped a few images of the interior.

As they approached the storeroom, he stopped and took more pictures of the blood on the floor. It had soaked in, staining the concrete a rusty brown color.

The storeroom door was open. Dermott stood in the

entry surveying the crime scene. Tom Krieg was on his back, one knee up, three neat holes in the front of his skull.

"What's Doyle got to say?" Dermott turned to his deputy.

"Came home. Couldn't find his father. Looked everywhere. The storeroom in the barn was one of the last places he thought to search."

"He have any idea who might have done it?"

"No, none at all."

"That's bullshit!" Doyle shouted from behind Brainerd.

Dermott whirled. "Told you to wait outside, Doyle. This is a crime scene."

"I know who did it!"

"What?" Dermott shot Brainerd a hard look. "Who did it?"

"That half-breed did it. I know it!"

"Be more specific." Dermott reached for the note pad in his pocket.

"Palmeras … Sandy Palmeras. He had to be the one."

"Why is that?" Dermott's eyes narrowed. "What's going on here, Doyle?"

Behind him, Brainerd scowled at Doyle, mouthing the words, "Shut the fuck up."

"Going on?" Doyle mumbled, his feeble brain beginning to comprehend that he may have said too much. He struggled for a way to explain why Sandy would kill his father without saying that Tom Krieg liked to keep young girls around and rape them.

"Well, I didn't say anything was going on exactly," he said lamely.

"You said Sandy Palmeras murdered your father. I asked what's going on. Well?"

"It's just that he always hated us. We had a fight out on the road outside Creosote a while back."

"Yeah." Dermott nodded. "Heard he handed your ass to you. Why would he want to come here and do this to Tom?"

"Well ... like I said, he always has had it in for us. Jealous, that's what he is. Because we got money and he don't ... lives in that piece of shit house in that shit hole of a town with his mother, and he won't never have nothing better."

"Jealous?" Dermott shook his head. "That doesn't sound like Sandy Palmeras."

"It's true, goddammit!"

Doyle had played his card and had run out of meaningful things to say. Dumb as he was, he knew he couldn't mention the girl and Sandy's promise to take her away. If he did, there would be more questions, ones he didn't want to answer. Some he couldn't answer since his father kept him on the ranch and away from the real money-making aspects of his affairs.

He was smart enough to understand that if he opened the door to everything his father was doing, he could lose it all. Visions of his family fortune floating off into space sobered him. The ranch, the trucking company, and everything of any value confiscated by the law.

"It's true," he repeated, feebly.

"That's not much to go on." Dermott motioned to Brainerd to come forward.

Brainerd stood behind Dermott staring into Doyle's eyes, trying to send a message for him to shut up before they all went to jail.

"Take Doyle outside and get a statement in full. Not likely that financial jealousy was a motive here, but there might be something else." Dermott knelt by the bloodstains on the barn floor. "I'll get an evidence kit and see if I can get a sample of this blood. Might take a while, but DNA may be able to tell us who was here with Krieg. Doesn't look like he was dragged into the storeroom after he was killed, so this could be another victim, or the perpetrator."

"Yes, sir," Brainerd said and motioned to Doyle to follow him outside.

With three deputies handling Emmett Brewer's murder, he and Brainerd were the only other on-duty law enforcement officers available to work the Krieg case. Pulling bodies from the river was one thing, but Dermott wasn't about to let Claude Brainerd within fifty feet of a real investigation.

He worked the crime scene alone, taking images of every inch of the barn and of Krieg's body from every conceivable angle. He dampened sterile pads from his evidence kit with distilled water and used them to soak up blood samples from the stains drying into the concrete. Then he took samples of Krieg's still wet blood from around his body and off the wall of the storeroom and recovered two of the bullets that had passed through Krieg's skull.

Outside, Claude Brainerd stood beside his county pickup with Doyle Krieg, staring intently at the barn from which he had been banished.

"Why don't you go in there and do something," Doyle snarled. "Isn't that what my father pays you for?"

"Do something like what?"

"Hell, you're the fucking deputy. Make the sheriff leave. Tell him you'll handle things. Find that half-breed son of a bitch, and we'll drag him down to the river and put a bullet in his head like he done to my father."

Brainerd looked at Doyle, eyebrows raised in disbelief. "You're an idiot, Doyle."

SEVENTY-FIVE

Very Unfair

He wouldn't do it here. Or would he? Pepe Lopez tried to reassure himself as he walked into Alejandro Garza's hotel in Monterrey.

He wouldn't kill me here. If he wanted to do that, it would have been much simpler out on the road where the ambush had taken place, he reasoned. After all, there were already so many bodies there. What would one more matter?

No, he wouldn't do it here, Lopez decided. There would be too many witnesses. They would leave too much evidence behind.

He stepped into the lobby elevator, feeling a little calmer. He pressed the button for the fifth floor and looked up to smile broadly into the security camera. Hopefully, the equipment was functioning correctly and recording, so there would be a record that he had come to visit a friend who was expecting him.

The elevator stopped, chiming softly that he had arrived at his destination. He took a breath and stepped into the plush hallway of the five-star hotel. No hail of gunfire greeted him, no men with knives to slit his throat. So far so good.

The door to Alejandro Garza's room was easy to spot. One of his scowling security guards stood in the hallway watching him approach.

"Here to see *Señor* Garza, as instructed," Lopez said, smiling and trying to appear confident, hoping that the man did not notice the nervous tic in his left eye.

The bodyguard tapped on the door, and the second one opened it. He motioned Lopez into the room then roughly pushed him against the entryway wall and patted him down.

"I would not bring a weapon here," Lopez said, feigning indignation. "I am among friends, no?"

The bodyguard ignored him. When he had completed the search, he escorted Lopez down the hall into the sitting room of an expansive suite. Alejandro Garza sat in an overstuffed chair, legs crossed, scrolling through screens on his phone. A bottle of Gran Patron tequila sat on the table beside him. There was only one glass.

The bodyguard positioned Lopez in the center of the room, facing Garza, like a director placing an actor on his mark on the stage. Lopez waited, eying the tequila. The thought of speaking did not enter his mind.

Now and again, Garza stopped scrolling to type an email or text and send it, then continued his perusal of the messages he had received during the day. After several minutes passed, Lopez began to feel lightheaded. Standing ramrod straight with his knees locked, he began to sway and worried that he might lose consciousness and topple to the floor.

Keenly aware of the two security men observing him

from opposite sides of the room, he wondered what would happen to him if he passed out. That thought cleared his head. He didn't want to find out.

Finally, Garza looked up. He spoke without inviting Lopez to sit.

"Do you understand why you're here?"

"Yes, I think so. I said I may know the location of the *gringo*, this John Sole you are searching for. You said to come here so we could make a plan."

"This is the last plan we will make together." Garza nodded, his gaze piercing through Pepe's chest like a hand grabbing his heart and squeezing. "Do you understand this?"

"Yes," Lopez managed to squeak out of his constricting throat.

"Tell me how you know where this man is."

"There was a man who worked for Krieg and Zabala. His name was Martin. He …"

"I don't care about his name," Garza interrupted impatiently. "Give me the facts."

"Yes, yes, of course." Lopez swallowed several times rapidly. "The man, John Sole, beat him and took his rifle away. It was a topic of conversation among all the drivers and men who work for Krieg and Zabala. They laughed about it because no one liked Martin." Lopez paled and mentally cursed himself—you *tonto*, fool—for mentioning the name again. "I mean the man who was beaten."

"Why did he beat this man?"

"Because he found him shooting at a family trying to cross the Rio Grande. The man shot one of them, and your John Sole stopped him from shooting any others."

"Sole did this?"

"He did not use that name. He called himself Bill

Myers, but he is the man in the picture. The one who killed your man Bernardo in Monterrey."

"And you say he helped the Mexicans?"

"Yes. Yes, he did." Lopez's head bobbed up and down for emphasis.

Garza considered this for a moment. He filed the information away for further reflection later and continued his questioning. "If he shot one of Krieg and Zabala's men, why did they hire him to ride the trucks?"

"I am told that Krieg respected his firmness, that he was a man willing to take action when needed. Krieg told the others they needed more men like him. At least that is what they told me. It was a topic of much discussion among the other men."

Lopez shook his head as if trying to decipher a puzzle. "Krieg is a strange man, a dangerous one. There were times when I feared he might shoot me even though I made money for him. I tell you he is crazy."

"Why should I believe you have any knowledge of Sole's location?"

Garza wondered if Lopez might actually have some insight into where Sole was hiding. The account of Krieg hiring the man who beat his employee would be unbelievable ordinarily, but Lopez was shaking too much to dare fabricate a false story.

"Because this morning, when we loaded the trucks with the K and Z men, one of the leaders, a man called Pearce, was annoyed that he was a man short. He said that Bill Myers failed to show up and was probably sleeping with one of the whores in Creosote."

"Creosote?"

"Yes." Lopez nodded. "Just a small town, a collection of shacks really. They say Sole was staying there. If he was not on the trucks today and not killed with the others, he must still be there." He feigned a confident, knowing leer. "Sleeping with a whore like Pearce said."

Lopez looked at Garza, hoping that he saw the logic of his reasoning.

"Or, he may not have been on the trucks because he is gone, disappeared," Garza said.

The look of hope faded in Pepe's eyes.

"Still," Garza conceded. "We must make an attempt to verify what you have told us."

They spent a half four planning how to find and capture the *gringo* if he remained in the place called Creosote. Garza left no doubt that if he was not there, Lopez's usefulness to them would come to an end.

The planning ended. A bodyguard escorted him to the door, and Lopez walked down the hallway, conscious of the man's eyes on his back. He rang for the elevator, stepped on and sagged against the back wall. He didn't bother looking into the security camera.

In the lobby, he nearly ran to the restroom, loosening his pants as he scurried into a toilet stall to empty his loose bowels. He lowered his head into his hands as he squatted on the toilet.

"It is not fair," he muttered.

Pepe Lopez offered another silent prayer, the fourth of the day, and the most fervent.

Please Dear God, I beg of you, make sure the motherfucking gringo is there so we can kill him for this man who makes me want to shit my pants! In the name of the Holy Mother, I beg this one small favor of you. In return, I promise I will go to confession and confess my many sins to a priest.

Pepe stopped short of promising the Almighty that he

would make an effort to cease his sinning. After all, he was only human.

He looked up at heaven, which he imagined being somewhere just above the restroom ceiling and bemoaned his fate.

"This is all very unfair."

SEVENTY-SIX

Suicide

The night Claude Brainerd committed suicide, most everyone in Salvia County was sleeping, including Brainerd. Like most of the people in the county, he lived in one of the outlying rural communities away from the county seat.

No one noticed the man in dark clothes park his pickup in a wash between two nearby hills. He moved silently in the dark through the brush until he came to the rear of Brainerd's house. He wore gloves and, in his pocket, carried a screwdriver, a small pry bar, and a pocketknife. He only needed the knife.

There were no deadbolts on the doors. Sliding the knife blade along the strike plate, he inserted the tip just enough to pry back the spring bolt. The door opened soundlessly. He smiled. You had to love country folk.

The intruder slipped his boots off on the back porch and moved silently into the small frame house in his socks. Sounds of snores came from a bedroom in the back.

He moved cautiously, a step at a time, careful not to cause the floorboards to creak. It wouldn't have mattered.

He crept into the bedroom and found Brainerd profoundly asleep, unaware of anything, dead to the world. The man paused to consider the irony.

His plan required a weapon that belonged to the deputy, and he had come prepared to force the issue. That turned out to be unnecessary.

Most people secure their firearms, or at least hide them away in a closet or nightstand drawer. Not so with Brainerd.

The enormous Sam Brown belt that he strapped around his bulk every day hung over a chair in the bedroom. His service weapon, a Taurus 24/7, sat snuggly in the holster.

It was an unusual choice of weapon for a law enforcement officer. The Brazilian manufacturer made pistols priced on the lower end of the market, which was probably the reason Brainerd selected it.

Sole took the pistol from the holster and examined it. At least Brainerd kept it clean. Pulling the slide back, he checked for a round in the chamber. There was.

Brainerd slept through it all. The man stood for a moment, watching him and feeling a little guilty about what was going to happen, but not much.

The deputy had been involved with Krieg in a business that kidnapped young women and girls, imprisoned them, raped them, and sold them into sexual slavery. He was the worst kind of cop. Justice was coming tonight, and Brainerd's mouth would be closed permanently.

The man tapped the sleeping deputy's foot with the barrel of the Taurus. Brainerd grumbled, snorted, and continued sleeping.

He lifted the gun high and slammed it down on his big toe. Brainerd jerked up in the bed and grabbed his foot, letting out a stream of profanity.

"Goddamn, son of a bitch, motherfucker!"

He rubbed his foot for a second, still groggy, trying to comprehend what had happened. Lifting his eyes, he became aware of the man in the room with him and of the pistol in his hand—his pistol—pointed at his face.

"What the fuck … you're…"

"Sit up."

"What?" Brainerd shook his head, trying to get his brain around what was happening to him in his own bedroom.

"Sit up straight in the bed. Put your back against the headboard. Do it."

The man holding his pistol advanced toward him. Brainerd complied and sat up, leaning back against the headboard.

"You're right-handed?" the man asked.

He already knew the answer from the side the holster was positioned on the Sam Brown belt, but he was a careful man. Details were important.

"Right-handed? Yeah, I'm right-handed. Now you get the fuck out of my house!"

There were no other details to confirm. The man stepped quickly to Brainerd's right side, placed the pistol an inch from his skull, and pulled the trigger. The deputy finally understood what was about to happen. At the last moment, he started to move, but the man was quicker.

The gunshot reverberated through the small house. Outside it was a dull popping thump. A hundred yards away, it was barely discernible among the night sounds of chirring insects and distant coyotes. If any of the neighbors heard it, they did not feel motivated to leave their beds and investigate.

Claude Brainerd slumped, blood pouring from the holes in his head, entry and exit wounds. The man took the pistol and wrapped Brainerd's dead hand around the grip to make sure his prints would be clearly identifiable.

Then he stepped to the side, lifted Brainerd's arm to shoulder height, and let it drop. The gun fell out of the dead man's hand, striking the floor hard. Taurus pistols had a reputation for discharging unexpectedly from impacts, but this one did not.

The man left the same way he had come in and made his way across the back fields behind the cluster of houses. Five minutes later, he pulled his truck back on the county road.

When Sandy and Jacinta revealed that Brainerd had found them and taken them to Krieg, Sole recognized immediately that the deputy presented the greatest threat to their plans. Isabella suggested that he was worrying too much because Brainerd would be condemning himself if he told what he knew.

Sole nodded and did not argue. He didn't want to worry Isabella, but he knew that, while Brainerd might remain silent because of his involvement with Krieg, it was only a matter of time before Sheriff Dermott put some of the links together, and Claude Brainerd was the weakest link of all. He would snap like a twig under any investigative pressure.

The clock on the nightstand showed three in the morning when Sole climbed back in bed with Isabella. She put an arm over him, rested her head against his chest, and held him close. She did not ask where he had been.

SEVENTY-SEVEN

Damnedest Thing

The days passed in relative quiet. The news of Tom Krieg's death buzzed through Creosote, raising all manner of speculation among the locals. Theories about the killer's motives were plentiful. The lord of Salvia County had no lack of enemies and, despite the deference shown from those intimidated by his bullying, few friends.

Isabella served beers at the café while the cowboys and locals tossed their theories back and forth. John Sole, whom the locals simply called Bill, spent most of his time with Isabella helping in the kitchen and working the bar with her.

He became an accepted member of the community. They walked side by side from Isabella's house to the café each day, talking and holding hands. The citizens of Creosote sat on their stoops and smiled as they passed. It was good that Isabella didn't spend her days alone anymore, they said among themselves, and this Bill Myers seems like a good enough sort.

A sort of domestic tranquility settled over Sole and

Isabella. He reminded himself he would leave one day. The need to complete his mission still nagged at him like a sore tooth, but the longer he stayed with Isabella, the less he felt the nagging. An uncomfortable thought crept into his mind. Maybe he should let it go.

Shaye's dead voice whispered to him in the quiet hours of the night as he lay beside Isabella, that he should let it go. Move on, be happy, find peace, she whispered. He had done enough. There was nothing else to do. Lying beside Isabella, he was almost persuaded.

His life became entwined with hers, and he kept putting off his departure. Next week would be soon enough to do what he had to do, he thought. Or, maybe even the week after. For now, he soaked up the time with Isabella, spending every possible minute with her.

"We have company." Isabella peered through the café's dusty window at the pickup, pulling up out front.

Sole was in the kitchen washing dishes. They had a working arrangement. She did the cooking, something she was an expert at. He did the cleaning, something he was learning to do to her standards.

He came through the door, wiping his hands on a towel. Outside, Sheriff Paul Dermott exited the pickup, stretched, gave a glance up and down the street, and headed for the door. He pulled it open, a look of concern replacing the customary smile for his constituents.

"Isabella," Dermott said, giving her a greeting nod. "And …"

"Myers," Sole said with a smile. "Bill Myers."

"Right." Dermott nodded. "Myers, the new man in town I heard about."

"Not so new now," Isabella chimed in, doing her best to smile. "Bill's been helping me out for a while."

"That's good." Dermott gave Sole the usual law enforcement scrutiny, alert for something out of place, a nervous tic, eyes that wouldn't meet his, Adam's apple that bobbed up and down in his throat from nervous swallowing.

There was nothing. Bill Myers apparently had no secrets to hide. Dermott turned his attention to Isabella.

"Need to ask you a few questions."

"Alright. Can I get you something? Some lunch? Coffee?"

Dermott stood by the counter without taking a seat. He hadn't come for lunch.

"Coffee would be good. Thanks."

She turned away to pour the coffee and hoped he didn't see her hand shake. Sole reached for it when the cup was full and placed it on the counter in front of the sheriff.

Dermott focused on the coffee and lifted the cup. "You always make a fine cup of coffee, Isabella."

"Thanks, Paul. You should come around more. We don't see you in Creosote much."

"Yeah, sorry about that. I stay pretty busy, county business, constituents, that sort of thing. It all ties up my time." He sipped the coffee and looked her in the eyes. "Something else has been tying up my time."

Here it comes. John had warned her that one day they would ask questions. Today was the day. The key, he emphasized, was to tell the truth, except for any truth that would come back to bite them in the ass. Remain calm and answer the questions—to a point, at least.

"What's tying up your time, Paul?" Isabella asked.

"This damned Krieg murder." He shook his head. "It's a puzzler."

"Really? I figured you'd have things wrapped up pretty quick. Krieg had a way of pissing people off."

"Yes, he did." Dermott laughed. "But so far, I haven't been able to figure out which one got so pissed off they put three slugs in his brain."

Isabella's face paled. She never saw the body before they rushed from the barn the day they rescued Sandy and Jacinta.

"Sorry. I shouldn't have said that to you." Dermott was sincere. He added, nonchalantly, "Haven't seen Sandy around in a while."

"He's on his great adventure." Isabella smiled and leaned on the counter as if excited to share her son's exploits with the sheriff. "I told him the time had come for him to go off and see some of the world."

"Want to get him out of Creosote, huh?"

"Not really. Just wanted him to realize there's more to this world than this old town."

"For sure," Dermott said with a nod. "How about you, Bill Myers? You strike me as a man who has seen a good bit of the world."

"I have." Sole nodded, his eyes on Dermott's. "That a problem?"

"Nope. Not at all." Dermott shook his head. "Just commenting. You know how it is. A new man in town. Prominent citizen gets murdered. Makes a person wonder."

"Wonder if I did away with Krieg?"

"Something like that. It's not unheard of," Dermott said, smiling pleasantly and added, "You worked for him, didn't you?"

"Briefly." Sole nodded.

"What sort of work?"

"Relief driver on one of his trucks. Picked up tomatoes down below Monterrey ... sometimes avocados."

"Anything ever happen on those trips?"

"Nothing out of the ordinary. Usually took most of the day. Got home late."

"You hear about what happened to their trucks down in Mexico ... the ambush?"

"I did."

The news of the K and Z trucks ambushed by hijackers in a mountain valley and the resulting bloodbath had spread like wildfire through Salvia County.

"But you weren't there?"

"Nope. I was here."

"You quit your job?"

"I did."

"Mind if I ask why?"

"Don't mind at all. Krieg was an asshole."

"Can't argue with you there," Dermott said, laughing good-naturedly. "But here's what I find interesting. Krieg's murder took place on the same day as the ambush, when you were here and not out on the trucks. That's curious." His brow wrinkled as if trying to decipher a riddle. "Don't you think that's curious?"

"It is odd." Sole nodded. "I'll give you that. Guess I'm just lucky."

Sole was familiar with this game, had played it many times himself. He decided it was time to stop playing games. The longer the back and forth went on the greater the chance they would say something to open a hole in their story, and Sole had no doubt the smiling sheriff would pounce on it if they gave him a chance.

"Now, I'll ask you a question, Sheriff," Sole said.

"Shoot." Dermott put the coffee cup down calmly and returned his gaze.

"Am I a suspect in the murder of Tom Krieg?"

"No," Dermott said honestly. "Not now, at least."

"Not ever," Isabella interjected. "Bill spent the day here with me … all day. He did not leave."

"Well, I guess that answers that," Dermott said. He looked at Sole. "You have my apology, Mr. Myers."

"No need," Sole said. "Doing your job. I get it."

"Yeah, I suppose." Dermott scratched his head. "Not too good it seems. Thing is there's some other murders I can't explain. Lucky Martin, Emmett Brewer and now old Sherm Westerfield." He looked at Sole, his eyes narrowed. "Now who would want to kill old Sherm? Most harmless fella I ever knew."

"That's a good question." Sole nodded. "He was my friend."

"How about Lucky Martin? Was he your friend?"

"Nope." Sole shook his head. "Only met him once, and far as I could tell he was an asshole like his boss."

Dermott laughed. "You damn sure got that right. Biggest asshole in the county." He shook his head. "Then there's Claude Brainerd."

"Word is that was a suicide," Sole said, his eyes never leaving Dermott's.

"Sure as hell looks like one." Dermott's lips pursed as if he was trying to work out a puzzle. "Thing is, of every person I have ever run across in my life, Claude Brainerd would be the last one I'd expect to put a gun to his head and pull the trigger."

"You said you had questions for me, Paul," Isabella broke in firmly, her intimidation fading and her annoyance rising. "What are they?"

"Oh, it was mostly about Sandy. You gave me the answers." He shook his head, a wry smile on his face. "You know, Doyle Krieg said some things."

"What things?" A knot formed in Isabella's belly.

"Said he was sure Sandy killed his father. Said Sandy was jealous of them, always had been, and this was the way he got even."

"Sandy? Kill Someone? Don't be ridiculous," Isabella snapped.

"Almost exactly what I told him." Dermott shook his head. "The boy is crazy and about as mean as his father was."

He turned for the door, stopped, and turned back to face them. "I'm sorry for the worry I've caused you, Isabella. It's not your problem, it's just this case is using up all my time. Things aren't adding up, and maybe I'm pushing a little too hard to figure it out." He shook his head "Don't have much to go on. Only pieces of evidence I have are Krieg's body and the slugs that killed him, and they don't match any gun I can find. Then there's the blood I scraped off the barn floor."

"Blood?" Isabella tensed.

"Yep. Blood in the middle of the barn, not in the storeroom around Krieg's body. Just got the lab results back this morning." Dermott ran a hand through his hair, shaking his head. "Damnedest thing. The blood is not Krieg's, but it has the same DNA markers in it. The lab report said it came from a relative, but the only relative around was Doyle, and he didn't have a mark on him."

They waited, knowing the sheriff was fishing again, hoping for a response. They gave him none. Dermott shrugged and turned to leave.

"Anyway. Sorry again, to have troubled you." The

sheriff pulled the door open and stepped out muttering, "Damnedest thing."

SEVENTY-EIGHT

More Comfortable

While the investigation surrounding the murder of his partner whirled through Salvia County like a tornado, Raul Zabala tried to carry on with their enterprises, for a time at least. He put out the word he was hiring drivers for their produce import business. Apparently, a mass exodus of staff around the time Tom Krieg was murdered left him shorthanded.

The *Federales* in Mexico were investigating an apparent hijack attempt involving three K and Z trucks and were asking questions about the large number of dead, heavily armed, men whose bodies littered a valley road near Monclova. Coincidentally, the battle in the Mexican valley happened at the same time Krieg and Zabala's employees walked out on them.

Eventually, Mexican federal investigators contacted the FBI about the abandoned K and Z trucks littered with dead Americans in their country. Agents came to visit Raul Zabala, and he stopped hiring new men long enough to answer their questions. Then he stopped hiring altogether and found himself a high-powered attorney out of Dallas. On the advice of his lawyer, he shut his mouth and stopped answering questions.

During the investigation, The FBI questioned Doyle Krieg about his deceased father's business. Doyle claimed to have no knowledge about the workings of his father's activities outside the ranch. The agents that interviewed him were inclined to accept his explanation and reckoned that Doyle Krieg might be the dumbest son of a bitch in Texas. They deduced correctly that Tom Krieg deliberately kept his son on the ranch and away from his other business endeavors because he was an idiot.

Authorities eventually discovered the hidden panels and false walls in the abandoned K and Z trucks. It became clear that Krieg and Zabala had been importing more than tomatoes and avocados.

Prosecutors pondered where they could find living witnesses. Everyone at the ambush site was dead, and the illegal immigrants who had made use of their border-crossing services felt no inclination to step forward and reveal themselves. As for the girls selected for sale to human traffickers in the sex industry, they had vanished so deep into the grimy recesses of that world that they might never be found—if they remained alive at all.

Raul Zabala's time as a free man dwindled to a few days. Even without the victims, the prosecution amassed enough evidence from the trucks at the ambush site and those remaining on the K and Z lot to bring charges.

Once the legal maneuvering ended, and the appeals settled, the federal prosecutor assigned to the case exuded confidence in a series of public interviews that Raul Zabala would spend years in prison for human trafficking. Even so, he would undoubtedly be more comfortable than his victims.

SEVENTY-NINE

Side by Side

"Which house?" the man Pepe Lopez thought of as Gordito asked.

They crouched beside a mesquite in the grassland just beyond the fringe of shacks that constituted Creosote's residential district. He still didn't know the names of the two scowling security men Garza had sent with him. He simply labeled them *Gordito*—Fat One, and *Flaco*—Skinny One. The nicknames were for his reference only, and he never said them to their faces.

The three men had crossed from Mexico earlier in the day at Brownsville, using the false identities on their forged Border Crossing Cards for a brief visit to the States. Garza told them to bring back the *gringo*, John Sole, alive if possible, or dead if not. Either way, he would be bound and stuffed in the false bottom of the trunk of their car.

"Which house?" Gordito repeated, his tone insistent.

"I brought you here," Lopez said. "He is in this village, but you can't expect me to know exactly which house, sitting out here in the middle of the night."

"We expect you … *Señor* Garza expects … you to lead us to the man. We will do the rest," Flaco said, in a menacing bass whisper.

Lopez swallowed. He'd been thinking fast, and mostly on the fly, since the ambush in the valley. There hadn't been time to come up with a real plan, not if he wanted to live.

Desperate to survive a few more hours, he told them he knew where to find this John Sole they wanted so urgently. He prayed he was right.

This rundown row of hovels was a gathering place for the K and Z men. Even more, the morning before Garza's men shot holes in him, Stu Pearce told Lopez that Bill Myers—John Sole—was missing and probably with a whore in Creosote where he'd been living the past few weeks.

Lopez figured the odds of finding Sole there at fifty-fifty. Not great, but they were far better than the one hundred percent chance Garza would have had his men slit his throat if he hadn't come up with some sort of plan.

He had bought time for himself. Now, his brain whirled in overdrive to find a way to buy more.

"Okay, I have a plan," he whispered.

Flaco snickered, "Your plans aren't worth much, *cabrón*."

Gordito glared at him.

"Just hear me out," Pepe insisted. "I didn't realize that we would be here after dark. I thought we would have time to observe during daylight and see which house he entered."

"This is not a plan." The threat in Flaco's tone was clear, and his eyes narrowed like a snake poised to strike.

"Listen to me!"

They huddled under the mesquite while Garza's men listened. When he finished, they looked at each other for a moment. Gordito shrugged as if to say, sure why not?

Moving along the back of the line of shacks in the dark,

they were invisible. It was a little before three in the morning with a forecast of a late moonrise at five o'clock. For now, the only light came from the soft glow of the stars. Flaco held up a hand, and they stopped midway down the row.

"This one will do," he said.

Gordito tried the back door and found it unlocked. In fact, there was no lock, just an old rusted knob. If security concerns in rural Texas were relaxed, in Creosote, it seemed they were nonexistent.

The door scraped the floor as they pushed it open and crept into the shack.

"Who's there?" a voice asked from directly ahead, not ten feet away.

Flaco crossed the space in a second and placed a hand over the old woman's mouth, his knife at her throat. An old man, her husband, stirred in the bed beside her.

"Mae, what's wrong?" Carl Chaney rolled on the creaking mattress toward his wife of forty-eight years. "What's …"

Gordito's massive hand clamped over his face. Like Flaco, he held a long thin-bladed knife at his victim's throat.

Pepe Lopez stepped to the foot of the bed and looked down at the terrified couple.

"Do not be afraid. We are looking for someone." Lopez reached into his pocket and took out the folded paper bearing the photo of John Sole. "Have you seen this man?"

Wide-eyed Carl Chaney nodded. Mae Chaney whimpered. Everyone in Creosote knew Bill Myers.

"Which house is he in? Can you tell us?" Lopez held his breath, his muscles tense, ready to bolt from the house and escape Garza's killers.

Carl Chaney nodded. Pepe Lopez breathed again and tried not to fall over from relief.

"Tell us." He put a finger to his lips. "Tell us quietly, and we will not hurt you or your wife."

Chaney nodded, and Gordito moved his hand away from the old man's mouth.

"He's in the big house, last one at the end of the street," Chaney managed to whisper through his trembling lips.

"Which way on the street?"

"Out our front door and to the left. All the way to the end. Biggest house in town. You can't miss it."

"Good. That's very good." Pepe nodded and folded the piece of paper.

"Please don't hurt my wife," Chaney said, looking into the icy stares of the men with the knives. "Don't hurt us."

Pepe smiled and put the paper in his pocket. He turned away without speaking.

Behind him, he heard the sound of a brief struggle. Feet kicked under the bed sheets, frail old bodies twisted to escape. There was no escape. Knives passed over thin, aged throats, and the struggling ceased.

Carl and Mae Chaney, husband and wife for almost half a century, lay side by side, their lifeless eyes staring at the ceiling that had covered their heads for more than half of those years. Pepe Lopez trailed by Garza's men left the house through the same unlocked back door they had entered less than five minutes earlier.

EIGHTY

Under the Stars

Sandy and Jacinta worked at staying out of sight, not always an easy task in the small house. Sole had explained the need for them to remain unseen. The investigation into Tom Krieg's death would be swirling around the county for many months. He told them that when their bodies had healed, and they were mentally strong enough, they would arrange a homecoming to Creosote, welcoming Sandy and his new bride back to his home.

They even concocted a cover story. Keep it simple, Sole cautioned them. Include too many details, and the holes in the story would be apparent.

For the truly curious, it was simple. Sandy met Jacinta sitting alone in a *taqueria* in El Paso while he was out seeing some of the world. She had crossed the border illegally with a *coyotaje* to find her uncle in Houston, but the *coyotaje* abandoned her.

For the residents of Creosote, the presence of an illegal immigrant would be of no great concern. Like many western states, Texas was full of immigrants crossing the border illegally.

Jacinta was beautiful, and Sandy naturally took an interest in her. They talked. He asked her out, and she accepted. Eventually, they fell in love, and he brought her home to Creosote to meet his mother and friends in town.

That was the story, simple and reasonably close to the truth. There would be no way to prove the connection to Tom Krieg and his human trafficking operations. Once her presence could be revealed, they would begin working to gain her permanent resident status and eventually citizenship.

For now, though and until they could emerge back into the world, healed from their injuries, Isabella told the more curious in Creosote that Sandy had gone to do some exploring and find some adventure. She said she encouraged him because a young man needed to get out and find that there's more to the world than a backwater west Texas town.

People nodded and agreed. Yes, Sandy was a fine young man. He should go out and see what there is to see, but will he be back sometime? She assured them that he planned to return. Creosote had always been home, after all.

Sandy and Jacinta lived together in his room and spent their days in the house. They slowly recovered from the beatings they had received from Krieg and Brainerd and grew stronger every day.

At night, while Creosote slept, they would sneak out of the back door and into the brush country stretching for miles in all directions. Sandy knew a path, and they would walk for a mile in the dark, with only the moon and stars to light their way.

Sandy always carried a blanket, and Jacinta would bring

leftovers from dinner in a sack. There in the dark, they would spread the blanket and lay back, munching the leftovers and looking at the night sky as they talked about their future together.

Sometimes they made love under the stars, the grass swaying over their heads. Other nights, they talked. Always, they returned to the house well before daylight. They waited anxiously for the time when they could arrange their "homecoming" and live together out in the open.

Their bodies and minds were healing. Sandy—Reynaldo as Jacinta called him—said he would ask John and Isabella in the morning if it wasn't time to plan the homecoming so that they could come out into the open.

But tonight, they lay on the blanket under the stars. They touched and kissed, exploring each other, thrilling each other the way young people do. Nothing else mattered.

EIGHTY-ONE

No Time

Sandwiched between Flaco and Gordito, Pepe Lopez stumbled through the brush in the dark as they made their way toward the house at the end of the road. Flaco raised a hand, and they crouched to examine the darkened windows. As Carl Chaney promised, it was the most prominent house in town.

Lopez listened as Garza's men planned. They spoke calmly, conducting business as usual. Clearly, they were not novices at breaking into homes in the night and killing or kidnapping people. Pepe was mesmerized and terrified by their matter-of-fact attitude about what they were going to do.

The man they sought was known to be dangerous, a man who had killed. Flaco and Gordito huddled and decided that a two-pronged attack made the most sense. They would flank him from two sides so he would be unable to defend against them both at the same time. Pepe Lopez remained silent, hoping to be forgotten in the planning.

"You will come with me," Flaco said.

Lopez nodded his understanding, unable to force words from his mouth.

His stomach churned. This John Sole had already killed two of Garza's drug dealers, Bernardo in Monterrey, and another in Atlanta the year before.

What was he doing with these men, he wondered? He thought of running away while they were busy trying to capture the *gringo*, then pushed the thought away. Even if he managed to escape during the turmoil, Garza would find him, a possibility that terrified him more than any other.

Gordito and Flaco agreed that speed was the critical element of their attack. They planned to move rapidly, trying the doors, Gordito in front and Flaco with Lopez in back. If they found them unlocked, they would creep into the house and do what had to be done. If the doors were locked, they would force them open with a kick and overcome the man they sought with sudden, overpowering violence, a tactic that had served them well in past assignments.

Lopez thought he saw a hole in their plan but was not about to interfere. Surely they knew better than he how to kidnap and murder someone. They were the assassins. He was only a simple *coyotaje*—and seller of women.

The plan in place, they moved to their positions at the front and back of the house. They would enter simultaneously, precisely one minute later.

Flaco checked his watch, put his hand on the doorknob, and found it unlocked. He pushed it open slowly and stepped into the small kitchen followed by Pepe.

An instant later, they heard a small sound at the front door, followed by an enormous crash. Gordito rushed into the living room and stopped, facing Flaco across fifteen feet of open space.

The failure in their planning, the hole that Lopez had noticed and kept to himself, became immediately apparent. Their target was not trapped between them. He was in a room down the hall, and the noise of their entry had undoubtedly alerted him to their presence.

Flaco and Gordito moved to the hallway. It was about fifteen feet long and narrow. Two doors opened into it, one at the far end, and one midway to the left. The sound of movement came from the room at the end of the hall.

Isabella lay spooning against Sole's back as they slept. When the front door crashed open, she rose on her hand, startled and started to speak.

"What the …"

Sole rolled off the edge of the bed to the floor dragging her roughly by the arm with one hand, as he retrieved the Colt from the nightstand with the other. When she was on the floor beside him, he pushed Isabella face down and motioned for her to get under the bed.

She hesitated only a moment, feeling she should help him somehow and face the intruders. He pushed her down, and she relented, wriggling and squirming until she was under the bed.

Though their plan had been flawed, Flaco and Gordito were not fools. They were skilled assassins, working for a master assassin.

Flaco got on his belly and began inching forward toward the door. If someone in the room fired a shot, it would have to be aimed at the floor to hit him.

Gordito rushed back through the front door, dragging

Pepe Lopez with him. At the side of the house, Gordito located the window that looked in on the room at the end of the hall. The killers had their target between them.

Inside, Sole moved away from the bed to draw fire away from Isabella. Crouching on the floor, his back in a corner, he could see the door and the single window into the room.

No shots had been fired, and he considered sending a round through the door to keep the intruders honest and not assume they could rush the room unscathed. He opted against firing to conserve ammunition.

The .45 held eight rounds including one in the chamber. The nightstand drawer held a spare magazine. He crawled toward it, wishing he'd remembered it before taking up his defensive position.

Gordito stood on his tiptoes but found he could not see into the window. The ground sloped away from the house, and though the front windows were at chest level, this one was over his head.

"Find me something to stand on," he whispered.

"To stand on?" The whites of Pepe's wide eyes were visible even in the dim starlight.

"Do it," Gordito ordered. "Now."

Lopez scurried toward a shed in the back. A minute later, he came running breathlessly across the yard, a five-gallon bucket in his hand

"Will this do?"

Gordito jerked the bucket from him and turned it upside down under the window. When he stepped on it, Pepe wondered if it would support the big man's weight. It did, and Gordito slowly lifted his head above the window sill, one hand steadying himself against the side of the house, the other holding the TEC-9 machine pistol, apparently the weapon of choice for close quarters assassinations.

Sole reached the nightstand, slid the drawer open, and retrieved the spare magazine. He was backing toward his corner just as a head appeared, rising slowly on the other side of the glass.

The forehead was broad with a mass of thick black hair above. Two eyes peered down into the room, searching in the darkness for him. Sole knelt and sighted along the Colt's barrel and waited to make sure the threat was real and not some local drunk or peeping tom.

The man's hand came up. The weapon was unmistakable.

Sole applied four pounds of pressure to the Colt's modified trigger, and the pistol bucked and roared in his hand. The head disappeared.

Gordito fell backward, landing with a resounding thud on the hard-packed dirt. Sole had fired from a crouching position near the floor, five feet from the window, and the .45 slug entered Gordito's head on an angled trajectory that sent it through his forehead and out the top of his skull.

The flash and roar from inside the house were enough to start Pepe Lopez running for his life. But not before gore and brain matter from Gordito's shattered skull sprayed over him, covering his face and clothes.

Arms flailing, he ran retracing their path through the grassland behind Creosote's row of dwellings. On reaching their car, he remembered Flaco still at the house in the hallway.

Fuck Flaco, he thought and climbed behind the wheel, reaching for the ignition key. It was gone, taken by Flaco when they left the vehicle.

"*¡Mierda!* Fuck Flaco!" he shouted this time.

In complete panic, Pepe Lopez was out of the car again and running through the brush. His feet now controlled his destiny, his brain was nothing more than a mass of quivering synapses overcome by terror. Pepe's only instinct was to run and keep running.

At the sound of the shot, from the bedroom. Flaco decided he had to offer some cover fire for his partner. He gave a quick burst with his TEC-9, spraying bullets through the door.

Crouched in his corner again, Sole watched them stitch holes in the back bedroom wall and continue out into the night. He checked the bed on the far wall, and Isabella put a hand out to indicate she was unharmed.

From the pattern of bullet holes in the door, Sole deduced that the shots had been fired from close to the floor. That meant the intruder was lying prone in the hallway.

He had fifteen rounds left and decided he could afford to put out some suppressive fire of his own. Hell, he might even get lucky and hit the son of a bitch.

He stood, intending to send some rounds on an angled trajectory through the door and down into the hallway floor. He picked three spots on the door, aiming so that a .45 slug should hit the hallway floor about three feet from the door, another six feet, and another at ten feet. It was pure guesswork, but if it caused the intruder to think twice, it might buy them time until he figured out what to do next.

He sighted the Colt, finger on the trigger and took a deep breath. He never fired the shot.

A deep roar thundered at them through the door. A moment later, Sandy called to them.

"Mom, John? Are you in there?" His voice was full of worry.

Sole shook his head to encourage her to remain hidden until he had a chance to check things out, but Isabella began crawling out from under the bed as soon as she heard Sandy's voice.

"We're here, son."

She ran to the door, but Sole stopped her, holding her arm and forcing her to wait. He called through the door.

"Where are you, Sandy?"

"At the end of the hall, by the kitchen."

"Anyone else there?"

"No, sir. J-just the man I shot."

He sounded shaken. Sole figured he had a right to be.

"Sandy, we don't know if there are others. Step back into the kitchen and put your back into the corner where the refrigerator and wall meet. I'm coming out."

"Okay."

Sole gave him a few seconds and then pulled the door open, easing his head out to peer into the hall. It was empty except for the man lying face down about ten feet from the door, the TEC-9 still clutched in his hand. The bloody hole in his back indicated that he never heard Sandy approach from behind and made no effort to turn and defend himself.

Sole moved down the hall. Sandy was in the kitchen as

directed, his back against the wall. Isabella followed and ran to her son.

"Mom, stay behind me," Sandy ordered.

"Where's Jacinta," she whispered.

"Safe ... I think. We were sitting out in the brush on a blanket and came heading back to be in before daylight when we heard the shots. I grabbed the shotgun from my pickup in the shed and put her inside with the doors locked.

"Let me have the keys to your pickup," Sole said standing with his back to Sandy and Isabella, watching for any additional threats. Sandy handed them over. "Stay here while I check outside."

Satisfied that there were no more intruders in the house, Sole moved through the kitchen to the back door. He found one more person, the man with the broad forehead that had made such a good target in the window.

Sole knelt by the body and retrieved the TEC-9, then moved around the yard, circling the house in widening arcs to make sure no else lurked in the dark. When he got to the shed at the back of the yard where they had hidden Sandy's truck, he used the keys to open the door.

He found Jacinta wide-eyed, but not panicked. A look of relief crossed her face when she recognized him.

"Reynaldo, is he injured?" she asked, starting to run toward the house.

"Wait," Sole ordered. "Stay beside me." He patted her shoulder. "He is fine. He saved us."

"I knew he would," she said with a nod. "When he makes up his mind, he can do many things."

"Yes, he can," Sole agreed.

They moved toward the house. Creosote's entire population approached, walking down the street toward them. Most were armed with rifles or shotguns.

"Bill," a voice called to him. "Bill Myers, is that you?"

"It's me, Ralph." Sole recognized the old man as one of Isabella's customers. "Everything's fine. Sorry to bother you all."

"Who's that with you?"

The crowd moved closer, not convinced. Isabella stepped out on the front porch.

"We're fine. Everyone go back to sleep. Bill was shooting at some coyotes. That's all."

There were murmurs among the crowd.

"Didn't sound like no one shooting at coyotes."

"Sounded like some kind of machine gun."

Right ... and a shotgun."

Skeptical, the crowd was still milling around in the road when they reached the house. Sole took Isabella by the arm and pulled her inside.

"We have to go ... all of us. Five minutes. Take what you can and then we leave."

"Wait a minute." She pulled her arm out of his grasp. "You can't tell us to do that. We can't just pack up and leave." Her eyes narrowed, and she demanded. "Who were those men? Tell us what's going on, now."

"There are people who want to kill me. They found me here. I don't know how, but now they will try to kill you too. I won't let them." He put his hands on her shoulders and looked into her eyes. "I'm sorry, Isabella. I've put you in danger, all of you. I was overconfident ... careless. That's inexcusable. Now, I have to get you someplace safe ... away from here."

"Who?" Isabella asked. "Who wants to kill you ... us?"

"There's no time to talk!" Sole's eyes begged her to trust him. "Please, pack some things. Travel light. I have money. We can buy whatever we need, but we must start moving and put distance between them and us before they send others. They won't stop. When we're gone … on the road, I'll explain."

Isabella's eyes never left his. Who was this man, she wondered for the thousandth time? She made her decision.

"Alright." She turned to Sandy and Jacinta. "Pack some things. Do it now. We leave in five minutes."

EIGHTY-TWO

Betrayed

It didn't take a genius to see she was pissed. Her back turned toward him, Isabella stared out the passenger window, her chin resting on her fist, elbow on the armrest. Sandy sat with his arm around Jacinta in the rear crew cab. They rode in silence.

He owed her an explanation. No, he owed her much more than that, and he knew it. Being with Isabella these past few weeks had been like pouring cool water on his feverish head.

Still, it was not enough to stop him from going to Mexico to meet Juan Galdo's cousin, a meeting that had allowed *Los Salvajes* to somehow track him to Creosote. If he had only resisted the need to end things his way. If his pride would have allowed him to walk away from it. If the memories did not burn so deeply in his soul.

If … if …. If. The ifs amounted to nothing. His foolishness had endangered those he cared for once again.

Yes, he owed her an explanation, but first, there was a

call to make. Sole checked the time on his phone. Just after four AM—a little past six in Georgia.

He punched in the number with his thumb. A voice answered, not asleep, but not completely awake.

"Hello." The man on the other end yawned, and Sole could hear him sip coffee.

"Semper FI. Do you know who this is?"

There was a pause, and then the man said, "Yes," whispering it into the phone.

Only John Sole would speak those words to William 'Billy' Siever, though Siever had never been a Marine. The Marine Corps motto was among the last words they exchanged after they buried John's mother decades earlier. Since then, it had become a sign of comradeship between them.

"I need your help, Billy."

"Tell me, John."

There weren't many people in the world John Sole could call on and ask for a favor. In fact, there weren't any —except Billy Siever.

They had been friends since their childhood back in Cassit Pass, Georgia. A night of joyriding in a local preacher's car had resulted in John's arrest, trial, guilty verdict, and subsequent enlistment in the Marine Corps while Billy's well-connected father managed to keep him out of court with no blemish on his record.

Since then, Billy, now William Siever, Attorney at Law, had established a successful practice in Dahlonega, Georgia. John had gone into law enforcement in Atlanta. They kept in touch until the day John lost everything and vanished from the face of the globe. That was over a year ago.

Siever's conscience had always been burdened with

guilt. He had gotten off from their escapade without even a slap on the wrist. John Sole had paid the price.

The judge presiding at his trial sternly advised John that he would allow him the option of enlistment in the military or prison. He had an hour to decide. John elected to join the Marine Corps.

Siever offered many times over the years to help his friend if the time came that help was required. That time had come.

Sole explained what he needed and why in as few words as possible. Siever asked some questions for clarification, but the request was straightforward.

"When will you arrive?"

"Three days."

"I'll have things ready."

The call ended. William Siever poured another cup of coffee and checked his calendar. He would have to reschedule a couple of client appointments, but he would tell his staff he was feeling under the weather. In reality, he was worried sick about his friend.

"What have you gotten yourself into, John?" he wondered looking into his backyard.

Outside, the sun was brightening the garden. Two hummingbirds buzzed, bumped, and fought each other for rights to the nectar from his wife's daylilies.

He had a good life, coasting through it with ease and without care. The call from his friend made him feel guilty about that. What would John Sole do to be able to sit and sip coffee on a pleasant morning while he watched hummingbirds flutter around daylilies?

With a sigh, Billy Siever picked up his phone and began making calls. He had a debt to repay to his friend.

Sole tossed his cell phone into the pickup's console and looked at Isabella. Sandy and Jacinta in the back of the crew cab watched him in the rearview mirror.

"It's time we talk."

They covered fifty miles in silence, each lost in their thoughts, trying to come to grips with what had happened and how they came to be in this pickup fleeing from—from what, Isabella wondered.

"Yes, it is, John." Isabella paused. "Let's start there. Is that really your name?"

"It is." He nodded.

"And your last name?"

"No." He shook his head. "It's best you don't know that."

Isabella sighed, shaking her head. "What the hell have you gotten us into, John-with-no-last-name?"

He began talking. For an hour, he explained about his past as a law enforcement officer, although he left out any reference to the city, people, or other officers involved. They listened, riveted.

When he described the deaths of his wife and children, tears rolled down his face, but his voice did not break. Isabella sobbed as did Jacinta. Sandy's eyes were wet as he fought back his own tears.

Sole left nothing out. He killed one of the cartel members after leaving the police department. He went underground to find the others responsible. For more than a year, he sank deeper and deeper out of sight. Secure in his anonymity, he became overconfident. He killed another in Monterrey but had no idea how they could track him to

Creosote. Krieg's operation had nothing to do with the cartel.

He wrapped up the explanation with a simple conclusion. "They will kill you. That is why we had to leave. These men, the cartel, will not give up. They found me. I must have been careless."

He paused to allow them to respond if they wanted. No one spoke.

He looked at Isabella. "I can't tell you how sorry I am. There, in Creosote with you, I thought I was far enough underground that they couldn't find me. I was wrong."

"So this is about your vengeance?" She looked into his eyes, trying to finally understand what drove him.

"No." He shook his head and then added, "Yes maybe, at first, vengeance was part of it. Now it's something more." He looked up trying to find the words. "There has to be a balance … a reckoning. My wife, children, all the others that have suffered and died at their hands, there must be some balance to things or nothing makes sense in the world." He struggled for a way to explain. Finally, he shrugged. "I don't know how else to say it."

"You mean justice."

"Yes, that too."

"Then stop and we'll call the authorities. Start with Sheriff Dermott, then the FBI or whoever else works on these things."

"I thought of that, but they would find out."

"Who?"

"The cartel … *Los Salvajes*—the savages they call themselves, and for good reason."

"I have heard of these people." Jacinta spoke softly from the back, and her hand tightened on Sandy's arm. "No one escapes them, and everyone fears them in my home."

Isabella wasn't convinced. "Still, they can't know what we say to the police ... to the FBI."

"They would figure things out when the investigators came knocking. It might take time, but eventually, they would find out who spoke and where they are." He shook his head. "You don't understand. People talk ... everywhere. In prison, on the street, even cops among themselves, but they talk. The cartel has money, more than you can imagine." He nodded with certainty. "Eventually they would get the information, whatever they had to pay for it, and they would find you."

"What about protection?" she asked. "Don't the Feds do that?"

"For witnesses, yes." Sole nodded. "But what have you witnessed? A home invasion and attempted murder. That is a local matter. Sheriff Dermott will not be able to identify the bodies. The cartel is too careful for that. The dead men back there will go to their graves as John Doe ... no names and no ties to the cartel. Besides, Dermott couldn't protect you, not from *Los Salvajes*."

Sole shook his head. "And you wouldn't get any protection from the Feds because you have nothing to offer to them in exchange. Some bad men broke into your home, for reasons unknown. That is not a federal crime, and despite what you see in the movies, they do not provide permanent bodyguard services."

"What about Krieg's operation," Sandy said. "That's a violation of federal law, isn't it?"

"It is," Sole agreed. "They will put that together through the murder investigation, and if you wanted to come forward, you could." He looked into the mirror. "What would you add? That you know who killed Krieg? That you wanted to kill him yourself. Would you give up

Reggie Prince? He helped get you out, saved your life, but it's your choice. I won't stop you if that's what you want to do."

Sandy was quiet, thinking it over. He shook his head. "No, but it seems like there should be something we can do."

"I agree," Isabella snapped. "You've painted this picture of the cartel with its money and killers and that they can reach anyone, but the government has money and can reach anyone too."

"It seems that way, but it's not that simple," Sole said, nodding.

"Why?" Isabella refused to accept that nothing could be done to get their lives back.

"Alright, let's say you had information to give them about a federal crime the cartel was involved in, which you don't, but assuming you did, the Feds would use it and move on."

"Move on? What does that mean? Abandon us?"

"They don't look at it that way, but yes, that would be the effect. Oh, they'd arrange new identities for you, set you up in a new city, help you find employment, but after a while, you and Sandy and Jacinta would be on your own. There won't be guards standing outside your house or driving you to work or shopping. It'll just be you."

He shook his head. "The cartel can wait. If it takes a year or ten years to find you, they will, and when they do, after the Feds are gone and no one is watching, you will disappear ... all of you."

"But you were there. You could explain it all." She stopped. "But then they would put you in prison for killing the cartel man after your wife died, and there was ...." She stopped short of mentioning Claude Brainerd's suicide. How many others, she wondered?

"I thought of doing that," Sole said. "Turning myself in would be the simplest way."

"No," she shook her head. "I don't want that either."

"It's my decision, not yours. I would do it to protect you all if it would help, but it won't."

He struggled for a way to explain "If I go to the FBI, confess, tell what I know, what I have found out, what I've done, they'll use that information. Other agencies will get involved, DEA, ICE, all of them and as they close in, the cartel will know it and eventually will find out who talked. It won't take much for them to piece it all together. They know I was with you in Creosote. You would become a target, a warning to others who might turn on them. I would be in prison, unable to protect you, and the result would be the same. You would disappear ... forever."

"Disappear? You mean ..."

"One more thing." He wanted her to understand everything. "This is more than cops and robbers, good guys and bad guys. This is personal for them. Forget the cartel drug dealer I shot. They will come for me because they butchered my family."

"No." Isabella shook her head. "That doesn't make sense."

"Think of it this way. If the situation was reversed, and I had murdered their loved ones, they would never stop looking for me ... ever. They assume the same about me, that I will never stop coming for them ... ever." He didn't mention to Isabella that their assumption was valid before he met her and she damped the fire inside him.

He continued, "It's how their minds work. They have to find me and eliminate me, and everyone I care about, or I will always be a threat, someone who could show up one day when they least expect it."

"A blood feud ... Hatfield and McCoy sort of thing ..." Isabella's lip curled in disgust. "They kill yours; you kill theirs until there is no one left to kill."

"Vendetta," Jacinta said.

"Yes. Vendetta." A thought came to him, a way to illustrate their predicament. "Have you ever heard of Whitey Bulger?"

"A gangster," Sandy said from the back seat.

"Right. A mob hitman. No one knows exactly how many men he killed, but with all the killing, he made enemies along the way. He was also an FBI informant for a while. The mob put a contract on him. He was a young man when he started killing people."

He paused and looked at her. "He was eighty-nine years old serving time for racketeering in a federal prison when another inmate put a padlock in a sock and beat him to death. The mob never forgets."

"But that's the mob, not the ones who are after you." Isabella tried to sound hopeful.

"The people looking for me, the cartel ... they're worse." Sole shook his head. "Even if I gave it up. They would not, and now they are looking for you so they can get to me."

He stopped talking. They tried to absorb everything he had said. Finally, Isabella spoke.

"This is bullshit." She was angry and had a right to be. "Our lives are over. According to you, we'll always be on the run." She glared at him. "All because you're on some quest, some road you think will lead to justice, but there won't be any justice, just more killing." She shook her head, tears in her eyes. "How could you do this to us?"

Her words cut deep into his heart. She felt betrayed. Isabella had come to mean more to him than he had dared admit to himself, and he had just lost her.

"I had no right to become ... to involve you in my life," he said stoically. "I'm taking you to a place where you should be safe. I'll leave you and go somewhere else ... leave a trail for the cartel to follow so they come after me and away from you. It's the best I can do, for now, Isabella. I'm sorry."

He looked at her, but she turned away, staring out the passenger window.

You did this, John, he told himself. Everything you touch turns to pain. He promised himself it would never happen again.

EIGHTY-THREE

The Saddest Part

Enrique Valera walked into Sheriff Dermott's office, formal and stern-faced. Dermott greeted him with a handshake and offered him a side chair where they could talk more informally than if the sheriff remained behind his desk.

"Thank you for coming, *Comandante*." Dermott took a seat across a small coffee table from Valera. He placed a folder on the table between them.

"There is much to discuss, Sheriff." Valera crossed his legs and waited for Dermott to begin.

Valera had contacted the sheriff regarding the shooting of the Mexican crossing the river. Since his visit from Emmett Brewer, information on the matter had dried up.

"Yes, there is." Dermott nodded, opened the file, and began going through the notes he prepared for the meeting.

As a matter of professional courtesy and in the interest of maintaining reasonably amicable, if uncertain, international relations, the sheriff included almost every detail of the investigation—almost. He explained that, while they had not been able to prove who pulled the trigger, it seemed likely that an employee of Krieg and Zabala was the shooter, and the most likely suspect was one Ralph 'Lucky' Martin.

"This man then, he is under arrest?" Valera asked.

"No. I'm sorry." Dermott took a breath. "He's dead."

"Dead?" Valera's brow furrowed. "You found *his* killer then, and this will perhaps lead you to a motive for the wounding of the father at the river. Whoever was behind the incident may have wanted the shooter dead and unable to talk."

"Yes." Dermott nodded. "That is the likely scenario, but we have not been able to determine who gave the orders to shoot at the family at the river or who killed the shooter. We agree, however, that the two are almost certainly linked together. At some point, we'll be able to connect the pieces."

"At some point." Valera frowned. "You'll excuse me for saying so, but that is not very reassuring."

"I know," Dermott said with an exasperated sigh. "*Comandante*, this is as frustrating for us as it is for you."

"I'm sure it is." Valera nodded and spoke his next words less formally. "And our friend and comrade, Emmett Brewer, is there any progress on finding his killer?"

"No, I'm afraid not." Dermott nodded. "He was a friend and a dedicated professional. We found him by the river. No doubt, he was searching for evidence regarding the shooting at the family and the murder of the shooter."

"So, once again, there is a connection, but the person who killed Brewer is unknown, and there are no suspects." Valera remained silent for a few seconds and then asked, "May I see the file?"

"Surely."

Dermott spread the file and its contents on the table between them. Both huddled over it, examining reports, looking at crime scene images, discussing their theories. They talked for more than two hours, reviewing every document and report.

When they finished, there was nothing more to review, and nothing more to say. Valera rose to leave. They shook hands.

"Thank for the courtesy of seeing me, Sheriff."

"I wish I could give you more. I promise you, we will stay on the investigations until there are answers."

Valera nodded without speaking and did not seem reassured. "Thank you, Sheriff. I am sure you are doing all that you are capable of."

He left. Dermott took the file and slumped into the chair behind his desk. The words stung. *All that you are capable of.*

With no hint of rudeness or confrontation, Valera managed to give him a solid slap in the face regarding his thoughts on the investigative capabilities of the Salvia County Sheriff's Office. Dermott had to agree. He rubbed his eyes and reached for his desk drawer, retrieving another file and a small plastic evidence bag.

The file contained the investigative report regarding the suicide of Deputy Claude Brainerd. He had been out on paid time off and never reported back to work for his next assigned shift.

The duty lieutenant sent a deputy to investigate. He found Brainerd, three days ripe, sitting up in bed, a bullet hole in his head, his duty weapon on the floor. There was no evidence of foul play, no signs of a struggle, nothing. Brainerd lived alone, and of all the fingerprints lifted from the house and the gun, not one matched anyone except the deputy.

Those same fingerprints were also all over the three .32

caliber shell casings in the plastic bag. They had been taken from Emmett Brewer's pocket by the deputies collecting evidence while Dermott responded to the Krieg murder.

He laid the evidence bag beside the investigative report. The key to the puzzle was there, and the only men able to answer questions and put the puzzle together, Tom Krieg and Claude Brainerd, were dead, one executed in his own barn, the other dead of an apparent suicide.

"What were you up to, Claude?" Dermott muttered out loud. "What did Krieg have you doing?"

That Krieg paid Brainerd to do his dirty work was entirely believable. That the deputy put a gun to his head and pulled the trigger? It was inconceivable.

Dermott shook his head. There was no way in hell he would ever believe that Claude Brainerd decided to end his own pathetic, moneygrubbing life.

Valera was right. They were doing all they were capable of, and that was the saddest part of all. It was not enough.

EIGHTY-FOUR

Dead Man Running

"Did you think you could hide?"

The old rags that had covered him in the night were ripped away. Pepe Lopez blinked up at the tall man standing over him. A terrified wail began low in his throat and rose to a crescendo, filtering out of the small shack into the morning air.

The shack belonged to his aunt, his mother's sister—*Tía* Ramira. His eyes darted around the one-room hovel and found her sitting in the small chair that was her only piece of furniture. Her head was tilted back, the wide gash in her throat smiling at him, bright red in the rays of light shining through the single window.

"Noooo!"

"Yes." Alejandro Garza nodded.

Pepe Lopez had run and stumbled and hidden for several days after leaving Garza's men dead at the house in Creosote. He knew only one direction to go and eventually found his way to the Rio Grande. Near starvation and with only creek water to drink, he barely had the strength to wade across a chest-deep ford in the river. Fortunately, crossing from the north into Mexico was not nearly as difficult as going in the other direction.

Once in Mexico, he worked his way along the bank until he came to a village and paid a local farmer to take him to a place he remembered from childhood visits with his mother. *Tía* Ramira never left the small settlement where she grew up.

She opened the door for Pepe, eyed him up and down, and shook her head in disgust because she knew he must be in trouble or he would not have come to her. Then she stepped aside and allowed him to enter. She asked no questions about his business, and he provided no information.

That was yesterday. This morning she was dead.

"Did you think you could hide?" Garza repeated his question.

"I—I was going to come to you. I had to find a way back to Mexico to report to you."

"I don't think so." Garza smirked and shook his head. "Your movements were predictable. We simply spread the word to villages along the Rio Grande. A reward was offered. You should know it wasn't an enormous reward. It seems your life is not as valuable to others as to you."

"It was him." Pepe spoke rapidly. "The one you are looking for. He was in the town. He killed your men."

"You think I don't know that?" Garza shook his head. "You become less valuable by the second."

"No, please," Pepe begged desperately. "I did everything you said. It wasn't my fault. I ran because there was no other choice. He killed your men and would have killed me."

"It may have been better if he had," Garza said matter-of-factly as he knelt and Pepe cringed away on the pile of rags.

Pepe's throat and mouth froze, unable to speak or plead for his life. He wept and turned, trying to scramble away on all fours. Garza put out a hand and pushed him face down in the dirt. With a knee on Pepe's back, he reached into his pocket and retrieved a knife. He thumbed the release, and the well-oiled blade sprang open.

As it did, he passed it across Pepe's throat, pulling back hard into the tissue to make sure he severed the carotid artery. Rising to step away from the spurting blood, Garza wiped the blade on Pepe's pants and watched.

For a minute, Pepe continued to move, ever more feebly as the seconds ticked by. He tried to crawl away, but he found he could not crawl away from death. When he ceased moving, Garza turned and left the shack.

Outside, three men stood facing outward. They were the new security detail replacing the men Pepe called Gordito and Flaco, who now lay nameless in a morgue in Salvia County, Texas.

One opened the door to their car, and Garza took a seat. The others kept an eye on the scattering of nearby shacks that made up the village. There was no movement. Everyone remained as far out of sight as possible while the men from *Los Salvajes* did their work.

The trip back to Lázaro Cárdenas took several hours. First, he rode by car from the village thirty miles across the

Sonora Desert to a small airfield the cartel occasionally used as part of its narcotics smuggling operations. From there, he rode by helicopter, making several stops for fuel along the way.

By the time he arrived at Bebé Elizondo's hacienda on the hillside overlooking the Pacific, he was fatigued. He had been gone since leaving to meet with Lopez and arrange the ambush in the mountain pass.

"It is good to have you back, Alejandro." Bebé greeted him on the veranda, a smile spreading wide across his round face.

"It's good to be back." Alejandro took a seat in a cushioned, rattan chair across from Elizondo.

"It seems our American is a difficult one to trap."

"It would seem so."

"Have we underestimated him?" Bebé examined Garza's face. The point of the question was clear, although Bebé would never say it so directly to his friend and partner. Have *you* underestimated him, Alejandro?

As always, Garza answered immediately and without equivocation or resentment. "Yes, I may have."

Bebé nodded without comment. Garza would be harder on himself for his failure to bring the American's head back to him than Elizondo could ever be.

"So, what shall we do about him?" Bebé asked. "Perhaps write him off and forget about him. It may be time to move on to other matters."

"We cannot. This is personal. What would you do in his place, if you found your wife and children murdered?"

"A valid point." Elizondo nodded, understanding. "If it took the rest of my life, I would rip the heart from the man who did it while he was still living. He would feel every cut of the knife."

"And that is why we must find him and end this, or one day we will look up, and he will be standing over us, with our blood on his hands." Garza looked into Bebé's eyes, an expression of remorse on his face. "I have failed you … twice now. Once when I visited his home and now here."

"You are too hard on yourself, my friend." Bebé shook his head. "He was not present on both occasions. That is not a failure on your part." Bebé shrugged the matter of failure away. "He is a lucky man. That is all."

"Still, I promise you I will not fail again."

"As I said, you have never failed me, Alejandro. Let us not speak further of failure." Bebé took his time lighting a cigar and puffing it to life before he leaned back in the chair and said, "This lucky *norteamericano*, this John Sole, he is on the run now. So we must either follow or find a way to bring him to us."

"He is running. This is true." Garza nodded and made a pledge. "The direction, away from us or to us, is of no importance. I promise you this. He is a dead man running."

EIGHTY-FIVE

Road to Justice

They drove for twenty-four hours, stopping only for gas, convenience store snacks, and restroom breaks. Sole paid for everything with the stash of cash he carried from the sale of his home in Georgia. In one small town, he found an old-style five and dime store on the courthouse square and bought everyone underwear, a change of clothes, toothbrushes and other necessities.

Since the discussion of the danger he had placed them in, Sole had focused on driving, ashamed, and aware they felt betrayed by the man they had trusted. Once or twice, he caught Jacinta looking at him in the rearview mirror. He thought he saw her smile, but couldn't be sure.

Sandy's face bore no expression. When his eyes met Sole's, they pierced, assessing, questioning, analyzing. He spoke little and watched everything Sole did.

Isabella's silence during the journey was deafening. Mostly, she looked out the window at the passing countryside. When she spoke, it was in answer to a question about food, or restroom breaks. Otherwise, she remained silent, lost in her thoughts and regrets.

By the time they pulled into Rochester, Minnesota, nerves were frayed. Fatigue had set in hours earlier. Sole found a budget motel and paid for two rooms.

He came out with the keys. "Two rooms," He said as he climbed into the truck. "One for all of you and one for me. Unless …" He looked hopefully at Isabella. "Unless you want to share one with me and give the young people some privacy. I made sure it has two beds."

Isabella stared at him. For a moment, he thought she might tell him to go to hell. She nodded.

"Alright. Separate beds. The kids should have their privacy."

Sole pulled the truck along the row of rooms and handed a key to Sandy. "We leave early in the morning."

Sandy took the key. "You going to tell us where we are going?"

"Tomorrow," Sole said. "When we are on the road. When I am sure no one is following, and there are no ears around, listening to hear what the strangers in the parking lot are talking about."

"Tomorrow," Sandy said firmly. "No matter who is following or what ears are around."

He helped Jacinta from the truck, and they went into their room. Isabella sat in the passenger seat, facing away from Sole and did not move.

"I know you're angry," Sole said.

"No. Don't do that." She shook her head. "You don't understand anything about how I feel right now, John."

His heart jumped in his chest, hearing her say his name. "You're right. I don't, but you can't sit out here alone in the dark." He stretched out his arm and offered her the key to their room. "Here, take it. If you want, I'll stay out here in the truck, and you can have the room."

She pushed the pickup door open and stepped out, carrying the plastic sack with the few items they had purchased. "Open the damned door and get inside," she ordered.

He nodded, and they entered the room. Once inside, he looked at the beds and said, "I'll take the one near the door. You take the other."

"You never stop, do you? On alert every minute. Doing things, saying things that telegraph the danger we are in." Isabella shook her head, incredulous. "You'll take the bed near the door, protecting me." A smirk flitted across her face. "Like that will make a difference."

"It might. Besides, I can't help it. I got you into this, and the danger is real."

"Fine, you take the bed nearest the door."

She went into the bathroom without saying anything else. In a minute, he heard her washing and brushing her teeth. He sat on the bed nearest the door, contemplating the mess he had made of things. When she came out of the bathroom, he looked up.

She was dressed in the sweats he had bought her at the five and dime. Pulling the covers back on her bed, she climbed in, propped the pillows up, and laid back. She turned her head toward him.

"You say I'm angry." She shook her head. "Maybe a little ... a lot at first, but I've had a day, and God knows how many miles to cool down and go over things in my head."

"Okay," he said softly, not sure where this was going.

"What happened with Krieg is not your fault," she said sighing. "Sandy would have met Jacinta, and Krieg would have been unstoppable. They would be dead, or we would be on the run anyway. You stopped that from happening, saved their lives." She nodded, looking into his eyes. "For that, I will always be truly grateful. I don't have the words to say how grateful."

"You don't need to …"

"I'm not finished," she interrupted, sharply, not willing to be thrown off course, now that they were talking on her terms. "It would be a lie for me to say that I don't have feelings for you. I do, John, and you know it. But too much has happened."

He listened without responding. Every word was true, and there was nothing to say.

She shook her head. "This mission of yours, it will be the death of you. Forget that we are on the run and will probably be that way, always looking over our shoulder, for the rest of our lives. Yes, I am upset about that … furious about it to be truthful."

Tears filled her eyes. "But I am also terrified that one day I will get a message or see it in the news that you have been killed … dead in some unspeakable way. I couldn't bear that, John." She took a deep breath and continued, "So, when we get wherever you are taking us, what there is between us will end." She shook her head. "It has to."

She turned over and pulled the covers tight around her. Her shoulders shook with silent sobs.

Sole lay on his back on the bed. His dreams of simple domestic happiness with Isabella were now dead.

He would continue on the path he had chosen. He had no other choice. It was the only way to protect those he loved.

They spent the second night in Cincinnati, after winding all day through back roads, ever alert to the possibility that someone was following. Sole was determined not to repeat his carelessness.

On the third day, they arrived in Gainesville, Georgia. Sole drove to the address Billy Siever had provided. When they pulled into the driveway of the small frame house, Siever came out of the front door, smiling.

"Right on time," he said and descended the porch steps as Sole and the others climbed out of the pickup. He looked at the plastic bags with their few purchases. "You travel light."

"Matter of necessity," Sole said and stepped forward to shake his friend's hand. "It's good to see you, Billy."

"And you, John." Siever looked at the others. "Introductions are in order, I'd say."

Sole introduced the group, providing first names only to Billy. When everyone had smiled and shaken hands, he suggested they go inside and get off the street.

Billy walked them through the small house. It was a rental property he owned, a small but lucrative side business of his. He showed them their rooms and made sure they were comfortable. There were two bathrooms, and the women immediately closed their doors and began showering off the travel grime. Sandy crashed on the bed in the room he would share with Jacinta.

Sole and Billy retired to the kitchen to talk things through.

"Here." Sole pulled a roll of bills from his pocket and handed them to Billy. "Should be enough for several month's rent, food supplies, and such. I'll send more when that runs out."

Billy did not reach for the money. "You have quite a way of insulting your friends, Johnny Sole."

Sole looked around and shook his head. "No last names, Billy ... ever. We can't allow anyone to discover who they are or that I was here." His eyes narrowed. "This is critical. No one."

"Alright." Billy nodded. "But I'm not taking your money. Give it to them if you feel the need, but not me."

"Fair enough." Sole laid the money on the table and continued. "There's something else I have to ask you to do." He reached in his pocket and put a slip of notepaper on the table between them.

Billy looked at it. The paper bore the logo of a motel in a place he had never heard of—Rochester, Minnesota. On it, Sole had printed out in block letters a name and telephone number.

"Luis Acero?" Billy looked up. "Someone I should know?"

"Someone from the past ... my past ... a snitch and drug dealer, but he owes me. I want you to contact him and find out about getting new IDs for them. He knows the street and can point you in the right direction."

"Hell, John. I'm a lawyer. I can get new names for them, no problem and without calling some shady underworld character."

"No." Sole shook his head. "New identities ... no court records of name changes ... untraceable. They'll need everything, Social Security numbers, driver's licenses, a Green Card for Jacinta."

"False identities? Forgery?" Billy took a breath. "Remember I am a lawyer, John. I could be disbarred, or my ass could end up in prison, or both."

"I know. I'm asking a lot, and I'm sorry. I understand if

you say you can't, but the only other way is for me to contact him, and that would be dangerous for them. I have to go in the other direction to make sure the people who are looking for me don't find them."

Sole waited while Billy thought it over.

"How do you know he will do anything for you?" Billy asked after a few seconds. "What does he owe you?"

"His life. I killed the man who was going to kill him."

"John, for the record, I did not hear what you just said. From this point on, consider me your lawyer." He looked at the roll of bills on the table and peeled off a twenty. "You've paid me, and now we have attorney-client privilege, but do not repeat what you just said to anyone under any circumstances."

A look of amusement crossed Sole's face. He had killed in cold blood, more than once in the last year, but now he had an attorney, along with the privilege of confidential communications. He almost laughed.

"I'm not kidding, John," Billy snapped at him, and then said more softly. "I'll do what you ask. They'll have new identities. I'll help them find work. I owe you that. You took all of the heat for that stolen car when we were kids. You're in the position you're in because you were a cop, and you were a cop because you were a Marine, and you were a Marine because the judge said join up or go to prison." He shrugged and smiled. "You see. It all goes back to two punks taking a joyride in that asshole preacher's car. I got off, you didn't." He looked Sole in the eyes and nodded. "I haven't forgotten, John. I owe you."

"You don't owe me, Billy. If you do this, do it because you're my friend."

"I am your friend, John." Billy smiled. "Always have been."

When Isabella came from the bedroom, showered and clean, she found Billy Siever still sitting at the kitchen table. He looked up from the notes he was scribbling on a pad of paper and smiled.

"Feel better?"

"Much," Isabella said, looking around the kitchen and into the living room. "Where's John?"

"Gone."

"But …" Her eyes widened in surprise.

"To protect you."

She shook her head. "No. He was … I wanted to tell him …"

"He said it was better this way. He told me what happened, some of it at least." Billy leaned forward, elbows on the table hands folded, speaking softly. "John's a good man. He never meant to hurt you … doesn't want to hurt you again. That's why he left without saying goodbye. He said it was easier for everyone that way." Billy smiled. "I think he meant it was easier for him. He has feelings for you."

She listened and blinked back a tear without speaking.

"Sit down, Isabella," Billy said. "There are some things he wanted me to go over with you."

By the time John Sole had driven an hour, Isabella, Sandy, and Jacinta were sitting in silence at the kitchen table trying to digest everything his friend Billy Siever had told them and what the future held for them.

Life would go on, but they could not go back to Creosote. As long as they used the new identities he would provide and kept a low profile, they could live ordinary lives, go to school, get jobs, have a career, do whatever they wanted, and they should be safe. John would check in from time to time, calling Billy so as not to worry them or draw attention to them. They would not know where he was, and there would be no link from him to them.

For the next week or so they would stay around the house. Once he had their new identities and papers, they could go out and begin to live normally again.

Isabella had laughed and said, "Normally. What's that?"

"That's for you to decide, Isabella." Billy looked into her eyes. "That's John's gift to you, the only one he can give."

Billy left them with the cash, telling them John wanted them to have it and would send more but not directly to them. It would always come through Siever. There would never be any contact with him again.

When they were alone, Isabella cried. Jacinta did too. Sandy put his arms around both and held them close.

John Sole was on the road. He drove without a destination at first, putting as many miles as possible between him and the small rental house.

A little over four hours after leaving Gainesville, he passed through Nashville and picked up I-40 west. He drove into the night.

In Memphis, he turned north on I-55 toward St. Louis. From there he exited the interstate highways and took back roads through Missouri, traveling ever west and away from Gainesville.

He found a farm road outside Otterville, Missouri and pulled off the asphalt to sleep. He woke when the sun popped up over the fields sending its rays through the windshield. He blinked in the morning light, sat up, and started the truck. He was on the road again.

The miles behind lengthened. The miles ahead stretched even farther. For the moment, he had no idea where they would lead.

In the afternoon, a storm brewed ahead, flashing streaks of lightning that seemed to touch the road. He stared at it through the windshield, driving directly toward it. Drops of rain spattered the glass. He turned on the wipers and pressed forward into the storm.

The words Isabella had spoken as they fled Creosote rang in his ears. She was disbelieving at first, then angry, then frustrated, then afraid. She had a right to be all those things and more.

Her eyes had flashed at him. "You're on a road you think will lead to justice, but there won't be any justice, just more killing."

He feared she was right.

Next in the Sole Justice series

vinci-books.com/targetdown

They took everything. There will be justice.

John Sole finds himself playing a cat and mouse game with the killers who took his family from him. When the cartel changes tactics and sends their enforcer, Alejandro Garza to hunt him down, he finally confronts the phantom killer.

Turn the page for a free preview…

Target Down: Chapter One

CAT AND MOUSE

The Drill

He knew the drill. Actually, he invented it, part of it at least —the important part.

Dressed in a worn Army battle dress jacket from the Desert Storm Conflict era, he wandered aimlessly along city streets, muttering to himself or giving harsh looks to passersby. Sometimes he would stumble into a wall and lean there for support, appearing to rest and catch his breath.

———

It was all an act and the first part of the drill. That wasn't the part he invented, but he had learned to play the role of the homeless vet to perfection. That was the setup.

The aimless wandering came to an end when he rounded a corner, and his target was in sight. He had selected it earlier in the day, driving the neighborhood. Sometimes he drove for hours to find just the right spot. Today he had found it just minutes after arriving in the city.

It was a place along a curb across the street from a Detroit bar. The dealers worked as a team. One stood near the corner, taking cash from buyers. His partner stood at the other end of the block, near a public trash can. The theory was that if the cash-man got stopped and frisked by police, it was no big deal. There was no law about having a wad of money in his pockets, and he never had more than a thousand or so on him. When business was heavy, he would step inside a nearby door and hand off some of the cash to a third man working with them. Business was light today, and there was no third man.

After handing over the money, the customer made his or her way down the block where the second dealer would make a standard street pass, their hands touching briefly in the exchange. The buyer moved on to get high somewhere. The dealers set up for the next customer.

If the police approached the drug man, he tossed the drugs in the trash can and played innocent. Sometimes they caught on. Sometimes they didn't.

John Sole caught on. He had seen the technique operate before in Atlanta and spotted immediately what was going down on this seedy block, in a rundown Detroit neighborhood.

He approached the cash-man and stood swaying before him as he reached into his pocket.

"Hurry the fuck up, man. What you tryin' to do, bring heat on us?" The dealer put a hand under his shirt resting it on the butt of a nine-millimeter pistol tucked inside his

Stone Island designer jeans. "And when you bring that hand outta your pocket, it better have cash in it and nothing else, or you one dead motherfucker."

"Naw, man," Sole swayed and slurred his words, looking up at the dealer as he pulled a wad of bills from the jacket pocket. "Naw … just cash … I'm good. Just wanna get high."

"Shit. You already high," cash-man said as Sole counted out three hundred dollars from a roll that contained several thousand.

Sole fumbled with the bills, slowly counting them out, giving cash-man plenty of time to salivate. Then he handed the money over.

"I need three."

"Three what?" The dealer snatched the bills from Sole's hand before he could answer.

"Grams … three grams."

"Shit, motherfucker, you light then. You tryin' to rip me off?"

"No … no." Sole shook his head. "No, I thought three hundred would cover it."

"Naw, man. Not tonight." The dealer grinned. "Tonight, that gonna be a grand."

"But …" Sole started then closed his mouth, playing the needy user who craved a hit. "Fuck."

He reached into his pocket for the wad of bills again and counted out another seven hundred.

"Fuck, man. Where you get that money? Must be ten thousand there." The dealer was transfixed by the crumpled wad of cash. "Who you rob?" He grinned. "That's it, ain't it. You robbed someone."

"Ain't sayin'." Sole shook his head and handed over the money.

"I bet you ain't." The dealer laughed and nodded down the street. "See the man at the end of the block." Then he pocketed the cash, lifted his hand to the flat-brimmed ball cap he wore, holding out three fingers.

It was the signal that the buyer wanted three grams. His partner made no signal in reply but turned to walk toward the trash can where they concealed the drugs.

Sole wobbled up the street. As he walked by, the dealer turned from the trash can and passed the three plastic bags. It was a clumsy pass because Sole made it clumsy, stumbling and bumping into the dealer.

"Shit, man. What the fuck's your problem. You fuckin' get me busted, and I'll find you and put a cap in your ass."

The dealer gave him a shove, and Sole moved away. He stood on the curb swaying as if he might fall over, looked across the street, and headed for the bar.

Inside, he found a single high-top table in a corner and sat. The bartender called out to him, "No sittin' unless you're drinkin'."

Sole looked up, his brow furrowed as if he was confused by the bartender's directive.

"I said, drink, or get the fuck out!" The bartender picked up a bat from behind the counter and moved to the end of the bar, ready to run the vagrant out.

Sole nodded. "Okay, okay. Gimme a Jack."

The bartender put the bat back in its hiding place and poured a shot of Jack Daniels. He called out, "No table service. Come get your drink."

Sole nodded and wobbled over to the bar. When he reached for the drink, the bartender put a beefy hand over the glass. "That'll be six-fifty ... cash ... now."

"Oh, right." Sole nodded. And fumble in his pocket for the roll of bills. He made the same show with it as he thumbed through the bills and pulled out a ten. "Here, keep it."

"I will." The bartender took the ten from his hand and turned away.

Sole returned to his table with the drink. He walked carefully, each step deliberate as if he were trying very hard not to fall over.

When he was seated again, he put the drink in front of him, and hunched over the tabletop, throwing a furtive glance around the bar. A few patrons noticed, said something to each other, and then returned to their drinks, pretending to ignore him, but nobody was ignoring him. The cash had everyone's attention.

When the eyes turned away from him, he pulled a plastic bag from his jacket pocket, looked around to make sure no one was watching, and poured some of the contents on the table, taking care to seal the bag again and stuff it back in his pocket. Then he pulled the roll of bills out once more and peeled off a twenty.

With the edge of the bill, he cut the white powder into two good-sized lines. Then he rolled the bill into a tight cylinder, hunched over, and snorted the powder, like a man desperate for it.

When he sat up straight, he shook his head as if to clear it and noticed a couple of patrons eying him. "What the fuck you looking at?"

The patrons looked away.

He didn't invent that either, snorting fake cocaine. Hollywood invented that. The white powder was actually Inositol, a B-complex vitamin, available at any health food store. Snorting it was harmless enough—at least as harmless as inhaling any powder into your lungs could be. Actors had been doing it for years to give the appearance of taking drugs on a movie set. It provided no high, although some claimed the vitamin B did give them an energy boost. Sole never noticed any boost.

Not long after he snorted the fake cocaine and returned the baggie to his pocket, the two dealers made their way across the street and entered the bar. They gave a surreptitious nod to the bartender who returned the gesture, unaware that the worn-out vet in the corner watched everything.

The dealers sat at the bar and ordered drinks. They spoke in low tones to the bartender. After a few minutes, they came over to Sole's table.

"Hey, man." It was cash-man. "You know I shorted you out there."

Sole looked up bleary-eyed. "Shorted me?"

"Yeah, I saw that roll of bills, and I got greedy … charged you a grand for that coke."

"Shorted me?" Sole repeated, trying to focus his eyes on them.

"Yeah, shorted. You fuckin' hard of hearin'?"

"No." Sole shook his head. "No, I hear good."

"Good, that's good," cash-man said. "Look here. I can see you a vet. You seen some shit, right?"

"Some shit." Sole smirked and nodded. "Yeah, I seen some shit." He reached for the empty shot glass and waved it at the bartender.

The bartender nodded, poured another shot of Jack.

This time he brought it to the table and walked away without asking for payment.

"So, like I say," cash-man continued. "We see you a vet. My uncle was a vet too. So, you see, we got that in common."

Sole nodded and reached for the shot glass without speaking, focused on getting the whiskey to his mouth without spilling any.

"Anyway, man, it got me feelin' guilty. We shouldn't a done you that way. We want to make it up to you ... you know bein' a vet and all."

"Make it up?" Sole turned his eyes from one to the other, as if trying to piece together a puzzle.

"Yeah, make it up. We got more shit ... better shit than the cheap-ass stuff we sold you. We want to even things up."

"Even things up?" Sole's said.

"Yeah, that's what I said. We gonna give you the good shit to make up for tryin' to rip you off."

Sole sat and stared at the table for a few seconds as if trying to make sense of everything cash-man had said.

"You want to even things up ... with some good shit?"

"That's right." The two dealers grinned, and cash-man nodded. "We gonna make it up to you."

"How much?"

"Like I said, we feel bad about cheatin' you. You already paid, so this is on the house. It's yours."

"Okay," Sole said and held his hand out. "Let me have the good shit."

The dealer laughed and looked around, pushing his hand back down on the table. "Not here, man. Never know who's listening." Cash-man nodded toward the bar. "Out back. We keep the good shit stashed behind a brick in the wall ... out in the alley.

"Okay." Sole stood and reached out for the table to steady himself. "Let's get the good shit."

"My man." Cash-man grinned and slapped him on the back.

The dealers led him behind the bar, through the kitchen, and out the back door. The bartender followed.

"It's just over here." Cash-man led the way to a point on the wall where the mortar around the bricks had crumbled with age.

They stood in front of him and turned together, pulling their pistols from their waistbands. The grins on their faces faded as they tried to bring the barrels up to fire.

With a barrel length of less than three and a half inches, the Walther PPK was almost invisible in his hand. Before they could raise their arms, he squeezed the trigger rapidly four times, sending two rounds each into their heads. At a distance of three feet, he couldn't miss. They dropped without ever knowing they were dead.

As they fell, he turned, the Walther held out in front. It happened so quickly that, at first, the bartender thought the dealers had done what they set out to do—shoot the coked-up vet so they could rob him.

The pistol pointed at his face, the bartender was outmatched, and he knew it. He held the bat up in front defensively, as if he could use it to swat away the bullets. He couldn't.

The .380 caliber Walther had four rounds left. Sole sent two through the bartender's forehead, then turned and walked from the alley.

The deaths of the dealers would send yet one more message to the *Los Salvajes* cartel. He was still out there. If they wanted to end his rampage, they would have to follow his trail, find him, and kill him if they could.

That was the part of the drill John Sole had invented. It was the part that kept him motivated. They would come for him, and he would be ready.

Target Down: Chapter Two

Find John Sole

No one sat. This was a council of war, and everyone stood before Alejandro Garza, like soldiers before their general, intent on every word he spoke.

"What information do you have on his location?" Garza looked from face to face waiting for an answer.

No one wanted to speak first. There was no news to give, not good news at any rate. The man they had been seeking for months had eluded them at every turn. A few times, they came close to laying hands on him, but not close enough. They closed in only to find him already gone, sometimes not more than an hour before their arrival.

Garza nodded at one of his senior lieutenants. "Speak Andres. I only want to hear the truth."

He was calm. Garza always remained calm. That was what worried his subordinates. They had no way to detect what might be boiling beneath the surface of his stone-like exterior. The one thing they all understood was that he did not tolerate failure, and the hunt to locate and capture John Sole had gone on for far too long.

Andres nodded. Appointed by Garza as the spokesman, he had no choice but to speak for the others.

"Our people spotted him in Colorado ... in Denver," Andres began. "Our information is that he remained there for at least two days."

"Two days? And no one contacted us."

"He made contact with a low-level street dealer, not one high in our organization. It was only after the dealer met with his local boss that he saw the photo and recognized the man, Sole, as someone who bought cocaine from him earlier in the day. The next day the man, Sole, met with the dealer again to buy more cocaine."

"And?"

"And after that, he was gone. No more contact with him." Andres hesitated a moment, intent on every hint of expression passing across Garza's face then added, "Perhaps we should eliminate this dealer to send a message to the others ... spread the word to the other cities that they cannot fail again."

Garza's brow slanted down in the way that they recognized as his only outward expression of displeasure. His voice remained calm.

"No. The dealer is not at fault here, but his supplier in Denver, his boss and our man, he should be held accountable."

"I'll see to it personally," Andres said, anxious to make up for the bad news he had delivered.

"Everyone is to be familiar with his picture. I thought I made that clear."

"You did, *jefe*. The photo from the newspaper was there.

It seems our man simply failed to show it to this small dealer. Otherwise, he would have recognized Sole."

"Alright." Garza's dark eyes signaled it was time to move on. A message would be sent. The other suppliers and dealers working for *Los Salvajes* would understand, if they did not already, that they would be held accountable for future failures to find Sole.

"After Denver, do we have any word of him?" Garza continued.

"Yes." Andres took a breath and prepared himself to deliver more bad news. There was no point in lying. The penalty for lying to Garza was the worst of all punishments. Those found guilty of deliberately hiding the truth had been known to linger for days, begging for death, before Garza would allow them to escape this world and their pain.

Andres, continued, "He stopped in Pueblo, another city in Colorado. It is one of our growing markets."

"And there he was recognized but not confronted."

"Yes, but he stayed only for a brief time … perhaps two hours, or less even. His behavior is strange, though."

"I'm listening," Garza snapped.

"Again, he bought cocaine from our dealer. The dealer did recognize him this time. He notified his supplier, who told him to follow the man. The dealer did and saw him go into a bar."

"A bar?"

"Yes. According to the bartender, he ordered one beer, drank it, and left within a few minutes." Andres shook his head. "They say it seemed he wanted to be recognized."

"And from there?" Garza's face showed no emotion, and Andres had no idea how he was processing the information he provided.

"The dealer followed him on foot to a parking garage. Sole got into his vehicle and left before our people could get to him. The whole incident lasted perhaps fifteen minutes, less even. It was not enough time for our people to get to him, and the dealer alone would not be equipped to confront a man like this."

"No, he would not," Garza agreed. "And after Pueblo?"

"No sign yet," Andres said frankly. "But he will show up somewhere. He always does."

"Alright. Nothing has changed. Find John Sole."

Target Down: Chapter Three

AN UNFRIENDLY SORT

At around ten thousand feet, he had to pull over. The low, high-altitude air pressure had the radiator coolant boiling and the pickup's engine overheating.

John Sole pulled onto the narrow shoulder, leaving the left two tires on the road. The right side of the truck almost touched the guard rail. Not the best place for engine trouble. He checked the rearview mirror as the truck came to a stop. There was no traffic in sight. In fact, he hadn't seen another vehicle for the last ten miles.

Pushing the door open, he stepped out into the road, raised his arms over his head in a luxurious stretch, and took a deep breath. In the valleys below, temperatures climbed into the nineties. At the top of the Sandia Mountains, the air blew fresh and crisp, carrying with it the scent of pine and cedar.

Sole went to the front of the truck and opened the hood. The engine popped and clicked metallically while the radiator coolant boiled over into the reservoir, bubbling as it cooled.

"Well, John-boy," he sighed. "Looks like you'll be here for a while."

He leaned against the truck, taking in the view. Beyond the guardrail, the mountain sloped away, revealing a spectacular vista across a valley to more mountains. She would like this, he thought.

"Which she?" the voice in his head asked. "Isabella or Shaye?"

"Both," he answered himself and laughed.

For a while, he had considered the possibility that he might be losing his mind. There were days when he carried on long conversations with himself. The more the miles piled up, separating him from the past, the more isolated he became. He didn't mind at first, but with the isolation came a nagging need to talk, to converse, to say something out loud, to remain human.

There was only one human in his life now. He'd learned that lesson the hard way. No friends, not even casual acquaintances, could be permitted to penetrate his shell. The dangers were too great for them and for him. It was better for everyone if he remained isolated from the world. That left him one person to talk to—himself.

Concern about his sanity faded in time. He was fine, he told himself. Conversing with the voice in his head was simply a defense mechanism. His brain used it to ward off the inevitable loss of reason that comes from complete isolation. It was the brain's way of saying, we're gonna keep you sharp and sane, John-boy, at least for a while, until things are done. That's the way he talked it over with the voice, and the voice agreed.

"Yes, they'd love this." He smiled and took another deep breath.

In the months since leaving Isabella in Georgia, the old pickup had taken him across thousands of miles of highway, back roads and, city streets. First, west through Missouri to Kansas City. Then north to Minneapolis, and from there, over to Chicago and Detroit. He considered crossing into Canada from Detroit but wondered if the *Los Salvajes* cartel would be able to follow him there. Probably, he thought, but he wasn't sure, and he needed them to follow. That was the point of everything he was doing.

He turned south and west again. Indianapolis, St. Louis, and finally Denver. In each city, he sought out the places where they might be searching for him.

The residents of the cities thought they were unique, somehow special. They gave themselves nicknames—America's Crossroads, Twin Cities, Motor City, Big D, Forest City, Mile High. He visited them all and found they weren't so special.

The same seedy underworld existed in all of them, lurking just out of sight of the people who thought their city was special. And that underworld was always the same, inhabited by the same demons, regardless of the city's nickname. Drugs changed hands. People killed for the price of a hit of meth or heroin. Women sold themselves to survive or to feed their drug habit. The same grinning faces laughed while others died.

These are the places John Sole found in each city. He made himself visible, bought drugs he didn't use, walked streets, sat in bars where his was the only strange face, just so they would take notice, recognize him, and pass the word —he's here, the one you are looking for we saw him here in Detroit, or Milwaukee or Denver. Then he moved on, leaving a trail for them to follow.

When it seemed the cartel may not be paying close

enough attention, he would leave a body behind. It was always someone tied to the cartel, whose misfortune was to be standing on a street corner while John Sole passed. He felt no guilt as long as he had their attention.

From Denver, he turned south. A newspaper there had said that Pueblo, Colorado had the highest per capita murder rate in the state, and attributed the murders and associated crimes to the local gang problem. Gangs in Pueblo. That meant drugs in Pueblo. It wasn't a place he would have considered visiting on his odyssey, but he decided he might as well leave no stone unturned and headed down the interstate toward Pueblo.

Once in the city, it didn't take long to identify the area he sought. He drove slowly, eyes scanning side to side. Two men in an alley passed each other, a word spoken, their hands briefly touching. The telltale signs of a drug buy.

A few minutes later, he found a city parking lot, left the pickup, and walked back to the alley. Heads turned. Eyes stared. Voices whispered.

Some figured he had to be a cop. Others said, "Naw, man. He just a stoner. Check out that doped up crazy look on the fucker's face."

A few simply shook their heads and said the white boy walking down the sidewalk was fucking crazy. Sole tended to agree with the latter.

Crazy or not, the dealer took his money in exchange for an eightball of cocaine. Sole walked away without speaking and entered a bar at the end of the alley. The chatter inside died out as he took a seat on a stool and ordered a beer.

"Five-O in the house," a voice called out.

"Fuckin' pig," another said.

The bartender stared into his face as he put the beer in front of him. Maybe he recognized him. Sole hoped he did, and sipped the beer slowly so the bartender had time to get a good look at him. With luck, he would report to the local cartel gangbangers that he'd seen the one they were looking for, the one in the newspaper picture.

His work completed, he finished the beer and left, walked to his truck, and headed out of town. That was how he ended up on the road over the crest of the Sandia Mountains. Albuquerque was the next big city on his route. He hadn't been there yet to leave his scent behind. After Albuquerque … well, he hadn't thought that far ahead. Just keep moving, always away from Isabella.

A car approached from the south. It was new, and the young couple inside were laughing as they passed without slowing. Good. He didn't want them to stop and offer help.

Another twenty minutes passed. The pickup engine had cooled now, the angry popping gone. Another vehicle came along, an old man in a pickup. He slowed and rolled the window down.

"Can I give you a hand?" He leaned toward Sole and smiled. "Looks like you overheated. Yeah, altitude will do that. Had the same trouble myself."

Sole closed the truck's hood. "No."

He got behind the wheel, cranked the engine, and drove away without another word. The man watched him leave, shaking his head as he scratched under his ball cap. "Well, he's a damned unfriendly sort."

"Remember," the voice reminded Sole. *"Keep moving. No friends."*

Grab your copy…
vinci-books.com/targetdown

About the Author

Glenn Trust is the author of the bestselling *Hunters, Sole Justice, and Journey Series* of mystery/thriller/suspense novels. He has also written standalone works, including *Dying Embers, Mojave Sun,* and short stories.

There are no superheroes or knights in shining armor in his stories. According to Trust, knights are for fairy tales. His books are gritty and based in the real world, with characters who face their frailties while dealing with their roles in the story. The heroes are average people doing the best they can.

The villains, as real villains often do, look like us. Trust's monsters hide behind the smiling faces that pass us on the street. They look like us, and this makes them more frightening.

He is a Georgia native but has lived in most regions of the country at one time or another. Varied experiences, from construction worker to police officer, corporate executive to city manager, color and provide insight into the characters he creates. His stories are known for detailed plots, solid research, and realism.

Today, he writes full-time and lives quietly with his wife and two dogs, Gunner and Charlie.